EVASION

SCATTERED STARS: EVASION BOOK 1

EVASION

SCATTERED STARS: EVASION BOOK 1

GLYNN STEWART

FAOLAN'S PEN
PUBLISHING

faolanspen.com

This edition published in 2021 by:

Faolan's Pen Publishing Inc.

22 King St. S, Suite 300

Waterloo, Ontario

N2J 1N8 Canada

ISBN-13: 978-1-989674-19-2 (print)

A record of this book is available from Library and Archives Canada.

Printed in the United States of America

1 2 3 4 5 6 7 8 9 10

First edition

First printing: November 2021

Illustration © 2021 Elias Stern

Faolan's Pen Publishing logo is a registered trademark of Faolan's Pen Publishing Inc.

Read more books from Glynn Stewart at faolanspen.com

1

"SO, THIS ISN'T GOOD."

Evridiki Bardacki—"EB" to everyone who knew him in his current life—scoffed at the observation by his navigator and executive officer.

"You mean the fact that there's supposed to be a *star* here?" EB asked, the solidly built fifty-five-year-old freighter captain glaring at the display screens on his bridge. The screens that showed only deep space. "How the hell did we miss that the maps were *that* wrong?"

They'd just made a six-light-year nova—an instantaneous jump across three-dimensional space—aboard the freighter *Evasion*. According to the maps EB had purchased at their last stop, that should have delivered the ship and their cargo to the Agasoft System.

Instead, his forty-thousand-cubic-meter nova freighter was in deep space, at least as far from the nearest star as they'd been *before* their jump.

"Depends on *how* wrong the maps were," his navigator, Vena Dolezal, replied. The dark-skinned and dark-haired man went by Vexer to most people, and he shook his head as he skimmed through the data. "In this case, I think our download overwrote a bunch of our local astronomical data to make our computer buy its modifications."

"Well, there's only one reason to have sold us a map like this," EB said grimly. "Charge the guns, Vexer. Get the scanners up and running at full power and wake the rest of the crew."

EB had once been Captain Bardacki of the Apollo System Defense Force, a star system a very, very, *very* long way away from there. None of the other members of his small crew were ex-military, though, and it wasn't like *Evasion* had a battle-stations alarm.

As Vexer focused on calling and waking each of their crew individually, EB focused on the scanners. His headware interfaced with *Evasion*'s systems, adding additional virtual displays around him that only he could see.

"Everyone's awake and I've got plasma feeding to the gun capacitors," Vexer reported after a moment. "Turret self-checks are running."

EB nodded distractedly. *Evasion* had been built in the Outer Rim and was underpowered by any standard *EB* could apply...except that they were now well past the edge of the Rim and into the only-locally-mapped Beyond. More than fifteen hundred light-years from the home star of the human race, out there, the only maps were those you bought from the locals.

And the only security was your own guns.

Since EB had known he'd been heading out this way, he'd made sure that *Evasion* was as good as the Outer Rim system he'd bought her in could build. The freighter had two dual-plasma-cannon turrets, each as powerful as the main guns on an Outer Rim destroyer.

Whoever was tangling with his ship was going to have a *bad* day, but EB had bigger problems than whatever pirate was chasing her. Those problems weren't quite as *immediate*, he had to admit, but they were *bigger*.

"Got her," EB said aloud as a flare of Cherenkov radiation marked the arrival of their problem. "Bandit is at three light-seconds. She just micro-novaed over to us."

"Guess she's not worried about *us* running away," Vexer muttered. "She's stuck with us for ten minutes, but we're stuck here for *twenty hours*."

"I know the damn cooldowns, Vexer," EB replied dryly. "Might be more than ten minutes, depending on how far our friend jumped. Voids, she may have followed us from the last trade route stop."

To nova somewhere, a ship needed *very* detailed maps of the target. The usual solution was designated spots where everyone jumped, each ship scanning the location and passing on their scan data. Those were the trade route stops.

Out there, though, those maps were closely held trade secrets. EB had paid through the nose for his map of the route to Agasoft, and he'd only got it in the end because he was carrying cargo there.

"Get us evading," he ordered Vexer. "They're not going to try to shoot us at this range, but let's not make it easy."

"No, they know we're fucked and are going to order us to surrender," EB's friend replied. "Anyone else want to die for a cargo of sushi?"

"I'm not dying today," EB said calmly. "I did not survive the clash of *battlecruisers* to be killed by some Beyonder asshole with a rusty gunship. Let's see what they have to say for themselves."

Vexer had touched on EB's bigger problem, though. Their cargo of refrigerated and vacuum-packed fish was *perishable*. If they didn't make delivery within the next forty-eight hours, they might as well dump the cargo into space.

Which meant he *couldn't* go back to the Tatare System and find a new map. They were three novas away from Tatare—at least *sixty* hours just to get back. He needed to correct his location and get a *new* map.

EB's gaze settled on the gunship closing with his freighter.

"Ten thousand cubic meters," he murmured, just loudly enough that he knew Vexer could hear him. "Probably built from the standard colonial database, so a Ten-X class one nova drive, standard Harrington coils, standard antigrav, probably six to ten single-gun turrets."

"Yes, if we get the drop on her, we can vaporize her," Vexer agreed. "But I *know* that tone."

EB chuckled. He and the younger man were occasional lovers. Vexer was more aware of EB's thoughtful tones than most people in the galaxy.

"Standard colonial database is *old* at this point, Vexer," he said quietly. As he spoke, he brought up a database buried in his headware that he rarely touched anymore.

When the Apollo System Defense Force had gone to war against the Brisingr Kaiserreich, one Evridiki Bardacki had flown a nova fighter for the ASDF. He'd *also* flown NEWACs—nova electronic warfare and attack craft—for them, both before and during the war.

Every nova fighter—every *combatant*—in space carried the multiphasic jammers that could render a battlespace impermeable to anything except optics. But a significant portion of war took place outside of actual battles, and it was in those quieter moments that the NEWACs had flown, fighting a silent war of hack and counter-hack as they strove for an edge.

"If they're running old hardware, I wonder how much better their *software* is," EB concluded, pulling up the old programs he never should have left Apollo with.

"Nope, now I have *no* idea what you're thinking," Vexer replied. "Should I loop Ginny in?"

Ginerva "Ginny" Anderson was their senior engineer, but EB knew he was a better programmer and a *much* better hacker than her. He shook his head.

"No, Vexer, this one's on me," he said.

"I see our friend is finally calling us," he continued as a new icon popped up in his view. "Let's see what they have to say for themselves."

"FREIGHTER *EVASION*, we have you under our guns," an anonymous voice proclaimed over the radio. A distortion program rendered the voice genderless and toneless.

"Our scanners can tell your nova drive hasn't cooled down yet and you have no ability to escape or fight us," the stranger continued.

EB eyed the charge metrics for *Evasion*'s turrets and multiphasic jammer. The freighter was no nova fighter, able to skip around a battlespace with a miniature FTL drive, but she wasn't *nearly* as defenseless as the pirate assumed.

"If you stand down your engines and peacefully surrender, we will only take your ship and cargo and deliver your crew safely to a neutral station without ransom," the voice declared. "If you run, we will disable you. If you resist, we will kill anyone who draws weapons against us and sell the rest into slavery.

"You have five minutes."

The message ended and EB shook his head resignedly.

"Such wonderfully nice people," he observed.

"You're being sarcastic," Vexer replied. "But by Beyonder pirate standards? That *is* nice. Normally, *surrender* just means they won't kill us."

"That only makes me doubt their honesty more," EB said. "What a damned mess."

He'd found what he was looking for in his headware database and was now loading the viral vector with the code to do what he needed.

"I assume we're not surrendering, so what *are* we doing?" Vexer asked.

"Stand by the guns and wait for my order," EB told his navigator. He issued a final compile order to the program he was assembling and then opened a channel to Engineering.

"Ginny, how are we doing in the guts?"

"I can't cover the Jianhong radiation, boss; they *know* we're cooling," she told him.

"I know that," he confirmed. "The pirates were counting on that. Can you conceal the capacitor charge for the turrets?"

There was a pause.

"It depends on how close they get," she admitted. "They're decently shielded as it is; Reggie and I can throw some EM blankets over them, but that won't buy us much."

"I just need them to buy that we're surrendering," EB told her. "They're not going to do that if our guns are glowing red."

"Depending on how much attention they're paying, I can cover us down to about fifty thousand klicks," Ginny said. "I can't promise closer than that."

"It'll do. Make it happen," EB told her.

"Surrender, EB?" Vexer asked, his face looking darker than usual. "I don't trust their promises."

"Neither do I," EB agreed. "We're luring them in and then we'll deal with them, one way or another."

"Isn't that…" Vexer shook his head. "Isn't that like a war crime or something?"

"Last time I checked, my friend, we weren't soldiers," EB replied. His hands flew across the panel in front of him while he gave mental orders through his headware.

The code package he'd assembled had compiled. There was no time to *test* it, not with the pirates' deadline rapidly approaching.

"The problem, Vexer, is that we need a map that can get us to Agasoft in two novas or less," the freighter captain continued. "And the only one I see around here is on that gunship."

"They're not going to just give us their maps, no matter what," Vexer said. "Maps are life and death out here."

"I know. And that is why I'm *taking* theirs," EB replied.

His program was now concealed in the formatting data for a video transmission and EB activated the recorder.

"Unknown ship, this is *Evasion*," he said, trying to sound as pathetic and afraid as he could. "This ship is my life, my business. I can't let you have her! But…I can't let my people die. I'm cutting our Harrington coils and awaiting your approach.

"Surely, we can come to some compromise?"

He ended the recording and sent the message.

"Kill the engines," he told Vexer. "Let's look as meek as we can until my code is done."

There was a long silence on the bridge.

"What did you just do, EB?" his navigator, executive officer and sometimes boyfriend asked slowly.

"Sent them a computer virus that will download their entire navigational database and transmit it to us," EB replied. "Even if they've upgraded from the SCD, it should work…but given the *rest* of that ship, I think they're screwed."

The standard colonial database was the archive of science, technology, literature, history, and schematics sent along with every colony ship. Every planet from the Rim inward—everything within fifteen hundred light-years of Sol—had access to a slowly advancing library of public information and open-source technology that formed the core of the SCD and the baseline technology of any human world.

Even in the Beyond, those updates would percolate, and it was reasonable to assume that any system had access to the full SCD— which meant that they could build antigravity coils, class one nova drives and Harrington coils. Any system with the SCD could reliably build cheap ten-thousand-cubic interstellar ships.

Like the gunship closing with *Evasion*.

"Any idea how long your virus is going to take?" Vexer asked. "Because they are coming in *fast*."

"We don't get a nice, neat loading bar for how fast the virus is proceeding," EB replied. "We'll know it's succeeded when it takes over the pirates' transmitter to send us the data it's searching for."

Another icon popped up on his screens and he sighed and hit Play.

"Maybe we can reach some kind of compromise," the toneless artificial voice told them—*lied to them*, EB was reasonably sure. "I'm glad you see reason. We're closing with your ship, and if we see any sign that you're not playing by my rules, we open fire.

"We'll be sending a shuttle over as we get closer. I expect to see all of your crew in the landing bay, *unarmed*. Then we can talk about *compromises*."

EB sighed.

"I think they're going to sell us into slavery," he observed. "They're being *far* too willing to accommodate."

"You're probably right," Vexer agreed. "So, what do we do?"

"Let them close for now," EB said. "And we do not, no matter what, let that shuttle board. I doubt we'd be lucky enough to fight off a pirate boarding team once they get aboard."

Luck didn't even have that much to do with it. While all eight members of EB's crew had blasters and stunners of their own, those were *sidearms*. None of them would burn through even half-decent armor.

There were only two heavy blasters on the ship, and the only *armor* EB was sure of was his. His shipsuit—the one-piece uniform-slash-emergency-spacesuit worn by every spacer—was the one he'd been issued as a nova-fighter pilot a long time before. It had the ballistic and energy-dispersal web layers to resist light blaster fire—and he had a suit of proper power armor, from the same system as *Evasion*, as the centerpiece of his limited "armory."

But he expected that pirates would be coming with heavier blasters and proper armor. There was no way his collection of freighter techs could hold the ship against a serious boarding party.

"If the virus fails, we need to force them to give us a map," EB said softly. "That means we blow away the shuttle and try to disable the gunship's weapons. I need to know if *she's* cooling down."

"I'm not detecting significant Jianhong radiation," Vexer warned. "I'd say she was waiting for us and then novaed over. I'd *guess* she still has ten to fifteen minutes of cooldown left, but…she's not trapped here with us."

"And that she was waiting for us with *that* much accuracy tells me we were set up," *Evasion*'s captain said grimly. "But by void and stars, I *will* make this damn delivery and I *will* get paid."

EVASION RESEMBLED nothing so much as a square loaf of bread held in a horseshoe. At her heart were four five-kilocubic cargo bays, stacked two on top of the other two in a twenty-meter-by-twenty-meter square fifty meters long. The engineering hulls were mounted "above" and "below" the cargo space, with a fifth pressurized cargo bay and the operations hull attached to the very front.

Each of the engineering hulls held enough reactors and Harrington coils to move the ship, plus one of the freighter's dual turrets, currently pretending to be locked down while the pirate ship closed.

"I'm not seeing anything special about this gunship," EB observed as the bandit closed. "Standard eighty-meter lozenge. Four guns on top, four guns on the bottom."

Vexer snorted.

"Unless she's hiding more accel than I think she is, we could *outrun* her," the navigator noted. "Though she does have twice as many guns as us."

"SCD cannon," EB pointed out as he distractedly ran through the electromagnetic spectrum from his scanners. *Evasion*'s guns came from a middling Outer Rim power that had owed an old colleague of his a favor.

Out there, they might as well be *Excalibur* against most of the ships he was running into, and Vexer *knew* that. They'd test-fired the guns since he'd come aboard.

"We've got at least three times their throughput and I'd eyeball twenty percent sharper focus. I doubt our friend over there even *begins* to realize it, but he is completely outgunned."

Even by the standards of the Beyond, a pure SCD gunship was trash. There might be sections of the Beyond where that *wasn't* true, but they were only a hundred light-years past the Rim. They were beyond both the official fifteen-hundred-light-year line of the "Beyond" *and* the unofficial line where the mapping companies stopped running automatic updates, but they were still in a region in communication with "civilized space."

"Range is a hundred thousand kilometers, and our friend is matching velocities," Vexer warned. "I expect... Yeah, here comes the shuttle."

EB took a moment to scan the data on the shuttle itself. It was about what he expected. Like the gunship, it was built with pure SCD tech. By the standards of the Mid-Rim navy he'd once served, it was slow, blind, stupid and toothless.

By Beyond standards, it was still a respectable threat, with a quartet of light plasma cannon and probably twenty armored troops aboard.

"ETA?" he murmured.

"About two minutes," Vexer replied. "I mark their cooldown as just about done, too, EB. And they're going to see through whatever Ginny and Reggie have done with the guns."

"I know," EB agreed. "You have control of the guns?"

"It'll take about three seconds to pull from locked position and target the shuttle," Vexer told him. "Half that to pop the jammer."

The multiphasic jammers would render all communication and

complex sensors useless for a one-light-second bubble around *Evasion*. EB assumed that the gunship had jammers of her own—any warship *should*—but they were almost certainly assuming that *Evasion* didn't.

The pirate would be confused as hell when *Evasion* started jamming. Unfortunately, once they started jamming, there'd be no way to get the transmission from the virus if it succeeded in its mission.

"Give it more time," he told Vexer. "But stand by the guns. The moment the shuttle twitches, we blow her out of space. Then we see if the gunship will talk."

EB was starting to run the numbers for an evasive course that would put *Evasion* in position to disable the gunship when the communications system chimed again.

"Burst transmission from the gunship," Vexer told him. "Looks like a couple dozen terabytes of data. Formatting *looks* like nav data, but it'll take the computer some time to crunch."

"Good enough," EB barked. "Bring up the engines and fire a warning shot at the shu— What the *void*?!"

The gunship had gone dark. Her Harrington coils cut off with a suddenness that would have taken dozens of hours off their operating lives, her active scanners died—even her *power* signature was rapidly falling off.

"My virus…shouldn't have done that," EB said slowly, mentally reviewing the code he'd plugged in and then grimacing. "Okay, okay, I forgot about that part."

"You *forgot* that part?" Vexer asked drily.

"The intrusion-code module I used has a default terminal code section that attempts to shut down the target ship," EB admitted. "I *forgot* because I've never seen it work—the core engineering computers and such to do so are usually separate enough to require an entirely new round of intrusion measures.

"So, not only is our friend a crap ship, she's a terribly *designed* ship."

He snorted.

"Warning shot at the shuttle, Vexer," EB repeated. "Time to wrap this up."

The shuttle was already flipping, shedding velocity as they tried to get back to their mothership. The blast of plasma that flashed through space in front of them definitely registered.

EB smiled thinly and brought up the video-transmission software again.

"Pirate craft, this is *Evasion*," he said calmly. "You are now under *our* guns. If everyone now plays very, very nice and leaves me and mine alone, you'll live. If your shuttle so much as *twitches* toward my ship, or your gunship attempts to repower her engines or guns, I'm going to vaporize all of you.

"I suggest you stick to *my* rules now."

2

"DEFINITELY NAV MAPS," Vexer confirmed a few minutes later.

EB's focus was on the pirates, continually updating the targeting on the dual turrets to keep one turret trained on each pirate spacecraft. The gunship would probably survive the first shot. The shuttle would definitely *not*—and since the shuttle was the concern for now, that was good enough for him.

"Do we have a route to Agasoft?" EB asked.

"I'm validating everything against our current position and making sure their star charts and ours align with the reality of where we are," Vexer said grimly. "That being what we *didn't* do with the charts we bought in Tatare."

"Good plan," EB agreed. "I'd say faster is better, but we still have hours left on the cooldown."

The pirates hadn't replied to his message yet, but the shuttle had cut her acceleration to a crawl and continued her return to the gunship. The gunship itself was still dead in space. The heat signature suggested that she had auxiliary power and life support, but that was it.

Without main power, the ship wouldn't even have gravity, and EB was doubtful of the likelihood that pirates flying *that* gunship had trained in zero gravity.

"There's always one other consideration, you know," Vexer said quietly as his analysis processed. "They're following instructions, but if we *have* the maps...we don't need *them* anymore."

EB checked the angles and projections on his targeting solutions again.

"What are you suggesting?" he asked.

"They're pirates, EB," Vexer reminded him. "We were set up by someone selling maps, even *with* the client backing us. That means this is organized and they've done this before...and they'll do it again.

"Out here, there's nobody to follow up or patrol this particular spot for them. We'd be doing everyone a favor if you just pushed that button."

EB winced.

"That button" would activate the targeting solutions he was coding and kill, at his best guess, forty or so people.

"At this point, Vexer, that would be murder," he told his lover. "I'll kill anyone who comes at me guns blazing, but there's no fight left in these people. We might not have locked them down, but they're basically prisoners.

"And I won't kill prisoners. I won't kill a helpless ship."

"They would," Vexer reminded him. "They were ready to take us down when they thought we didn't have the firepower to fight them. And now we have the upper hand and they're relying on your mercy.

"A bit hypocritical of them, don't you think?"

"We report them in Agasoft," EB replied. "Depending on how decent their engineers are, the ship might well still be there by the time Agasoft can send someone out to pick them up."

"Agasoft won't have anyone to send out, boss," Vexer said. "They *might* have a few gunships of their own. They'll be *better* gunships, but that's a low bar. If we don't deal with them today, they're going to kill and kidnap more people."

EB grimaced and glanced at the disabled gunship. He'd expected the dilemma to be easier, if he was being honest. They'd steal the data they needed, the pirates would try to fight, and his people would vaporize them.

"We are not murderers, Vexer," he said, firmly. "I *will not* fire on a helpless ship. Though…I'll admit I expected them to get their reactors back on by now."

"Is it any better to leave them to die of suffocation?" his XO asked.

"No," EB said with a chuckle. "But I don't think *anyone* is *that* incompetent."

"Fair," Vexer sighed. "I've got the map pinned down. We're only about five light-years from Agasoft, a single nova. I'm programming it now, though it'll still be ages until we can jump."

"One jump also means it's more likely Agasoft can spare whatever nova ships they have to check on the bastards," EB pointed out.

"Hope springs eternal when you weren't born out here," Vexer said with a sigh. "You're the boss, EB, but…these guys don't deserve your morals."

"Maybe not, but *my* morality isn't about *them*," EB told his lover. "It's about who I am and what I choose to do."

And when push came to shove, EB wanted to make it through the rest of his life without ever killing another human being. The war had been bad enough.

"If they stay nice and quiet until the cooldown, then we leave them and we never think about them again."

"You're the boss," Vexer repeated. "I'm selfish enough to hope that it isn't *us* that gets bitten by this."

"HOW ARE WE DOING, GINNY?" EB asked as he walked into the nova-drive compartment.

Evasion's general technological level was significantly above the standard colonial databases, except in one important area: her nova drive was still only a Ten-X. Four thousand cubic meters of technology EB didn't pretend to understand, it filled two-thirds of the upper engineering hull and a chunk of the forward operations hull, too.

"Ten hours to cooldown," she replied, leaning against one of the tanks of coolant that seemed to exist only to allow engineers to judge the electrostatic level. "Are we still being stalked?"

"I'm not sure a disabled gunship with what appear to be the most incompetent engineers for fifty light-years in any given direction is able to 'stalk' anyone," EB said drily. "I mean, how long would it take you to reboot the cores from an unexpected cold shutdown?"

"I wouldn't *let* some idiot with a computer worm force the cold shutdown," Ginny replied. "My reactor core is on a complete stand-alone system, air-gapped from the rest of the ship."

"Most are," EB agreed. That wasn't even a warship precaution. Not all civilian ships did it, but most expecting trouble did.

The redheaded woman shook her head at him. Ginny was a slim woman of his own entirely average height. She kept her hair cut short and spiked with product, well out of the way of her work.

"Look, boss, I just keep this girl running," she murmured. "But I can't help but look at that floating junkheap over there and think everyone would be better off if it ceased to exist."

"Vexer said the same," EB admitted. "And I'll tell you the same thing I told him: I don't kill helpless people, no matter what they might do in the future. I'm not a murderer and I'm not making you lot murderers.

"So, we watch them, and when we're ready, we leave them behind. We're only one nova from Agasoft, as it turns out, and we've got twenty thousand cubic meters of vacuum-packed refrigerated fish to deliver.

"*That* is my priority today."

"You ain't wrong, I suppose," Ginny conceded. "Just…fuckers like that, boss. They deserve what they get."

"They might," he allowed. "But we're not them and we won't sink to their level. This is a merchant ship, not a privateer or a crusader. We do our job, and our job does not involve killing people, Ginny."

"Even when they come right at us?"

"I'd have shot them down without blinking if they'd fired," EB said cheerfully. "But leaving them dead in space… They've already lost this fight, and I can hope it makes them rethink things."

"And if it doesn't? Who's to blame for the folks they kill next?"

EB let that hang in the air for a few seconds, then sighed and shook his head.

"They are, Ginny," he told her. "I can't control what anyone else does. Only what I do—and there's an old saying on this one."

She gave him a dirty look, but he smiled and continued anyway.

"You kill a murderer, the number of murderers in the world doesn't change," he said softly. "It's not about them. It's about *us*. So, we keep the guns warm and watch the nova drive until we can get the void out of here.

"Ten hours, you say?"

"Ten hours," she confirmed. "What do we do if the pirates manage to get the ship online and start shooting at us?"

"We vaporize them," EB conceded. "But we're safe and we have what we need. I won't make us all murderers for that."

"Your call, boss. Should I be pulling the EM blankets off the guns?"

He chuckled.

"Is it a problem if we leave them on?" he asked.

"Eventually. They're catching electromagnetic radiation and heat, and trapping it. They're *supposed* to melt before they trap enough heat to damage the ship's systems, but I don't trust that."

"Pull them off whenever it's safe," EB decided. "Don't risk yourself or Reggie, but let's not risk the guns, either."

Reginald Kalb was *Evasion*'s weapons tech, a native of the Redward System that had built *Evasion*. He was the *only* original member of the crew other than EB now. The rest had slowly drifted away and gone home over the last two years.

Fortunately, there were enough people like Vexer and Ginny that EB could keep *Evasion* flying.

"We'll be out of here soon enough," EB told Ginny. "And there'll be no blood on our hands when we leave."

No new blood, anyway. EB had made ace in the war against Brisingr several times over. *His* hands weren't clean—but there was no point in dirtying his people's hands, either.

3

AGASOFT—TECHNICALLY Agasoft III, but it was common enough for a habitable planet and its star to share a name that everyone dropped the number—was an interesting planet to EB's eyes.

Not many habitable planets had natural rings, however small. Agasoft's ring was only a few hundred kilometers thick, but it made navigation around the planet more difficult than most.

It also meant that the system's defensive fortifications were harder to see than most. EB assumed they were *there*—he'd never seen a system that wasn't fortified enough to stand off a carrier group, even out there—but the only thing he could see was the normal counterweight asteroid fortress attached to the orbital elevator.

"You realize, Captain Bardacki, that the pirate was almost certainly lying doggo by the end?" the local security officer he was speaking to asked. "Whatever maintenance or systems failure they had, it is unlikely that it was completely unrepaired after twenty hours."

"I realize that," EB agreed. "But is it really going to hurt to send a ship to investigate?"

He doubted that the very junior woman on the other end of the video call had the authority to send so much as a paper airplane anywhere. If Agasoft Orbital Security had been going to send anything, they'd have done so when his message arrived.

They wouldn't have waited until *Evasion* was close enough for a real-time conversation and tasked a junior officer to take his statement.

"Captain Bardacki, that is not my decision," the young woman told him. She couldn't have been more than twenty-five, and it was taking a solid amount of EB's self-control not to either condescend to or patronize her.

"I realize that, Lieutenant..."

"*Leftenant* Maimu Dumitru," she told him precisely. "I am only taking your statement, captain. More senior officers will review the report you submitted and decide what action the AOS will take."

She paused, then sighed.

"I don't think I am betraying any great confidence, though, by saying that I don't think we will be doing anything immediate," she told him. "We have the record from your sensors of the ship's emissions signature. That will go on file, and if she shows up in Agasoft in future, her crew will be detained.

"However, my superiors already judge it unlikely that the ship will still be at the ambush point. I... I can't speak for my superiors," Leftenant Dumitru told him. "But *I* wouldn't want to send a gunship after a gunship, which means the only vessel we could send would be *Agasoft Gloria*, the *flagship*.

"I don't see that happening, Captain. I assure you, we will distribute your information to our allies and the pirates will be caught, but we don't have the resources to chase every lead reported to us by a freighter captain."

EB nearly had to bite his tongue to control his reaction. He wasn't handing them a *lead* so much as a *blood trail*. Even if the pirates had been playing dead, there'd been a decent chance that the AOS could have caught the gunship before the pirates got their nova drive online.

If they'd responded when they received his report...an hour earlier.

"I understand, Leftenant," he finally managed to get out, hopefully politely. "Thank you for taking my statement and considering the situation."

He still wasn't a murderer...but damned if he hadn't figured that handing the locals a pirate on a *platter* would get a better response than this!

"TOLD YOU," Vexer said bluntly as EB walked out of his office. Clearly, the navigator picked up the result of the call from EB's face.

"You did," he conceded. "So did Ginny. So did Lan."

Lan Kozel was *Evasion*'s doctor. EB had never asked them *why* a fully qualified MD had decided to ship out on a ship that was explicitly never planning on coming back to their system, but he was pleased to *have* a full doctor aboard.

"Almost everyone on this ship except you is a Beyonder," Vexer said calmly, sprawled across one of the bridge control chairs in a manner that looked ridiculously uncomfortable to EB. "We know damn well how things work out here.

"If you aren't in a star system, they can't do anything. Not even *won't*, boss. *Can't*." The elegantly lanky man shook his head. "Agasoft is pretty well set-up as places out here go. A hundred million-ish souls, decent industry, real orbital defenses...but I was surprised to realize they even *had* a corvette."

"*Agasoft Gloria*," EB agreed, pulling what was publicly available on the ship. "Sixteen thousand cubic meters, sixteen guns."

That was a small but real warship. Probably overgunned for her mass, which meant she likely wasn't as capable of taking a hit as a Mid-Rim ship...but even Mid-Rim powers tended to admit that anything smaller than a destroyer's thirty kilocubics wasn't going to survive a real hit.

Gloria could take *Evasion*, most likely. The freighter was over twice the corvette's size, but the corvette was a dedicated warship.

"How does anyone out here get *anything* done when random pirates have ships on par with the local system fleets?" EB finally asked.

"Mercenaries and protection money," Vexer said bluntly. "And the line between the two gets *real* vague." He waved a hand at the scanners. "Take a look. *Agasoft Gloria* isn't the only corvette in Agasoft orbit."

EB hadn't really looked at who else was in orbit. He did now and raised an eyebrow as he saw the truth of his XO's words. Agasoft Orbital Security had four nova warships—three gunships and *Agasoft Gloria* herself—but there were *ten* nova warships in orbit of the planet.

Including two corvettes.

"You're telling me there are more mercenary warships here than system warships?" he asked.

"It's not usually quite so unbalanced, but the system governments are inherently insular," Vexer told him. "When your own system and citizens are secure, why spend the resources to run a nova-capable fleet when you can just rent one if you ever need it?

"That's the logic a lot of Rim powers use," EB admitted. "A bunch of friends of mine set up as mercs there."

EB had fled his home system one step ahead of a hostile kill team. It turned out that part of the peace treaty between Apollo and Brisingr had been clearance for Brisingr's assassins to terminate many of Apollo's top aces—including the entirety of the Apollo System Defense Force 303 Nova Combat Group.

His old CO had sent a pile of resources out to Redward and arranged for most of the Three-Oh-Three to escape…but it hadn't been enough. Most of them had died. EB himself had met with his former colleague, Kira Demirci, there.

She'd been setting up a mercenary fleet based around stolen Apollon nova fighters. She'd offered EB a slot in her fleet. A slot he'd declined.

If EB could make it through the rest of his life without ever getting into a firefight, he would still have seen too many.

"I'm heading onto the orbital in person," he finally told Vexer. "I need to meet up with the client's delivery end. They still owe us for this."

He had a grim suspicion why the contract had been one-third on pickup, two-thirds on delivery now. No one had expected *Evasion* to actually *make* the delivery.

Getting paid might be *interesting*.

4

"I'M HERE to see Em Mirja Skov," EB told the young man sitting behind the desk.

The reception area for the trade brokerage was surprisingly nice. Most of Agasoft's main orbital gave the vague impression of being held together with duct tape and hope. The space station had arrived with the colony fleet in prefabricated chunks and never been updated since.

Skov & Partners Limited's office did its best to conceal that. The walls had been recently painted, the carpet was new and a cloth cover hung from the ceiling, disguising the necessary piping and wiring of a space station.

All of it was done in a tranquil blue and green that did nothing for EB's mood.

"Do you have an appointment?" the youth asked calmly. His clothing and position said *receptionist* but his body language screamed *bodyguard*. If there wasn't a blaster under the desk, EB would eat the desk.

"I've only been in-system for a few hours," EB told him. "I have a twenty-thousand-cubic-meter perishable cargo for Em Skov, though, that I suspect she'd rather we closed the deal on *before* it expires."

"I see," the guard said. "And your name, em?"

"Captain Bardacki of *Evasion*," EB replied. "Carrying a cargo out of Tatare System for Em Skov. I have the invoicing and paperwork on this datastick."

He dropped the chip—a copy of documents that lived in *Evasion*'s computers—onto the youth's desk.

"Of course. Let me check with Em Skov," the other man replied, his eyes unfocusing in the manner of someone taking a virtual headware call.

The visible nod that followed a few moments later suggested the young man wasn't as practiced as he'd like to pretend. Or their software sucked. Both were options, EB reflected, but no gesture in the virtual discussion space should leak to the person's body.

The guard swept the datachip into a scanner wordlessly as his eyes refocused, his gaze settling on EB.

"Em Skov will need to review the documentation, but she has a slot clear to see you in about fifteen minutes," he said. "May I get you a coffee, Captain Bardacki?"

MIRJA SKOV'S personal office was several steps farther above her brokerage's reception area than the reception area was above the rest of the station. Decorative tapestries—*handwoven,* if EB judged it right—covered the walls around a large wooden desk. The metal station floor had been covered with a hardwood stained dark red, and a dropped ceiling covered the station fixtures.

The dropped ceiling made the space a bit claustrophobic even for someone of EB's size, but Mirja Skov didn't look like she'd be bothered by it. She was a tiny woman of clear Chinese descent, with near-black eyes that locked onto him like chips of obsidian.

"Captain Bardacki, a pleasure to see you," she told him, gesturing him to a seat. "You already have a coffee, good, good. Refill?"

"I'm good," he said. "My understanding is that the delivery of this cargo is somewhat time-sensitive."

"Not so much that we cannot be polite, captain," Skov replied, but she returned to her seat and took a sip of her own coffee.

Facing the woman across her desk, EB could tell that she hadn't been expecting him. It was subtle, but he was looking for it too. So, either she'd never *ordered* this cargo—which raised questions about the Tatare factor who'd sent him—or she'd never expected him to *arrive*.

"You have all the paperwork from the factor in Tatare," EB told her. "Is there a problem?"

"No," she said instantly. Too quickly. "My factor is authorized to engage shippers at his discretion to get supplies here. I don't have the shipping in place to handle your cargo immediately, but I will be able to sort it out in time."

"Good. I'd rather not have a few thousand tons of fish rot on my decks," EB replied drily. Given that the fish was vacuum-sealed, *in* vacuum, and stored at a controlled temperature, that wasn't going to happen.

The *worst* case from EB's side was that his team moved that temperature to *frozen* sometime in the next eighteen hours, preserving the fish effectively indefinitely—but also cutting its value in half.

Never frozen apparently meant something to Em Skov's clients, even when it was all being carried in vacuum.

"We will be able to prevent that, I am certain," Skov told him. "There are no concerns with retrieving your cargo. I presume it is stored in standard TMUs?"

The standard ten-meter unit—or ten-meter-equivalent unit—was a unitized shipping container designed to make transport across the stars easier. Ten meters long and five meters on a side, it held two hundred and fifty cubic meters of cargo.

Each of *Evasion*'s four unpressurized holds held twenty of the containers. EB *could* load the containers into his pressurized hold, in which case it would hold another twenty, but the point of the pressurized hold was to hold less-organized cargo.

"Eighty of them, yes," EB confirmed. "We will be delighted to help your people off-load. Of course, there is one matter outstanding. That of our payment."

He smiled thinly.

"Em Lorraine paid one-third in advance and committed to a two-third payment on delivery," he told her. "There was *also* a twenty-five percent premium if *Evasion* was forced to engage or flee from pirates.

"Since the maps we were provided by one of Em Lorraine's associates led us directly into a pirate ambush, I am activating that clause."

"You were attacked?" Skov asked. "I'm impressed you're still here."

"We were lucky and clever," EB replied. "We managed to evade the pirates sufficiently that they overloaded and shut down their own reactor in their attempt to pursue. It appears that AOS has no interest in following up, but that doesn't change the situation.

"The final accounting is on the chip I provided," he noted. "Thirteen kilograms, seven hundred and fifty grams of third-party-stamped platinum ingots."

There were no banks handling interstellar transactions out in the Beyond. In the Rim, there was usually *someone* who'd made themselves the local bank of choice for those transactions, providing the baseline currency for all trade deals.

EB had grown up with his own system's new drachmae being that currency around him. The realization that there *wasn't* a currency like that in the Beyond had been an...adjustment.

Payment for interstellar deals out there was in precious metals. There were exchanges that would handle currencies for a half-dozen local star systems, but they would also all exchange against the gold, platinum and rare-earth elements critical for technology.

"I don't have fifty-five ingots on hand, Captain Bardacki," Skov noted calmly.

"That's unfortunate," he told her. "In the absence of payment, I, of course, have to seize and auction the cargo to cover my costs. That would take more time than I'd really like to spend in Agasoft and would require it to be sold frozen."

He shrugged and smiled.

"Of course, I'd probably come at least a bit ahead in that case, I suspect."

"Please, Captain." Skov waved a hand in the air. "I am noting an absence of immediate resources, not refusing to pay. I acknowledge the piracy clause and accept that charge," she noted formally.

"If you are prepared to take partial payment in Agasoft dinar, I can pay you five kilograms of platinum plus one million dinars right now," she told him. "If you require payment in platinum, it will take me at least twelve hours to arrange the ingots, in which case I would ask that you take the five kilograms as a good-faith payment and permit us to begin unloading."

EB blinked as he quickly checked the current exchange rate of dinar to platinum. Skov had clearly expected him to do that, as a million dinar against eight point seven five kilos of platinum was almost exactly the exchange he saw.

It would be a pain to make the conversion…but less of a pain than risking a delay in getting the fish out of his cargo bays.

"I'll take partial payment in dinar to get this moving," he agreed genially. "Shall we get that in motion?"

EB ENDED up waiting in the reception area for another twenty minutes, drinking mediocre coffee patiently. He'd never had a particularly refined palate for coffee—he reserved his specific tastes for beer—but even he'd taken some time to adjust to the general quality of coffee in the Beyond.

Or lack thereof.

Eventually, the receptionist slash guard looked up from his console and gestured EB back over.

"She's ready for you, Captain Bardacki," he said. "You can head right back."

EB looked around the reception area. He had a bobbing light in front of him for a virtual guide that would take him to Skov's office—apparently he was trusted to make his way alone this time—but the whole place still seemed…excessively quiet.

"Does anyone else actually work here?" he asked.

"Sometimes," the guard replied. "I…won't say how many *partners* there are in Skov and Partners—we like to keep our confidences here—

but there are several others who work in the office outside of our admin staff."

"I won't pry; I was just curious," EB conceded. "Thank you."

The floating ball of light led him directly to Skov's office again, though this time he paid more attention to the rest of the place. He passed two of what looked like doors to similar offices, and he *thought* he could see a lunchroom-esque space at the end of the corridor. He guessed that whatever admin staff Skov employed were past that.

It was a small office, but it still seemed *very* empty.

But that wasn't his business, so he told his curiosity to shut up and put an honest smile on his face as he entered Skov's office and saw the secure carrying case on her desk.

"Check it," she suggested, sliding the metal briefcase across the wood. "Carefully, please. It's heavy."

There was a cloth mat between the case and her desk to prevent damage to the wood, too. Skov was being careful.

EB opened the case as suggested and quickly skimmed the contents. Twenty ingots, each stamped by a third-party assessor agency verifying weight and purity. Each was ninety-nine percent pure, two hundred and fifty grams.

Five kilos of platinum. The rest of the payment was in a single credit chip, tucked into a faux-velvet packing section on one side of the case. He waved his hand over it and his headware linked in. There was a quick pause to confirm his identity, and then it happily informed him of the amount.

"Everything appears correct," he told Skov. Closing the case, he plugged in a random number sequence as a lock code. His headware would tell him what it had been later.

"I don't usually miscount, but validation at transfer is always preferable to later retribution over mistakes," the petite woman told him. "My first team should be making contact with your ship in about twenty minutes, so you'll want to give them a heads-up."

"Thank you. I believe that concludes our business," EB said.

She raised a hand.

"That concludes *that* business," she said precisely. "If you're interested, I'd like to make you an offer."

EB swept the case off the desk, carefully leaving the cloth mat behind, and settled it between his chair and his right leg.

"I'm just a freighter captain, Em Skov," he noted carefully. "I'm listening, though."

"I'm not looking for anything else, Captain Bardacki," she told him. "But I am looking for a freighter captain with gumption, fortitude and competence. A good-sized ship to go with all of that is also useful."

"*Evasion* is...not small," he replied.

Skov laughed aloud, a delicate wash of cheer that he hadn't heard from her yet.

"I can count the number of forty-kilocubic ships that come through Agasoft in a year on my fingers, Captain Bardacki," she noted. "You're not unique, no, but your type of ship is uncommon out here. That draws attention—attention you have clearly proven yourself able to handle."

"I've been in the Beyond for a year and a half, Em Skov," EB said. "We're surviving."

"And that means you have the gumption, fortitude and competence that I am looking for," she told him firmly. "I need a delivery made, Captain. To a place where someone lacking those three things will be eaten alive."

EB leaned back in his chair and steepled his hands.

"I'm not sure you're selling this as well as you're thinking," he pointed out.

"Danger increases compensation," Skov said bluntly. "And it is a warning as well. Not all danger is obvious."

A holographic map of the area around Agasoft appeared above her desk. She lifted a delicate hand and pointed at a section of it.

"Here, we have Agasoft. Tatare. Legence. A few other systems," she said calmly. "None of them really close to each other, but at least within the usual six novas before you have to discharge."

A nova drive built up tachyon and electrostatic charges in direct proportion to the distance jumped. Around thirty-six light-years, the buildup became strong enough to interfere with navigation and even threaten to overload the most hardened of systems.

That meant a ship had to discharge that static into a gravity well and atmosphere of some kind. Gas giants served quite well, though even a regular inhabitable world would never notice the discharge.

But that six-nova / thirty-six-light-year limit was solid. A ship *had* to discharge the buildup before passing that line.

"If you look *here*"—Skov pointed at another section of the map—"you have the Nigahog System. Poberin. Blowry. A few others, again, of less importance. All within thirty-six light-years of at least one other.

"Neither group of stars is a cluster by any reasonable standard, but they have communication with each other and enough trade that someone from any one of the worlds in each group can expect to get to one of the others easily enough."

"And between them is a fifty-five-light-year gap," EB said quietly, processing the scale of the map.

"Exactly. A gap with no actual stars in it," Skov explained. "A trio of novas swept it clean about fifty million years ago. Locals call it the Fasach Expanse."

EB's headware recognized the Gaelic word and he chuckled in amusement.

"The desert desert?"

"Humanity lacks imagination as often as not," Skov told him. "Going around the Fasach adds weeks to any trip. It, in fact, renders any route between Agasoft and Nigahog economically nonviable."

"And?" EB asked. "What was the answer?"

She tapped a point in the middle of the Fasach and the map zoomed in. *Way* in, narrowing in on two icons and then to a representation of a large planet and a small station.

"The Diomhair," she told him. "A rogue gas giant, ejected from one system by the nova of another before its original star novaed. Far too small to ignite under its own gravity, it isn't even a brown dwarf.

"It's 'just' a super-Jovian planet wandering around in deep space in exactly the position needed to make the Fasach Expanse traversable. Some braver-than-smart scout found it thirty years ago," she said. "She made a *killing* just selling the map—enough to fund her setting up a space station and her own security force.

"Now her heirs charge a toll to discharge at the Diomhair and run

Star Plaza, a privately held space station twenty-seven light-years from anything resembling authority."

"I've seen trade route stations before," EB noted. "But that sounds...*special*."

Hence her wanting someone who would survive its dangers.

"Star Plaza is a space station with a permanent population of about twelve thousand people whose entire economy is built around emptying the pockets of the spacers who stop there," Skov said bluntly. "It's the *only* way through the Fasach, which means it sees more traffic than any individual system on either side of it.

"But you can guess, I suspect, the limitation of an independent space station in the void almost thirty light-years from the nearest star."

"How's their food production?" EB asked.

"Insufficient," Skov said bluntly. "Usual array of hydroponics with chickens. Last I heard, they were expanding, but they only really had enough in place to feed about three-quarters of the population—and vegetables, soy and chicken don't *really* make for the kind of food they want to be selling at luxury hotels and casinos."

EB had an idea of what kind of "luxury" a trade route stop station was going to have. There were advantages to being the only option, after all.

"So, you want me to haul food there?" he asked.

"Your ship has, what, thirty thousand cubics capacity?" she said.

"Twenty-five," he told her. "Twenty thousand unpressured and ungravitized, five thousand with pressure and gravity."

If she knew ships, Skov could probably put together that the math didn't quite add up for what *Evasion* was supposed to be. Four thousand cubics of nova drive and twenty-five thousand cubics of cargo storage left *eleven* thousand cubics of...other stuff.

Standard power, life support, crew space and Harrington coils should only consume about five to six. *Evasion* was generously supplied with all of that, plus her guns.

She was faster, tougher and better armed than she had any business being. Just because EB never wanted to get into a fight again in his life didn't mean he wasn't *prepared* to.

"Twenty-five thousand cubic meters of supplies is about two weeks of necessities, luxuries and assorted other supplies for Star Plaza," Skov said. "I have a running contract to provide whatever I can to the station, and, well, it's cheaper to send one ship than five."

EB grinned.

"Are you sure about that?" he asked.

"I *lose* one ship in five, captain," she said bluntly. "I don't expect to lose *Evasion*, which means it's definitely cheaper to send you. Do you understand?"

"Fair. But you're not helping your negotiating position here," he said, echoing his earlier comment. "This sounds riskier than I'd like."

"The route to Star Plaza is probably the single most known route in the region," she told him. "It's also one of the few that is actually patrolled—by mercenaries under contract to the Plaza. It's safer in some ways than many nova routes...but it's also a far richer target for pirates.

"But you've already handled one set of pirates. I'm confident in your ability to deliver the cargo."

"So am I," EB agreed. "If you make it worth our while."

He tapped his foot against the secure case underneath his leg.

"Given our recent...issues, you'll forgive me if I do require payment for this in stamped elementals. In advance."

"That will affect the total I can afford to pay you," she said.

"Will it?" he murmured. "Because it won't affect how much I'm prepared to do the job for."

5

EVEN WITH ALL eight members of *Evasion*'s crew in it, the freighter's mess was spacious. The entire ship had been built for about twice the crew that EB ran it with, which meant the mess was sized for sixteen crew plus eight passengers.

It also meant that each of his crew had a set of personal quarters intended to be shared between two spacers. They might be doing half again the work that they would normally be doing, even with the extra artificial stupid robots EB had acquired to make up the numbers, but he didn't hear very many complaints.

"We have a new cargo contract already," he told them as Reggie, the last in, joined them.

EB was holding a chilled bottle of local beer as he spoke. Of the four local beers he'd tried since arriving at the station six hours before, Agasoft Havana Ale was the most tolerable. It didn't quite qualify as *good*, but it was definitely drinkable.

The local microbial life of a world gave every planet's beer its own distinct taste. The varieties of hops and yeasts and so forth that the brewers used to try and control the flavor of their beer couldn't avoid at least *some* of the local taste.

Agasoft's was a soft edge of tartness, almost berrylike. The first three beers he'd tried had attempted to overwhelm that taste. Havana Ale rolled with it, creating a fascinating interplay of flavors.

EB wasn't sure he *liked* it, but it was the best so far.

"That's fast for a contract," Vexer said. "Same person we delivered to, I'm guessing?"

"Vexer got it," EB agreed, saluting the other man with his beer. "And not because I told him. He knows as much about this as the rest of you."

That got him a few chuckles. That the gay captain and bisexual first officer on the ship were amicably on-again off-again lovers was about the worst-kept secret EB had ever encountered. They were only really *trying* to keep it secret from people off the ship.

Some of the people who'd ended up in the Beyond had done so because they were...opposed to the general mores of humanity in the age they'd left behind.

"We're still going to be off-loading the last cargo for another few hours," Tate told them all. Tatiana MacNeal was a heavily built woman whose shoulders packed more muscle than any other two crew members combined.

Tate handled all of their administrative paperwork and was their cargo handler. Most of the work was done by robots, but she'd get in there when she needed to.

"And that's for the best," EB agreed. "Let's get the perishable cargo on its way. What theoretically perishables we'll be bringing aboard in the next load gets vacuum-frozen."

He snorted.

"Trade route station restaurants aren't going to care if the crab legs were frozen before delivery," he said drily. "We're delivering food, fuel and other supplies to a station called Star Plaza.

"It's apparently the only stopping point between Agasoft and Niga-hog, middle of something called the Fasach Expanse."

"The Diomhair," Ginny said instantly. "I've heard of it."

From what EB understood, Ginny was from one of the systems near Nigahog. He'd met her several hundred light-years away from her homeworld and wasn't sure yet if she'd be staying aboard when they passed her star.

"It's a rogue gas giant, well away from any star, but it's convenient for novaing through the Fasach," EB told the others. "So, there's a station there that charges a toll and maintains some level of security."

"I've heard of Star Plaza," Tate said grimly.

"Me too," Vexer agreed. "That place has a *reputation*, boss."

"So it was made clear to me," EB agreed. "Casino station that provides a base for mercenary security that *sort of* secures the route through the Fasach. When they're not selling the schedule to pirates to avoid them."

"You're probably underestimating the degree of collaboration between the pirates and Star Plaza's mercs," Tate said. "There are few places in the Beyond with reputations that spread. Star Plaza is...*infamous*."

"I figured," EB replied. "But we're getting twelve kilos of stamped lanthanum to make the trip. In advance."

The rare-earth element was about as "high-denomination" as the stamped elemental metals used for trade out here got. The payment for this mission was almost double what he'd been paid for the damn sushi.

"It may be a hive of scum and villainy—so far as I can tell, it's a shithole full of backstabbers," EB noted cheerfully, "but we're being well paid to deliver food there. From the sounds of it, we may have some problems finding a cargo there, but we can bounce on through the rest of the Fasach and see what we can find in Nigahog if we can't find anything on the Plaza."

"All I really know is a bad rep," Vexer admitted. "Nothing in detail. So...I guess we're careful and we watch each other's backs?"

"Exactly," EB replied. "All that said, Tate, I want you to do me a favor."

"What's that, boss?" she asked.

"When we were looking at the pirates, I realized we have one blaster rifle and one heavy blaster pistol on the ship," he said drily. "Can you check and see what's legal on Agasoft? I wouldn't mind stocking up the armory, just in case.

"Nothing any of you has said has made me feel any *safer* visiting this place!"

EB STOOD on *Evasion*'s bridge, watching with a careful eye as the container units were stacked into his cargo bays. The containers went in "sideways" relative to the main holds, layered in two high and then ten deep.

Bay One was both more and less of a headache in many ways. The entire "roof" of the pressurized cargo bay could be opened up and ten cargo containers laid in at once. It was the only time that the accesses to Bay One were ever set up as airlocks.

No one wanted to accidentally vent the ship's atmosphere, after all.

"All going to schedule, boss," Tate told him over the radio. "Give me another hour and I'll have all five cargo holds stuffed full and checked against the manifest."

"Good to hear, Tate," he said. "Any problems?"

"Not a one. The locals seem disturbingly competent." She paused. "You realize the other end isn't going to be nearly as useful, right?"

"My expectations of Star Plaza are low and I expect the locals to fail to meet them," EB replied. "Did you have any luck with the guns?"

"Not as much as I'd like," Tate admitted. "Agasoft restricts personal energy weapons pretty hard. I can't even get you military-grade stunners, let alone armor-piercing blasters. Not above the table, anyway."

"I'm not wedded to following *every* law, Tate," EB said. "What do you need?"

There was a pause, interrupted by Tate shouting an order at someone on the other end.

"Sorry, boss," she said when she came back. "Someone wasn't watching their safety margins, and I'd rather *not* wreck Bay One's airlocks by ramming a container into them."

"Appreciated, Tate," EB replied. "So. Should I leave you to the work? Or…the guns?"

"I need one of those stamped lanthanum ingots," she admitted. "And I'm not enthused with what I think I can get for it. And even *that* is only if my contact is playing me straight."

"Given our last few encounters, I'm not sure we can trust that," EB told her. "Take Reggie with you when you close the deal."

The one heavy blaster pistol EB knew of on the ship belonged to Reggie, a leftover from the weapons tech's days as a Rim mercenary. Or...that was what he'd *told* EB he'd been doing before he signed on, anyway.

EB wasn't going to dig too hard into his people's pasts. Everyone on *Evasion* had proven themselves worthy of his trust by now.

"I will," Tate promised. "We don't have much time now, though, do we?"

"Finish loading up, close your deal for guns and we'll get on our way," EB agreed. "Always moving on, my friend."

The cargo handler chuckled at him.

"You are, anyway. Some days, I have to wonder what you're running from, boss. The rest of the time, I know better than to ask."

"Nobody asks anybody about their past, Tate," EB said quietly. "That's why the ship is named *Evasion*."

6

THIS TIME, *Evasion* was using the maps they'd stolen from the gunship. EB had taken the maps Skov had offered for the trip, but their stolen maps actually stretched all the way to Nigahog via Star Plaza.

Skov's maps lined up too, which suggested that *this* trip was aboveboard. So far.

"Nova complete," Vexer said aloud. "We are now away from the Agasoft System and on our own."

"Who else is out there?" EB asked. He was already going through the sensor data, but multiple eyes never hurt.

"I have eyes on one twenty-kilocubic freighter at just over a light-minute," Vexer said. "That's it."

"I see the same," EB agreed, checking what *Evasion* could see of the stranger. It was hard to tell at this distance, but she seemed normal and innocent enough.

"Drive cooldown is in progress; we'll be on our way again in twenty hours," Vexer noted. "Anything in particular you want to do while we wait, boss?"

Vexer waggled his eyebrows enthusiastically at EB, and the older man couldn't help but laugh.

"Not *right* away," he told the other man. "But check in again in a few hours, hey?"

His sometimes-lover laughed.

"I'll hold you to that, EB," Vexer said. "But for now, everything looks quiet. *I* am going to go nap, since my alternative plans have been rejected."

Vexer sighed overdramatically and bowed his way off the bridge while EB laughed at him.

The younger man was darkly attractive in a dozen ways, but the thing that most drew EB to Vexer was that Vexer could make him laugh. With the scars EB carried on his heart, that was more important than many realized.

In the quiet, EB ran through a list of automated reports that let him know what was going on aboard the ship. There really wasn't anything to worry about, not at this stop. Not yet, anyway.

He was surprised Agasoft didn't seem to patrol any of their surrounding mapped trade route stops, though. That was the usual purpose of a nova-capable fleet, after all. If the system government was going to just defend their own territory, they might as well just have the monitors and asteroid forts.

Presumably there was *something* they'd send the nova fleet out for...but he wondered if the Agasoft System had a nova fleet because they *needed* one or because they felt that a "major" system *should* have one.

It didn't matter for him, he supposed, but if even the best systems in the Beyond only had nova fleets as trophies...it really did factor into his threat analysis for his trips.

And at the end of the day, all EB ever planned to do was keep moving.

GENERALLY, EB took the time at a quiet nova stop to tour the ship and check in with each of his people. With only seven other people aboard, each of his crewmembers was a critical cog in the machine that kept the ship going.

It took him longer to find Tate after the first nova than he was expecting, and he finally tracked her down in the storage closet that acted as *Evasion*'s joke of an armory. A single suit of full body armor—sized for EB, though he'd worn it exactly twice since being sized for it in the Rim—held pride of place, flanked by mostly empty cases designed to hold weapons.

There'd been a single blaster rifle and two military heavy stunners in the room the last time EB had been in it, but a second rifle was now spread across an impromptu workbench assembled of ration crates.

"Tate?" he asked, glancing around the cramped space. "How we doing?"

"Checking the guns," his admin assistant and cargo handler told him, gesturing at a waist-high silver case next to the door. "I didn't quite buy this lot sight unseen, but the black-market dealer I was giving a quarter-kilogram of stamped lanthanum to was being *really* pushy about making the exchange and getting gone."

She shrugged immensely muscular shoulders.

"So far, this one checks out," she told EB, gesturing at the dismantled rifle. "It's not quite up to spec with that one"—she gestured at the rifle mounted next to the combat armor— "but it's not shabby.

"Throughput is decent, focus is decent. It'll punch through most armor you'll see out here, and I can rig it to do better."

"And what does it cost if we rig it to 'do better'?" EB asked carefully, examining the silver case and sliding its top open. A quarter-kilogram of stamped lanthanum would have been enough to equip an entire squad of elite commandos with powered armor and heavy weapons back home.

The exchange rate of stamped elementals to dinar to Apollon new drachmae to high-tech weapons was not...that clean-cut. Especially not when the black market was involved.

Still, he picked out three more blaster rifles and what he hoped were the cases for four heavy handheld blasters. It wasn't a terrible deal, he supposed.

"I'll need to check with Ginny and Reggie before I try to do that," Tate admitted. "I figure I could rig them up to overcharge the capacitors and increase the throughput—but since I *have* a weapons tech and a proper engineer to hand, I figure we should put our heads together."

"But...roughly?" EB asked dryly.

"When was the last time you had to swap a blaster cell, EB?" Tate asked. "They run, like...two hundred shots a cell. If I overcharge these, they'll run more like...ten. You'll have a much better chance of burning through armor, but you're giving up the usual endurance."

"This is a freighter, not a commando transport," he pointed out. "If we have to fire more than ten shots in a fight, we've already screwed up *real* bad."

She chuckled.

"Fair enough, boss."

"Put your head together with Reggie and Ginny, though," EB continued. "If we can find a better compromise, I won't complain." He tapped one of the heavy blaster cases. "And since we *have* heavy blasters now, I might even take one when we board Star Plaza."

"If they pass your scrutiny, that is."

"Five more novas," Tate observed. "Anything that *doesn't* meet my standards today *will* by the time we reach the Plaza. You just get us there alive, and I'll give you something flashy that goes boom well."

EB chuckled.

"Let's...not describe it to Reggie that way, shall we?" he suggested. "I think that might hurt our dear weapons tech's soul."

7

THERE WAS something about novaing into an expanse of space with no stars or planets that felt different from usual. Sections of the galaxy like the Fasach Expanse were rare, so far as EB knew, and he'd never traveled through one before.

In the mapped areas of the galaxy, within fifteen hundred light-years of Earth, a ship was rarely more than two or three novas at most from a star with *people*, let alone a star system where you could discharge nova static.

Even in the Beyond, it was rare to be more than a dozen light-years from a system that had a planet large enough to absorb the tachyon and electrostatic buildup on the nova drive. Most crews preferred to discharge in systems with planets, stations and people—discharging being a long and boring process, having somewhere to send the crew for leave for a day never hurt—but any rock bigger than Mars with a half-decent atmosphere would serve.

Three novas into the Expanse, though, EB's maps told him there was *nothing* around him. Following the route map he'd been given, Agasoft was now fourteen light-years behind him, and the Diomhair and Star Plaza were thirteen light-years ahead.

"The weirdest part is that we're not alone out here," Vexer said aloud, the navigator's thoughts clearly following his captain's.

"That same twenty-kilocubic ship?" EB asked. "We're four hours behind them. I worry we're making *them* suspicious."

His XO snorted.

"And vice versa," he agreed. "We also picked up a sixteen-kilocubic friend at the last stop who's joined us here. Got close enough for me to confirm she's *definitely* a freighter. If she's even got popguns, I'd be stunned."

EB nodded, considering the two icons on the display. Three ships sharing a trade route stop wasn't *that* many, though it was busy for the Beyond. From what Skov had told him about this route, though, that made sense.

"Think we could charge the little guy a fee to keep him under cover of our guns?" he asked.

"They almost certainly wouldn't trust us if we offered," Vexer admitted. "This isn't exactly the safest of neighborhoods, EB."

"Fair." The Apollon studied the chart and shook his head. "Not like I'd leave them to it if anyone *did* jump them, either. Would be easier to protect them if they were tucked in closer."

"You, my dear, really need to think more like a Beyonder," Vexer told him. "If those guys get jumped…"

"Do *you* really have it in you to sit over here and watch a piece-of-shit gunship we could take out in our *sleep* murder or enslave another crew?" EB asked. "I don't want to get in any fights out here, Vexer. But I'm not going to sit back and watch *that* go down."

Vexer looked at the display with the other two freighters on it and sighed.

"Not used to having the oomph to *make* a difference," he admitted. "But out here…you look to yourself first, EB. None of us are on *Evasion* because we want to get into trouble. We're all running from something."

"So am I," EB said genially. His lover knew that much, even if nobody—not even Reggie, the longest-standing member of the crew—really knew the story of the war and assassins that had sent him to the Beyond.

"But if we could get those two to come in closer, I'm pretty sure we could intimidate any pirate off," he continued. "And then we don't have to kill anybody."

EB had left enough wrecked ships and dead bodies in his wake. He wouldn't add to the list if he could avoid it—by action *or* by inaction.

"*Nobody* out here is going to trust the most heavily armed ship at the trade route stop," Vexer told him. "So, let's just…keep moving."

"I know, I know," EB allowed, still watching the icons. He tapped a command, firing the Harrington coils on low for a few seconds, sending them drifting toward the smallest of the three ships.

They wouldn't get close enough to threaten them before *Evasion* novaed, not without a far more active approach, but it would give them a start if things got messy.

Vexer said nothing, but his silence spoke volumes. Entire libraries, in fact, and EB flashed him a giant grin.

"What? I'm not getting close to anyone except you," he said.

After the last few days, it was clear that they were in one of the on-again phases of their on-again, off-again relationship. It was mostly friends-with-benefits… Mostly.

EB wasn't even sure if he *wanted* it to be anything more. But he certainly wasn't objecting to the help relaxing as they dove into the unknown void!

"NEW CONTACT."

EB chuckled after he realized habit had made him speak aloud. He was alone on the freighter's bridge. He and Vexer traded off watches and sharing watches, but they were the only two actual qualified watch-standing officers on the ship.

Both Ginny and Tate could do enough to keep problems from arising, but EB and Vexer had both qualified as merchant officers according to at least one star system.

And if EB's qualification "exam" had basically been an Outer Rim system's merchant officer academy taking one look at his former military commission, well, who knew or cared this far out?

Still, EB was the only one on the freighter's bridge as another ship emerged from nova. There was no real way to judge which way a ship was coming from, except for the fact that EB hadn't seen this one at the last nova stop and he was reasonably sure they were down to a single chain of mapped stops now.

That meant the ship was coming from Star Plaza and was a new unknown. EB's headware interfaced with *Evasion*'s systems, drinking deep at the well of her passive scanners as he tried to identify the stranger.

Twelve kilocubics. That was a dangerous range. It *might* be a small freighter. But it could also be…

A gunship. An eighty-meter lozenge shape gleamed on the display as *Evasion*'s finely tuned optical pickups focused on the ship.

"Power signatures," he murmured aloud. "Six guns on top, six guns on the bottom. *Not* SCD."

Evasion's guns were better, but it was twelve guns in single turrets to four guns in dual turrets. EB figured the odds were in his favor if he picked a fight with the gunship, but…

He double-checked the coordinates. He was between the gunship and the other two freighters. A few more commands into the system adjusted his ship's vector, making sure she *stayed* that way.

For a couple of minutes, the four ships continued to float along. The stranger wasn't in range of *Evasion* and would basically have to go through the big freighter to reach the smaller ships.

"What are you thinking?" EB murmured. He would wake his crew up if the gunship started moving toward him, but right now he wasn't even powering up the guns. He was just using vectors and positioning to make it clear to the stranger that he *was* prepared to fight.

It was the starship equivalent of body language, a silent message that none of the other three captains were going to miss.

His mental focus was hovering over the command to start charging the capacitors for his plasma cannon when the stranger started transmitting. Standard beacon code, declaring the ship to be a mercenary patrol out of Star Plaza.

EB relaxed and shook his head.

"You're not pretending to be a merc," he murmured. "But you weren't pretending to be a *pirate*, either, were you?"

He'd been warned by Tate that the mercenaries employed by Star Plaza were often as willing to prey on their supposed charges as they were to protect them—but by making his willingness to fight clear, he'd convinced the gunship's captain that it wasn't worth it.

He was a long way from home, far enough that the Kaiser's assassins would never find him, but there were days EB wasn't convinced running to the Beyond had been the right call.

8

"AND HERE WE ARE," EB announced.

"I *did* push the button, you know," Vexer told him, the navigator almost giggling.

The giggling was probably because Vexer had done so from EB's console, since he was currently sitting in EB's lap. It was probably only the second or third time their relationship had progressed to cuddling outside the bedroom, but EB wasn't complaining.

He'd mostly left the exact level of public affection of their relationship to Vexer. In truth, he was letting the younger man control basically the entire pace and level of their personal relationship on an ongoing basis. EB was the *captain*, after all, which gave him authority over the other man in a way he was trying hard not to abuse.

"You did," EB conceded, looking over his lover's shoulder to check out the scanners. "I guess we should *probably* take a look at what's around us."

Evasion's computers were smart enough to flag if there was anything close enough to actually pose a threat, which was allowing them to wallow in the cuddle for a few extra moments. Still, they *were* at their destination and EB *probably* should have ejected Vexer to work before the jump.

Instead, the other man slowly shifted away, stealing a kiss as he moved, and they settled to work with a comfortable warmth on the bridge.

The time had also allowed *Evasion*'s sensors to complete their first initial sweep of their surroundings, and it was clear that Vexer's jump had brought them in well away from the Diomhair and its single orbiting space station.

The first thing EB really noticed was that everything in the area was just...*dark*. He was used to the void, but his brain still objected mildly to the presence of a *planet* without any light. The Diomhair was an immense gas giant, almost two hundred thousand kilometers across, but it wasn't a star. It emitted some infrared radiation but no visible light.

And with no stars for dozens of light-years in any direction, it wasn't reflecting much light, either. Everything around the Diomhair was dark, and only the light of a thousand distant suns gave them anything to see by.

That faint starlight and the heat signatures of human technology at least allowed EB and Vexer to locate the rogue planet's moons. Both were airless chunks of ice, with surface installations that likely only served to provide Star Plaza with water.

Star Plaza itself was almost impossible to miss. In a space with almost no natural light or heat, Star Plaza was a blazing artificial sun of both. Brought to the Diomhair in chunks small enough to be carried aboard nova freighters, it had been assembled into a behemoth that dwarfed the largest nova ships ever built.

Glittering with ten times the lights of a regular space station, Star Plaza was a ring just over two kilometers across, rotating once a minute to maintain an artificial gravity of one gee in the ring itself.

That was odd to EB's eyes. Anyone with access to the SCD had access to antigrav and grav coils. Given the amount of effort necessary to build a station of Star Plaza's size, why would they have built it without gravity?

"Interesting economizing," Vexer said softly.

"The spin gravity?" EB asked.

"Yeah. They chose size and lights over...well, everything," his navigator told him. "No artificial gravity, just spin. Not enough food production, just flash. Not even..."

Vexer flicked his screen over to EB with a thought and a hand gesture. It was an infrared scan of the station, and EB instantly saw what Vexer meant.

Only about half of the station was actually occupied. Large chunks, entire *skyscrapers* assembled from prefabricated panels and sticking out from the outer ring, were showing minimal heat.

There were lights and signs on those buildings, but they were a façade. A relatively *obvious* façade, at that, one any starship would see through with ease.

"I suppose it gives them room to expand and makes the place look impressive right now," EB murmured. "But why the lack of gravity?"

"It is cheaper to spin up a ring with a tow and a few ships than it is to provide artificial gravity for, what? Two million square meters?" Vexer sighed. "*Interesting* economizing," he repeated.

"Plus, as I understand it, rotational gravity is different," EB noted. "That gives their security personnel, who are used to it, a serious edge over strangers."

"That too," Vexer agreed. He ran more numbers. "We're about an hour out. Any reason to hold off?"

"Who's out there for ships?" EB asked. "I make about half a dozen ten-kilocubic ships running ice from the moons. Looks like a handful of other freighters."

"Yeah. I make it...two docked, three in space," Vexer agreed. "Two gunships just...hanging out. Not really needed. See here?"

EB nodded as Vexer highlighted the three installations, equidistant around Star Plaza's perimeter. They looked like towers, each rising a hundred meters from the "top" of the ring. They were heavy plasma cannon, each of them the size of one of the gunships.

Even built with the standard colonial databases, those guns would vaporize most nova ships with a single hit. The ships that could survive those massive cannon wouldn't come this far out.

"Take us in, Vexer," EB finally ordered. "If nothing else, we can be reasonably sure that Star Plaza doesn't want to shoot down their groceries!"

"FREIGHTER *EVASION*, this is Star Plaza Control. Please be advised that there are discharge tolls to be paid for the use of the Diomhair as a staging point," the station controller told EB in a faux-perky voice.

From the sounds of it, she had the spiel down to a fine art.

"Your officers and crew are, of course, more than welcome to enjoy the amenities of Star Plaza herself," the woman continued. "The standard toll includes docking for one shuttle at a time at the Plaza and a small number of Star Plaza digichips for you to distribute amongst your crew.

"Please note that while the discharge toll may be paid in stamped elementals, the only legal tender aboard Star Plaza itself is the Star Plaza digichip. On boarding the station, we recommend you contact a currency trader who will provide the current exchange rates versus Nigahog marks, Agasoft dinars and stamped elementals."

EB let her get the standard spiel out of the way before activating his side of the video call.

"Star Plaza Control, this is Captain Bardacki aboard *Evasion*," he told them. "We are operating under Star Plaza replenishment contract seven five nine D. Per the contract, our docking and discharge fees are waived.

"I request a docking slot to off-load our cargo."

Skov had paid them in advance for the delivery, which at least avoided *one* potential problem. He wasn't entirely sure he believed her that her contract with the station waived the docking fees, but that was what she'd told him to say.

There was a definite pause as the controller looked things up before she replied.

"Replenishment contract confirmed, Captain Bardacki," the controller told him. "Agents of the Plaza will need to review your cargo before accepting delivery. Please proceed to docking bay twenty-four.

"As per your contract, you are welcome to discharge static once your business aboard the station is complete," she continued. "I do remind you that digichips are the legal currency of Star Plaza, and if you and your crew wish to enjoy the amenities of the station, you will need to acquire some through a licensed trader."

"Understood, Plaza Control," EB conceded brightly. He could think of half a dozen ways that particular restriction could be used to siphon money away from him to the station's owners—and he'd bet that *all* of them were being used.

"I'm forwarding our manifest now and look forward to discussing with the Plaza's agents," he continued. "Locking in a course for bay twenty-four now."

"Welcome to Star Plaza, *Evasion.*"

EB dropped the channel and chuckled.

"Boss?" Vexer asked.

"I do believe they intend to make us much, *much* poorer before we leave," he noted.

"Are you surprised?"

"No," EB admitted. "It very much fits with what I expect of the station. Even if I could convince everyone not to gamble, just testing to see if I can find a cargo here is going to cost money in meals and drinks."

"Such a harsh part of your job," Vexer said with a chuckle of his own. "I make it five minutes to dock. Anything else?"

"Yeah. Get everyone in the mess straightaway," EB ordered. "Time for a family meeting."

THE NATURE of a small crew like *Evasion* was that literally half the crew were technically "officers." EB was the captain, Vexer was the navigator, Ginny was the engineer and Lan Kozel was the ship's doctor.

EB then had one administrator slash cargo handler, Tate, and three techs. One weapons tech, one environmental tech, and one engine tech —Reginald "Reggie" Kalb, Yijun "Joy" Parisi, and Aurora Narang, respectively.

EB was older than his entire crew by a significant margin. Old enough to add another layer to his occasional discomfort with his relationship with Vexer—if not old enough for anyone *else* to question the ten-year age gap between the two men.

With everyone in the mess hall, he always had to resist the urge to be excessively paternal. *Some* space-dad approach was expected, but he couldn't afford to patronize his crew.

"Tate, how'd our box of guns work out in the end?" he asked her.

"We're up to five blaster rifles and five heavy blasters," Tate told him. "Reggie and I up-charged them all, so they'll punch through more than people expect, but...you might want to carry extra power cells."

Reggie chuckled, the blond tech tapping his own blaster as Tate spoke.

"You also want to be *careful*," he observed. "They're not going to blow through, say, a ship's hull. But they'll put some ugly holes in interior bulkheads, and in a place like this, that'll piss off the wrong people."

EB accepted one of the blasters from Tate almost automatically. The woman had brought the four new ones to the meeting.

"Which brings me to my point," he told them all. "I have about five minutes before the Plaza's agents show up to go over our cargo, which will hopefully start the offloading. I *don't* expect that to be fast, but there's not much we can do to help.

"So, you're at liberty at your discretion." It was a small-enough ship to get away with that. "But we need to be *careful*. No more than half the crew off the ship at a time. No one goes alone and no one goes unarmed.

"It might not be a bad idea to see if we can track down concealed body armor, too," he noted, almost thinking aloud. "If there's anywhere around here that's going to sell that, it's going to be somewhere on this damn station.

"We'll sort out some of the local currency for everyone pretty quickly here—or you're welcome to try to exchange your own cash. I doubt any of us are getting an actually reasonable rate."

"Not in this kind of place," Ginny agreed. "There's a lot of ugly behind the glitz, boss."

"And I don't expect the glitz to be overly impressive," EB said. "Gamble if you want, but expect to lose. I'm going to check out food and traders myself once I'm done dealing with the Plaza agents, see if I can find us a cargo heading toward Nigahog."

"What do you figure the odds are?" Reggie asked.

"Fifty-fifty at best," EB admitted. "This is a stopover, not an origin point. Nothing gets produced here, so I can't see them having much to ship anywhere. But…worth the attempt, at least."

"Same rules apply to you, boss," Ginny reminded him, his engineer looking grim. "Take Vexer or Reggie with you. No one goes alone, no one goes unarmed."

EB had been *planning* on sweeping the station on his own…but she had a point.

"I'll take Reggie, leave Vexer in charge," he told them all. Reggie also had the advantage of being the other person on the ship he knew to be combat-trained.

"Be careful, everyone," he reiterated. "This place *should* be safe, but it's designed to separate spacers from their money. Let's not run too low on cash while we're here, all right?"

9

THERE WAS A CERTAIN... *TONE* to the decoration in the section of Star Plaza *Evasion* had easy access to. Someone had seen the concept of luxurious decorations in a database image somewhere and tried to duplicate them.

Except they'd tried to duplicate all of them.

Which meant there was a casino with a faux-Greek white marble—trying and failing to ape the style that EB's homeworld of Apollo had more successfully copied for their public buildings—next to a hotel with a concrete sphinx painted to look like sandstone next to a strip club with dancing male and female holograms out front.

Holograms were *everywhere*, advertising any service or good EB could possibly want to acquire, backed by physical signs in a dividing line down the center of all the main corridors.

This section of the station alone probably had the capacity to handle several thousand spacers passing through...but from what they'd seen outside, there were *maybe* a few hundred non-locals on the station right now.

Which made all of the decoration and advertising gaudy, over-whelming...and desperate. The corridors had enough traffic to count as occupied, but were far short of busy. The impression was that there was far more demand for the station's services normally and…yet…

EB was beginning to understand why the station had rotational gravity. Despite the station's population and determination to be a linchpin between two regions of the Beyond, it likely wasn't making enough money to justify the gravity coils to build artificial gravity into the structure.

Star Plaza was meant to be so much more than it was.

A woman—a girl, really, at *maybe* twenty—emerged from a hologram advertising cheap drinks as he passed. Wearing nothing but a *very* short skirt, she waved him over with a *visible* lack of enthusiasm, and EB tried to hide his shiver as he apologetically shook his head at her.

The pout was probably more honest than the invitation, but she vanished back into the advertisement to wait for her next ambushee.

Through all of the advertising targeted at bored and lonely crew, it took EB and Reggie a few minutes to locate his destination.

"There, I think, boss?" Reggie suggested, pointing past a restaurant that was pretending to conceal itself behind "silk" hangings with Chinese characters.

EB's headware was capable of translating the characters for him. Despite the attempted decorativeness of the hangings, the fake gold characters on the hangings were advertising the same cheap beer, cheap food and naked servers as half the other establishments on the promenade.

But past the hangings there was a door tucked into the wall of the corridor with a far plainer sign marking it as a trade nexus. Theoretically, the nexus's job was to provide commodity-price listings and a job board.

In practice, in the Beyond, where things were much less formal, it served as a networking hub and would let captains talk to potential clients. Whether there *were* any such clients on Star Plaza was up to EB to figure out, he supposed.

He wasn't hopeful. The station was exactly what he'd expected, but he was starting to wonder if the half-dozen ships he'd seen there were a quiet period…or the normal.

If it was the latter, the station was in trouble. And stations in trouble weren't generally hiring shipping.

THE INTERIOR of the office was a relief from the promenade outside. There were still faux columns lining the reception area, but the only holographic ads were those visible through a window looking out onto the ring station.

There was enough of a step into the office that EB nearly tripped, his balance still thrown by the nature of the rotational gravity on the station. Gravity coils produced a sensation roughly equivalent to being on a planet.

Rotational gravity did not, and his brain was *not* okay with it.

"Welcome to the Star Plaza Commodities Office," an artificial stupid hologram greeted them from behind the desk. Almost certainly plaster, the desk had been carved and painted to resemble stone.

Sadly for the intended feeling of the office, both the desk and the columns were chipped, flaking bits of paints onto carpet that was showing its age and wear. Given the age of the station, everything in the trade nexus had to be original installation and un-updated since.

"I'm Captain Bardacki off the freighter *Evasion*," EB told the stupid, gesturing for Reggie to take a seat. "I'm looking to talk to the factor or someone else who can put me in touch with potential shippers."

The hologram paused, gears almost visibly grinding for a few seconds.

"Welcome to the Star Plaza Commodities Office," it finally replied.

EB sighed.

"Is there anyone here?" he asked the program.

"Factor Jessica Magellan is on duty," the hologram replied cheerfully. "She will be delighted to assist you."

"Can you let the factor know we're here?" EB asked.

There was another pause.

"Factor Jessica Magellan is on duty," the program finally said. "Welcome to the Star Plaza Commodities Office."

EB glanced around the office and found the door into the back offices. Ignoring the AS as it continued its cycle of useless information, he walked over and knocked on the door.

"The back offices are private," the hologram told him. "Please do not enter without an appointment with the factor."

"Can I speak to the factor?" EB asked.

"Please make an appointment. Factor Jessica Magellan is on duty. She will be delighted to assist you."

"Can I make an appointment with you?" EB demanded.

Pause.

"Welcome to the Star Plaza Commodities Office," the glitching hologram finally said.

Sighing, EB pushed the door open.

"The back offices are private," the hologram said, but EB ignored the rest of its words as he stepped into the offices.

There was a chill stillness to the air that was familiar to him. It meant that the life-support system was scanning for oxygen content and otherwise not moving the air at all. The door had just enough of a seal that the air could have been...left.

The four office doors that EB could see were all closed, but the privacy glass was set to transparent on them all. None of the offices were occupied, and two of them had dead potted plants. No one had been in there in a while.

EB stepped back into the main office area and looked at the AS.

"Where is Factor Jessica Magellan?" he asked.

"Factor Magellan is on lunch break and will return shortly," the hologram told him.

"And how long has Factor Magellan been on lunch break?"

"Eleven thousand four hundred and eighty-three hours," the hologram replied cheerfully. "She will return shortly."

No one had bothered to report into the trade nexus in over a year. That was a bad sign for EB's ability to find work.

"What now, boss?" Reggie asked.

"We head back to the dock, and I poke the lady who checked our cargo," EB said. That woman had been efficient enough, even if the unloading had looked to live down to his expectations. "This is a mess."

Reggie snorted.

"Can I grab a beer somewhere?" he asked plaintively.

"No one goes anywhere alone," EB told his companion. "So, no. Because I'm not doing anything *else* until I've either found a cargo or given up."

He was pretty sure he knew which it was going to be now.

EVASION WAS LARGER than any docking bay that Star Plaza had. That wasn't saying much, though, as most space stations wouldn't attempt to internally dock a forty-thousand-cubic-meter starship.

It might have been useful on Star Plaza, with the rotational gravity, but instead, EB's ship was linked by a personnel transfer tube and several larger cargo transfer elevators. Getting from the ship into the station ended up involving climbing a ladder, with ninety-plus percent of the work of transition between ship and station handled by the freighter's gravity systems.

There was *supposed* to be someone in the office at the end of the corridor the personnel tube linked to. The corridor was set up to provide foot access to six ships, after all, and part of what their docking fees paid for was security.

EB wasn't entirely surprised to find the office completely empty. He sighed as he glared at the locked door.

"Even for the Beyond, this is a shit-show," he muttered. "There has to be *someone* to talk to."

"First time on the Plaza?"

EB looked up at the speaker, his hand falling to his blaster as old paranoid habits activated. The speaker was a sharp-faced stranger with shoulder-length hair, in a worn-looking dark gray shipsuit.

"Yeah," he admitted. "I'm Captain Bardacki. You?"

In many systems, he'd be receiving a personal profile from the other spacer, receiving a name and pronoun at the very least. The spacer's headware was completely locked down in privacy settings, though, even more than EB's—and *EB's* just gave his last name and nickname.

"Chance," the stranger introduced themselves. "I'm a courier. Been flying this route for Nigahog for...five years? Maybe six? I don't keep a lot of track."

"Is it always this quiet?" EB asked. He was surprised there were any couriers there. They were uncommon enough in the Rim, small ships with crews of five or less that existed solely to carry information.

The only way to send data between stars was by ship, after all.

"These days? Yeah," Chance told him. "PlazaCorp kinda shot themselves in the foot. Ten years ago? There's sixty ship docks and a hundred shuttle bays on this station, and ten years ago, they were talking about doubling that."

EB glanced down the corridor. Chance's courier would be in an actual docking bay, but there were two of those on the same section.

"What happened?" he asked.

"There was a spike in piracy and PlazaCorp hired mercs to secure the trade route," Chance said. They shrugged. "'Cept it didn't help. And a lot of folks think that the mercs PlazaCorp hired *are* the pirates. If you don't pay the right people, you only get through half the time.

"And if your ships don't get through...why come by the Diomhair? And since no one is quite sure *who* to pay off yet..."

"Everything slows until the protection racket becomes clear," EB noted drily.

"Bingo. I think my bosses worked it out," the courier pilot admitted. "Certainly, I don't get trouble, and I don't think the couple of ships that fly under our flag do, either. But...even who to pay protection to is a trade secret out here, Captain.

"Watch your step."

"Thanks," EB said. "Appreciate it. Speaking of 'paid off,' though... Any idea who around here might be looking for shipping? Our delivery was *to* the Plaza."

"Not that comes to mind," Chance admitted. "That said, when my bosses visit, they hit a place called the Solitaire Lounge. If there's any bigwigs, they'll be there."

"That's more than I had five minutes ago," EB told the stranger. "Can I buy you a beer or something?"

"Nah," Chance shook their head. "I'm on a schedule and need to get my ship out to discharge. But when I see a man looking lost and angry, I figure I can drop a few words down the right ears."

They smiled thinly.

"A bit of positive karma. Stars and voids know I need it."

And on that...nerve-wracking note, the stranger turned and walked away down the hall.

The corridor outside the locked office was silent, and EB shared a long look with Reggie.

"You're being set up, boss," Reggie said bluntly.

"I agree," EB admitted. "On the other hand, if I'm being set up with *work*, I'm willing to give it a shot. For now, though..."

He shook his head.

"I need a damn shower."

10

THE SOLITAIRE LOUNGE was on the same promenade as the gaudy casinos and hotels EB had passed while looking for the trade office. Amidst that cacophony of holograms and distractions, it had been easy to miss the hand-stenciled sign with the gameplay spread of the titular game and the single word SOLITAIRE.

The entrance beneath the sign was closed by a single heavy curtain hanging across an open standard station door. EB pushed it aside and stepped through, Reggie trailing hesitantly in his wake.

"Good afternoon, sir," the young man standing behind a host station greeted him. "Welcome to the Solitaire Lounge. May I have your name?"

The youth looked conservatively well dressed at first glance. The second glance revealed that he wasn't wearing a shirt underneath the dark blue suit jacket, which exposed the kind of chiseled chest that required either hours of work every day or a skilled surgeon.

"I'm Captain Bardacki of *Evasion*," EB told the host. He paused, waiting to see if that triggered any kind of response.

"Ah, I see," the host replied, clearly checking against a list in his headware. He then glanced down at something on his station.

"I'm afraid I'll have to ask you and your guest to surrender your weapons," he said apologetically. "Solitaire has a strict no-armaments policy."

EB hesitated for a second, then shrugged. Whatever was going on there, he doubted that a stunner and heavy blaster were going to get him out of it.

He unhooked his stunner and blaster holsters, one with each hand, and passed them to the host. Reggie followed suit a few seconds later, the weapons tech looking even more uncomfortable to hand over his guns than EB felt.

A printed flimsy receipt emerged from under the station, and the host handed it to EB. It included the time, a picture of all four weapons, and a picture of the host himself.

"They'll be returned to you when you leave, on the security of PlazaCorp itself," the host told them. "If you'll follow me, please?"

EB had not, he mentally noted, said so much as "we're looking for a table." Either the host was making assumptions...or the Solitaire had instructions for when EB arrived.

He'd been expecting the latter, though, so he fell in behind the host and gestured for Reggie to follow him.

Setup? Reggie silently messaged him via their headware implants.

Yup. Someone's expecting us.

EB wasn't one to insist on being armed everywhere he went, but something about this situation was making his *lack* of weapons itch-inducing.

It wasn't the restaurant. The Solitaire was the most tasteful place he'd seen so far aboard Star Plaza. The wait staff, regardless of gender, wore the same dark blue suits exposing most of their upper torso. The furniture and decorations were a low-key mix of dark grays and burgundy. The lights were bright enough to provide clarity on anything EB looked at, but dark enough to provide a sense of privacy.

He'd held business negotiations in nicer restaurants and *definitely* in classier ones, but he suspected the Solitaire might be as classy as Star Plaza got.

Their host led them to the very back of the Solitaire, where a row of hydroponic planters held well-maintained living bushes of some kind. The air was perceptibly fresher around the plants, but their main purpose was to divide a semi-private section of the Solitaire Lounge from the rest of the restaurant.

As soon as they passed through a gap in the artificial hedge, a skinny stranger in an anonymizing black mask stepped up to EB, running a scanner wand up and down the two merchant spacers with practiced speed.

There was no audible pronouncement, but the bodyguard disappeared back into a corner of the closed-off section as quickly as they'd appeared. The host had paused, clearly expecting this, and now led EB and Reggie to the single table in the space.

Two people were waiting for them. The closer was a shaven-headed man of about EB's width but a far more towering height, a tad under two meters and packed with muscle. He'd turned his chair half away from the table to stretch out his legs, almost sprawled across his seat...but positioned to watch all of the entrances into the bush-concealed area and with one hand idly tapping on the grip of his blaster.

The gunslinger's eyes and fingers moved with a speed and twitchi-ness EB had seen before, though rarely this far out. He was boosted to the nines, though EB couldn't tell if the boosts were cybernetic or biological implants.

"Soldier boosts" was a generic term anyway, one that covered anything from additional adrenal glands to nanotech-delivered combat drugs to cybernetic organ and bone replacement.

EB figured that the man wasn't responsible for bringing them there, though. He read the man as a top-tier hired gun or a security chief. Troubleshooter, with emphasis on *shooter*.

Still, the big man caught his attention first and it took him a second to register the woman at the table past her companion's intentional attention-grabbing.

She was significantly smaller than the gunslinger. Sitting made it difficult to judge, but she was slimly built, with mousy brown hair drawn back in a ponytail that he suspected made her look younger than she was.

Once he saw her eyes, however, he realized just how much trouble he was in. The lines around them were those of someone who smiled easily and often...but the hard agate chips of her eyes stared into his soul like a hungry predator.

"Have a seat, Captain Bardacki," she instructed softly. "I suggest that Em Kalb allow us some privacy. Cedar will find you a table."

She gestured to a woman in the dress of a Solitaire server who'd materialized out of nowhere at a silent command.

"Go with her, Em Kalb," the stranger ordered.

Do it, EB said silently. *We're in danger here.*

If nothing else, EB figured the gunslinger could draw his blaster and kill EB and Reggie before they even reached the hydroponic hedge.

REGGIE RETREATED with the server and left EB alone with the two strangers. The mousy woman with the hard eyes gestured him to a seat, and EB obeyed instantly.

He strongly suspected that there'd be times to play games in this conversation, but right off the bat was the time to establish an assumption of obedience on the part of the other side. The whole situation smelled wrong to him, and he was well aware of how thin the ice he'd been led onto was.

"I believe you have the advantage of me, Em...?"

"You may call me Lady Breanna," the woman told him in a warm and friendly tone. She gestured to the big man sitting with her. "This is Ansem."

Lady Breanna, EB suspected, was a name at least some people would know. It probably wasn't the name on the warrants, but it would still be one to conjure with.

On the other hand, he would eat his *ship* if Ansem was known to anyone except Lady Breanna and his own immediate superiors. From his easy confidence, the name Breanna was dropping wasn't anything EB could use to trace him, at least.

EB decided to play at least a *little* dumb. It definitely seemed the wisest course at the moment.

"A courier I met said that there might be some people in the Solitaire Lounge who would be looking to hire a starship," he said carefully. "I'm not...entirely sure why I was seated with you, but I'm guessing you might be looking for a ship?"

Lady Breanna smiled. It was a practiced warm thing, a *teacher's* smile that was both forced and sincere at the same time. Everything about the woman was a practiced façade of warm schoolteacher.

Everything except her eyes...and the smile didn't reach her eyes.

"I keep an eye on ships that visit Star Plaza," she told him. "And the staff here have certain names that they are supposed to bring to me. Persons of interest, let's say. The captain of one of the largest ships to ever visit the Plaza is definitely such."

"*Evasion* is a common size for the Rim," EB told her. "I know it's rarer out here in the Beyond, but we're hardly the largest ship to travel through here."

"Few who fly such ships would risk them in the Fasach Expanse, captain," Breanna said. "It's been a dangerous journey for some time. You impressed one of PlazaCorp's suppliers, or you would never have been sent out here...but this is a dangerous route for a stranger to fly, Captain Bardacki."

EB nodded, a bright, understanding smile plastered on his face and a chill running down his spine.

Lady Breanna's implicit threat was clear. If she wasn't in control of *all* of the pirates raiding the Fasach Expanse nova route, she was in control of enough of them to be quite sure that EB wouldn't make it through.

"I was warned about the route," he admitted. "But that was factored into the price that Em Skov offered for the shipping contract." He arched an eyebrow. "It should, I suppose, be factored into any shipment from here.

"If you have a cargo heading toward Nigahog, I'm interested, but we'll need to talk price."

"Of course." Lady Breanna waved a hand dismissively. "You'll find I am quite generous, Captain Bardacki. The exact terms of our arrangement will take some discussion, however, before we speak on price."

A server materialized through the hedge, delivering three plates and three tall glasses of beer to the table. Despite the theoretically high-end fittings of the restaurant, the plates held a galaxy-wide standard burger and fries.

"I'm not sure what terms there are to discuss," he said calmly. "I'm an owner-operator; I only accept carriage contracts at agreed-upon rates per cubic-meter. Loading and offloading are at your expense, and after some bad experiences lately, I'm afraid I have to insist on full payment in advance."

Ansem chuckled and shifted position slightly—tensing up to move toward EB. The lady gestured him back down and the gunslinger relaxed again.

The ice was even thinner than EB had feared.

"That won't work for me," Breanna told him bluntly. A hologram appeared above the table from a hidden emitter. A hologram of *Evasion*.

"Your ship," she said, unnecessarily. "Forty kilocubics. Two dual turrets. She's faster than I would have expected, too, from the footage I've seen. She's not the largest ship to ever dock at Star Plaza, but she may well be the most capable non-warship to."

It had, EB reflected, taken a massive amount of luck to get this far without his ship being someone's target. Now he just had to extract himself from the situation safely. And he wasn't entirely sure how to do that.

"I appreciate the compliment, Lady Breanna," he said carefully. "But if you don't have a carriage contract for me, I'm not certain we have business to discuss."

"Captain Bardacki, no one else on this station has any work for you," Breanna told him. "Very little leaves this station, and almost none of it does so in sufficient quantity to justify a ship of your scale.

"There are more reasons than one that the trade office you visited has been abandoned."

There was a long silence. Ansem was tense enough that EB knew he wouldn't even finish standing before he was shot. *Probably* with a stunner, but...no guarantees there.

"What did you have in mind?" he finally asked.

"I want you to work for me, Captain Bardacki," Breanna told him calmly. "You will be generously compensated and given codes to declare yourself as one of my captains. Those codes will clear your way past many threats, and open doors and stores that would otherwise be closed to you.

"You will not find working for me to be particularly arduous," she continued. "I ask for loyalty and obedience, Captain. In exchange, you will have the most powerful patron you can find in the Agasoft or Nigahog Clusters."

Neither group of systems was actually called that, EB knew, but her point stood. If she cast her web out from Star Plaza, Lady Breanna could exert at least some control of the underworld in twenty or so systems.

That also meant that *running* from her was going to be a pain. A pain better started at the edge of her territory than in the heart of it.

"I am prepared to consider it," he said slowly. "That's a more long-term arrangement than I was anticipating, Lady Breanna. It's a generous offer but not one I can commit to immediately.

"We could, perhaps, carry a cargo for you from Star Plaza and then reassess at the end of that shipment?"

The agates got sharper.

"That won't be acceptable, Captain," Lady Breanna murmured. "The Plaza itself is a reminder of why I have learned not to be so patient. PlazaCorp's owners continue to drag out the negotiations for the buyout."

EB managed not to visibly nod as the pieces fell into place. Star Plaza had very little government, and what governance it had was provided by the corporation that owned it. If PlazaCorp—mostly held by the founder's family, he assumed—sold their ownership of the station to a local crime lord, that would give that crime lord a powerful legal front.

So, Lady Breanna had unleashed her pirates on the station, driving down its revenues and values. Once she took control, the routes would become safe again and she would build it back up over time.

A crime lord as strong as she was implying she was could probably nearly guarantee safe transit through the Fasach Expanse, providing her organization with both vast revenues and a legitimate face everyone would have to respect.

But it also meant that she likely had the power to make sure he couldn't escape her. If EB refused her now, he'd never leave the Solitaire Lounge.

Lady Breanna might not own the Star Plaza yet, but she very clearly owned the Solitaire. No one here would question her if EB was shot dead in the middle of the restaurant.

"I understand," he finally said, looking down at the plate of food in front of him. Strangely, he had no appetite at all.

"Is there a cargo you want us to haul from here?" he asked.

"We use Star Plaza as a relay point to obfuscate the origins of our ships and cargo, so, yes," Breanna said, her tone relaxed now. "Scans can't tell me your cargo capacity, Captain. The information on your delivery says it was twenty-two thousand cubics?"

"It was," EB confirmed. "We can carry twenty-five thousand, but there wasn't that much of the Plaza's supplies ready to go, and storage in the pressurized cargo hold can be complex."

"I see. And passenger capacity?" she asked.

The chill in his spine settled somewhere in the back of his stomach, an icy pit of fear and anger EB didn't dare show. Calm and quiet as this restaurant was, he was realizing this conversation was as dangerous as any fighter strike he'd ever flown.

"Limited," EB said slowly. "We can carry maybe twenty people if we stack them four to a room in the spare quarters. More than that, we'd need to convert the pressurized hold, and that would take time."

"That won't be necessary," Ansem said cheerfully. "The security detail can hot-bunk four to a room, so that will get all forty of them in. We can set the volunteers up in the pressurized hold with basic gear, and they can arrange themselves relatively easily."

"The rest of the cargo should only fill two of your unpressurized holds," Breanna observed. "I assume they have the hookups to provide power and atmo to properly equipped containers?"

"They do," EB conceded. *Volunteers.* Containers that required power and atmosphere. A security detail. He knew what he was being expected to carry. But...he had to be sure.

"Just what am I carrying, Lady Breanna?" he asked softly.

"Voluntary and involuntary indentures," she said calmly. "Ansem

will confirm the numbers over the next few hours, but my understanding is that we have a bit over a hundred voluntaries ready to go,
and five hundred cryo-stasised indentures we should be able to hook
up in your regular cargo bays."

The ice weighed down EB's spine, but it barely held back the fury
that surged through him. Breanna was a human trafficker. "Indentures" meant kidnapped people, lied to and deceived into finding
themselves trapped on a strange world, usually with no identity.

The lucky ones would find themselves trapped in the dangerous
and dirty jobs too complex for an artificial stupid. The...others
would find themselves forced into prostitution and other forms of
abuse.

"That won't be a problem, will it?" Ansem asked calmly. "We can
arrange to replace your crew if necessary."

A process EB was sure that none of his people would survive. He
couldn't allow that.

"That won't be necessary," he said, his voice as level as he could
manage. "I will need...some time, Lady Breanna. Em Ansem. Time to
convince them of the value of this retainer."

"You have six hours, captain," Breanna told him, still in those
gentle, warm schoolteacher tones. "Then you'll receive your first
payment and the datacodes you'll need as Ansem's people commence
loading.

"If there will be any problems, let Ansem know and they will be
handled," she continued. "You won't be required to interact with the
indentures, Captain Bardacki. The security detail will handle all of
that."

"And will the detail be a problem for my crew?" EB asked grimly.
He could guess what kind of people ran security for transporting trafficking victims.

"You have my permission to shoot and space any of them that
cause trouble," Ansem replied instantly. "If they haven't learned what
the limits and rules are, they're worthless to all of us. You'll be doing
me a favor."

Out there, any captain had the effective authority to execute anyone
aboard their ship, passenger or crew. EB had no illusions about that,

but he also had a spectacularly low opinion of any captain that actually *did* it.

Explicit instructions to kill any of the passengers who stepped out of line went against the grain…even if he'd been *intending* to actually take the cargo.

"All right," he said, surprised at how level he was keeping his tone. "It'll take me some time to bring my crew around, so if I have a time limit, I should get back to my ship ASAP."

"The food is actually good here," Breanna told him with a chuckle. "The burger, at least. But I understand. I promise you, Captain Bardacki, that while you may feel strong-armed right now, this *is* the better choice.

"You'll realize that soon enough. I take care of my people—and you are now my people."

"I understand, Lady Breanna," he said quietly, bowing slightly as he rose. "But if I am to earn that retainer you've promised, I need to get to work."

11

REGGIE DIDN'T SAY a word as he trailed his captain all the way back to *Evasion*, which EB was more grateful for than he could admit. The weapons tech had been with him for the longest out of his crew and knew him as well as Vexer, if in a very different way.

The tech clearly recognized that EB was in turmoil.

"Get everyone together in the mess," EB finally told Reggie when they got back to the ship. "I'm going to shut down a few things out here, then join you all."

He'd spent the entire trip rolling concepts and plans around in his head. He was a little surprised, if he was being honest with himself, that actually accepting Lady Breanna's retainer had never been an option.

One of the options he was considering was taking the poor bastards he was supposed to transport aboard and then freeing them—but that would pit his half-dozen civilians against forty armed thugs.

It wasn't a winning scenario, which drastically reduced EB's options and time.

For now, he plugged one of his old software worms into Star Plaza's systems and initiated a sensor loop. The last hour should have been quiet enough on all of *Evasion*'s access points, so he picked up that recording and fed it back into the station.

Every sensor, including the physical locks on the station itself, would now spend the next twenty-four hours looping that one hour of footage. He doubted he'd *get* the full twenty-four hours, but it bought him time.

He'd take all of that he could make.

A second sweep confirmed that there *was* an extra connection between the station and *Evasion*. It wasn't a particularly complicated thing, but it was passively eavesdropping on the ship's internal surveillance feeds.

The bug's lack of complication would make it harder to deal with. For now...EB shut down *Evasion*'s internal sensors with a single command. He wasn't going to need them for the next couple of hours, and blinding Breanna's people was worth it.

They might ask pointed questions later...but he suspected the crime lord would also respect his desire to have the conversation with his people in private.

He *wasn't* actually going to try to sell them on being human traffickers. But if he was, that wasn't a conversation he'd want any recordings of.

Ever.

BY THE TIME EB reached the mess, everyone had gathered there. It didn't look like Reggie had told anyone much of what was going on—he hadn't been present for the conversation, anyway—but everyone looked nervous enough.

"We have a problem," EB told them quietly. "A big, we're-all-kind-of-fucked problem."

"Reggie said you got yanked into a meeting with a crime lord?" Vexer asked.

"Yeah," EB said. "Goes by Lady Breanna and she is a piece of work. She's the reason Star Plaza is going downhill. She's waging a pirate campaign to force the owners to sell the station to her."

"That will make getting out of here harder, won't it?" Ginny said.

"That was her implicit threat," EB agreed. "If we don't work for her, she controls enough of the pirates around here to make it impossible for us to get out. Ginny, how's our discharge levels?"

They couldn't discharge into Star Plaza, and they weren't close enough to the Diomhair to loose much of their static into the gas giant. "Not much" wasn't the same as "nothing," however, and they'd been there for over a day and a half.

"Fifty percent," she said instantly. "If we're sitting here, we need another thirty-six hours. If we drop into proper orbit of the Diomhair, maybe twelve."

"How close would we have to dive to dump the charge in six?" EB asked.

Ginny and Vexer traded a long look.

"We might *bounce* before we manage that," Ginny said slowly. "If we did a minimum-distance six-hour powered orbit...that might do it, but that's not safe at all."

"I can fly that course," Vexer said calmly. "So could EB. So...EB... what's going on?"

"The Lady Breanna gave me a choice," EB told them. "Take a retainer to work for her as a member captain of her syndicate...or be killed, along with all of you, and she'd seize *Evasion*."

"I've heard worse offers," Reggie muttered.

"So have I," EB said. "But most of them don't require me to get actively involved in the human-trafficking trade, people."

The mess was deathly silent.

"That's the work she wants us to do, my friends," he told them. "We'd be hauling forty guards, a hundred conscious and presumably cooperative victims, and five hundred uncooperative victims in cryostasis containers.

"That would just be our first cargo. Give it six months, and we'd probably have helped ruin more lives than the average planetary dictator," he continued quietly. "We'd get rich enough — I don't disbelieve her when she says she's generous — but I can't do it."

"I wouldn't let you," Reggie said bluntly. Every eye in the room was on the Outer Rim ex-mercenary, and he shrugged.

"I wasn't a *nice* merc, people," he admitted bluntly. "I worked for whoever paid and got involved in at least one protection racket. But I bailed when they wanted me to kidnap people for this shit. I'll break a man's leg if I'm being paid, and I'll shoot anyone who draws a gun on me, but I *won't* sell some damn kid so a rich fuck can get his kicks.

"If you're in this shit, I'm out."

"We're not in this shit," EB said flatly. "Anyone have a problem with that? We're about to piss off what I suspect is the most powerful crime lord in fifty light-years. Anyone who wants out can stay on the Plaza, though I'd ask that you not tell the Lady Breanna what's going on for a day or two."

"If she's that powerful, she's got eyes on us already," Vexer warned.

"I have control of the dock surveillance," EB told his crew. "It's looping right now, which means that they won't realize we're gone until someone comes to physically check. Things are quiet enough that we should be able to get clear to the Diomhair without running into anyone."

"Station security will see us go, no matter what we do," Ginny warned.

"But she doesn't own the station *yet*, and the current owners *don't* like her," EB noted. "We have a decent chance that they aren't telling her shit. I can obfuscate the station scanners a bit, but mostly, I'm relying on them not talking to her."

He looked around his crew and was reassured by the gazes he got back. No one even looked afraid. Just...angry and determined.

"This isn't the easy path," he told them quietly. "I'm not sure it's even the *right* path, because we aren't saving those kids. We're just running."

"We can't save those kids," Reggie said flatly. "Forty security, you said? We can't do *shit* against forty security."

"Exactly. So, we run." EB shook his head. "I, for one, have plenty of practice at that. Anyone got a better plan?"

12

IT HAD BEEN a *long* time since EB had truly flexed his hacker muscles. He'd almost forgotten how wide a variety of worms and hacking programs he'd buried in the datavault in the back of his skull.

Technically, keeping some of those programs had been treason. On the other hand, EB's government had allowed enemy assassins to hunt him through their capital city. He didn't feel particularly guilty for the minor treasons he'd committed on his way out.

Now those programs, the best electronic warfare suite of the Mid-Rim, gave him a near-godlike view and control over Star Plaza. Apollo might be an eighth-rate power at *best* by the objective standards of all humanity, but his home system was *decades* ahead of what was available to criminals and corporations a hundred-plus light-years into the Beyond.

"We're clear to move," he told Vexer. "A few people might notice, but they're not going to be able to confirm *which* ship is moving."

"That seems...unlikely," Vexer replied.

"They *should* have their primary sensors air-gapped from their communications, yes," EB agreed cheerfully. "But neither Star Plaza nor PlazaCorp's mercenary gunships do."

It wouldn't matter in an actual fight, of course. In a fight, the gunships would fire up multiphasic jammers and render all communications and complex sensors useless. Then, there'd be nothing EB could do to impact the warships.

Right now, though, he could mess with the sensors of everyone near the rogue planet.

"Overrides in place; all umbilicals and clamps retracting," Vexer reported. "Where did you even *get* this shit?"

"Another time and another life," EB replied. "Some of it I coded myself; some of it I stole. All that matters is that we need it and we have it."

"Fair enough," his lover agreed. "Clear of the station, bringing Harrington coils up to twenty-five percent and diving for the Diomhair. Let's see if they're as blind as you say they are."

EB was watching the sensors, his mental "cursor" hovering over the command to bring *Evasion*'s turrets to full power. If there wasn't at least one gunship in the system that answered to Lady Breanna, he'd eat his command chair.

He didn't want to kill anyone. That wouldn't stop him doing whatever he had to do to get his people out.

"That's right," he murmured as the display remained steady. "Ships leave Star Plaza all the time; why would this one be more important?"

EB still held his breath as the power levels on the Harrington coils increased toward full acceleration. Once they were at full thrust, nothing at Star Plaza could catch them—but "catch" was a very different metric from "fire on."

"Coils at full power; we are on course for a close orbit of the Diomhair and a full discharge," Vexer announced. "Ginny, check the distance metrics I'm sending you. Let me know if we need to get closer. I don't think we want to try for a second pass."

"No," EB agreed. He checked the time. "In four hours and forty-six minutes, Lady Breanna's chief thug is going to be checking in to make sure my crew has bought in and that they can start loading—and I doubt I can conceal that we're gone at that point."

"It's going to take just over six hours to discharge everything we need to, boss," Ginny warned. "If I'm reading these vectors right, we should be clear enough of the Diomhair's gravity to nova as soon as we've dumped everything, though."

"Time on that, Vexer?" EB asked. His focus was still on Star Plaza and the ships there, though part of his attention was now turning to the half-dozen ships orbiting the Diomhair itself.

"Ginny's nailed it. Unless we need to change the course, we can nova in six hours, eleven minutes," Vexer replied.

"Course looks good to me," Ginny replied. "All depends on how much trouble we get in when someone works out what we're doing."

"I'm still hoping no one will," EB said with a chuckle. His humor faded almost instantly, though, and he sighed. "But I'm reasonably sure that they'll notice at the point they were supposed to start loading those poor bastards into our holds."

His chill spread across the bridge and he felt his people share his distress.

"I wish we could do something for them," Ginny said.

"Me too," Vexer agreed. "But Reggie was right: we couldn't do anything against a platoon of merc security. They'd be expecting us to try to vent atmosphere, ready for that. And we couldn't win a straight fight."

EB nodded silently. He wasn't going to *help* ruin six hundred–odd lives, but he couldn't do anything to save them, either.

"Keep an eye on the ships orbiting the Diomhair," he told Vexer. "They're the bigger worry right now, even if they all *look* like freighters."

He couldn't assume that Breanna didn't have any converted freighters at her command. It wouldn't take much for a twenty-kilo-cubic freighter that no longer carried cargo to be a real threat to *Evasion*.

"I'm watching *everybody*, darlin'," Vexer told him. "I'm not as good at reading the sensors as you are, but I can pick out guns and charging plasma capacitors. You need to *breathe*."

EB exhaled a sigh and nodded.

"Maybe," he conceded. "But I don't think I'm going to be able to until we've novaed."

"Not to put too fine a point on it, boss," Ginny said, "but from what you said, we're probably not safe until we hit Nigahog."

"Probably not," EB said. "But we'll have some margin to work with once we're clear of the Diomhair."

He rose from his seat, setting up a mirror of the sensor feed in his headware.

"I'm going to do a walkabout of the ship with a hand scanner," he told the other two. "The one bug I saw was piggybacking on our internal surveillance and nothing is transmitting to the station, but that doesn't mean we're clean.

"I don't trust Breanna's people not to have bugged us in all kinds of fascinating ways."

THE MOST LIKELY location for bugs was the pressurized cargo hold, a yawning void at the heart of EB's ship. There weren't even any supplies for *Evasion* herself in the space right now—it could be used for that, but there were specific storage sections for *Evasion*'s consumables located throughout the ship.

The hand scanner was a fifteen-centimeter screen attached to a small handle and a bundle of sensors that extended another thirty centimeters out. It was a beast of a device, more in line with the mass of a blaster rifle than a standard sidearm, but it was also capable of picking up surprisingly faint signals.

As it was at that moment. None of the bugs EB was detecting were transmitting—they were, he guessed, "call-and-response" style beacons that would activate when pinged by a specific signal—but they *were* recording and consuming power.

The signatures of the four devices were faint and well concealed, but not concealed *enough* for the tool. EB had upgraded this particular scanner himself, and it was actually *better* than Apollo's standard.

It led him directly to the first bug, but even with that, he was staring at the wall for several minutes before he finally found it.

The electronics and optical pickups of the bug had been spread out across a ten-centimeter-square area of the wall, concealed inside a thin layer of plastic that mimicked the color and texture of the wall perfectly.

Having *finally* located the bug with the scanner, EB peeled it off the wall. It was impressive as Beyond tech went and surprisingly tough for its nature. The hand scanner had a small EMP tool attached to it that made short work of the electronics.

Tossing that bug in a garbage bag, EB headed for the second one. That was a more-traditional pinhead camera and recorder dropped in a corner, only difficult to find because of its size. He accidentally stepped on it before finding it, scraping up a tiny pile of silver dust with a bit of paper as he laughed at himself.

The other two bugs were each different again. Someone had put a good deal of thought into making sure there were multiple ways to surveil and track EB's ship.

He'd have to check the main cargo holds as well, though offloading had been sufficiently automated that there was a lower chance of bugs left behind. For now, he'd sweep the main body of the ship.

Some bugs, after all, looked even more like their namesakes. Legs could let a camera or locator beacon find itself all *kinds* of corners to hide in, and EB had no interest in letting that happen.

Plus, it gave him something to do that *wasn't* watching the sensor feed that was telling him everything was fine.

13

BY THE TIME he'd spent an hour patrolling the ship, EB had come to the conclusion that his paranoia had been a *very* good idea—and that whoever ran Lady Breanna's intelligence-gathering operations clearly compensated for the mixed quality of their hardware with sheer *quantity*.

He'd found seventeen mobile bugs scattered through the ship and linked his hand scanner into the ship's sensors to see what he'd missed. For the first time since he'd taken possession of *Evasion*, he figured the internal surveillance system might actually be less dense than he'd like.

Most of the time, he barely used anything except the security cameras at the airlocks. The rest of the system was quite sparse, mostly just security cameras on the links to the docks and in the hallways of the living quarters.

Those were the only places strangers were likely to be. There weren't any extra sensors near the currently empty suites he'd use for passengers, because those were all technically crew quarters. *Evasion* wasn't designed to carry passengers. There was some extra space, but mostly, EB had space for passengers because they ran the ship with significantly less crew than it was designed for.

Still, linking together internal and external sensors and comparing them against his hand scanner told him that he had missed a bug. There were a few random power signatures floating around the ship, but he knew he didn't have *every* piece of personal electronics belonging to the crew flagged.

But there were certain key indicators he'd use for a bug. The power level would be low, small enough to be concealed. It would generally be on the floor or a wall, places where a personal computer or other powered toy wouldn't be.

All of that said there was a bug hiding in the environmental plant, probably having scuttled underneath the hydroponics racks.

As instructed by Vexer, EB took a moment to breathe as he stepped into the main environmental facility. The air was always just a bit fresher in there, the smell of the fertilizer concealed under the scent of the hydroponically grown vegetables.

Everything in the rows of sludge-fertilized hydroponic racks was genetically engineered to the nines for this purpose—and included in the default standard colonial database, too. Potatoes, wheat, canola, soy and mushrooms. Five plants that would be found on every ship and space station in the galaxy.

EB's understanding was that they didn't smell anything like they had on Earth centuries earlier, adjusting their scent to cover the use of human waste as fertilizer having been part of the modifications, but they still *tasted* the same once they'd been processed.

The environmental plant was a multi-purpose facility that both provided oxygen for the ship through the plants and high-tech carbon scrubbers *and* supplemented the food supplies on the ship with fresh vegetables.

Like most ships, *Evasion* had a small plot of almost-actually-dirt tucked in the corner of the room with a berry bush. In their case, puckberries from Apollo. Those formed in purple seed clusters that could, if properly managed, reach the size of a human thumb.

Joy did a good job of managing them, and there were usually several puckberries ready to be eaten when EB wandered through Environmental. Between that and his scanner, the berry bush was the first place he checked.

The scanner part was correct—the bug had embedded itself *in* the fifteen-centimeter-deep box of dirt, though it wasn't enough to stop EB finding it—but there were sadly no berries on the bush. It looked surprisingly denuded, in fact.

Joy normally left the smaller berries to see if they would grow, but it looked like she'd stripped everything and that…wasn't right.

EB wasn't even surprised, not really, when he heard movement deeper in the hydroponics racks. His scans had been looking for electronic bugs…not a more old-fashioned kind of stowaway.

The light in Environmental was carefully controlled. The grow lights usually provided more than enough illumination for work in the space, but there were standard ceiling lights for when Joy was working on the machinery.

Some of those lights hadn't been turned on in months, if ever, but they all responded quickly enough to the silent command from EB's headware. The whole room was suddenly lit with the brilliant stark light of standard spaceship illumination.

He still couldn't see anything in the room, but he *heard* the muffled gasp from the far end of the space and sighed.

"I know you're there," he said loudly. "You may as well come out."

Nothing happened for a moment, and EB instructed the door to lock itself. He was about to move into the labyrinthine arrangement of oxygen-generating plants when a figure slowly shuffled out, their gaze on the floor.

EB kept his sternest look on his face as the kid stepped out into view. She was a gangly young woman of an awkward age, easily anywhere from twelve to eighteen. She was wearing a plain white shift that would do *nothing* for her in the case of pressure loss.

"What the *void* are you doing on my ship?" he demanded.

"Hiding," she said calmly, with a tiny but audible tremor in her voice.

That was obvious enough, but the plainness of her response almost made EB chuckle. It was an effort to keep the stern expression on his face—but stowaways could be dangerous, and there was very little he could do to send her home now.

"'Hiding,'" he repeated back to her. "How did you even get *on* my ship?"

"I snuck onto the dock and no one was watching the door," she told him. "Came here and hid after."

And he'd turned off the surveillance systems to avoid Lady Breanna's people eavesdropping on him, handing some idiot kid the perfect opportunity to get on his ship. He sighed.

"I'm not running a passenger service," he told her, intentionally roughing up his voice. "And if I were, I don't think you could afford it. This isn't a game, little girl. I'm not seeing any reason I shouldn't toss you in a bubble and tell Star Plaza to come get you.

"Someone's got to be looking for you, right?"

She was still looking at the floor, which made it hard for EB to judge what she was thinking, but he saw her tremor as he suggested someone was looking for her. He wasn't *actually* going to throw her off —not unless he *knew* someone was going to come pick her up, anyway —but he needed her to understand just how much danger she was in.

"I can't drop you off, so I'm not seeing any other way to send you home," he concluded after a second of silence.

The silence endured for another few moments, then she reached up to the collar of her shift and undid a single connector. To EB's shock, the entire garment slipped open and fell to the floor, puddling around her feet and leaving her completely naked in his life-support plant.

He spent long enough looking at her to realize that she was quite well developed for her age in some ways—and very definitely on the *young* end of his age guess, *maybe* fourteen. Then his attention was very firmly focused on the bright yellow flowers of the canola plants behind her.

"I can't go back," she whispered, still staring at the floor. "I'll do anything you want. Be your...pet... Just get me away from Star Plaza."

EB stared at the yellow flowers in silence from his own shock. He could put together a good chunk of the story on his own now, and his shock was rapidly being replaced with anger.

Ginny. He pinged his engineer via the headware. She was the oldest and most...motherly of his female crew members. There was no way in void or stars EB was bringing another man into this room right now.

Ginny, I need you in Environmental. We have a problem.

On my way, she sent back immediately.

"Miss, put your clothes back on," EB told the girl. "I have no inclination to start molesting children, and I like my bedroom companions enthusiastic, not *terrified*."

He chuckled softly.

"And even if you were forty years older and ecstatic at the idea, I don't like women in the first place," he concluded. "So, you are about as safe right now as you could ever be."

She was on her knees, pulling the shift up around her shoulders, when Ginny walked in and stopped, staring at the kid.

Part of EB's logic in calling Ginny in proved out. The kid was *maybe* a third of the engineer's age, but the two women were of a height and build. The stowaway had long blond hair instead of Ginny's short red spikes, but he suspected—*hoped*—that they wore much the same size of clothes.

"Stowaway," EB told Ginny, as calmly as he could. The girl was still on the floor, crouching like she was expecting yelling or possibly even blows. Nothing about the situation was making *Evasion*'s captain less angry...but not one iota of that anger was directed at the child on his ship.

"I don't think I want any of the men near her just yet," he continued as Ginny crossed to the girl and knelt down beside her. "Can you take her back to your quarters, get her washed up and dressed in something more decent? Something that belongs on a fucking *starship*?"

"I think we can squeeze her into one of my shipsuits until we get her scanned to have the fabricator run one off," Ginny agreed. As she spoke, she reached over and did up the connector at the girl's neck.

Their stowaway's hands were trembling too hard to do it herself.

"Listen to me, kid," EB said, keeping at least a meter distant from the girl. "Ginny is going to get you washed and dressed. Then she'll bring you to the mess and get you fed—and when all of that is done, we'll talk about why you're on my ship and why we're going to help you, okay?"

For the first time since she'd emerged from the maze of plant racks, the girl finally looked up at him. She had brilliantly green eyes, glittering through unshed tears as she nodded.

"Take care of her, Ginny," EB instructed. "Then check on the discharge capacitors."

He didn't need this, not while he was running for his life and the lives of all of his people, but there was nothing else he *could* do.

14

"I HEAR WE HAVE A NEW WRINKLE?" Vexer asked as EB returned to the bridge.

"Yeah," EB confirmed. "Good news is that I've swept all of the bugs. Bad news is we apparently have a stray."

"So, we give her a ride to Nigahog and hope someone there can help her?" Vexer said.

"Pretty much," EB said. "We'll see what she has to say. Ginny's getting her cleaned up and fed. She was looking pretty exhausted and terrified, so I'm expecting her to fall asleep before we can really ask her questions."

His lover chuckled.

"I see we continue on our trend of being the great terrifying privateer crew, as always," the navigator said.

"Oh, yes, we are very terrifying," EB agreed with a shake of his head. "Anyone on Star Plaza figured out that we've run yet?"

They were now into the time frame where EB figured Ansem had a good chance of checking in on the ship to, if nothing else, see if EB needed the gunslinger to "deal with" any of his crew who weren't buying in.

"I've been picking up the edge of what looks like active sensor sweeps from the station, so probably," Vexer admitted. "We're on the wrong side of the planet for them to pick us up, but, well... That they *can't* pick us up will tell them where to look."

"What are our chances of getting jumped by a gunship before we nova?" EB asked.

"Pretty low at this point," Vexer said. "I mean, theoretically they could cross the distance in the hour and a half left before we nova, but there is a *planet* in the way. It's a minor obstacle and one no one wants to go *too* close to."

EB nodded but mentally measured distances.

"And if they nova?" he asked.

"I'm not sure I'd trust *Evasion* with a million-kilometer nova," Vexer admitted. "I certainly *wouldn't* trust a gunship with an SCD class one nova drive to do that safely.

"No, EB, we're safe. The problem will be after we nova. There's only so many places we can go from here, and they're probably going to guess we're headed to Nigahog."

"I'm half-hoping they think we'll try to run for Agasoft," EB noted. "A lot of people would try to run to known space, after all."

"When was the last time this ship went back to somewhere we'd been before?" Vexer asked drily.

"Never," EB told him. "I've never turned back. Never looked back. We're running *away*, not *to*."

Vexer snorted.

"And you never even asked what any of us were running from," he murmured.

"I had no intention of telling any of you what *I* was running away from," EB replied. "I can guess what our new passenger is running from, though, and her presence does render the whole affair that much more...personal."

"Darlin', Reggie and I were ready to start vaporizing gunships as soon as you told us what was going on," Vexer said. "I mean, we can't exactly take over Star Plaza, but we could make our displeasure known."

Star Plaza's massive defense cannon were probably direct contributors to Lady Breanna's slow and steady plan to force the owners to sell.

The situation was a microcosm of the usual problem in dealing with planetary governments—nova ships were *small* and it was easy to build defenses that could outclass anything a nova ship could carry.

Those same cannon limited EB's ability to cause trouble within range of Star Plaza, too. He doubted Star Plaza's owners would care if he picked a fight with Breanna's people, but he couldn't pick Breanna's people out from PlazaCorp's. Which left him with one option—the one he was quite comfortable with at this point in his life.

"No, we get away," EB said quietly. "Leave Star Plaza and the traffickers to rot with each other. They deserve each other."

The innocents caught in the crossfire didn't deserve any of it...but EB was just one man.

There was a long silence on the bridge, then Vexer sighed and nodded.

"Nova in sixty-five minutes, EB," he said. "We should probably have Reggie get the guns cleared before we make that jump. The next stop is our most likely point of trouble."

"I'll talk to him," EB agreed. "We'll deal with the stowaway once she's in a state to talk and realizes she's not going to have to sleep with anyone on this ship to stay."

He *saw* the shiver of anger that stiffened his lover's spine at that, and smiled grimly.

At least his crew looked to all be on the same page on *that* point.

EVASION'S two plasma-cannon turrets were entirely remote-controlled. Any of the stations on the bridge could run them, though they would be set to mostly automatic as well.

As they ran, EB was sending control of them to his own console. Vexer was flying the ship and, well, they didn't *have* a second officer in the traditional sense. One of the several downsides of how EB ran his ship.

The upside was smaller payroll for him and larger shares and quarters for the crew. Plus, EB was always going to be happier with a smaller crew. He'd been a nova-fighter pilot, after all. In the chaos of a battlespace, with multiphasic jamming everywhere, the only person you could rely on was yourself.

"Discharge is complete," Ginny reported up from Engineering. "Our 'guest' did exactly as you figured, EB. I warmed up a towel for her while she was showering and wrapped her in it when she came out.

"She sat down on the edge of my bed and was out like a light."

The engineer sounded *very* pleased with herself.

"Is the room secure?" EB asked.

"Yeah. I rigged the lock. I can get back in there if I need to, but otherwise, she has the key and nobody else is getting in. She's safe... and I'll get an alert the moment she leaves, and can make sure she doesn't cause trouble."

EB nodded. That met both his meanings of "secure"—and Ginny had known he *meant* both of them, too.

He had a good crew.

"Thank you, Ginny. Vexer, ready to nova?" he asked.

"We need a couple of minutes to get a bit farther from the Diomhair," Vexer replied. "But there is nothing in position to give us grief."

EB checked the gun status anyway. Reggie did a lot of odd jobs around the ship, but the weapons tech's main responsibility was making sure those four plasma cannon were in perfect condition on the occasions they were needed.

According to the status checks he was getting, Reggie had done a *very* good job.

"Boss, this is Reggie," the tech said in his head. "I'm at the lower turret-control section. I can take control of the guns from here and run them, but it's your call."

EB hesitated. He was feeling twitchy and wanted his finger on those triggers. On the other hand, it was his job to watch *everything* and make sure all eight of them—nine of them!—got out of this safely.

"We'll check over the best place for you to do that from later," he said aloud. "Transferring shipwide fire control to lower turret-control. Don't shoot anyone I don't tell you to."

"If I shoot someone without orders, boss, it'll be because I *knew* they were going to shoot us," Reggie replied.

"Fair enough. Finger on those triggers," EB ordered. "Vexer?"

"Ready to nova," his lover replied.

"Get us out of this shithole."

The universe flashed bright blue and then returned to normal. New scan data was pouring into the systems, and EB was running through it as fast as he could.

"We're on the very edge of the mapped zone as our database has it," Vexer reported. "Shouldn't be anything within a half a light-hour at least."

"That was risky," EB said softly. They novaed to mapped zones for a reason. The closer they jumped to the center of the zone, the safer the nova was. On the edge, something unmapped might have a material effect.

"Yeah, but take a look at who's at the center," Vexer said grimly.

EB was already looking at scans. There were four freighters scattered around the trade route stop. The largest was thirty kilocubics, a solidly sized transport by Beyond standards—and one traveling with her own escort, a ten-kilocubic gunship that clung to the freighter like a friendly barnacle.

Everything he was seeing was almost thirty minutes out of date, but at that time, a pair of gunships had been approaching the freighter. Flying without identity beacons, they may as well have run up a skull and crossbones.

"Pirates," EB agreed. "Fortunately, Lady Breanna *probably* hasn't sent out orders to hunt us yet—and they won't see us for a while yet, either."

Unfortunately, whatever had happened to that freighter had happened thirty minutes before. Even if EB had some way to cross half a light-hour fast enough to intervene, the vectors he was seeing told him the situation was already over.

"The other two freighters are gunning it, away from the pirates and the big guy," Vexer said quietly. "It's just the freighter and her escort against those pirates."

"I know," EB agreed. He didn't need to tell Vexer about the lightspeed delay. His navigator already knew. "We record everything. It might be useful if anyone in this region ever decides to remember what law enforcement looks like."

"They won't," Vexer told him.

"I know. But it's all we can do," EB admitted. "So, we watch, and we keep ourselves quietly over here while our own drive cools down."

Even as he spoke, though, the entire area around the conflict disappeared into the chaos of multiphasic jamming. At this distance, even a telescope could no longer sort out what was going on.

"Guard gunship fired her jammer," Vexer noted. "Gutsy bastard. If she's doing that…"

"Then her captain is going for it," EB agreed. Part of him almost wished he could see it. Two-on-one wasn't likely to end well for the defender, but they clearly weren't going to surrender, either.

"Keep us well clear of everything," he reiterated. "Worst case from our perspective is that those gunships are going to be too busy looting their target to come for us, even if their main backer sends orders."

"And best case is that the merc over there turns two pirate gunships to debs," the navigator said with some satisfaction. "I can live with that one."

"We can hope," EB agreed, his gaze resting on the impenetrable bubble of jamming half a *billion* kilometers away. "But that's all we've got."

At least his people were safe.

15

TRACE WOKE up wrapped in thick blankets, warm against the chilly air of the room. For a moment that rapidly turned painful, she thought she was back at home, probably due to get yelled at by her foster mom for sleeping in again.

That lasted about, oh, five seconds. Then the memories of the last few months came crashing in on the teenager, and she pulled the blankets closer around her with a whimper.

Nothing happened in response to that, though, and she took a long, deep breath. She'd got away. She was on a ship... She didn't know the name of the ship, or of the captain who'd calmly rejected her desperate offer.

The woman who'd guided her to this room was named Ginny. She remembered that. She remembered the shower—the shower in the bathroom that the woman had firmly closed the door of.

Pulling herself a bit more together, Trace rose to a sitting position with the blankets still wrapped around her. The lights in the room turned on automatically, staying at a gently low illumination that still allowed her to look around the room.

It was...not what she'd expected from being aboard a starship. The dresser with the full-length mirror looked like it had different handles than she was used to and might be attached to the wall, but otherwise, it was almost identical to the one Trace's foster mom had had.

There were several chairs, one of which was clearly in the middle of being reupholstered by hand. Trace wasn't sure if the two fluffy bright pink chairs were the pre-work or post-work products, though the similar texture and color of the throw blanket on the bed did suggest that the reupholstering project would result in more pink chairs.

Still looking around the room, she saw that there was a table by the two pink chairs—and that the table had a full set of clothes spread out on it. Practical underwear and...

Trace shivered at the sight of the shipsuit. She couldn't help herself. She wouldn't have recognized the single-piece garment—other than as "that suit everyone wears in space vids"—six months before.

Now she knew that it doubled as an emergency spacesuit. She knew *that*, however, because her captors had never let any of the indentures wear them. Only the guards wore shipsuits. Only the guards were safe if something breached the hull of the ships and stations they'd been transported through.

Swallowing her fear, Trace dressed. None of the clothing quite fit, but the shipsuit automatically tightened in key spots. It didn't have *much* flex, just enough to make sure it would keep her safe.

Unless she missed her guess, the clothes belonged to Ginny. Like the room. Despite the initial threat from the captain, Trace was surprised to realize that she felt...safe? That was a new feeling.

She wasn't even sure she'd felt safe in her foster home. She certainly *hadn't* felt safe while in the hands of the *people* who'd brought her to the space station she'd escaped on.

Trace's feeling of safety fragmented a bit when she approached the door. There was no mechanical handle and it didn't respond to her pushing on it. There wasn't a visible control panel or anything, and she realized she was just as much a prisoner in there as she was with the traffickers.

Except...

She stared at the door silently for a moment as an impulse hit her.

"Computer, do you take verbal commands?" she said aloud.

"Yes," a calm artificial feminine voice replied. No further explanation.

Trace knew she was brighter than the norm but had ended up being worse-*educated* than the norm...but she knew what an artificial stupid was.

"Is this door locked?" she asked.

"Yes," the AS replied.

"Who can unlock it?"

"You can, Jane Doe."

Trace blinked as she processed the name, then giggled. She'd watched enough crime dramas to understand *that* reference. The giggle surprised her, though. She'd learned to fake laughter *very* well over the last few months, but that tiny genuine giggle had been new.

"Who else?" she asked.

"The door is currently secured to Jane Doe only," the AS told her. "Engineer Ginerva Anderson has a physical override key. No other persons have access to this door."

They hadn't just locked her in. They'd also locked themselves *out* so that she was safe.

"Ginny" had probably assumed that Trace would get that information automatically through her headware—except that Trace's headware was completely disabled.

"What is this ship's name?" Trace asked.

"This is the independent merchant transport *Evasion*, owner-operator Captain Evridiki Bardacki commanding."

"Okay." Trace exhaled a long sigh. "Can you...let Engineer Anderson know I'm awake? I don't want to wander without checking in."

She'd learned that cooperating initially made it *far* easier to fool people later on. She had hope that this might be better and safer than her *last* set of voyages...but she couldn't assume that.

A SIGNIFICANT PART of the safe feeling that had fragmented when Trace realized the door was locked was restored when Ginny, who the AS had told Trace had a key, knocked.

"Computer, unlock the door please," Trace told the AS. There was no audible change, but the door slid open a moment later to allow the stranger in.

Trace took a moment to study the woman whose clothes she was wearing. She had a pretty good idea of how bad she was at judging adult's ages, but she figured Ginny was at least into her forties.

Everybody she'd seen on this ship was *old* by Trace's thirteen-year-old standards. But she wasn't sure that was a bad thing. Especially as Ginny carefully gave her her space, standing just inside the door and waiting.

"You sent me a ping?" she asked. "How are you doing, kid?"

"Awake, terrified," Trace said. It didn't take much effort to sound pathetic and small. She'd made it this far, and this was a *vast* improvement over her prior situation...but she really didn't know what was going to happen now.

"Is...the captain actually going to throw me off?" she whispered.

"We're a nova and change away from Star Plaza, so that's not happening," Ginny said bluntly. "May I come in?"

"It's your room."

"Yes, but right now it's the closest thing *you* have to a safe space, so I'm going to protect that," the engineer told her.

Trace found herself suddenly, *fiercely* fond of the much older woman. The spiky-haired redhead wasn't much taller or curvier than Trace herself, but the age gap was clearly visible, looking at Ginny.

Ginny wasn't much to hide behind, but she'd clearly volunteered as human shield. Trace would *use* that...but she'd also appreciate it.

"Yeah, you can come in," Trace said—and then her stomach growled, loudly.

"When did you last eat, kid?" Ginny asked.

"I...uh...stole a bunch of berries in the life-support plant," Trace admitted. "That's how the captain caught me."

"Yeah, EB would check the berry bush first," the older woman said with a chuckle. "Come on, let's get some real food in you. No questions till after," she said firmly. "But realize that we're going to have questions.

"Stowaways aren't free for us. Captain figures he's got a good guess at your story and that's enough to get us all started. But you're going to need to tell us what's going on, kid, and if it's half what we think it is, that's going to hurt."

Ginny had *no* idea.

"So, if you want a word of advice?"

Trace nodded silently.

"Tell the truth the first time," Ginny told her. "No one on this ship is going to hurt you, but the more we know, the better we can decide how far we'll go to help you. It's the difference between you getting dumped at Nigahog and you going home.

"Understand?"

16

WHEN THE MULTIPHASIC jamming finally cleared, EB had to admit his surprise.

"All right, I owe that captain a beer if we ever have a chance," he told Vexer as he looked over the updating sensor feed. When the jamming had gone up, there had been three gunships and a freighter dancing toward an inevitable conclusion.

When the jamming came down, all that was left were the freighter and her escorting gunship. From their current range, it was impossible to tell if either of the surviving ships had been damaged, but they were still around.

And the two pirate gunships definitely *weren't*.

"Looking," Vexer murmured. "There...and there."

Two debris fields lit up on the screens.

"Definitely the pirates," Vexer concluded. "I don't know what the defender pulled on them, but I'd say only one side was actually ready for that fight."

"Agreed." EB looked at the scans and shook his head. "That helps us out a lot, too," he admitted. "Those pirates were the most likely people to follow orders from Lady Breanna to hunt us down."

"Right now, the only people left in this chunk of void with guns are very clearly *not* her friends," his navigator said. "But who knows who'll come out of Star Plaza?"

"I was expecting somebody already," EB admitted. It had been over an hour since they'd novaed away from the stopover station. "Not that I'm *complaining*, mind."

Every hour they were left alone there increased the chances they'd make it to Nigahog unharassed. And once *Evasion* made it to Nigahog, their options for destinations expanded dramatically.

Unless Lady Breanna had a lot more pirate ships than the local economy could ever support, pursuing them after Nigahog would be almost impossible.

"Boss, it's Ginny."

"How are we doing, Ginny?" EB asked the engineer as her voice sounded in the bridge.

"Our guest is awake. I'm taking her to the mess and feeding her pancakes. Give me fifteen to fatten her up, then swing down for the questions?"

"Take twenty," EB told her. "Let the kid breathe before we demand she explain everything."

"Fifteen or twenty, minutes or hours, I'm not sure waiting is going to make anything easier on her," Ginny warned. "But I'll try."

"I'll let Lan know to expect to examine her later, too," EB said quietly. "I *think* they should be pretty nonthreatening."

"I'm not sure *any* of us are going to qualify as 'safe' to her for a while yet," Ginny said. "She's pretty scared, EB."

"I know," he admitted. "And we'll handle her gently. But I need to know what her story is."

"Like I said, let me feed her. Swing by the mess in fifteen or twenty, your call."

THEIR PARTICULAR CHUNK of void was still calm and quiet when EB headed down to the mess. He had a link to Vexer on the bridge in case that changed, but he also needed to find out what the stars was going on with their stowaway.

Neither he nor Ginny had issued any particular order to keep the mess clear, but the only occupants when he paused at the door to the space were the engineer and their stowaway.

The kid looked a lot less ragged with her hair tied in a ponytail and wearing a proper shipsuit. The poorly fitting clothes made her age even more obvious, and EB had to control a spike of white-hot fury at whoever had made her think that offering sex was even an *option* for her yet.

She was polishing off what looked like a second plate of pancakes, and he chuckled softly. Healthy teenage appetite, if nothing else.

"Do we have more of that coffee?" he asked Ginny as he finally entered the room, using the request as a way to announce his presence.

Their stowaway still looked like a deer trapped in vehicle lights for a moment. Her gaze flickered up to him, then back down to her mostly clean plate.

"Yup," Ginny replied. She grabbed a carafe and filled a new cup for EB—and refilled her cup and the kid's at the same time.

There was a moment of hesitation, then the kid added cream and sugar to hers, stirring it with a dedicated focus as EB took a seat across from her.

"This is my ship," he told her gently. "I'm Captain Evridiki Bardacki. You can call me 'Captain' for now."

"Okay," she said in a small voice, staring down into the coffee cup.

EB took a sip of his own coffee to cover his sigh.

"What's your name?" he asked.

"Tracy," she whispered. "Tracy Finley. My…friends call me Trace."

"Okay, Trace," he said. *Hopefully,* she'd take that as an olive branch, not patronizing. EB wasn't sure. The "kids" EB was used to dealing with had been twenty- to twenty-two-year-old hotshots out of the Apollo pilots' academy. The youngest and dumbest of them had been older than Trace.

"I need to know where you're from, Trace," he told her. "And how you ended up on my ship. I'm not going to toss you off in deep space, but there's only so much I can easily do for you.

"If we're going to help you, I want to know what's going on," he said gently.

She nodded slowly, still staring into her coffee.

"I'm from a place called Black Oak Island Sanctuary," she said. "Terraformed bio preserve on…Denton? I didn't pay enough attention to the planet. It was just…home."

That was common enough for people who didn't expect to leave their homeworld, EB knew. And for kids in general.

His headware ran a database search and popped back the *planet*, at least. Denton was in the Icem System, some thirty-six light-years past Nigahog. Trace had come a *long* way to end up on his ship.

"Parents died when I was little," she said softly. "Lot of folks' parents did. Plague."

She shrugged with the fatalism of someone for whom a devastating crisis that had changed their community and their own life had occurred before their real memories started.

"Bunch of orphans running around Black Oak," she continued. "I was one of them. They tried to find us homes; some of us went to the mainland, but they wanted to keep us there."

EB grimaced. If the adult population loss was as bad as she implied, someone had probably been actively keeping the kids to rebuild the long-term population of the island. The consequences of that on the *kids* probably hadn't occurred to them.

"But…big crisis, handling us all. You wanted to be seen doing what you could," Trace said bitterly. "Ended up with a foster family, the Vortanis. They…weren't bad people. Did everything expected and a bit more. But…"

She took a long swallow of coffee.

"Sarah Vortani was running for planetary parliament," she explained. "I was in their home to mark off a box expected by the people she needed to vote for her. Nothing more. They *tried* but they didn't *care*."

EB wasn't entirely sure he bought that explanation himself, but he was no parent. Taking on that task for *any* reason seemed insane to him. From what he could tell, raising a teenager was harder than running a nova-fighter squadron.

But he could also begin to see how a disgruntled foster child had ended up on his ship.

"So?" he prodded after Trace had been silent for a minute.

"So, I caused trouble," Trace admitted bluntly. "The Vortanis wanted a perfect poster foster child, and I refused to be it. Skipped school. Did drugs. Met what Sarah called 'a bad crowd.'"

She sighed.

"I should have listened," she said. "But I was determined not to listen to a word she said. And when it started getting twisted, I wasn't paying attention."

EB drank his own coffee silently, waiting for Trace to get to the next part on her own.

"Amelie was *so* glamorous," she finally continued. "She was older, not local. But she listened and she had a flashy aircar and access to drugs and money." Trace shook her head. "Listening to *her* was dumb. Dumb. Dumb. *Dumb.*"

The room was silent again. EB couldn't argue with that assessment.

"She said there were ways we could make our own path," the teen whispered. "Away from foster parents. Places we could get ourselves legally emancipated and live our *own* lives. She said she could help us."

"Be easy on yourself," EB told Trace as she glared down at her hands. "If she's what it sounds like she was, she likely had a lot of practice."

"Probably," Trace agreed. "Six of us, in the end," she continued. "Both of the boys were older; pretty sure Amelie was sleeping with them. Three of 'em, including one of her boytoys, were hooked on one thing or another.

"Two of us just wanted to be gone. We were sick of the foster care, sick of the island, sick of...everything. We were all dumb."

"I'm guessing things looked fine until the first nova?" Ginny asked.

"Yeah," Trace agreed. "It was made clear we were going to have to *work*, but that was fine. We were dumb enough not to question what kind of work they had in mind. I was the youngest by a few years, so..."

Not all trafficking was for sex abuse, EB knew. The older boys Trace mentioned had probably been destined for the kind of dangerous and changing but repetitive tasks that artificial stupids were bad at and no one really *wanted* to do.

"Once we made the first nova, there was no way we could get out or call for help," she said, the last vestiges of emotion draining from her tone. "That was when we realized that Amelie *hadn't* novaed with us. She left the ship just beforehand.

"They split us up almost immediately afterward," Trace continued. "There was no pretending anymore. We were to follow instructions or be punished. Submit to…degrading exams. I was quickly completely separated from the rest."

She shivered.

"They told me I had *special value*," she whispered. "That if I followed instructions and did as I was told, I'd be comfortable. I'd just have to be a *very good girl*."

EB held his coffee cup tightly enough that he was worried about breaking it. He could guess what kind of "special value" a young woman like Trace would have to the human traffickers.

"So, what did you do?" he asked quietly.

"I was a very good girl," Trace said, her voice still toneless. "Realized they didn't want to ruin that special value, so I was protected from some of what they could do to me. Some of what they *did* to the other girls."

She shivered.

"I had to watch 'educational' vids and such, but I didn't have to demonstrate what I was supposed to learn. The other girls did. So did the boys, I think. I know…"

Trace trailed off, staring at the coffee cup in front of her.

"Take your time," EB told her. "It's all right."

"Ben got chipped, in the end," Trace told them. "Something in his headware. Last time I saw him, he was…almost robotic."

"Fuck." EB couldn't stop himself from swearing, even in front of the child. He'd *heard* of headware-control implants, but only in the most distant and vague of theory. Even research into *related* areas was carefully regulated in any sane star system.

"Khasan, the other boy, cooperated, like me," she said. "But I think he'd have done anything to get his next fix by then. Two of the girls got...put on ice? I didn't understand."

"Cryo-stasised," EB told her. "Only unfrozen in areas the traffickers know they control. Plus, it means those victims end up completely unaware of where they are or how they got there."

"I was awake and I didn't know where we were," Trace said grimly. "We ended up at a space station where I was put through more *training* by a series of older women.

"Still...theoretical. My *special value* kept me safe."

Her tone was dripping acid now.

"But you knew what was happening to everyone else," EB said. It wasn't a question. "Fear was how they controlled you."

"If I stopped being cooperative, I could end up on ice or chipped. Or just...expected to service the guards."

The toneless lack of hope that undercut Trace's words fanned the flame of EB's anger, but he bit it down and carefully put his cup on the table.

"I think that's enough on that part," he told her softly. "How did you end up on *Evasion*?"

Trace stared blankly across the room for a few more seconds before shaking herself.

"They were moving a bunch of us somewhere," she said. "I was as close to a *favorite* as the lot of us had, and no one told me anything. But several hundred of us were shifted from that station to a ship and delivered to the space station I found you on.

"I'd been cooperative, gone along with everything and was generally regarded as *easy to handle*," she explained. "But I eyeballed that station as being a big-enough port I *could* hide somewhere.

"So, I took a chance. But I couldn't trust anyone on the station not to turn me in straight away, so..." She shrugged. "There was no one guarding your ship when I saw it, so I snuck aboard. Then I needed to eat and found the berry bushes...and then you found me."

"And here we are," EB said. "Thank you, Trace. I'm sorry you had to go through that."

He was apologizing for having her explain it to him, though he realized the apology also covered the hell the poor girl had been put through.

"I'd like to have our doctor examine you," he told her. "From what you've said, I understand if that's not…something you're okay with. Lan is…"

EB stretched for a description that would cover what he needed to say.

"Not male," Ginny finished for him, bluntly. "They're an asexual nonbinary physician from the Kolter System. They're as safe as can be. I'll come with you if you want."

Trace looked down at the table.

"I…don't like doctors," she said quietly. "They're—"

"The ones you've dealt with are monsters," EB interrupted. "I won't make you see Lan, Trace. Ginny will get you fitted out with some clothes from the fabricator and a room of your own for the next few days.

"Your headware will only have limited access to the ship, passenger-level," he continued. "That's standard. You'll be able to ping myself or Ginny at any time if you feel you're in trouble."

Trace sighed.

"My headware's disabled," she admitted. "The traffickers poked at it a few times while I was with them, to make sure of it. We weren't allowed data or coms access."

EB grimaced.

"May I attempt a direct network link?" he asked quietly. "If it's a software lock, I may be able to undo it."

A direct network link would normally require her to set up specific protocols on her side, and he wasn't sure it would work with the headware disabled. Headware had wireless connections, but the fact that the implants were in people's *brains* meant that there was more focus on security than functionality.

"You can try," she allowed, her voice even quieter.

EB closed his eyes, focusing on his implant and sweeping the networks around him. He could feel the ship. Feel Ginny. But…there was nothing where Trace was. He attempted a connection several different ways, then sighed.

"It's been physically disabled," he told Trace. "But you knew that." She nodded.

There was no way to *miss* someone physically disabling headware. It was outright brain surgery, if a nonintrusive one usually carried out with magnetic manipulators, lasers and remote-controlled microbots.

"Dr. Kozel—Lan—can undo that," he promised her. "I understand that you don't trust doctors, but they're as good as doctors get. I trust them. Ginny trusts them.

"Above all else, Em Finley, you have my word, as *Evasion*'s captain, that no harm will come to you while you are aboard my ship and under my protection," he told her, hoping that she felt the weight of the words.

"I swear it."

17

THE SICKBAY ABOARD *Evasion* had identical bones to the one on the space station Trace had undergone her last examinations on. The layout was similar, the equipment was similar—everything about the two spaces clearly spoke to the same intended purpose and ideals.

The similarities sent a chill down her spine, but there was something about *this* sickbay that still eased her mind.

She was pretty sure it was the stuffed animals. The first one she noticed was a human-sized golden bear, recognizable from a dozen storybooks. Even a terraformed bio preserve didn't go so far as to introduce *bears* onto new worlds, after all.

Once she got over the giant bear, she saw there were more regular-sized toys standing watch on half a dozen surfaces around the room—and once she was looking for them, tiny, fist-sized, stuffed animals hiding inside cupboards and machines.

"Em Finley?" a voice asked. The speaker emerged from the attached office, the stuffed cat in their hands still steaming from a run through some kind of sterilizing process.

Dr. Lan Kozel was a shaven-headed individual of middling height. They were *shorter* than Trace, with a wide-hipped body shape the young woman associated with a certain type of schoolteacher, except flat-chested.

"I'm Trace," she said faintly. Ginny's hand was suddenly on her shoulder, squeezing gently in reassurance.

"I'm Dr. Lan Kozel," Lan told her, their smile flashing brilliant white. "And *this* is Mistopheles. Hold him."

The stuffed black cat was suddenly in her hands, and she instinctively pulled the toy to her face. Still faintly damp, Mistopheles was also warm and soft.

Suddenly, without even a conscious thought, she was clutching the stuffed cat and trying to swallow sobs. Both Ginny and Lan had her a moment later, stabilizing her and guiding her onto the gurney as she bawled into the fake fur.

"Sorry, I'm sorry," she gasped.

"For what?" Lan asked. "That's Mistopheles's job. My dear heart, you have nothing to apologize for. In this room, in this space, you are safe. Ginny will remain with you to make certain of that. Do you understand me, Em Trace?"

Trace nodded, feeling ridiculous as tears streaked down her face onto the warm stuffed animal.

Ginny offered her a tissue and she took it.

"Now, I need to examine you to make sure you aren't injured or ill," Lan told her gently. "This will be entirely nonintrusive, but I will need to do several scans that would be blocked by the shipsuit.

"They will *not* be blocked by normal clothes, so I took the liberty of running off a set of pants and a T-shirt in Em Ginny's size from our fabricator." They gestured to a curtained-off alcove.

"Please change in private," they continued. "And, Em Trace?"

"Yes?" she asked, still clinging to Mistopheles.

"If I ask you to do *anything* that makes you uncomfortable today, tell me and we will stop," they told her. "I would *like* to get a solid assessment of your general and specific health before we proceed with reactivating your headware, but while the aggregate of the tests will be extremely valuable, no single test is essential.

"Do you understand?"

She nodded.

"Good. Now take Mistopheles with you and get changed," they instructed.

SOMEWHERE BETWEEN THE STUFFED CAT, the clean and comfortable clothes, and the instruction to raise any complaints, Trace found enough confidence not to instantly flinch away when Lan approached her with a palm-sized scanner.

"I prefer a stethoscope," they told her brightly. "But this will allow me to listen to your heart and lungs from about twenty centimeters away. Are you okay with that?"

She squeezed Mistopheles tightly to her and nodded, feeling very young and small.

She'd *used* that feeling and the ship's crews' reaction to it to protect herself, but it was a very real feeling. Trace didn't even feel particularly *bad* for manipulating the crew...not least because she wasn't entirely sure she *was* manipulating them.

Lan slowly circled her with the device, their attention entirely focused on the screen in front of them and the earpiece they were wearing. The whole process took about two minutes, then they cheerfully nodded to her and put the scanner down.

"Heart and lungs are healthy," they said. "Pulse is elevated, blood pressure is elevated, classic white-coat syndrome. Nothing to worry about."

"White-coat syndrome, doc?" Ginny asked, a bit of concern in the engineer's voice.

Lan chuckled.

"You're scared of doctors and medics, correct, Em Trace?" they asked.

She nodded silently.

"Her pulse and blood pressure are elevated by that fear," Lan told Ginny. "White-coat syndrome. It's normal; it just helps me look at some of the numbers and recognize the elevation isn't a concern.

"Now." They turned back to Trace. "I'm going to set up several scanners on a rail that runs up and down the bed. None of them will touch you, but I will need you to lie back and remain still as the rail moves."

Hesitantly, Trace lay back on the table. She could hear the doctor setting up their tools but she couldn't see anything. She inhaled sharply—and then Ginny was sitting next to her head.

"I can see all of the scanners, Trace," the older woman told her. "Can I help?"

"No," Trace admitted. "I just need to…"

She wasn't sure what she needed. She clung to the stuffed cat even tighter, then felt Ginny's hand cover hers and squeeze.

"I'm here," Ginny said quietly. "EB would be here if we didn't think that would hurt more than help."

"Are you familiar with the Hippocratic oath, Em Trace?" Lan asked.

"Not…really," she admitted.

"Not a lot of doctors swear the actual original version," Lan told her. "But almost all of us swear some descended oath, calling on us to do no harm, to protect our patients above all else.

"You are safe with me," they said quietly. "But if you are not comfortable, I will find a different method."

"No…this seems best," she told them, lifting her head to look at the mobile rail he was setting up. It would run almost thirty centimeters above her, a far cry from the intrusive touching and examinations she'd undergone at the hands of the traffickers' doctors.

"Okay," they assured her. "Starting the first scan now. We'll be doing two sweeps with this set of scanners, then swapping for a different set and doing another two sweeps.

"After that, I'll need to do a contact scan of your head before I can attempt any kind of work on your implants. Ginny will be with you until we're done. I will be as well.

"And trust me, Em Trace, the captain will break my legs if I hurt you. Hang on to Mistopheles—he's specifically designed not to interfere with these scans.

"Are you ready?"

Trace looked at the rail with its intimidating scanners…and then focused on the ten-centimeter-tall stuffed fox sitting on the left end, grinning at her. The stuffed animal was reassuring. If nothing else, it told her just how different *this* sickbay was.

"I'm ready," she told Lan.

AFTER ALL OF the scans and preparation, the final procedure was shockingly quick.

"Hold still," Lan told Trace. "This is the most intrusive thing we'll be doing today."

She inhaled sharply and nodded. She *still* flinched as the warmed metal syringe entered her ear. The feeling as it touched the top of her inner ear was almost indescribable, like concentrated pins and needles.

The buzzing sensation remained as Lan withdrew the device, examining a tablet which Trace suspected contained a map of her brain. They tapped something on the tablet with one hand...and the world woke up.

The first implants of Trace's headware had been installed when she was a single standard year old. Upgrades and additional modules had been part of her annual examinations as she'd grown older, and the Vortanis had made sure she had the best hardware available on Denton.

She'd had computers helping her process the world and reinforcing her memory since shortly after she could walk. The last two months without her headware had felt...numb, with much of the color and depth of information washed out of the world around her.

Suddenly, all of that came back. Her implant instantly identified Mistopheles as a surgical-grade emotional support device. A fancy name, she recognized, for a stuffed toy designed to survive sterilization.

It also flagged that the name was derived from some old play she'd never heard of, but she let that flag fall away as she glanced around the office. Both Ginny and Lan were transmitting standard limited personal beacons, giving used names and pronouns to anyone around them who inquired.

Trace checked her own personal beacon. She'd turned it offline long before her headware had been disabled, but she turned it back on now. She made sure it was sending the same information the two *Evasion* crew members' beacons were sending—the name and pronoun she used.

"It's back on," she said aloud.

"It's a fascinating choice they made," Lan told her. "Usually, headware isn't designed to be turned off. They installed a module that allowed them to do so. Once I found that module, telling it to turn your headware back on was easy enough."

They shook their head as Trace looked at them.

"The module is still there, Em Trace," they warned. "Removing it will be significantly more intrusive and potentially harmful. I would recommend we leave that for a planetside hospital when we get you wherever you're going."

That was…a small problem, Trace realized. *She* didn't know where she was going. She wasn't sure where she even wanted to go. She'd been running away from the traffickers, not toward anything.

This ship seemed safe enough for now, but she knew her safety and presence there were on tolerance. They were going to help her, but she wasn't sure how *much* they were going to help her.

"Come on," Ginny told her. "Change back into the shipsuit and we'll head down to the fabricator. Should be able to do some measuring scans, then get you into a proper 'suit of your own."

The engineer shook her head with a smile.

"Then I need to actually get to work. You're welcome to go rest or tag along, your call."

Trace considered that for all of about five seconds.

"I'll tag along, if you'll let me," she said.

Despite the last few months, she was still a kid…and how many opportunities did a thirteen-year-old *get* to see the inner workings of a starship, after all?

18

EB WATCHED the footage of Trace following Ginny through Engineering. Ginny had the route to check on all of the key systems down to a fine art, an almost random-seeming path that he presumed was the most efficient.

Their young stowaway followed quietly, watching everything the engineer did with sharp and fascinated eyes. Ginny, EB judged, was nurturing what could easily turn into a lifelong love of starships.

"If she stays with us for long, we'll need to pick up an education stupid somewhere," Vexer suggested. "Not the same as a live teacher, but it'll be better than her not getting any formal education."

"She has a home," EB reminded his navigator.

They were back on the bridge, neither of them really willing to spend much time away from the control center as they continued their flight from Star Plaza. EB was surprised they'd made it even a single nova without being obstructed.

Evasion would still be there for another ten hours, though. There was still time for things to go sideways.

"Fair, fair," Vexer conceded. "Wasn't really thinking... I don't know what I was thinking."

"She's smart and brave and a manipulative little shit and we all respect that," EB told the other man with a chuckle. "But she's also a traumatized thirteen-year-old who needs her home and her people."

"Didn't sound like 'her people' were much help," Vexer muttered.

"Remember that you're listening to the *teenager's* story of that relationship," EB said. "I've never met a teenager yet who thought their relationship with their parents or caretakers was good."

"That's because you've mostly met military brats," the navigator replied. "There's a *lot* of teenagers who love their parents. With the kind of comparison Trace now has? And she's still down on these Vortanis?"

"Maybe," EB conceded. "But I bet you, lanthanum to donuts, that they cared about her more than she thinks and are heartbroken by her loss."

He snorted.

"They wouldn't have to care much more than she thinks to be heartbroken," he added. "Just be fucking human, and I don't think even Trace would argue that they aren't that."

"You've...*met* politicians, right?" Vexer asked drily. "If they needed a trophy foster to keep their office...I'm not sure I'd be betting on the political family being human."

"I'd bet on them taking her back and being able to afford damn good therapists," EB said. "But for that, we need to get her back to Denton."

"Feel like it should be her call," Vexer said mulishly.

"If she was older, maybe, but she's *thirteen* standard years old, Vexer," the captain said. "I'm prepared to take responsibility for getting her home now she's fallen in our lap, but I'm not going to do anything except take her back to her family."

"Fair," Vexer agreed. "Icem System is an awkward distance on from Nigahog. If we had the right maps, we might be able to make a direct flight."

"We don't have *any* maps past Nigahog," EB said with a sigh. "That's the limit of what we stole from that pirate. We'll need to buy maps and find cargo in Nigahog. Keep our heads down as best as we can, but that's our next step."

"If we make it to Nigahog," his lover said.

"We'll make it to Nigahog," EB said. A grim chill ran down his back. "It's a question of how many pirate gunships get left behind in pieces."

After all he'd done and how far he'd run, the fact that violence was key to his next steps *hurt*. But he wasn't going to fail his people, either.

Vexer gestured an astrographic map into existence in the middle of the bridge.

"After that, there are two systems that will make sensible stopovers between Nigahog and Icem," he noted. "Poberin and Blowry. Both decent-sized colonies, forty-million-plus people. We should be able to find cargo in Nigahog to either of them."

EB nodded, his attention back on the video feed of Engineering as Ginny coopted Trace as a second set of hands for some project.

"Then that's what we'll do," he confirmed. "I don't think any of us care much where we go, so we may as well go somewhere that lets us bring that poor kid home."

19

BY THE TIME *Evasion* reached Nigahog, EB could easily split his crew into two groups. The first, led by Ginny and Lan, were clearly taking the absence of a follow-up threat as a sign that they'd got away with their flight. If no one had shown up to harass them in the five days and six novas since Star Plaza, clearly the crime lord hadn't been as determined to chase them as EB had thought.

The second group, which consisted of EB himself, Vexer and Reggie, *knew* that the quiet simply meant that Lady Breanna was mustering different resources.

"We're entering orbit in twenty minutes," EB told the gathered crew plus Trace. "We don't have a cargo aboard, so orbital control is being vaguely confused at us. It won't be a problem, though. We can cover the traffic-control fees."

"So, what's the next step?" Ginny asked.

"We're not docking with an orbital here," he told them. "Vexer is negotiating with Nigahog Orbital Control over our orbit, but we should be about twenty thousand klicks from any of the stations.

"That should put us safely clear of everything, including strange ships and the orbital defenses."

Nigahog had one of the more impressive sets of the latter EB had seen since leaving the Rim. Almost every inhabited planet had an asteroid fortress built into the counterweight for their main orbital elevator. Often, the first additional defenses were built on the counterweight asteroid for the second elevator.

Nigahog only had the one orbital elevator, but they'd augmented that fortress with an array of battle stations and defensive satellites. They hadn't pulled entire asteroids into orbit the way many systems did—and EB suspected that most of the "battle stations" were actually monitors, capable of moving quite swiftly under their own power, at least inside the system.

"That seems a bit paranoid, boss," Lan noted.

"That seems insufficiently paranoid, boss," Reggie countered. "Just because nobody has come hunting us from Star Plaza yet doesn't mean we aren't being hunted."

"Exactly," EB said quietly. "At least for the next few systems, we need to assume that Lady Breanna can reach us and is angry enough to try.

"It seems the timing didn't work out for her to send her own people after us in deep space, but that doesn't mean that we're free and clear. Places like this have bounty hunters, and those hunters don't ask questions."

Though, fortunately for EB, he'd clearly outrun any news of the standing bounty on the members of his old squadron. There'd be too many middlemen involved in collecting that bounty from his homeworld's enemies for it to be worth it out there, but that might not stop someone *trying*.

"So, what's the plan?" Reggie asked.

"Vexer and I take the shuttle down to the surface, the capital," EB replied. "We've got a few potential next stops while heading in the direction of the Icem System, and on a planet of over a hundred million souls, I'm figuring *someone* is shipping that way."

The mention of the Icem System sent several gazes flickering toward the teenager sitting quietly at the back of the room. Clearly recognizing the attention, Trace cleared her throat and looked up at EB.

"What about me?" she asked. She now wore a shipsuit that had been sized properly to her and looked her actual age instead of too-young wrapped in hand-me-downs or too-old wrapped in traumas.

"That's at least partially up to you," EB admitted. "If you're willing to stick with us for a bit, we can see you home to Denton. That's why I'm aiming for the Icem System. If you'd *rather*, we could take you over to the orbital and give you cash for a private ticket, but…"

"I'd rather stay with you," she said in a rush of words. "Seems safer than a liner."

EB wasn't sure that she was happy with the idea of going back to Denton, but she was at least going to stick with his crew. That would help keep her safe for now.

"I hope so, at least," he admitted. "So. Everyone except Vexer and I stays aboard, watches everything like we're hauling solid gold. Tate, I want you to run up a list of what we need in terms of supplies.

"We'll need to dock with the orbital to take on cargo and supplies when everything is settled, but I want that to be as short a stop as possible."

"I'm on it, EB," Tate replied.

"The rest of you, let's keep our heads down," EB ordered.

He met Reggie's gaze, arching an eyebrow at the ex-mercenary. Reggie nodded once. The weapons tech understood *his* role in this.

If someone tried to pull a fast one on *Evasion* while EB and Vexer were gone, they'd have a rude surprise waiting for them.

BETWEEN THE CASH that his old wing commander had buried at the edge of the Rim and the resources an old colleague had assembled based on the nova fighters she'd taken to the same place, EB had been lucky in what he'd been able to acquire for a ship.

After cramming everything he'd wanted into *Evasion*, though, he'd functionally run out of money. When he and *Evasion* had left Redward, he hadn't *had* a shuttle aboard. Their single parasite runabout craft was a later acquisition, and for all of his complaints about the concept, it was a dirt-cheap standard colonial database spacecraft.

Barely three hundred cubic meters total, the thirty-meter-long craft had no nova drive—it was smaller than any class one drive could be built, after all, and the SCD didn't include class two drives—but was packed with antigrav units and Harrington coils.

It was designed to get to the surface and back or vice versa as cheaply and efficiently as possible.

"Talson City Spaceport Control, this is shuttle *Evasion*-One," EB said. "We have the beacon and are inbound to the designated pad. I make estimated landing in six minutes."

"Understood, *Evasion*-One," the controller replied. "A spaceport official will meet you at the pad. Please do not leave without making proper arrangements for storage and payment with TCS personnel."

"Understood, Control," EB told the stranger. "Looking forward to seeing your city."

That got him an amused snort—but it was an *appreciative* amused snort. Everyone wanted to think positive things of their home city, after all.

And Talson City deserved at least *some* of those positive thoughts. Like most diaspora capitals, it had been planned from the beginning. A perfect grid had been laid along the coast of a sheltered bay in the shadow of the orbital elevator.

Nigahog was colder than many human-settled worlds, but the equatorial regions were apparently a delight. EB could see rippling purple-blue seas stretching away to the south and expanses of pale blue sand wrapping around the bay.

There was an industrial port on the bay, but the builders had done a good job of siting it to avoid damaging the natural beauty of Talson City's surroundings. The same logic had been applied to the grid. There were places where the terrain wouldn't conform to the grid— and those places appeared to have been turned into parks, some with local plants and some with imported Terran trees.

"It's a pretty city," Vexer said calmly as they swept toward the port. "I haven't seen any ugly planetary capitals, as a rule, but they picked a good place for this one."

"Let's hope the people are half as welcoming as that bay and beach look," EB replied.

THE OFFICIAL WAITING for them was an older woman wearing a conservative black suit of a type known the galaxy over. Despite head-ware meaning she didn't need anything of the sort, she gave off an undeniable vibe of holding a clipboard as she studied EB's shuttle.

"Any cargo aboard, Em Bardacki?" she asked before EB had even said hello.

"Nothing, ser," he told her crisply. He could push back on the title, but she was using it to establish power, and it probably wasn't worth the fight. "We're at sixty percent fuel and carrying personals only."

"Weapons?" she snapped.

"Standard personal arms," EB replied. "Two personal blasters, two personal stunners."

He opened his jacket to show the gun belt with the two weapons.

"Blasters are forbidden for civilian ownership inside the limits of Talson City," she told him. "They'll need to stay on your ship. Stunners are permitted without licensing for apertures under two millimeters, dispersal under two degrees, and ranges under ten meters."

The heavy military-grade stunner EB was carrying after the last few weeks met...none of those restrictions.

"What are the licensing requirements for heavier stunners?" he asked.

"Thousand-mark application fee and range test with a certified instructor," she told him. "Current turnaround on the datawork is about three weeks. Are you staying that long, Em Bardacki?"

"No," he conceded. He glanced over at Vexer. "Do we even *have* light hand stunners on the shuttle?" he asked.

"No, ser," his lover admitted.

"Leave any weapons that are not light stunners on the shuttle," the woman told them. "Landing fee is five thousand marks. Standard eighty-percent deuterium fuel is five thousand marks a cubic."

EB checked his headware for the exchange rates against stamped elementals, the closest thing the Beyond had to standard currency. The landing fee was rich...but the fuel was actually on the cheaper side. A cubic meter of hydrogen there on Nigahog had almost certainly been shipped from the gas giant Nigahog IV.

"Is third-party stamped gold acceptable?" he asked. "If not, I will need to visit a currency exchange before I can make payment."

"May I check the stamp?" she replied.

EB removed a quarter-kilogram bar of stamped gold from inside his jacket and passed it over to her. That should be more than enough to cover the fee and the fuel they'd need.

The woman—who hadn't given her name and didn't have a personal headware beacon transmitting—flipped a hand scanner out of the wrist of her suit in a practiced gesture. The scanner flashed a series of small lights over the ingot and then she flicked it away.

"I'm not familiar with the stamping agency, but their code checks out," she told him. "This will more than cover the landing fee. I will put the balance on account for fuel costs for your shuttle. The remainder can be paid out upon request in Nigahog marks.

"The Talson City Spaceport does not carry a significant quantity of stamped elementals and will be unable to pay out in elementals."

Or provide change, EB gathered. The shuttle would run enough costs that he expected to use up most of the value of the ingot, so that was fine, and he nodded his agreement.

"We'll be looking for cargo and nova-route maps," he told her. "Any suggestions on where to look?"

"You will need to register with the Transporters' Guild," she said instantly. "Guild operators are generally preferred by local shippers. They would also be your most reliable source of nova-route maps.

"Any autocab can take you to the Guild Tower. Welcome to Talson City, Em Bardacki."

20

THE GUILD TOWER wasn't noticeably different from the other hundred or so skyscraper offices in the downtown of Talson City at a distance. As the automated groundcar pulled up to the building, though, its main distinguishing feature came into view.

Most of the towers had a small courtyard in front, providing at least a small green space in the middle of the city. The Guild Tower's garden was no exception there, except that its main decoration was a ten-meter-tall model of a standard colonial database cargo transport.

The sign above the main entrance simply said TRANSPORTERS' GUILD. Everyone who needed to know what the Guild was clearly already knew.

"Monopoly?" Vexer muttered as they entered the garden. The auto-cab, thankfully, could draw on the account they'd set up at the space-port for payment.

"Or close enough," EB agreed. "If no one will hire a non-Guild ship, then you have to be a Guild ship. I just hope that doesn't end up costing us too much."

"Maybe we're lucky and the cost includes their maps," Vexer suggested.

EB looked around at the hundred-meter-tall skyscraper and its manicured gardens and its statue of a starship, all of which spoke to money and wealth and power, and shook his head.

"Don't count on it," he told his lover. "Not as strangers just paying for memberships to get work. If they even *let* us get a membership, we'll be at the bottom damn tier."

"What happens if they don't let us buy a membership?" Vexer asked.

"We find someone who hates the Guild and needs a cargo hauled," EB replied as they reached the old-fashioned glass doors. "But for now, game faces. We are very impressed with the Tower and would *love* to become members of an organization of such repute and ability."

Vexer chuckled—but did as instructed. They stepped through the main doors with level and respectful expressions on their face and approached the front desk.

"Good morning and welcome to the Transporters' Guild," the older man sitting behind the desk greeted them. "My name is Mohinder Nunes. How may I assist you today?"

"Good morning, Em Nunes," EB said. "I'm the captain of a ship that just made the transit from Agasoft, and I'm looking to acquire new nova-route maps and a cargo. My understanding is that the best source for nova maps and the best broker for contracts here is the Transporters' Guild."

"We are the only non-government source for nova-route maps, captain," Nunes told him. "And all sensible merchants arrange their shipping routes through us. Of course, access to our maps and our contract brokers is limited to members of the Guild only."

"Of course," EB agreed cheerfully. "And how does one become a member of the Guild?"

Nunes's dark face split in a broad white grin.

"I'm glad you asked. Allow me to page one of our initiation specialists, and we'll see what we can do for you, shall we, captain?"

EB WASN'T SURPRISED that "Initiation Specialist" Vivian Lamarre had a high-floor office, with a view that covered the gorgeous bay and beach that anchored Talson City. She ushered EB and Vexer into the office, closing the door behind them as they took seats.

"Em Nunes tells me that you wish to become members of our Guild," she finally said, crossing the office to lean against the window and face them. "You understand, Captain Bardacki, that is not something that we simply sell, yes?"

"So I presumed," he told her. "I don't want to cause any trouble here, Em Lamarre."

The dark-haired official nodded and gestured at the city out the window.

"Look out there, captain," she told him. "Every trucker. Every cargo ship you see in the bay. *Everything* on Nigahog is run by Guild members. We keep this system running, keep goods and people flowing.

"We are neither able nor willing to just blithely pass membership out to everyone who wants it. There is generally a period of apprenticeship and coworking, where a new member works under an existing member with experience at the role they are taking on.

"Starship captains are among our most respected members, with the attendant cost of membership in terms of money, time and proven experience."

EB waited for her to get to the point. She, on the other hand, seemed to be waiting on him to say something.

He leaned back in his chair, met her gaze and smiled. If the barrier to entry for him was as high as she was trying to imply, she would never have brought him and Vexer up to her office.

"It is the interests of the Guild, our members and even Nigahog itself that we maintain tight control of our membership and the transportation networks around our system."

He was reasonably sure they weren't managing the latter. If the Guild had any kind of lock on shipments even *coming* to Nigahog, he'd have seen some sign of it in Agasoft or on Star Plaza.

"And?" he finally prompted her.

"Without far more history of your ship and yourself, captain, we would require you to undergo a period of apprenticeship with one of our captains," she told him. "That could be aboard your ship if you wish, but that would be nonnegotiable."

His smile widened.

"That is impossible," he told her. "I'm not staying in Nigahog for any significant length of time, Em Lamarre. I'm *certainly* not surrendering command of my ship to *anybody* ever. I suppose what you're expecting is to put one of your captains in a sinecure, aboard my vessel, claiming the captain's share of payments while we do what we would have done anyway.

"If you want my history, I can give you that," he continued. "I was a military officer for the Apollo System in the Rim. I can provide a full personnel profile from that, if you want. I've run *Evasion* as an owner-operator for eighteen months.

"She's my ship, crewed by my people, and that's not changing." He shook his head gently at Em Lamarre.

"I sincerely doubt that my position is unusual, Em Lamarre. Owner-operators from other systems must arrive in Nigahog all the time—and, at the very least, captains arriving through the Fasach Expanse will never have heard of you.

"I want to make a positive deal here," he concluded. "As I said, I have no interest in causing trouble for the Guild. I'm perfectly happy to pay reasonable membership fees and contract commissions, and to work within Guild confines in the systems they operate in.

"So, what is the *actual* process we're looking at here, Em Lamarre?"

EB was pretty sure he heard Vexer inhale sharply as he calmly tossed aside "game face" in favor of speeding the process up.

"That is quite presumptuous of you, Captain," Lamarre replied. The smile flickering around her lips suggested that she found his forthrightness amusing, though.

"It is," he agreed. "But am I wrong that there is another process?"

"There may be," she admitted. "There is, however, a significant push against the Guild certifying many out-system owner-operators. Most locally based spaceship captains feel that the purpose of Guild certification is, in fact, to keep out-system owner-operators from carrying cargo for Nigahog businesses."

"So, the price is high," EB said.

Lamarre snorted.

"There is a special certification process, yes," she confirmed. "The easiest way to access it, of course, would be to carry a cargo no one else in the system currently can."

"How many nova ships with twenty-five-kilocubic capacity do you have?" EB asked.

There was a silence.

"Currently in-system? None," she conceded. "The size of your vessel does give you certain advantages. If there were to be a cargo of such scale, the client would be able to sponsor you for membership.

"The cost would still, as you guessed, be significant," she told him. "I will, though, roll the cost of our nova maps into that membership. Updates are an annual cost, but I don't see that being one you're worried about."

"I take it you have a client in mind?" EB asked.

"That depends," she told him. Her hand stretched out toward him in a universal gesture of fingers rubbing together. "I may know some shippers who would always like to ship in the largest quantities possible."

EB knew Vexer well enough to know that his partner wasn't surprised by the blatant demand for a bribe. Even *EB* wasn't, not really. He'd expected somewhat better from the organization that appeared to control Nigahog almost completely, but he supposed power corrupted.

He slipped a hundred-gram ingot of stamped platinum out of his jacket and dropped it onto the coffee table in front of him. Lamarre studied it from a distance with a focus that suggested she had augmented vision of some kind.

"That'll do, Captain Bardacki," she told him. "I'll set up an appointment between you and Nadzieja Victor. She is the chief operating officer of Victory Chemical Solutions, which is primarily owned by her uncle, German Victor.

"Blowry's gas giant has lower deuterium concentrations than many, whereas Nigahog IV actually has one of the highest natural deuterium ratios ever recorded," Lamarre noted. "VCS is one of several organizations that provide enriched deuterium fuel to the Blowry System.

"With that underlying base trade, VCS and others have expanded to manage a multi-point trade network of assorted chemicals and gasses. Such a trade moves in bulk, which requires a lot of ships."

Lamarre shrugged.

"It is *always* in Em Victor's interest to hire the largest ships she can find to transport their products as efficiently as possible. She will insist on meeting you in person before she signs sponsorship papers, but I suspect she will be pleased to bring you aboard to handle her cargo."

"Then I look forward to meeting her," EB replied.

And he hoped that Nadzieja Victor's goals meant that she'd be cheaper to bribe than the Guild had been!

21

EB'S BRIBE was apparently enough to get them Em Lamarre's full attention. He and Vexer barely had time to find and acquire locally legal hand stunners before he received a message inviting him to a meeting with Em Victor.

To his not-quite-amusement, EB realized that Vexer was getting a lot more looks than he was as they wandered Talson City's streets. It wasn't that Talson City had a homogenous population—no city on a diaspora world ever would—but it was much more so than many, with a tendency toward a mix of classical European and North African features.

Vexer—Vena Dolezal by his birth name—was darkly attractive, with features clearly shaped mostly by the populations of Earth's Indian subcontinent. EB certainly couldn't argue with the taste of the people eyeing his navigator as they crossed downtown Talson City on foot toward VCS's office, but he had a flash of envy.

Their relationship was most definitely open, not least since Vena had a far broader sexual inclination than EB did, and EB wasn't a jealous man. But he *did* envy his ofttimes lover the attention, he had to admit that.

Not everyone went for the solid-older-man look, he was afraid.

"Are you grumbling because I'm getting all the looks from the pretty boys, or are you grumbling because these hand stunners are garbage?" Vexer asked.

"Both," EB confessed. "Trying not to *think* about the stunners, though."

A hand stunner of the type that was legal in Talson City could be built in a million forms. EB had even seen one version of about that power built into a ring. *That* weapon had come from the Fringe worlds inward of his home, but a light hand stunner should be a delicate and even somewhat decorative thing.

But since EB hadn't had a lot of time to *find* an appropriate shop, he'd ended up with the local default, which was a blocky thing with an odd bend in the middle. It wasn't gun-shaped, it didn't have sights, and EB wasn't sure he could even reliably *aim* the thing.

He hadn't thought to bring light stunners down to the surface, though, so the two local stunners were what they had. Hopefully, they'd go unneeded, but EB was feeling paranoid enough.

"Where are we meeting this client?" Vexer asked as they drew within sight of their destination tower.

"VCS apparently operates the forty-fourth through forty-sixth floors of the Sandoval Building," EB told his companion. "There's apparently a mid-building mezzanine on the fiftieth floor with restaurants and a food court. We're meeting Em Victor in one of the restaurants in the mezzanine."

"Who's paying for lunch?" Vexer muttered.

"Well, *she's* a billionaire looking to hire us, so I'm assuming her," EB replied. "But still, let's keep the steak and expensive whisky to a minimum."

"What about the expensive local beer?" Vexer asked with a chuckle.

"*That*, my dear, is a necessary part of sampling local culture!"

EM NADZIEJA VICTOR was instantly recognizable from the picture EB had been given. She was a stocky older woman, probably around his own late fifties, wearing a carefully styled practical skirt suit in navy blue, with silvering blond hair done in an updo that added at least fifteen centimeters to her not-inconsiderable height.

The restaurant she'd picked was an interior patio, a fenced-off area of the eight-meter-tall mezzanine level in the direct light from the windows. It wasn't the fanciest or most expensive place in the mezzanine by a long shot, which meant EB figured it was probably Em Victor's favorite.

A single younger woman in the shipsuit of a spacer under a formal black suit jacket sat with Victor. Except that the "shipsuit," EB realized, was actually light body armor. The "spacer" was Em Victor's bodyguard.

"Captain Bardacki, Officer Dolezal?" Victor greeted them as the host escorted them over. "Have a seat."

"I appreciate you meeting us on such short notice, Em Victor," EB said, pulling a seat out for Vexer before seating himself.

"Em Lamarre tries to stay bought," Victor said drily. "And, as it turned out, my lunch appointment canceled." She gestured to the younger woman with her. "This is my assistant, Em Liv Ross."

EB was still figuring bodyguard. Hiring veteran noncommissioned officers as personal assistants with a bonus for bodyguard duty was a long-standing tradition in his experience.

"Em Ross," he greeted the assistant with a nod.

"I took the liberty of ordering for the four of us," Victor continued. "It saves time, and this restaurant only does three things on its menu well."

A waiter was already approaching with a tray, delivering plates of steaming pasta and glasses of water. The pasta, at EB's first glance, appeared to be ravioli in tomato sauce. Simple enough, he supposed.

"For all my complaints, they do make the ravioli themselves," Nadzieja Victor noted. "It is *very* good. Now. While I start on the food, please give me the rundown of your ship's capabilities."

Em Victor had only ordered wine for herself, EB noted, though Ross was nursing a chilled beer. Most negotiators would buy alcohol for their counterparts and try to stay sober themselves. The gesture was small, subtle...and a positive sign about his potential client.

"*Evasion* was built in the Redward System in the Outer Rim," he told her crisply before pausing to swallow down a single ravioli. Victor was correct. The pasta was *excellent*. He couldn't identify the meat inside it—usually the case when eating on a strange world—but they'd done an amazing job of spicing all of the ravioli pasta, its contents and its sauce.

"I had, at the time, contacts who were in extremely good favor with the Kingdom of Redward," EB continued after taking a moment to savor the food. "She doesn't look like it, but *Evasion* carries Outer Rim military-grade Harrington coils and inertial compensators. She is also armed with destroyer-grade plasma cannon for self-defense.

"We have four unpressurized and ungravitized five-thousand-cubic cargo holds and a fifth fully pressurized and gravitized five-thousand-cubic hold."

He took a sip of his ice water.

"I'm not sure what else you need to know, Em Victor," he admitted. "We run with a crew of eight, all of whom have extensive experience in their specialties. Em Lamarre said that I needed a client sponsorship and a likely contract to get Guild membership, which seems to be the only way to get nova-route maps and shipping contracts here on Nigahog."

While he'd been speaking, the executive and her bodyguard had been plowing through their lunches with a speed he had to respect. They were clearly *enjoying* the food, but they were also eating quickly.

"The speed and armament are always useful out here, though not many people attempt to steal deuterium fuel," Victor noted calmly after finishing her last bite. "Can your open-space holds be converted to act as storage tanks?"

EB considered for a moment, glancing over at Vexer.

"My understanding is yes, but we have never done so," he admitted. "I'd recommend in favor of shipping in your tanks, in all honesty."

"Except for a few specialty ships, we mostly transport the deuterium in thousand-cubic-meter storage tanks holding nine hundred and fifty cubic meters of liquid," Victor replied. "I'd love to get that five percent back on my shipping, but I understand that most ships aren't rigged for liquid transport.

"Are there any problems loading cargo units of that size into your pressurized hold?"

"It depends on the dimensions," EB admitted. "But if we can't load your tanks into the pressurized hold, we can't load them into the unpressurized holds. Dimensions for both storage and access are the same, if aligned differently."

"Of course," Victor agreed. She leaned back in her seat with her wine glass, taking a sip with unreadable eyes.

"We ship approximately two million cubic meters of deuterium-enriched hydrogen fuel to the Blowry System every year," she told him. "Our largest transports can haul about what your ship hauls, but by and large, we are coordinating a minimum of a ship every single day for that route. A standard ten-kilocubic transport only has the capacity of one of your cargo holds.

"On the other hand, my impression is that you're not planning on sticking around here, are you?"

EB was about to concede that point when Ross moved.

"Down!" the bodyguard snapped at EB and Vexer as she swept the legs of Nadzieja Victor's chair out from underneath her. Ross rolled with her boss, pulling the woman to the ground as a blaster bolt crashed into the middle of the table.

EB was on the ground a moment later, the awkward hand stunner in his grip. That bolt had been aimed at *Vexer*, and he wasn't sure where it had come from.

Ross had drawn a blaster. *She* was licensed for real weapons, EB presumed. Before she could use it, though, a second blaster shot slammed into her. The armored shipsuit dispersed the blow, but it took her breath away—and a stunner blast caught her face before she recovered.

The only really armed member of their dinner party was out, her boss half-trapped under her unconscious body. EB and Vexer were using the tomato-sauce-streaked table as cover as the rest of the restaurant's patrons started to panic.

"Where?" Vexer hissed.

As if in answer, a third blaster bolt hammered into the table. Its lightweight construction wasn't intended to act as cover—and the wide-aperture blaster bolt vaporized a half-meter-wide hole in the middle of it.

"Go left," EB snapped.

Vexer obeyed, running left for the host station—hopefully heavier cover than the tables!—while EB ran right, diving for cover behind a heavy-looking stone plant feature.

The buzzing sound of the heavy stunner echoed again, and EB watched his lover go down in a tumble of nerveless limbs. *He'd* made it to his cover, but he still had *no* idea what was going on—and all he had was the terrible local stunner.

But it was what he had, and Vexer was unconscious. Plus, he felt *some* obligation to the potential client!

He glanced around the edge of the stone planter to get a sight picture of the scene, pulling back before anyone managed to shoot him. A bolt of some kind *definitely* hit the other side of the planter, though, which was a bad sign.

There were two people, wearing anonymizing digital full head masks, advancing across the mezzanine floor. Both were carrying military-grade stunners, and one was holding a lighter blaster in their right hand.

EB looked down at the stunner in his hand and sighed. Whoever had designed it had *not* expected it to be aimed, so he had to hope.

He popped up, turning to target the attacker with the blaster, and fired. He knew the moment he pressed the button that he'd missed; it was *impossible* to aim properly with the awkward handle on the stupid weapon.

To his surprise, the beam didn't go where he expected. Instead, it went off at at least a ten-degree angle from the direct line of the stunner's tip and *directly* at the man he'd been aiming at.

The beam took the stranger in the center mass and he lurched. There was clearly armor of some kind under the regular clothes the stranger wore, so EB fired again, trying to get the stunner aimed at the man's face.

Instead, the beam hit in center mass again as the auto-targeting made up for the weapon's impracticality. The attacker's armor clearly held, but the aura effect made him stumble backward.

His companion, though, very nearly got EB with their return fire. The stunner bolt slammed into the edge of the planter, close enough to give *EB* the same floaty-aura effect he'd just inflicted on the attacker.

He held his breath, trying to clear away the effects of the weapon and readying himself to move again—but there was suddenly shouting from the far end of the mezzanine and the shooting stopped.

Security was there. Somehow, he doubted they'd manage to catch the attackers—but he *also* figured that meant the attack had to end.

What the *stars* had just happened?

22

"AND THIS *PARTICULAR* STUBBORN *FUCKNUGGET*," Ginny explained colorfully, "is one of our three primary sensor resolution modules."

She finished extracting the meter-long chunk of circuitry from the open bulkhead and passed it back to Trace. The teen took it willingly enough, though the sheer weight of it surprised her.

"Mix of fiber-optics and picometer circuitry," the engineer continued. "Not a full sealed module but almost impossible to repair in place, as it requires specialized tools. That's why we have a spare—swap that one for the one on the cart, please?"

Trace *carefully* put the removed module on the tool and supply cart behind the two women and removed the antistatic-cloth-wrapped replacement piece. There was a clear tab to open the package, and she pulled on that as she returned to Ginny.

"Thanks," the engineer said, reaching into the opened package and slowly easing the module out.

"*Evasion* isn't the most advanced ship I've worked on," Ginny noted as she aligned the big piece of circuitry. "In the top three, *maybe* four, but I've helped run maintenance on a few Outer Rim warships that were a bit more top-line. That said, she's better designed than most, especially for this kind of maintenance.

"Most of her likely-to-fail systems are built like this. Key components can be removed, swapped for replacement parts, and the broken parts fixed in the shop—hopefully before the *next* one of those components fails, because we don't have many spare parts."

"Seems like repair-in-place would be better, wouldn't it?" Trace asked as she helped wrap the antistatic bag around the module that had unexpectedly failed in Nigahog orbit.

"When you have the hands, yes," Ginny agreed. "But some of the tools, especially for the picometer circuitry, are even more finicky than the parts themselves. Better to work in a clean room for a lot of parts. Plus, by always having a part ready to drop in, actual downtime is low and we level the true repair work out over time.

"Half of the crew are techs and maintenance jockeys of some kind, but spreading that work out keeps the ship running and stops anyone getting crushed by a crisis unless something really goes wrong."

Ginny shrugged.

"It's not how most militaries do it, but they've got the hands for real damage control. We don't. There's eight of us aboard."

She tapped the side of her head and addressed the air.

"Hey, Reggie, sensor res three should be back up," she said. "How are your eyes?"

To Trace's surprise, the other tech included her in the response. He must have been tracking where Trace was to know to loop her in.

"Eyes are bright and shiny, Ginny," Reggie replied. "We were doing okay before, but I'm liking the extra sco— Huh. That's funny."

"No engineer alive likes that phrase, Reggie," Ginny said. "What's going on?"

"EB *just* said he was going into his client meeting," the tech replied. "So, if he and Vexer aren't coming aboard, why do I have a shuttle headed our way?"

Trace froze.

"We shouldn't," Ginny said grimly. "Warn 'em off, Reggie. I'm coming up to the bridge to back you up. Let everyone know we might have ourselves a problem."

"Wilco."

Trace was still frozen in fear when Ginny met her gaze for a long and thoughtful few seconds.

"Yeah," she murmured. "With me, Trace. Whatever this is, I don't want you out of my sight!"

———

EVASION'S BRIDGE wasn't big. It was a two-level room roughly five meters long and four wide, the higher back level lifted above one of the ship's fuel tanks. That increased the apparent overall height of the room, but the ceiling sloped to provide three meters' height in most places.

There were two seats on each level, and Trace could tell that the back seats were rarely used. The auto-adjusting seat audibly *groaned* as it activated and shifted the chair around to conform to her body in an ergonomic fashion.

Ginny joined Reggie in the front two chairs. Trace had no idea what the official chain of command on the ship was, but it was pretty clear to her that the weapons tech was a generally acknowledged "first among equals" of the four specialists.

The engineer, on the other hand, was the only officer left on the ship except for Dr. Lan—and no one really expected the ship's doctor to take command of anything except their sickbay.

"Shuttle Meridian-Six-Five-Five, this is nova freighter *Evasion*," Reggie was saying. "Please check your navigation beacons. You are *well* off course and straying into the safety zone for my ship."

He looked up at Ginny and shook his head.

"They're saying the right things, but they keep coming toward us."

"Have you checked with orbital control?" Ginny asked.

"Couple of times now," Reggie agreed. "They are definitely off course. OrbCon recommends we adjust our orbit to increase our safety margin but doesn't seem otherwise concerned."

Trace had enough access to the console at her seat to bring up the visual of the shuttle. They were less than five thousand kilometers away, the range dropping by the second. There was nothing about the shuttle that *she* could identify as unusual, but the approach still left her wanting to hide under the seat in fear.

"Make that adjustment," Ginny ordered. "If they divert to *follow* us...then we have a problem."

"We weren't expecting to need to deviate from our assigned safe orbit," Reggie admitted. "I'm not actually qualified to fly the ship, Ginny. Nobody aboard is except Tate and she's still asleep."

"The stupid is smart enough to move us up five thousand kilometers on its own," Ginny replied. "Let the computer do it."

Trace didn't have full access to *Evasion*'s internal network, and that had never been more obvious than on the bridge in the middle of a potential crisis. She could tell that *someone* had issued the order to the computer, but she couldn't be sure which of Reggie or Ginny it was.

She had enough access to tell that the shuttle was adjusting course to match them, and she shrank backward into her seat.

"Fuck."

"What do we do?" Reggie asked as Ginny's curse hung in the air. "I most definitely do *not* have permission to blow them away. At what point does that become okay?"

"It doesn't. I'm locking down all external airlocks and accesses," Ginny replied. "Get us moving, as much as you're comfortable with. I'll hail them again."

Trace wanted to help...but there was literally *nothing* she could do. She definitely wasn't a pilot, that was for sure. And a shuttle would probably be faster and more maneuverable than *Evasion*.

"They're coming for me," she whispered, barely realizing she'd spoken aloud.

"I'd *guess* they're here for the captain, actually," Ginny admitted. "He may have pissed a few people off as we were getting the void out of Star Plaza."

The engineer's response was distracted, though, and her focus was clearly on the main coms system.

"Shuttle Meridian-Six-Five-Five, stop being a fucking joker," she snapped. "You are maneuvering to match course and vector with this ship. You have neither authority nor invitation to do so."

The range was now down to barely a thousand kilometers, and

Trace couldn't keep herself from staring at the shuttle's image on the screen.

"If you approach within one hundred kilometers of this ship, I can and *will* destroy your craft and argue self-defense in Nigahog court," Ginny continued. "I don't know what game you think you're playing at, but it ends *now*. Stop endangering my ship!"

The shuttle did not break off—but they did finally reply.

"*Evasion*, we have reason to believe you are carrying a wanted fugitive by the name of Tracy Finley," the strange shuttle replied. "You will stand down and permit boarding to enable the apprehension of this fugitive."

Trace stayed frozen. How did they know she was there? Why did they even *want* her? The traffickers had to lose a dozen runaways a year. What was one more...? And yet, she'd somehow *known* they weren't going to let her go.

Ginny shook her head and fired up the com again.

"You are not authorized Nigahog police, and you have neither authority or jurisdiction over my ship," she replied. "My warning stands. Break off or I will destroy your shuttle before you endanger this ship."

There was a long silence and Ginny looked back up at Trace.

"I'm going to guess there aren't actual warrants out for your arrest, right?" she asked drily.

"No," Trace whimpered. "No. They're... They've got to be hunters."

"Working for the traffickers," Reggie said grimly. "May I *please* vaporize them?"

"We've given them plenty of warnings," Ginny replied. "Hundred kilometers, Reggie. Spin up the turrets."

The shuttle continued to approach, but new icons on the screen Trace was watching showed that *Evasion*'s turrets were online.

"Target locked," Reggie said. "At three hundred kilometers and closing. If they don't have some serious juice in those engines, they may already be locked in to an unsafe approach."

"Can we make it obvious we're targeting them?" Ginny asked.

"My guns are designed for multiphasic jamming battlespaces,"

Reggie pointed out. "They don't *have* active targeting scanners. But we took the extra shielding off the capacitors. They *know* we've charged the guns."

Two hundred and fifty kilometers, according to Trace's screen. Her heart was crawling up her throat and her stomach was trying to run away down her left leg. The traffickers apparently valued her more than she thought...but surely the bounty hunters wouldn't push enough to get Reggie to fire?

Trace realized, to her shock, that she had absolutely *no* fear that Reggie wouldn't blow the shuttle away to protect her. *She* might not be sure that she was worth the consequences of that, but *Evasion*'s crew hadn't even hesitated.

"Harrington coils flaring," Reggie snapped. "They are breaking off. Vector is ninety degrees up, away from the planet."

"Will they clear the hundred-kilometer zone?" Ginny asked softly.

"Probably," Reggie admitted. "Can I shoot them if they don't make it?"

There was another long silence, then Ginny chuckled.

"Sadly, they're making a good-faith effort, so no," she told him. "We let them go. This time. Any further coms?"

"Nothing. They're just breaking off and running away."

"Okay." Ginny looked back at Trace. "They're leaving, Trace," she reassured the girl. "And if they come back, they'll get the same damn answer. That shuttle isn't going to succeed in sneaking up on *Evasion* or in threatening *Evasion*.

"They don't have the gear to go head-to-head with us. The situation is under control, Trace. And it's *staying* that way. I promise."

"Thank you," Trace whispered, aware of just how small and pathetic she must sound. "I didn't... And yet... But I didn't..."

Her words were stumbling incoherently, and she was staring at the shuttle as it broke away.

"They came after you," Ginny said grimly. "You said yourself they regarded you as more valuable than most of their victims. But I doubt they're putting up enough money to bribe cops or for anyone to play suicide charge."

Trace nodded, but the chill didn't fade.

"What happens if they get a ship that *is* big enough to threaten *Evasion*?" she whispered.

"I don't know," Ginny admitted. "But I do know this: EB promised we'd get you home safely to Denton. And I don't want to be the idiot bounty hunter who puts herself between EB and keeping that damn promise; am I clear?"

The teenager inhaled a long, shaky sigh as the distance to the shuttle finally began to tick up and nodded.

"Okay," she whispered. "I believe you."

And to her shock...she realized that she *did* believe them. Whatever else happened, she believed that *Evasion*'s crew would do everything within their power to keep her safe.

What she *didn't* believe was that, when the chips were down, *Evasion*'s crew had more power than the people who'd stolen her life.

23

EB CHECKED ON VEXER FIRST, making sure that his lover was still breathing and still had a pulse. Stunners weren't *supposed* to cause long-term damage, but they did trigger several nerves to force an involuntary blackout.

Just the fall could kill someone, let alone the effects of the weapon itself!

He only spent ten seconds or so checking on Vexer, though, before he crossed over to Ross and Victor. The executive, to her credit, was performing the same quick first-aid check on the bodyguard and looked up as he came near.

"I don't know shit about armor," she said bluntly. "You?"

"Let me see," EB replied. He knew quite a bit about armor, enough to know that Ross's armor should have protected her completely against a single light blaster bolt.

"Should have" didn't mean "had," however, and he knelt next to Victor to examine her bodyguard. The shooter had clearly had the same training as the auto-targeting system in his new stunner and had put the blast into the woman's mid-torso.

The armor surface was blackened and cracked, but EB's examination showed that the inner layer was intact. The dispersal web between the two layers had done its work, spreading the remaining heat and force across Ross's entire torso to prevent it from burning through.

The armor appeared rated for a single heavy blaster shot and could probably have taken another blast from the light weapon in play. *Probably.*

Most unpowered armor was only really rated for one blaster bolt. The purpose wasn't to stand up to sustained fire. It was to survive a surprise shot and let you get to real cover—exactly what Ross's armor had done.

"She's fine," EB told Victor. "That was a heavy stunner, so she'll be out for a few minutes, but she's fine."

"Thank you," the executive told him. Security was converging on them with drawn blasters, and Victor sighed. "I will talk to security, but I can already guess what happened."

"Em?"

"I make a very clear and purposeful effort to keep our business entirely aboveboard and avoid enemies," Victor told him. "So does the rest of the executive at Victory Chemical Solutions. So, I am reasonably certain, Captain Bardacki, that those bounty hunters weren't after me or Ross."

EB swallowed a curse as he nodded grimly.

"The Trackers' Guild lacks the power of the Transporters' Guild, not least because many of their activities are frowned upon by governments and police alike, but they are spread over several systems, where the Transporters only truly have power here," she explained. "If there is a bounty on you, Captain Bardacki, I'm afraid we can't do business."

"I'm not even sure—"

She cut him off with a raised hand, gesturing the security team's commander over with the other.

"Captain, even from our short conversation, I do not believe you did anything to attract their attention that I would disapprove of," she said calmly. "But I *cannot* risk the people and businesses that I am responsible for.

"I will tell Em Lamarre to either find you a new contact or give you back your bribe," Nadzieja Victor told him firmly. "I wish you luck, Captain Bardacki. But I cannot help you."

With that, she gave him a calm nod and finally turned to the waiting security woman.

"CAPTAIN, WE HAVE A PROBLEM," Reggie's voice echoed in EB's head the moment he stepped away from Victor to focus on Vexer again.

"What kind of problem?" EB asked. Like Reggie's voice, his words were entirely inside his headware. "We just got jumped by bounty hunters on the surface, Reggie. My problems are already growing."

"Someone just tried the same stunt up here with a boarding shuttle," Reggie said bluntly. "Ginny managed to get them to back down, but we very nearly had to vaporize somebody in Nigahog orbit. OrbCon is *not* happy with our threats."

"Fuck," EB said aloud. "Everything is under control?"

"So far," Reggie agreed. "I'd be happier with you back aboard. Do we have a contract?"

"Negative," EB admitted. "Our potential client won't take the risk of getting on the wrong side of the bounty hunters—the Trackers' Guild, they're apparently called.

"I need to poke the Transporters' Guild again and hope for better news there."

Silence answered him.

"Vexer got stunned as well," EB told Reggie. "I'm waiting for him to wake up, then I'm probably going to end up talking to building security and Talson City police. I'll try to get clear before local night, but my focus has to be on finding us work."

"Understood," the weapons tech conceded. "Ginny has everything in hand, but this is a bigger mess than I like. We should probably start checking in regularly. Both ways."

"Fair," EB agreed. "We're not allowed real guns down here, Reggie, but I'll back whatever you have to do up there. I'll deal with official displeasure before I'll deal with bounty hunters on my ship."

"Figured. I'll check in in an hour," Reggie promised. "Trace is terrified, boss. That's the other wrinkle," he concluded. "They weren't after us or the ship. They were after the *kid*."

"That's a wrinkle," EB agreed. One that made...some sense. The traffickers might not put a *huge* bounty on Trace, but she was supposedly a high-value asset to them. One that could justify a moderate conditional investment in getting her back.

Bounty hunters made for a handy tool that way. The client only had to actually come up with the money if they brought the target home.

"We'll deal with it," EB told Reggie. "Keep everyone on the ship safe, Reggie. We both know you and I are the only actual *fighters* aboard."

"Always, boss."

SECURITY HAD their own questions for EB—and Vexer, when the navigator woke up. One of the oddities of a modern stunner was that the feeling wasn't even particularly *unpleasant*. The aura effect of a near-miss was overstimulating and uncomfortable, but waking up from being stunned was more of a haze.

At its worst, it was pins and needles. For a significant minority of people, it was actually pleasant. Not enough so that most people would intentionally get stunned, but it was certainly disconcerting the first time you were stunned.

From Vexer's confused expression, this was the first time he'd been stunned.

"You okay?" EB asked as he helped his lover to his feet, glancing over at the security chief as he spoke.

The older woman in charge of the Sandoval Building's security was clearly drawing the same conclusion on Vexer that EB was. That meant, to EB's amused curiosity, that *she'd* almost certainly been stunned in the past.

"Yeah. Weird damn feeling, though," Vexer admitted. "What happened?"

"That is what we are attempting to work out," the security chief said. "Yamuna Haupt," she introduced herself to Vexer. "I run security for this building and coordinate with the Talson City Police Department.

"You seem to have caused quite a bit of trouble, the two of you."

"We were having a business meeting," EB pointed out.

"And then someone decided to shoot at you," Haupt replied. The woman was one of the few people with Vexer's coloring EB had seen in Talson City. "That doesn't happen much here. I'm going to send some displeased commentary to the Trackers' Guild office, since this whole mess seems to fall into their alley."

"Is that *legal*?" EB asked.

"A properly registered Tracker, a member of the Guild in good standing, has certain authority with regard to apprehension and detention of fugitives," Haupt told him. "And certain obligations as to how they *do so*."

She waved around the wrecked restaurant.

"This didn't meet those obligations," she concluded drily. "But given the gear and skill they operated with, I am assuming Trackers. So, Captain, why are the Trackers after you?"

"I don't bloody know," EB told her. "I'm not sure why we're being interrogated when we were *shot at*."

"Oh, you're not in trouble," she said. "Not...really. But if there's a Tracker bounty on you, that's going to be a headache. I'm probably going to have to ban you from the premises for our safety."

"That's *nuts*," Vexer said. "We were *attacked*."

"Yes," she agreed. "And it sucks. But if there's a bounty on you, standing next to you is going to be dangerous for a while. And my responsibility, bluntly, is not to you. It's to the owners and regular residents of this building.

"That means that unless you can confirm that you *don't* have a Tracker bounty on you, I'm afraid I have to ask you not to enter the Sandoval Building again."

The Trackers' Guild might not have formal power, EB reflected, but just *fear* of them appeared to give some interesting clout.

24

"I'VE SPOKEN WITH EM VICTOR," Lamarre said quietly.

She'd seated EB and Vexer and provided coffee without saying anything committal. Now she stood at the window of her office, looking away from them and out over the city.

"And?" EB asked. "She said she'd speak to you."

Somehow, he didn't expect that he was getting his bribe back. He was intrigued to see what Lamarre tried to do to make up for the hundred grams of platinum that had vanished into the ether.

"Em Victor and her company are unwilling to engage in contracts that *will* come with known enemies," Lamarre told them. "Few clients are. If I'd known you had acquired a Trackers' Guild bounty, our discussion earlier would have been quite different."

"We didn't know ourselves," EB pointed out. "It's not like you generally expect the illegal bounty hunters to have a formal guild that terrifies everyone, even if you think you might have an illegal bounty on you."

Lamarre chuckled.

"That's fair, I suppose," she allowed. "I've lived in a system with a healthy Guild system my entire life, Captain Bardacki. The Trackers, the Transporters, the Builders, the Accountants…"

She shook her head.

"About a dozen Guilds control everything on Nigahog," she told them. "I'd say…seventy-five percent of our planetary assembly has an explicit Guild allegiance. The Transporters and the Commercial Guilds have the largest blocs.

"But the Trackers' Guild make people nervous. Only they and the Transporters have armed nova ships, and ours are freighters with defensive guns. The Trackers have real gunships and even a few corvettes that fly under their members' command.

"So, even people like Em Victor, who is a member in *exemplary* standing with the Commercial Guild, tread lightly with the Trackers." She sighed. "I don't want to give you false impressions, Captain Bardacki. If you have a Tracker bounty, the chance that I can get you a client sponsorship for Guild membership is almost nil."

"So, what *can* you do for me?" EB asked. "Not to draw too much attention to things, but you have been *well* compensated for your help."

The bar of stamped platinum was probably three months of her salary. Maybe more, if the Transporters' Guild wasn't generous with its mid-level manager type employees.

"I said *almost nil*, not *nonexistent*," she said softly. "But to create any chance, you will need to exit the realm of safe and enter the realm of *political* and *dangerous*."

"Half of the last group we had lunch with were shot with blasters," EB said drily. "How much worse can it get?"

"A lot," she said flatly. "There are no Commercial Guild members who will risk Tracker attention. There may be non-Guild civilian operators out there with maps of their own, but I wouldn't know who they are and they wouldn't be able to sponsor you for membership."

Someone who didn't care about the Transporters' Guild but was willing to give EB maps to work for them sounded fine to him. It was only the lack of local nova-route maps that was keeping him from buying a speculative cargo and disappearing off to Blowry on his own.

"Civilian, huh?" Vexer observed. EB winced as he caught the same detail his lover had.

"Yes. There are a number of government and military contracts that are run through the Transporters' Guild," Lamarre told them. "We have few captains that are willing to take on their more dangerously political operations.

"I will arrange a meeting," she promised. "With the agency I am thinking of, they will likely want to meet in space. I suggest you return to your ship and await further word."

"If it's dangerous, it better be *worth* it," EB warned.

"It's still cargo hauling, Captain Bardacki," she told him. "It will be cargo that is more explosive than normal...both literally and metaphorically. You will be paid appropriately, as I understand, and if they sign the paperwork, you can purchase a Guild membership. And the attendant map access."

EB sighed and nodded.

"Very well, Em Lamarre," he said. "But my patience is not...infinite."

"This is a niche situation, Captain, but I am *very* good at my job," Lamarre said firmly. "You will not regret working with me. I promise."

As Nadzieja Victor had said, it appeared that Vivian Lamarre preferred to *stay* bought once someone bribed her.

25

EB DIDN'T EVEN BOTHER to conceal his sigh of relief as he stepped off the shuttle onto *Evasion*'s decks. He didn't *mind* planets, not in the slightest, but after a career on warships and almost two years living on board the freighter, it was a relief to be somewhere he controlled.

He was surprised, however, to find Trace half-bolting across the deck to wrap her arms around him and bury her face in his shoulder.

"Thank god you're back," she said. "It was... I was terrified."

He awkwardly patted her back, looking up at Ginny still waiting by the bay door.

The engineer shrugged and crossed.

"It wasn't fun, I'll say that," Ginny told them.

After a moment, Trace released her hold and sniffled.

"Sorry, I..."

"No apologies," EB told her firmly, taking her softly by the shoulders and studying her face. "It's been a stressful couple days for us all. You okay?"

"I think so," she said in a rush. "Thank you. For..."

She trailed off and sniffled again. He judged that she was fine, just stressed and thirteen.

"Everything's under control," he told her. "Reggie and Ginny took care of everything. Right, Ginny?"

"For now," the engineer said grimly. "Gods only know what those idiots were thinking, though. It's going to be a mess."

"They're thinking the Trackers' Guild can operate with near-impunity in multiple star systems," Vexer said. "From what the locals said, they know it was the Guild, but since they can't ID individuals, well…they can't do anything."

"I've *heard* of the Trackers," Trace said. "They're in the vid shows. But…they really are like that?"

"I don't know what the vid shows say about them," EB replied. "They're supposed to be following a bunch of rules on how to come after the people they're paid to arrest—and they're apparently supposed to stick to legitimate bounties."

"Which they aren't doing, I'm guessing?" Ginny asked. "It's not like someone can hang an actual crime on you or Trace."

"Pretty much," he said. "And you can't access their bounty lists if you aren't a Guild member. Vexer checked while I was flying us up."

"So, what do we do?" Vexer said. "Wait for Lamarre's contact?"

"Nothing else we *can* do," EB warned. "We don't have nova-route maps for this side of the Fasach Expanse. I didn't expect to get this far and be a target, people. I'm sorry."

"Who would?" Ginny said. "Most places, you can find *somebody* to sell you a map."

"And I want us to start looking, hard, for off-registry map sellers," EB told his two senior officers. "Trace, how are you at net-crawling?"

The teen raised her hands in a shrug.

"I can learn?" she suggested.

"Stick with Vexer," EB told her. "See if you can follow what he does as he searches for the kind of people we need, then back him up where you can. Sound good?"

"Of course!"

The teen threw him a comic-vid-series idea of a fleet salute and EB chuckled.

The traffickers had done Trace no favors, but they had *not* broken her—and the Trackers' Guild wasn't going to manage it if EB had anything to say, either.

BACK IN HIS TINY OFFICE, EB ran through the full detailed recording of the bounty-hunter shuttle's attempt to board *Evasion*. It had come pretty close to the wire, all things considered, and he suspected that even Nigahog Orbital Control didn't realize that Reggie had been perfectly willing to push the button.

OrbCon had made complaints—several directed explicitly to EB—about "excessive threats of force," but their tone wasn't where he figured it would be if they'd realized his people had come within seconds of vaporizing a five-hundred-cubic-meter shuttle with probably a dozen people aboard.

The problem was that even a cursory review of the scan records of the ships in orbit told EB why everyone was nervous about the Trackers' Guild. Nigahog was a wealthy system by Beyond standards, with over a hundred million people.

Their tech base wasn't up to building anything except class one nova drives and he doubted they could manage a four-kilocubic Ten-X drive, which meant that *Evasion* was bigger than anything they could build, but they were definitely managing twenty-five-kilocubic freighters.

There were also a handful of two-hundred-kilocubic sublight ships for in-system transport—and where there were two-hundred-kilocubic *transports,* there were two-hundred-kilocubic *monitors.*

EB hadn't seen any of them, though there were definitely armed space stations capable of maneuvering under their own power that were *basically* monitors. His personal guess was the mobile portion of Nigahog's in-system security fleet was mostly positioned at the gas giants, covering the cloudscoop infrastructure.

But their nova fleet, the ships of the blandly named Nigahog Extraterritorial Enforcement Agency, was in orbit of the planet. Two twenty-five-kilocubic corvettes and a dozen gunships of around twelve to fifteen kilocubics.

Except that as had occasionally been pointed out to him in other systems, there were *five* corvettes and twenty-seven gunships in Nigahog orbit.

Three corvettes and fifteen gunships belonged to mercenaries, private security…and the Trackers' Guild. Despite Lamarre's claim that the Transporters only had armed freighters, four of the gunships were flying Transporters' Guild transponders.

But two of the corvettes and six of the gunships were definitely bounty-hunter vessels. The shuttle that had tried to board *Evasion* had come from one of those gunships, the *Ambrosian Honor*.

EB was confident that his ship could probably take on basically *any* gunship in the Beyond. *Evasion* probably had heavier guns than any of the corvettes, even the NEEA ships that edged toward the fuzzy line between corvette and destroyer.

But any warship had *more* guns than *Evasion*, and the corvettes might even have some level of armor and dispersal webs—defenses he hadn't been able to get installed on a freighter.

And then, of course, there were the battle stations of the Nigahog Orbital Security Command. They *probably* wouldn't join the Trackers' Guild in shooting at him, but he could imagine several scenarios where everyone would try to keep him *in* Nigahog to turn over to *somebody*.

He tapped his com open.

"Ginny, the drive is fully cooled and discharged, right?" he asked her.

"Yes, for all the good that does us with no maps," she replied.

"Worst case, we might have to jump back into the Expanse for safety," EB admitted. "But in that kind of situation, we're going to have a lot of people objecting and arguing with us over the idea.

"Do me a favor," he continued. "Sit down with Aurora and Reggie and go over everything with a microscope. I want to know exactly how far out we need to be to nova…and I want to be as certain as we can that the multiphasic jammers are working without turning them on."

If he turned on multiphasic jammers in orbit of a planet, he was going to ruin a *lot* of people's days and make himself *extremely* unpopular.

But if he needed to get the void out of Nigahog, that might be the best way to protect his ship and people.

"I'll have some chats," Ginny promised. "Are we in that much trouble, EB?"

"I don't know," he said. "But my shoulders are itchy and it's *my* job to keep you all safe."

26

"MY NAME IS LEAR NAUMOV," the stranger in the video call told EB. "You were referred to me by the Transporters' Guild. I'm told you can handle some *discreet* work for my employers."

EB arched an eyebrow at Naumov.

"I can be discreet," he agreed. "As can my people. What I don't do is *no questions asked*, Em Naumov. I've been burned a few too many times."

"I can't discuss anything further on even a secure channel, captain," Naumov told him. "Can we meet in person?"

"Of course," EB allowed. So far, he was finding the man in the video's attempt at cloak-and-dagger rather amateurish. Naumov was visibly older than EB was, though, which suggested that was at least partially intentional.

"I see that your ship has not yet docked with any of our system's fine transshipment orbitals," the stranger said.

Naumov hadn't, EB noted, said who he worked for or what he did. He was dancing around a few points.

"I suggest that you dock with Iridium Everlasting," Naumov said. "I will make arrangements and you will be updated once you have docked."

"Until I have a cargo to pick up, I'm not sure I want to pay the docking fees to actually bring my ship in," EB told the stranger. He also had security concerns over linking his ship to one of Nigahog's orbitals, given the clear and present threat from the Trackers' Guild.

"Arrangements will be made, Captain," Naumov reiterated. "Not everything can be discussed on this channel. We will speak soon."

The video call shut off and EB sighed.

"Dangerous, political and about two meters up their own ass," he said aloud. Then he pinged the com for the bridge. "Vexer, you on deck?"

"At the moment, darling," his lover replied. "Want me somewhere else?"

EB could *hear* the eyebrow waggle that came with that question.

"Sadly, no. I'll be joining you on the bridge momentarily," he told Vexer. "Do you have a location on the Iridium Everlasting station?"

"Not to hand, but I'll have it by the time you're here," Vexer replied. "Give me a minute?"

A minute was about what it took for EB to reach the bridge from his office. The operational hull of *Evasion*—the "horseshoe" wrapped around the cargo holds—wasn't that big, after all, and most of the captain's spaces were close to the control center.

The quarters were closer than they'd be on a warship, but the office was farther away. It was mostly a wash in EB's opinion.

It gave Vexer time to look up the orbital station before he made it to the bridge, and the navigator had a model of the facility up on the screen when EB entered.

"Iridium Everlasting, EB," Vexer said with a wave as the door slid shut. "Fueling station in a polar orbit. One of the smaller ones, run entirely by VCS, actually."

"And our interactions with Em Victor's people continue. Anything particular about Iridium I should know?"

"Not much I'm seeing. It's a quiet station, no military use."

"Any of the Tracker ships docked there?" EB asked.

There was a long pause.

"No," Vexer confirmed finally. "There is *a* gunship docked at the station, but it appears to be running a mercenary transponder instead of a Trackers' Guild one."

"Somehow, I get the feeling that trying to claim a bounty in this system *without* being a member of the Trackers' Guild is unhealthy," EB said drily. "Let's hope their jealousy is strong enough to keep us safe.

"We're meeting our new potential client on Iridium Everlasting. Set a course."

"Does everything in this system feel like it's aiming at us to you, too, EB?" Vexer asked as he started plugging commands into consoles and the air—his headware translating the latter into instructions for the ship's computer.

"Unfortunately, yes."

The last time EB had felt quite *this* hunted, he'd just discovered that his government had sold his entire military unit out to their enemy's assassins…

"CAN WE TRUST THIS NAUMOV?" Reggie asked.

"I have no fucking idea," EB admitted on the all-crew channel. "The station is pretty clear of everything and everybody *else*, but it could be a trap. We were told to expect contact from a government agency, and it all fits right, but…I have no way to validate."

Trace wasn't on the shared communication network, but he could *guess* how the teenager felt. Certainly, the rest of his crew—who *weren't* recently escaped from a criminal human-trafficking network—were nervous and uncomfortable enough.

"Without maps, we have nothing," EB reminded them. "We're ready to pop jammers and run like hell, but we can't nova from polar orbit. We'll be too close."

"If we pop multiphasic jammers in planetary orbit without calibrat-ing…" Ginny's voice trailed off. "A lot of people could get hurt. There's got to be another way."

EB sighed, considering his options. He had a few nasty toys locked away in the vault in his head, but he wasn't going to have the access he needed to deploy most of them. He'd had *time* on Star Plaza to set up hard accesses.

At Iridium Everlasting, he was going to be meeting people and doing work.

"I've got one, maybe," he finally said. "Ginny, I'm going to need your help. Vexer, how much longer do we have?"

"Fifteen?" his lover replied.

"Right. Ginny, meet me in the fab workshop," EB ordered. "It's time to work up something *clever*."

27

IRIDIUM EVERLASTING WAS A STOPOVER POINT, a gas station in space for ships taking the polar launch route up from the surface. With antigrav units and Harrington coils, lifting off didn't take *that* much energy, but it was still one of the most fuel-consuming maneuvers a ship could undertake.

Given the station's purpose, form followed function. The actual "station" was a hundred-meter-wide disk that acted as the cap on a half-kilometer-high tank. Eight docking ports were spaced around the edge of the disk, three of them currently occupied.

"Iridium Everlasting, this is *Evasion*," Vexer said into the com. "Requesting docking clearance."

"Request received, *Evasion*," the station replied. "You are cleared to Port Six. All fees have been paid in advance, including for one thousand cubic meters of ninety percent deuterium-enriched fuel.

"Welcome to Iridium Everlasting."

EB's lover glanced over at him and EB shrugged back. He'd just returned to the bridge and was wiping machine oil off his hands as he listened to the conversation.

"Naumov said he'd make arrangements, and I'm not looking a gift horse in the mouth," he noted. "*Scan it*, carefully, but fill up the tanks."

"Isn't being paranoid about it basically *literally* looking the horse in the mouth?" Vexer asked with a chuckle.

"I'm prepared to trust that the horse has been paid for," EB replied. "I'm not prepared to trust that no one has fed the horse bombs."

"That is abusing the *void* out of that metaphor, hon."

"Then consider the dead horse flogged, and get ready to scan the fuel supply for bombs," EB said brightly. "Ginny, how's our toys?"

"Give me five and I'll send them out," she told him.

"Keep me informed," EB said. "I'm watching for contact from Em Naumov."

He checked the network link to the station, but the first contact he got was from aboard *Evasion*. Trace was calling him?

"Hey, what's up?" he asked their passenger.

"I watched over Vexer's shoulder like you said," the teenager told him. "You grabbed him for other stuff, but I thought I'd grabbed the gist of it, so I kept poking the planetary datanet."

EB had to pause for a moment to remember what she was talking about. With Naumov's call and the questions and paranoia about docking at Iridium Everlasting, he'd basically forgotten about asking Vexer and Trace to source nova maps.

"You found a source for nova maps?" he asked.

"Sketchy as anything, but yes," she confirmed. "There's a semi-concealed forum on the datanet for young pilots." She coughed embarrassedly. "They used the same concealment tricks as the drug dealers on Denton," she admitted.

"Most of those pilots *really* have it in for the Transporters' Guild, even though half of them are Guild apprentices," she continued. "So, a couple of black-hat-net map sellers advertise their services there."

Trace paused, a verbal shrug that EB was starting to pick up on with her.

"I contacted the one the forum thought best of, pretending to be a crew member on a nova ship," she said. "She was happy to send me a price list. I'll pass it to your headware?"

"Send it over," EB instructed. "Well done." He paused, and chuckled.

"And it seems, Em Trace, that you weren't pretending. We're taking you home, but you seem to be working your passage. You're *definitely* a crew member on a nova ship!"

EB HAD enough time to glance at the price list and recognize the *other* aspect of the Transporters' Guild's control of the nova-route maps— non-Guild maps were expensive as stars—before he got a mailbox-update ping from Iridium Everlasting's net.

There was a standard electronic mailbox attached to each docking port at a station. It would feed mail to the ship's captain in a relatively controlled manner. Often, the only things that hit it were advertise-ments for services on the station, though *most* docking controls insisted on a minimum level of *usefulness* to those ads.

This time, though, the mailbox was only mostly ads. The seventh piece of e-mail in the box was a note giving him a time and location, signed simply *LN*.

The location appeared to be one of the coffee shops being adver-tised in the junk mail. The time was…very soon.

"Bastard," EB muttered, but with no real heat. "Vexer, take a look at the price list and contact info Trace pulled from the system datanet. I want the seller's broadest map, but see if you can argue her down.

"We don't have that much digital cash on Nigahog accounts, and I don't see an easy way to send her stamped elementals," he noted.

Trace had found a seller whose maps offered routes to the nearest ten inhabited systems and thirty or so officially uninhabited ones. The full map, though, cost the equivalent of half a kilogram of platinum.

"What about you?" Vexer asked.

"I'm strapping on a heavy blaster and a heavy stunner, since Iridium Everlasting *doesn't* seem to have weapons laws, and heading to meet our contact," EB said. "Reggie will have the airlock. You have command.

"Try not to break my ship, hey?"

"If it's a choice between *our* ship and *my* boyfriend, I will ram *Evasion* through the station to come get you," Vexer said calmly. "So, try not to need rescuing, hey?"

EB chuckled and leaned in to kiss Vexer. This particular on-again of their on-again, off-again relationship seemed to be sticking harder than it usually did. EB wasn't sure why...but he was sure that he didn't mind.

"Watch the kid," he told Vexer when he came up for air. "I don't know how big the bounty on her is, but it's clearly enough to get some attention. Keep her safe."

"Will do."

28

EB'S largest concern proved to be a paranoia too far, at least. Lear Naumov arrived at the coffee shop at the same instant he did, gesturing for the freighter captain to join him at a table on the edge of the green-toned restaurant.

"Captain Bardacki," the presumed spy greeted him. "The caliber of your enemies speaks well of you."

"You may have an advantage over me," EB replied as he tapped an order into the screen on the table. "You seem to know who those enemies *are*."

"I'm not going to tell you who I work for, Captain," Naumov said bluntly, confirming EB's suspicions. "But we wouldn't be doing our jobs if we didn't know almost as much about the Trackers' Guild bounties as the Guild does.

"The Guilds, as an aggregate, may own the government I report to…but no *individual* Guild is above the authority of the Republic." He shrugged. "So, I know that the bounty on your head was placed by an individual known as Lady Breanna, through her usual intermediaries."

"You *know* one of your Guilds is taking bounties from the head of an organized crime syndicate?" EB asked.

"Know? Yes. Are able to prove? No," Naumov told him. "Plus, to be perfectly honest, my employers would *rather* that someone like Breanna work through the Trackers' Guild than send her own people.

"Trackers may be available to the highest bidder—well, *some* Trackers, anyway—but they follow a code. Breanna's direct operators do not. One of them would have just blown the entire mezzanine floor of the Sandoval Building with everyone in it."

EB winced.

"That would have got me, yes," he murmured.

"And about three hundred innocents. One of Breanna's operators wouldn't have cared. A Tracker does. Do you see my point, Captain?"

"Yes, but speaking as the person being hunted by your semi-legal bounty hunters, I'm not sure I agree with it," EB said. "Neither I nor anyone on my ship committed any crimes."

"And that is the unfortunate downside of the only interstellar law enforcement or extradition being the paid bounty hunter," Naumov said calmly. "There is nothing I can do about that, Captain Bardacki. That is simply the way of the world out here."

"And this isn't what you wanted to hire me for," EB noted.

"No," the spy agreed. "This is…free information. A professional courtesy, you could say."

Their coffees arrived, along with a slice of some kind of sweet loaf for Naumov. The old man took a bite, leaning back in his chair and studying EB.

"You were a soldier once," he said. It wasn't a question. "I can see it in how you stand, how you walk." He shook his head. "You may have told Lamarre or Victor more, but both of those worthies are surprisingly good at keeping confidences."

"I was a nova-fighter pilot," EB said. "Squadron XO."

"So, you're familiar with war," the spy said quietly. "There's a ground war going on in the Estutmost System, captain. The government in First Landing finally pushed too far, and the farmers of Dachaigh a Deas had been shipping in guns and gear for years."

"I don't know much about Estutmost," EB admitted. The only thing he could be sure of, in truth, was that it would send *Evasion* in the rough direction of Icem and Trace's home. It wasn't as convenient as

Blowry or Poberin, but it would at least leave him within one discharge cycle of the system.

"The Cinnead—the Clan, the rebels—are a faux-communist group of families that provide most of Estutmost's food," the spy told him. "The government in First Landing, on the other hand, is a hereditary Board of Directors descended from the people who funded the original colony.

"The Guilds, for all their many and obvious flaws, have generally declined to get involved in mercantile colonialism; otherwise, Estutmost's internal divisions would have left them vulnerable for us abusing their economy years ago," Naumov noted. "As it stands, however, the Board has taken a generally protectionist stance, and the Trackers' Guild are the only people with any kind of presence in Estutmost.

"*Their* presence there, however, is linked to the problem. The third faction in the Estutmost System is the Spacers. There are several moons and a two-planet system that have been decently opened up for mining, and the people who live there have their own opinions on most things."

Naumov shrugged.

"The Spacers have taken a 'pox on both your houses' attitude to the war on the planet and blockaded all shipments to Estutmost itself. A number of Trackers and other mercenaries have been hired to reinforce the Spacers' small monitor fleet in maintaining the blockade."

EB sighed.

"You want me to run the blockade?" he guessed.

"Exactly. You have a nova drive, so you can evade monitors, and if my people's estimate of your ship is correct, you should be able to outmaneuver the Trackers and other mercs. Can your ship land, captain?"

"With difficulty," EB admitted. He'd never done it, but he had more faith in his ability to land and take off in *Evasion* than he had in the theoretical ability to transform the cargo holds into liquid tanks.

"There are specialist TMU containers that can hold two heavy tanks and an array of other gear sufficient to equip roughly a company of medium infantry," Naumov noted. "The base of what we want to ship is one hundred heavy tanks. Plus additional equipment, infantry vehicles, artillery, and such... Seventy-five TMUs and roughly fifteen TMUs' worth of non-containerized equipment."

EB bit down his initial reaction.

He doubted Nigahog's "heavy tanks" were worth crap by his standards, let alone anyone closer to Sol's, but everything he'd seen suggested they'd be decent for the Beyond. A hundred of them, backed by artillery and the transport for...probably a division or two of infantry, he estimated?

That twenty-odd thousand cubic meters of military equipment was a significant investment for Nigahog—and while it might not turn the tide of the war on Estutmost on its own, it would definitely have an impact.

If EB could get it through.

"Part of the deal, as I understood it, was to get me membership in the Transporters' Guild," he said. "On the other hand, I'm told that the Nigahog government is the other reliable source of nova-route maps—and if you're contracting me for deliveries, that covers the other part I needed from the Transporters.

"The rate scale for this contract, though, will need to take into account the fact that I can't exactly pick up a cargo from Estutmost after running the blockade, can I?"

"I have faith in your ingenuity," Naumov replied. "However, I recognize the multiplicity of risks and problems inherent to this task. We are prepared to negotia—"

EB had been watching everything behind Naumov, concerned about the risks on the station. He had *assumed*—in error, it turned out—that the spy was keeping similar watch behind him.

The stunner beam barely missed EB's head as he bent down to drink his coffee—but it took Naumov directly in his open mouth. Spasming from the unexpected nerve stimulation, the spy went down in a pile of limbs around his chair.

EB was on the ground a moment later, a second stunner bolt flashing through the air where his torso had been. *This* time, he had his own heavy military-grade stunner, and trained muscle memory moved smoothly to draw the gun.

He barely registered the two attackers before he opened fire. They had set up a decent crossfire, and EB didn't see *any* way out of the situation. He'd kicked over the table as he went down, and it *should* cover him from stunners—but not from anything heavier.

Worse, he wasn't going to guess *these* people as Trackers. They wore light powered body armor that covered them from head to toe and absorbed his stunner beam without even noticing it.

The only good news was that *their* blasters appeared to still be holstered—but that also meant that *EB* would have to be the one to escalate to lethal force if he wanted a chance of getting out of there.

"*Evasion*," he commed the ship. "I'm under attack by mercenaries. Lock down the ship; prepare for attack. Ginny, make sure the surprise is running."

"Surprises are spreading out across the station," her voice replied instantly. "Need ten more minutes."

"We may not have them," EB warned as more stun beams flickered across his cover. Aura was starting to affect him, but he was still present in his own head. "Lock it down and hold until I get there."

"Too late," Reggie said grimly. "Someone was in position. They overrode the station airlock and rammed a work cart into ours. Even if I override the safety protocol, I think that cart will survive the doors crushing it.

"I'm moving to the airlock with everything I've got. Get to us, boss."

"Understood," EB said, swallowing a curse. His skin was tingling from the stunner aura, but he could tell from the sound that his attackers were spreading out for better angles.

Worst of all, at that moment, Naumov began to spasm again. EB was no medic...but he could *damn* well recognize the beginning of an electrostimulation seizure.

The spy was old enough that that was bad. *Really* bad.

29

TRACE WASN'T sure she felt safe on *Evasion* anymore. She didn't know what the klaxoning alarm that cut through the bridge was, but the way Vexer *froze* told her something was wrong.

"Vexer?" she asked. The dark-skinned man was one of the people she was expecting to keep her safe now. She'd admitted to several of the secrets of the gray net on Denton to him as they dug into the forums and went over the price list of their potential contact.

Before he said anything to her, Vexer was on his feet and opening a cabinet on the wall. Trace didn't get a good look at what was in there before he pulled out a visibly armored jacket and a blaster pistol.

He clearly considered both for several seconds before he tossed the jacket to Trace.

"We're under attack," he told her. "Put that on and stay here."

"What about EB?" she asked.

"He's under attack on the station, but there's nothing we can do if we lose control of the ship," Vexer said quietly.

"Can I help?" Trace demanded.

"I am *not* giving you a stars-fired blaster, Trace," Vexer told her. "But..."

She felt the ship's network suddenly interface more tightly with her headware implants. For a moment, she thought that Vexer had given her crew access…and then the full datafeed hit her.

He'd just given her *bridge-officer* access. There were only two higher tiers of access on *any* ship, from what the crew had taught her, and *Vexer* didn't have chief-engineer or captain access while Ginny and EB, respectively, were alive.

"We may not be able to hold them at the airlock," he said grimly. "You have access to the surveillance and the crew coms now. Can you help coordinate?"

"I can," she promised fiercely. There was a new fire burning in her chest, and she started assembling an array of virtual screens around her.

"I have to go," Vexer told her. "But you'll have me on surveillance and coms. You going to be okay?"

"Okay? Hell, I'm going to help you burn these assholes to *ash*," Trace snapped. "Go. I've got this."

She was so immersed in the surveillance feeds that she registered his weak attempt at a salute as much through the bridge cameras as her own eyes.

Part of her attention followed him as he left the bridge, but she spent most of her energy locating the rest of the crew and learning just where *Evasion* even *had* surveillance cameras.

There weren't as many as Trace would have liked at that particular moment, but most of what there was had been positioned in the areas around the airlocks. Three fully armored figures were now *inside* Evasion, and she flagged them in the system, highlighting them in red and sending their locations to the entire crew.

She located all of the crew except Reggie quickly enough. They were scattered through the operation hull, none of them close to the airlock and thankfully all moving toward the mess. Trace hadn't even realized that *Evasion had* an armory.

Now her new access informed her that one of the storage lockers next to the mess served that purpose, currently containing a stack of weapons and a suit of powered combat armor per the inventory.

The crew were falling back to pull arms, but her check of the data said that only EB could use the armor—and she still hadn't located Reggie.

A second wave of mercs was entering the ship, and the first was now definitely cutting toward Engineering. They had stunners out, but Trace guessed that the guns at their belts were true blasters.

She could recognize the stunners, at least. But she wasn't afraid. She wasn't sure *why* she wasn't afraid, but she wasn't.

"Everyone, I've unlocked the armory from here," she told the crew network as Joy—who *didn't* have access authority to that storage closet —reached it first. "I'm highlighting our intruders through the com, but I haven't found Reg—"

The first wave reached the edge of her surveillance network, near the crew quarters, and then a rapid pulse of heavy blaster fire walked across the hallway. Only one of the mercenaries managed to return fire before the plasma bolts cut them down.

Trace suspected the gun had done a number on the ship's *bulkheads* as well, but she couldn't complain—and wasn't going to say anything to Reggie in any case, as the fully armored weapons tech emerged into her field of view, carrying an immense, ugly blaster weapon she was quite sure *wasn't* on the inventory list for *Evasion*'s armory.

"Found you," she said unnecessarily. "Reggie, I'm pinging the location of our remaining intruders to everyone else. I don't know if any others are coming—I don't have any cameras outside the ship."

"But you have the internals and the coms?" Reggie asked.

"I gave them to her," Vexer said. "We need eyes and we need every blaster hand we've got. And I am *not* using a thirteen-year-old as a blaster hand."

"Look, we can argue age and usefulness *later*," Trace snapped. "Right now, there are three people in armor sweeping toward the mess. Since I guess that no one *except* Reggie has secret armor, that means folks have got to get guns *before* the boarders get there.

"And someone has to hold the main lock."

"I've got the airlock," Reggie replied. "Really don't want to fire an assault cannon inside the ship." He took a breath. "Again."

There was a long pause on the general channel.

"I'm going to try to take the team heading for the mess from behind," Vexer said slowly. "And when this is over, Reginald Kalb, we are going to have a *long* talk about what's appropriate to be in your *personal baggage allotment.*"

"Yes, yes, I've heard that before," Reggie replied. "Moving."

Trace saw both men moving through the ship. She took a moment to map the route for their boarders and growled in the back of her throat. They were going to make it to the mess before most of the crew *and* before Vexer could take them from behind.

"Vexer, what's the software for controlling the doors?" she demanded.

"...I don't even know," he admitted. "I only know which sections control the airlocks."

"It's the Internal Systems Control vee Three-Point-Six suite. Operations code is K-B-C-Five-Nine-One-Two," Joy snapped. "Does no one else on this void-ridden ship *read the damn manual*?"

Trace didn't bother to answer that—she was too busy opening the software the environmental tech had told her about and plugging in the o-code she'd been given.

That opened a virtual map of the ship. The teenager surveyed the controls and commands as quickly as she could, then took a breath as she realized the attackers were less than two corridors from the mess.

She tried three different commands on three different doors, sealing them all against the advancing mercenaries. From the codes that the software promptly gave her back, she might have permanently broken one door.

That told her what she needed, though, and she started sealing doors, forcing the mercenaries down a route *she* chose.

"I'm buying you time, but I can only do so much without making them suspicious," she guessed aloud. "Vexer, I'm opening doors as you reach them. We should be closing the trap."

"I've got your highlights," Vexer replied.

"Me too," Joy replied.

"And me," Tate replied. Surveillance showed that the stocky cargo handler had acquired one of the blaster rifles. "XO...should we be trying to take these guys alive?"

"They boarded this ship without legal authority," Vexer snapped. "Burn them down."

Trace looked at the situation and then twisted her hands together, slamming two doors shut.

"All right, they're trapped in the corridor between Vexer and the mess hall," she told the crew. "...and one of them is already pulling out a fusion cutter, so you do not have very much time."

"Ready," Vexer snapped, positioning himself next to the door in Trace's camera.

"We're ready," Ginny said, the engineer grabbing a gun tossed to her by Joy as she joined the two women already in the mess. "Fuck these bastards."

"Opening the doors," Trace said, her voice surprisingly calm to her.

The cameras couldn't track what happened over the next five seconds, but it ended the only way it could: with three dead mercenaries.

"Status?" Vexer barked.

"Joy took a flesh burn; grabbing a medkit," Ginny replied. "Otherwise, we're fine."

"Reggie?" Trace asked, trying not to look at the bodies on her cameras—and registering that the assault cannon had just opened fire.

"They had backup," the weapons tech said calmly. "Backup is now running. Got at least two of them."

"Okay. Now...what about the captain?" Trace asked.

"We cannot take heavy weapons onto the station," Vexer said grimly. "What we've already done is enough to draw a *lot* of attention and questions we can't afford. I'm... I'm not sure. Can we raise him?"

Trace poked at the half-understood system and grimaced as a blaze of static assaulted her ears.

"I'm the furthest from an expert, Vexer...but I think we're being jammed," she told the others.

30

STUNNER BOLTS FLASHED against EB's impromptu cover, but his focus was on Lear Naumov. The old spy was spasming around the chair, and EB could *see* him starting to foam at the mouth. The freighter captain knew the things the man needed, but he couldn't *get* to him.

Another salvo of stunner beams sent him back to cover as he started to make it to Naumov. The attackers were determined to take him alive, spreading out to flank his position—and whatever security Iridium Everlasting had was ignoring the situation, which said ugly things.

EB looked down at the gun in his hand and then back at Naumov. A stunner took a measurable amount of time to fire. So long as he played by the same rules as his attackers, the odds were in their favor. He figured had a decent chance of getting the flanker before he was stunned, but if he failed, *he* was down and stunned.

And either way, Naumov was dead. The spy needed attention in the next minute at most.

EB didn't want to kill anyone. He'd chosen to take a freighter instead of signing on with his old comrades' mercenary company to avoid that. He'd *wanted* to be a civilian, to avoid getting blood on his hands. That had driven so much of what he'd done, so much of what he'd run away from.

But if he tried to get through the next sixty seconds without killing anyone, he was going to end up Lady Breanna's prisoner—and Lear Naumov was going to die.

He dropped the stunner. He didn't even consciously go for the blaster, but it was in his hand as he rose over his cover.

Evridiki Bardacki had been a fighter pilot, and his kinesthetic sense was almost unsurpassed. He knew *exactly* where his attackers were, and his first blaster bolts went *exactly* where he intended them to. One shooter was down before they even registered that he was out from behind cover.

The flanker was reacting, their stunner rising as they adjusted for EB's movement—but a stunner took a measurable amount of time to fire.

A blaster didn't. A second burst of fire took the flanker in the chest as the stunner lined up with EB, sending them sprawling backward.

It was possible that one or both of the attackers was alive. EB didn't check. He was already at Naumov, pulling the chair out from the spy's limbs and turning the man into the recovery position.

Airway, breathing, circulation.

He rolled Naumov onto his side, clearing the spy's airway. EB heard his breathing clear up as the foam dripped away from his mouth. He checked the man's pulse. Weak, strained by the stunner beam, but present.

EB's headware triggered an emergency alert, calling for medical and security personnel to that location. Then he grabbed his stunner and blaster and got back to his feet.

He'd done what he could for the spy—the seizures seemed to have faded, and Naumov wasn't going to drown in his own saliva before he woke up.

Now it was time for EB to take care of *himself*—and get *off* this station!

THE LACK of an immediate perimeter of security personnel trying to contain the firefight was the clearest sign EB needed to confirm that the attackers had bribed Iridium Everlasting's people to stay out of the mess.

That definitely reduced his discomfort with his plan for getting *away* from the station!

When he finally spotted a security team, they were hustling toward the mezzanine and missed him completely. Wrapped in his jacket, his guns didn't draw attention, and the security troopers were focused on the direction of the emergency call.

Iridium Everlasting needed to work on their security people's training, but EB wasn't complaining today. He was almost all the way to his ship before he ran into any actual problems.

That problem, though, was very large and doing its best to be impenetrable. Emergency security bulkheads had slammed shut, sealing off the dock from the rest of the station. Warning signs flickered across the bulkhead, advising of pressure loss and telling people to get in touch with station security for a timeline on repairs.

"Ginny, what's your status?" he asked.

"We think we're clear," she replied. "We've thrown them back from the ship, and Reggie appears to have armor and an assault cannon. You need to talk with him about that. Preferably either before Vexer does or *with* Vexer."

"Right. Didn't realize I was everyone's dad," EB said drily.

"Starship. Captain." Ginny's voice was sardonic. "Look, at least a dozen mercs are dead from storming the ship. We're dumping the bodies on the dock, so the sooner we're out of here, the better."

"I'm on the wrong side of an emergency bulkhead, Ginny," he told her. "It's saying there's reduced pressure on the dock."

There was a long pause.

"I haven't *noticed,* but Reggie definitely fired off an assault cannon in here," she said quietly. "It's possible we breached the station."

And *that* was why assault cannon—rapid-firing, high-aperture, *barely* person-portable blaster weapons—were generally not *used* on space vehicles you wanted to keep.

"Check the pressure," he ordered.

There was a pause.

"Reggie says it's dropped one point four percent in the last ten minutes," she warned. "Slow leak, but the hull is definitely breached."

EB exhaled a hard sigh.

"Okay. I'm going to reseal the bulkhead behind me," he told her. "Our surprise?"

"Ready on your order, to *my* surprise," she admitted. "I just let the little shits go after people boarded and wasn't tracking them."

"Good," EB said. He was already loading up intrusion tools as he laid his hand on the wall next to the bulkhead, searching for the control network. "I'll be there in a moment."

Emergency bulkheads weren't *supposed* to open to anything except commands from the central control center. Safety designers understood that panicking people could all too easily doom an entire station trying to save themselves.

EB didn't necessarily agree with that logic, though he understood it. Unlike a panicky spacer, however, *he* had the tools and software to hijack the command center's signal. It took longer than he would have liked, but the bulkhead slid open in front of him.

He dove through, leaving his code on a deletion timer that would slam the bulkhead closed behind him.

"So, Reggie," he said conversationally as he finally linked into the crew network. "Is anyone going to try to kill me as I get back to the ship?"

"Well, *I* won't," the weapons tech told him. "And there's nobody left that I can see, but that doesn't mean there aren't mercs left."

"Wonderful. Cover me."

"EVERYBODY BACK ABOARD?" EB demanded as he dropped into his seat on the bridge. Trace and Vexer, he noted, were both watching him like they were worried he was an illusion that might pop if they touched him.

The looks were *very* different, and yet... And yet...

Both were clearly worried and both touched his heart. Weird.

"You were the only one who ever left," Reggie told him. "I'm in; just have the cannon trained on the airlock for the next wave."

"We're going to talk about that cannon," EB replied. "But for now, I'm glad you have it."

He ran through a sequence of commands.

"Iridium Everlasting Control isn't answering my hails," he said aloud after a moment. "Think they're bribed, scared or pissed?"

"All of the above," Vexer replied. "Let's get *out* of here."

"Working on it," EB replied. He tapped another command and *finally* got a response.

"Iridium Everlasting Control, this is *Evasion*, requesting emergency undock procedure," he told the controller before anyone could say anything.

"Denied, *Evasion*," the controller finally replied. "We have reason to believe your crew is responsible for breaches in the docking area and a firefight in the main mezzanine. You are specifically restricted from leaving the station."

"We just got jumped by fucking mercs," EB snapped. "What are you doing about *them*?"

"*They* are *also* specifically restricted from leaving the station," the controller told him. "You are *all* staying right the fuck where you are until an NFBI crisis unit arrives to take over the situation!"

Nigahog Federal Bureau of Investigation, EB's headware helpfully explained the acronym. The system-wide highest tier of police. They might be helpful. They might not.

Either way, EB wasn't prepared to sit in one place for that long... but he *was* prepared to let the station controllers think he was.

"Understood, IE Control," he said begrudgingly. "You keep those fuckers locked down and I'll play nice—but the moment *they* twitch, I'm *gone*, you get me?"

"You're locked down, *Evasion*," the controller told him bluntly. "You aren't going anywhere."

EB cut the channel and looked back at his lover and their teenage guest.

"They're going to come for you and Trace if we stay here," Vexer said, vocalizing EB's own thoughts.

"Yup," EB agreed. He wasn't planning on staying there that long, but he could see the concern in Trace's eyes.

"Don't worry," he told the kid. "We're not staying. Regardless of what I just told them."

He grinned.

"Ginny, do we have a hard link into the clamps and umbilicals?" he asked aloud.

"Of course," she said. "We don't have *control*, but we have hardware links."

EB grinned again and transferred an executable from his vault to *Evasion*'s computers.

"We have control," he told his engineer. "Activating our surprise. Once you've confirmed it, let's get the hell out of here."

Any properly designed station or starship kept their sensors, computers and communications well secured from each other. The trick he'd pulled on Star Plaza had been solely focused on the systems at the dock itself. To *actually* disappear from sensors was impossible.

Unless you'd fabricated a dozen or so small drones and set them across the outer hull of a space station, seeking out every sensor cluster on the station and its docked ships and inserting your viral code directly into the sensors itself.

The moment their "surprise" activated, every ship that had been docked at Iridium Everlasting and the station itself could only see *Evasion* as properly linked up with the station, exactly where she'd been told to remain.

"Surprise is active," Ginny said quietly. "Do you trust that code, EB?"

"Against the Brisingr Kaiserreich Navy? No," EB said cheerfully. "Against VCS's orbital gas station and a Beyond mercenary gunship? Eighty-twenty."

"Eighty-twenty," Vexer repeated from behind him. "And what happens in the twenty?"

"We probably have to shoot the gunship down at a minimum," EB admitted. "And I'd *really* like to get out of this without more dead people. Get us moving, hon."

Vexer called *EB* assorted pet names. EB hadn't realized he'd returned the favor until after it had slipped his lips—but it got him a brilliant smile and a renewed focus from his navigator.

Apparently, there was something to the habit after all.

THERE WAS something eerie to blasting away from a station without anyone around reacting. At least when they'd fled Star Plaza, the ships around the station had known. For that matter, the *station controllers* had known—they just hadn't cared much, Star Plaza being what it was.

None of the ships docked to Iridium Everlasting could see *Evasion* leave. To all of their sensors, the forty-kilocubic freighter was still docked to the refueling station.

"How are we doing?" EB asked Vexer, stepping over to squeeze his lover's shoulder.

"So far, so good," the navigator replied, sparing a hand to cover EB's. "We even got the fuel before things went to hell.

"Now? Nobody on Iridium is reacting to us. Everyone else is treating us as normal. The question is how long it takes for them to get a message out or send someone to physically check on us."

"The slow leak Reggie created will buy us some time," EB replied. "I'd rather have *not* shot a hole in the station, but it serves today. They'll patch that before they start looking for us."

"What happens when they realize what we've done?" Vexer asked. "Screwing with a station's traffic-control sensors…leaving a dozen or more mercs dead on the docks."

He shook his head.

"We don't really look like the good guys here."

"No, we don't," EB agreed. "We're not coming back to Nigahog. If we aren't officially persona non grata here when this is over, we won't be much short. No one is going to stop the Trackers' Guild wrapping us in a bow and sending us all over to Breanna."

He looked back at Trace.

"So, we won't be coming back here," he promised her. "Did you get those maps you were looking for?"

"There wasn't enough time," she admitted, looking scared. "We needed to get our hands on digital currency to pay, and…everything went to void."

Vexer's hand tightened on EB's to calm him, but there was no need. EB wasn't upset with either of them—and especially not the scared teenager!

"Where are we novaing, hon?" he asked Vexer, poking at the mental sore tooth of the pet name again.

"No choices," Vexer admitted. "Back into the Expanse. I don't know where to go from there, darling. We can't go to Star Plaza and we won't be able to come back here."

"And we need to nova soon," EB said grimly. "I guess we can ask ships coming through if they're willing to sell maps at a premium. Offer *enough* money and someone should take it."

He shook his head.

"If we can get a map, we should be able to get to Poberin," he noted, considering the map of the region in his headware. "From there, we can find a cargo and get to Icem and find Trace's foster family."

Something flashed across Trace's face, but he wasn't sure what to make of it. The kid would be safer with her foster home than with them—a nova freighter was no place for a teenager!

"Novaing in ten minutes," Vexer told him. There was an edge to EB's navigator's voice, too. One that hadn't been there when they'd been talking about being trapped between Star Plaza and Nigahog.

"All right." EB shook his head.

"Trace, come with me," he told the teenager. "Vexer gave you bridge-officer access, which, sorry, you don't get to keep—but we can set you up with crew access, and I want to walk you through the system and the o-codes."

That way, next time there was trouble, she might be able to start up software without needing someone to hold her mental hand.

31

TRACE WAS...CONFUSED. She'd freely admit she wasn't always the sharpest knife in the shed, test scores and intelligence assessments notwithstanding. She was *very* smart—she knew *that*—but that didn't always translate into fully understanding the people around her.

Especially adults. They were often manipulable, often dangerous, but not always fully understood.

Most especially, at that moment, she didn't understand Captain EB. One minute, he was treating her like a member of the crew, the next like a protected cargo they were honor-bound to deliver—and the next like a child.

His child, in some ways.

That thought...left Trace feeling both warm and guilty as she sat carefully on the seat in EB's office, listening to him lay out the dozen most common sub-softwares of *Evasion*'s main operating system.

"And, if you look here, you can see that we're not alone at this nova stop," he told her, bringing up the main sensor feed in the air above his desk. "Any of the crew can access this feed from anywhere in the ship, though detailed information is a bit more limited.

"That's not really a *security* thing so much as just straight habit," EB admitted. "I was a soldier once, and we worried a lot about operational security."

"Where were you a soldier?" Trace asked before she could stop herself.

EB paused thoughtfully, then shook his head.

"You haven't noticed yet, have you?" he asked. "None of us on this ship talk about our pasts, Trace. We're all running from something or someone."

He shrugged.

"That said, I'm pretty sure *you* aren't an assassin for the dictator of a hegemonic military state two hundred–plus light-years from here," he said drily. "I served in the Apollo System Defense Force, a long way away from here. I was a nova-fighter pilot, and as the saying goes, there are old pilots and bold pilots but very few old bold pilots."

He shook his head and smiled at her.

"I was old and not bold," he said cheerfully. "But my wing was in the heart of the war, so when the war ended, our enemies sent assassins after us all. So...that's what I'm running from.

"*Don't* ask the others what they're running from," he instructed.

Trace got that much. She *also* understood, much as EB didn't say it, that there were other things he was running from.

Void, there were things *she* was running from. Most of them were Lady Breanna's thugs...a thought that brought her attention back to the sensor feed.

"We're safe here, right?" she asked. She felt safe with EB. More than anyone else in her life, she felt safe with him.

"For now," EB agreed. "I'm going to wait until our nova drive cools down and then start contacting freighters, see who has a map of a route to Icem they're willing to sell."

A chill ran through the warm sense of safety she'd been indulging.

"What if someone causes trouble before that?" she asked.

"We deal with it," he promised. "Nobody harms my ship or my people. No matter what it costs."

Trace knew there was a weight to what he was saying...maybe even a fresh weight. She didn't know what it was, though.

Her own thoughts were a storm. She was afraid of Breanna's

people. She did *not* want to go back to the Cage, the space station they'd "trained" her aboard. She...didn't really want to go back to her foster family, though she knew they'd take her back.

Anything else would be *improper*, after all, and the Vortanis would never *dream* of appearing to be less than perfect. It must have hurt their image when she'd run away. She shivered at the thought of Sarah Vortani's reaction to *that*.

Going "home" would be safe, but it wouldn't be pleasant. Part of her wanted to ask if she could stay there, on *Evasion*. But...EB was so determined to get her home. She was a burden—one he'd protect to the end, she knew *that*—but a burden still.

"What are those?" she finally asked, pointing at two icons flickering orange in the display.

"A gunship and a corvette," EB said immediately. "The software flags warships until we tell it they're friendly. Or not, as the case may be, in which case it flags them differently."

"Trackers?" Trace asked.

"Or mercs. I don't know from here," he admitted. "They're over a light-hour away, Trace. They can't be here quickly and they won't surprise us."

He smiled gently at her.

"I'm keeping an eye on them; you have my word," he told her.

Trace believed him, and yet... She was afraid.

———

BACK IN HER ROOM, Trace poked at one of the things that was terrifying her. Something about that corvette on the sensor feed had looked...*familiar*. Which was insane, because she didn't know *anything* about corvettes, certainly not enough to recognize one based on the vague data on the main sensor feed.

Not that she'd ever seen a corvette enough to recognize one, for that matter.

And yet that corvette had flagged something in her head. Something that wasn't quite right.

It wasn't the first time. She'd known the right keywords to get into shadowy networks on Denton and those had got her half of the way into the shadow-net on Nigahog. And then...she'd thought she'd just guessed *right* as to which forums and sites to poke harder the first few times.

Except she'd kept getting it right. Again and again, she'd made choices that she thought were random or guesses, and they'd been the *right* ones for what she was looking for.

There was something in her head. Something she didn't consciously have access to—but it was linked to her nervous system, and that meant it couldn't fully *be* blocked off from her unconscious mind.

She pulled up the sensor feed again, trying to focus on the corvette. It was...*Zeldan Blade*. Twenty-six kilocubics, eight guns.

Trace shouldn't even know *that* much about a random warship floating around the Fasach Expanse, and she wasn't sure how she knew it.

The teenager didn't even know enough about headware to know if what she thought was happening was *possible*. EB might. Lan would— but then she'd have to admit that something was going on that might well risk the very people who'd put so much effort into helping her.

She didn't *want* to put *Evasion*'s crew at risk. But she didn't want them to decide she was a danger, either. She was stuck. They were her only way anyway, her only hope of getting back to Denton or...

Or what?

Trace snorted at herself.

"What do you think you're getting out of this, Trace?" she asked herself. "A real family? Not your kind of luck."

The Vortanis had taken care of her every need, except the need to be loved. She'd always known she was a *foster*, not an *adoptee*. Someone they took care of. Not someone who had become their child in any permanent sense.

They'd been her longest-lasting foster family, but they hadn't been her first. They'd wanted the perfect foster, so they'd found a kid who aced all of the aptitude tests and then taken over the fostering.

Trace might have blamed them more for that if she'd been any happier with any of the foster families *before* the Vortanis.

Right now, though, she just knew that a "real family" was a myth, a fairy tale when it came to kids like her.

And the *last* time she'd chased that fairy tale, she'd ended up in the hands of human traffickers...traffickers who appeared to have *put something in her head.*

32

A GOOD NIGHT'S rest put a new gleam on the world for EB. Of course, using headware codes to put himself into forced dreamless sleep wasn't something he could do long-term, but it would buy him some time before the nightmares really started kicking in.

"I've got the bridge," he told Vexer. "Had a chance to talk to Reggie yet?"

"Not yet," his lover replied. "You want to take first crack at it? I know you needed to sleep first."

"He did enough good that I'm not *really* inclined to rip a strip off of him," EB admitted. "Now that I've had a night's sleep, I can smack his hand for not telling us he had that kind of gear in his baggage."

"We probably should have scanned people's personal baggage," Vexer pointed out.

"Uh-huh," EB said. "And how many secrets do *you* have, hon?" he asked his lover. "Because I know scanning *my* baggage would probably give up a few I'd rather keep quiet."

Vexer was silent for several seconds.

"Okay, point," he conceded. "Up to you, then, darling. Good luck."

"Thanks. Go sleep," EB ordered. "Thanks for covering the watch until I rested. I needed it. Any trouble?"

"Nothing yet," Vexer said. "But I have the distinct feeling that corvette is watching me."

EB snorted.

"She's a corvette. She's almost certainly watching *everybody*. I just hope she looks at us and sees guns, not a payday."

"The problem, EB, is that at this point? Every merc and bounty hunter within fifty light-years of Star Plaza knows Lady Breanna wants your head," Vexer reminded him. "I did some digging while we were in Nigahog."

"And?"

"She *met* you. She doesn't *meet* anyone," Vexer said. "She wasn't just after our ship, EB. She wanted *you*. A new top captain, maybe? She wasn't expecting us to run."

"So, what, I know what she looks like and that's not okay?" EB asked.

"You met the most powerful crime lord in a dozen systems face-to-face and you *turned her down*," his lover replied. "I... I fucking *adore* you for that, EB, but you painted a target on yourself.

"And the kid? Trace? She's a brilliant little thing, going to be more trouble than she's worth to somebody—but they want her back, and to a degree that doesn't make sense."

Vexer shook his head.

"So, yeah, if that corvette has IDed us, her captain is thinking *payday*," he warned. "I mostly leave the paranoia to you and Reggie, darling, so *listen to me*.

"Watch those damn warships. Keep your finger on the button for the jammer. I don't like this."

"All right," EB agreed, closing the distance with Vexer to give his navigator a solid kiss. "I will," he promised. "Last thing I'm going to do at this point is *not* listen to you.

"I'm watching them."

And he meant it, too. If Vexer was getting twitchy, either things were getting too much for the navigator—which EB did *not* buy—or things were bad.

EB would watch the corvette and every other warship in the area. Because Vexer asked him to...and because Vexer was *right*.

NO MATTER how determined he was, EB couldn't maintain hypervigilance forever. He recognized that and paced himself. He'd done more than one patrol of a nova point that had involved jumping to random waypoints and hanging out for an hour, watching to see what the fighter's sensors picked up.

He suspected he had a better idea of how to keep watch in the military sense than any of his crew. Maybe not Reggie. EB was reasonably sure he understood the *shape* of Reggie's secrets, but he didn't know the details.

He didn't want to. That was the implicit deal when you signed on to a ship that wasn't coming back. EB's crew provided their skills and knowledge, and he never asked them where it came from.

EB was pretty open with his crew that he'd been military, but only a couple knew he'd served in the Apollo-Brisingr war. Only Trace, he realized, knew he'd fled the Kaiser's assassins.

And why, he wondered, had he told their teenage guest that? In the end, she was a passenger. Working her way, trying to be helpful, but still a passenger. They'd get her back to her foster family—maybe even get a reward, if they were as rich as she said—and part ways.

He shook his head. That thought felt...uncomfortable. But it wasn't like they could *keep* her. A ship that never came back was no place for a teenager. No matter how useful she was turning out to be.

Focusing on the corvette was a safer train of thought. And *everything* was a safer train of thought than the new deaths added to his conscience. He'd saved Lear Naumov—but he'd killed two mercs to do it.

His people had stacked another seventeen corpses on Iridium Everlasting's dock before they left, too. EB was responsible for those, if less directly. They'd weigh on him, but they wouldn't join his nightmares the way the people he'd killed face-to-face would.

He shook his head *again*, returning his focus to where it belonged: the scanner data on the pocket warship just over a light-hour away. There wasn't that much information *Evasion*'s sensors could get on a ship at this distance. They were better than most civilian ships in the Outer Rim, but they still weren't military sensors.

They couldn't even give him a decent reading on the Jianhong radiation emissions of the ship. *Those* would tell him how close the ship's nova drive was to cooling down. All he could really tell was that there *were* emissions.

He paused thoughtfully, considering that piece of information.

Everything he saw on the corvette was over an hour old. When they'd novaed out of Nigahog, the mercenary corvette had already been here for an hour. Now, ten hours later, she was still showing Jianhong radiation.

That meant her drive was still cooling down. She'd been in the area for less than twenty hours...but *also* for more than ten. As of an hour before.

A chill ran down his spine. If the merc had nova fighters, they could have sent them over to investigate. But no one in the Beyond had nova fighters, so the only way the corvette could investigate *Evasion* was by crossing the intervening space herself.

She could have reached *Evasion* by now if she'd traveled sublight. But EB would have seen her coming hours away and made his own maneuvers.

If the mercenary captain wanted their payday, they'd nova to him as soon as their drive was cooled down. Or they might be perfectly innocent, already on their way to Nigahog or Star Plaza or wherever.

EB wasn't buying innocence.

"Reggie," he said quietly into the crew net. "Get to the gun control center."

"Already there with my feet up on the targeting console while I drink my coffee and eat a sandwich Ginny kindly made me," the weapons tech replied. "The hairs on the back of my neck are holding a dance party.

"What do you need?"

"Capacitor status?" EB asked.

"Standard underway load," Reggie said. "Thirty percent. Two shots per gun, then we're into charge cycles."

It took roughly twenty seconds for the freighter's main fusion core to feed enough plasma into the capacitors for each cannon to allow them to fire. The *cannon* themselves could fire once every *two* seconds, and at full charge, their capacitors held enough plasma for eight shots.

Holding the capacitors at full charge was both obvious to anyone scanning the ship and bad for the capacitors in the long run. On the other hand, it was the best way to ready *Evasion* for the kind of fight she was built for.

"Charge them to full," EB ordered. "*Somebody* is going to make a jump for the payday we represent before we get out of here, and I want to make a *point* when they do."

"Wilco, EB," Reggie replied.

EB returned his attention to the corvette and gunships. Vexer had novaed them to the edge of the mapped zone, which meant everyone was millions of kilometers away. That also meant, unfortunately, that he had very little maneuvering room.

Without a star to use as an anchor, *Evasion* needed to nova *from* mapped space as well as *to* mapped space. EB couldn't take the freighter outside of the trade route stop and still make the jump to FTL.

He *could* move them around the edge of that mapped sphere, though. He brought up the Harrington coils to do just that—and *then* a pulse of Cherenkov and Jianhong radiation flashed across his sensors.

His clever idea had come too late.

"Everybody wake up," he snapped into the main network. "Contact at half a million kilometers. We have a *guest*."

33

SOMEHOW, EB wasn't surprised it was the corvette. Her captain had kept her nova careful, dropping her outside weapons range of the armed freighter, but was now heading directly toward *Evasion* at high thrust.

EB was heading *away* from them at equal acceleration, a capacity that he hoped was a surprise to the mercenary warship. Maybe even enough of a surprise to put some hesitation in their pursuer's mind.

"It's the big guy?" Vexer asked as he charged back into the bridge.

"The corvette, yeah," EB replied. "What do we know?"

"*Zeldan Blade*, Captain Lisa Zelda commanding," a small voice said from the back of the bridge. "Eight plasma cannon, the heaviest she could afford."

EB turned in his chair to look at Trace.

"What?" he asked bluntly.

"Scans match the description," Vexer said slowly. "I see two dorsal dual turrets and two ventral dual turrets. Bigger than ours—a *lot* bigger. Throughput probably isn't *that* much higher if she built them out here, though."

"How do you know that?" EB asked Trace.

"I don't know," she admitted, looking at the ground in distress. "But I recognized the ship from the sensor feed."

"Take a seat in the back," he told her. "Let me know if you recognize anything else. This might be scary, Trace, but it may help us, too."

"Okay," she promised, taking one of the spare seats.

The bridge systems informed EB she was linked into the main sensor feed, and he turned his focus back to their pursuer.

"Her guns are twice the size of ours," Vexer finally concluded. "Not that it will matter. Not unless this ship has armor and energy webs I don't know about?"

"She's a freighter with guns, but she's still a freighter, hon," EB replied. "Keep us dodging. We've still got the lightspeed lag on our side. She's got to get a *lot* closer to actually have a chance of hitting us."

A flash of energy on the screen proved EB's point.

"That was at least five hundred klicks clear of us," Vexer said.

"Warning shot," EB said. "She's about to hail us. Reggie?"

"Boss?"

"Return the warning shot, if you please. Let's make our position clear."

Another flash of energy lit up EB's screens as his own ventral turret rotated and fired a single pulse of plasma.

Like the shot at *Evasion*, it was obviously not aimed to hit. It bought EB a bit more hesitation, another minute of silence as the two ships danced.

Zeldan Blade could match *Evasion* for acceleration, which he hadn't expected. She had a slight velocity edge that she'd carried through the nova with her. It wasn't much, but it was, he calculated, enough to bring them within real combat range before *Evasion* could jump.

"Incoming hail," Vexer told him. "What do we do?"

"Link them a channel; make sure our video excludes Trace," EB said. "Let's see if I can talk my way out of this."

A holoprojection of a two-dimensional video image appeared in front of him. The woman in the screen bowed slightly as she saw that he was receiving, then met the gaze of the camera levelly.

She was certainly a distinctive individual. At some point in the past, she'd lost her left ear. Now, a purple niqab veil hung from a gold chain wrapped around her entire head just below the level of her eyes, hooked on her right ear and a piercing where her left ear had been.

The sides of her head were shaved to draw attention to the missing ear, the rest of her jet-black hair drawn through a slim hijab scarf into a braid that she let hang down in front of her right shoulder.

"I presume I am speaking to Captain Bardacki of the freighter *Evasion*?" she said in an unfamiliar, precise accent.

"Would it do either of us any good if I said you weren't?" EB asked brightly.

A few seconds passed as the messages crossed the void between them, and then the woman chuckled behind her veil.

"No," she told him. "Your ship is distinctive and I have imagery of you, Captain. I am Captain Zelda. You will surrender yourself and Em Tracy Finley to my custody."

It appeared Trace had correctly identified the ship. EB didn't glance back at the teenager, but he doubted that was a *good* thing in her mind.

Something very odd was going on with his passenger, but that was a problem for *after* this mess.

"That's quite the request, Captain Zelda," EB said. "One I fail to see any benefit in for myself."

"If you do not surrender yourself and Em Finley to me, I will disable your ship by fire and board her," Zelda told him. "While I need you and Em Finley alive, the rest of your crew are worthless to me.

"My preference, Captain, is to do what must be done at the minimum cost to all involved. If you surrender yourself and Em Finley, your ship and crew will be spared."

EB raised an eyebrow at the woman.

"Do you even know what we're accused of, Captain?" he asked. "Or what fate awaits us if you deliver us for the bounty?"

"No and no," Zelda told him. "As a lawyer must adopt a moral vacuum to defend a client who may or may not be guilty, a bounty hunter must adopt a moral vacuum to deliver a target who may or may not be innocent.

"That is for the Trackers' Guild and the courts to establish."

EB let that hang for several seconds.

"And so, you find yourself pursuing illegal bounties, to deliver children to their abusers?" he asked, his tone very soft. "Is your vacuum *that* strong, Captain Zelda?"

"If it must be," she replied, but he could tell he'd struck a blow. "Such is the nature of the world and the Beyond. We have little space or time for the niceties of the Rim, captain. A ship must survive and a captain must look to her crew."

"I agree," he told her. "And I will defend my ship and my crew, Captain Zelda. You may be able to *destroy* my ship, but I do not believe you will be able to take us intact."

"You underestimate me, I feel."

"That feeling is mutual, then," EB murmured. Zelda clearly didn't expect *Evasion* to have military-grade multiphasic jammers. To successfully disable EB's ship inside a jamming zone would require the corvette to get within fifty thousand kilometers—which would require *Zeldan Blade* to endure *Evasion*'s fire for a quarter-million kilometers.

The corvette had better guns than *Evasion* did. Zelda's ship almost certainly *had* armor and dispersal webs—but there was no way she had the defenses to survive that kind of approach.

"Of course, if you force me to destroy your ship, you and all of your crew will die," Zelda said calmly. "The bounty for *you*, Captain Bardacki, has a partial payment for that situation. On the other hand, I see a potential compromise."

"Other than my calmly surrendering myself to you?" EB asked. He doubted that he was going to agree to whatever compromise the mercenary offered, but every moment he kept the mercenary talking was a moment closer to being able to nova.

He doubted he could buy the hours upon hours that would take, but talking wasn't shooting.

"Finley is worth nothing to me dead," Zelda told him. "And she is worth more to me alive than you are dead. She is little to you but an inconvenience, I imagine.

"Turn her over to me and I will allow you and your ship to leave unchallenged."

EB couldn't even look at Trace. That would have given away that the kid was on his bridge.

That won't *happen*, he sent her silently over the crew network before he even verbally replied to Zelda.

"You don't know what they want her for, do you?" he asked, his tone flat and cold. "I don't know what you believe about your job, Captain Zelda, but if you are prepared to return a teenage girl to the people who would make her a rich man's sex toy, *you* are a monster.

"I once swore an oath to stand between the galaxy and people like *you*," EB said flatly. "I've retired from that career now. But if fate puts me between a thirteen-year-old child and the monsters of the night, I will *die* before I will *move*."

He cut the com channel before Zelda could speak, new commands flowing from his hands and his mind into the system.

"Multiphasic jammer online," he barked. "Vexer, close the range. She can't *disable* us at more than fifty thousand kilometers, so let's punch her in the *fucking nose* and see what she does."

"You want to pick a *fight*?" Vexer demanded.

The sensor data was disintegrating. The jammer broke their scanners as much as anyone else's. The bubble was only a light-second in radius—*Zeldan Blade* wasn't currently inside it, for example—but *Evasion* could barely see out of it.

"We've got a line on *Blade*," EB replied. "But she's got shit on us. Reggie—open fire. Cycle-time shots."

That meant a shot every twenty seconds from each cannon. They weren't likely to hit at this range—but they were *more* likely to hit than *Zeldan Blade* was, and EB was surprised at just how angry Zelda's "compromise" had made him.

"Engaging," Reggie said in a calm voice. "Alternating guns, ten second salvos."

That meant that every ten seconds, each of *Evasion*'s turrets was firing a single plasma packet from *one* cannon. That cannon wouldn't fire for twenty seconds, allowing the capacitor to recharge back to full, but the other cannon would fire ten seconds later.

EB didn't have a solid lock on *Zeldan Blade*, and his lock was degrading by the moment. Still, it was enough for Reggie to put the near-lightspeed energy pulses in the region of the corvette.

At this range, with the jamming bubble wrapped around them, EB couldn't tell if Reggie was *hitting*...but that wasn't actually the point.

"There she goes," he murmured as even his existing lock shifted—and then disintegrated into chaos.

"EB?" Vexer asked.

"*Zeldan Blade* just went to her maximum acceleration away from us and popped her own jammer," EB told his lover. "It appears that Captain Zelda is less prepared to fight a real enemy than we are."

"What do we do?" Vexer asked.

"Break off the pursuit; vector away from her at max thrust," EB replied. "Open the range until there's no way she can catch us before we nova.

"Reggie, pause charging of the capacitors and empty them down to fifty percent charge. Then cease fire," he continued. "That will give us some reserve if she changes her mind and has a clever idea, without straining the systems."

There was a long silence on the bridge, and EB spent it staring bleakly at the displays.

"Thank you," Trace finally said, her small voice the only break in the silence.

"We were *not* giving you up to her," Vexer snapped before EB could say a word. "Not in this world or the next. You're *ours*, kid, and we don't give up our own."

"No," EB agreed. "We don't."

He turned to look at the teenager with a sad smile.

"We do sometimes ask awkward questions, though," he told her gently. "How did you know what ship that was?"

34

TRACE STARED BLANKLY into the datafeed. She'd heard EB's question but she wasn't even sure what the answer *was*, let alone how to explain it.

And yet...*Evasion*'s crew had just gone to the wall for her in a way no one ever had in her entire life. She was *theirs*. One of them, not an awkward passenger. Not a burden to be dumped at a planet along the way.

Theirs.

She owed them everything she could manage.

"I'm not sure," she finally said, slowly. "I saw the scan data in the sensor feed and I just...knew. But I never studied ships, let alone individual ships or individual *bounty hunters*."

"To be fair to our rapidly departing friend, I believe Captain Zelda is primarily a mercenary," EB said. "Not that that would stop me vaporizing her to protect my people. To protect *you*."

"Would Lan know more about how that kind of knowledge would happen?" Vexer asked.

Trace exhaled a sigh.

"I do," she half-whispered. "I know...a lot more about headware than I think the traffickers realized. They were…John's hobby? Obsession? Career?"

She shrugged with open palms.

John Vortani might have gone along with his wife's political career and its attendant needs—like a poster perfect foster child—but his focus had been on maintaining his status as one of Denton's top neurosurgeons.

It was the money from his career and success that had funded Sarah Vortani's rise to power. So far as Trace could tell, he'd accepted the child into their home as a requirement of his wife's political plans and promptly hired a nanny to do the work.

But he'd still spent time with Trace, at least as much as Sarah had. Most of that time had been him talking about headware and neural implants—and a young child who had *wanted* the Vortanis to be her parents, at least at first, had listened to it all.

"And?" EB asked.

"There's no way to put storage in an implant that can't be accessed by the brain," Trace told him. "You could put a standard memory chip inside someone's skull, but the only way to access it would be to remove it.

"To allow for remote access, the memory has to be standard neural hardware. And then, even if it isn't linked to the main implant, the brain will still interface." She shook her head, stretching for half-remembered lectures.

"Even when the carrier doesn't have the memory on their headware operating system and can't access it consciously, it's still accessible by the *subconscious* mind."

"You think the traffickers put a datavault in your head?" EB asked.

Trace hadn't heard her foster father use that particular term, but it fit.

"Those of us who were…cooperating got special privileges," she said quietly. "We got rooms, a cafeteria, some limited privacy and socialization time. We talked. There were rumors. None of us had our headware turned back on, but the rumors said that part of the physicals was the doctors poking at the headware. Adding things. Sometimes control chips for the uncooperative.

"Sometimes…other things. We didn't know what. But…"

"The perfect secure courier," Vexer said flatly. "The poor kids wouldn't even know for sure that they had a vault in their head at all. And only the people who *knew* to look would find it."

"The data is almost certainly encrypted and shielded, too," EB agreed. He was looking at Trace quietly. "It's still a problem, though."

"Why?" Trace asked. "It's not a threat, is it?"

"No, not directly," the captain told her. "But if they're after you for the data they stuck in your head, Trace, someone like Breanna will *never* trust that we didn't copy that vault. We wouldn't give you up, no matter what…but even if we did, she can't let us live."

"I'm sorry," Trace whispered as the weight of that crashed in on her. The moment she'd sneaked aboard *Evasion*, she'd doomed every member of the ship's crew. That wasn't…*fair*.

"I should have ju—"

"No," EB cut her off, not letting her finish the thought aloud or internally. "You did the right damn thing, Trace. You came to us and we took you in. Nobody did anything wrong or anything less than the right thing to do.

"And now you're our responsibility and I *won't* let you blame yourself," he continued. "But…kiddo…we need to know what they put in your head. I know you don't like doctors. I know the thought of that vault has to *terrify* you.

"But Lan and I need to go into your head and find it."

Trace shivered in fear, her hands clenching at EB's words.

"I…can't," she whispered. "Last time… They could have put a control on me. I… I…"

EB was in front of her, the big gray-haired man kneeling and taking her hands in his. His skin was warm and reassuring against hers, his gaze firm and level as he met her eyes.

"Tracy Finley," he said, his tone level. "I will move the stars and void itself to keep you safe. I will fight traffickers and bounty hunters and mercenaries to watch your back. But I need to know why they're hunting you.

"It's the only way I can protect you. I promise you I will be there every moment of the way. I may not know the surgery and the hardware, but I know the software involved and I'll be the one pulling stuff from the vault.

"I *know* I can identify any safety measures or traps in the vault," he told her. "I *know* Lan and I can keep you safe. I won't make you do this, but…these people are prepared to kill for what's in your head."

He squeezed her hands and Trace felt unshed tears burning at the corner of her eyes.

"Let us help you."

She blinked, squeezing the tears out to fall on EB's hands, and then looked up to meet his gaze as calmly as she could.

"Okay," she said, her voice sounding tiny and pathetic even to her.

This time, she wasn't trying to manipulate *anyone*.

35

"SHE'S UNDER," Lan said calmly, the enby studying the reports from their artificial stupid robot anesthesiologist. "Heart rate, stable. Blood pressure, stable. Brain waves, stable. Implant self-check, green."

EB nodded, looking at the girl on the table. Unconscious, with a heavy blanket draped up to her neck, she looked frail and insignificant. Still, he squeezed the small hand in his and looked up at the doctor.

"There *will* be security measures on the vault," he warned the doctor. "Once we're into the software, I can locate and disable the triggering code. But I can't stop anything that's hardware-based."

That was the risk inherent in this.

"I know," Lan told him. "Setting up the scanners now. I want a full three-dimensional layer scan before I even consider taking probes in. *Any* physical work with a headware implant is finicky, Captain."

"I know," EB said. "And so does she. So, we owe it to her to do it *right*."

The doctor chuckled, laying a U-shaped scanner around Trace's head and then running their hands through a sterilization field.

"She's one of ours, isn't she?" Lan asked. "Still planning on dropping her off in Icem?"

"No idea," EB admitted. He opened up a virtual display, loading in some of his old software. His implant made contact with Trace's, a gentle poke that would normally be rejected.

Headware was the most secured thing in existence. Rejection was default. Only specific authorization with specific codes was permitted, and that authorization expired rapidly. The code Trace had plugged into EB's implant would be active for less than ninety minutes.

"I'm into her headware," he told Lan. "Looking for unusual software connections."

"And I'm scanning for unusual hardware," the doctor replied. "Hopefully, we'll meet somewhere in the middle."

EB nodded in distraction, his attention now entirely on the task in front of him. They knew there was at least one piece of unusual hardware, the physical lockout the traffickers had installed in Trace's head.

The entire data infrastructure in Trace's implant was odd. It wasn't just that it was a Beyond structure versus a Rim structure. This was...

"Son of the void," he whispered.

"EB?" Lan asked.

"Her headware data infrastructure is completely experimental," EB told the doctor. "An entirely new custom operating system." He shook his head. "If I'm reading this right, any control chip they installed would have *failed*.

"But...that's because her foster father was using her as a void-cursed *experiment*."

"That may be part of why the datavault was disgorging information to her subconsciously," Lan noted. "The human brain is notorious for doing odd things with neural-format hardware, but if her mind has already been trained to access data in multiple different ways, the additional neuroplasticity could easily have made that access easier."

EB glared at the operating system code on the feed. It wasn't anything that would have caused Trace problems. He'd interfaced with her implant before and not noticed it, so it wasn't like it would impede her day-to-day implant use.

But there were very clear signs of multiple versions of operating systems installed, uninstalled, updated and replaced. That was *not* something he'd ever seen in headware before. That kind of work was normally done with sample headware that wasn't *installed in anyone*. Let alone installed in a child.

"All right, so I'm angry at this John Vortani," EB said slowly. "But I'm *not* seeing signs of any additional software locks or secured data storage beyond what I'd expect."

Even with the level of access Trace had given him, there were sections of her headware and digital memories that the operating system simply would *not* give him access to. No one who wasn't Trace could access the digital backup of her personal memories, for example.

And while there were ways to get *past* that, none of them would work on Trace. Sickening as the thought was of using an unknowing child for tests like this, her unusual operating system would defy most attempts to *do* anything to her implant.

Given where she'd ended up, that was a good thing. EB still wanted to break Trace's foster father's fingers.

"What about hardware?" he finally asked Lan.

"The physical lockout is just that, a lockout," the enby doctor replied. "It's installed on the main ATP converter, the headware's power source. It just turns off the power supply. But it gives me a starting point as to where to look and…"

Lan trailed off and EB resisted the urge to metaphorically—or *literally*—kick the doctor.

"Fascinating," they finally said. "There's a layer of cloned neural tissue around the chip to disguise it. Young Trace's brain has grown into and taken over that tissue, but it still makes it harder to detect the vault.

"It's also been quite carefully sculpted to aid in the disguise. But it still has to draw power from the ATP converter."

EB knew enough biology to follow that. The human body produced ATP—adenosine triphosphate—as the product of the consumption of sugars and fats. It was one of several molecules used as a power source to fuel the actual cells of the body.

The converter stole a portion of the fuel produced in the brain and converted it to electricity to run the silicon implants present in every modern human's skull. The process noticeably increased the caloric need of a modern human as well. Brains and computers were demanding things—but the body knew how to handle needing more calories.

"Can we remove it?" EB asked. "I don't want that thing in her head anymore."

Lan was silent for at least ten seconds.

"With the way the cloned tissue has grown into her original tissue and the way that tissue is integrated into the chip itself, I'm not certain I can remove the datavault without inflicting some degree of brain damage.

"Based off my initial scans, I do not believe that the vault was intended to remain inside Trace's head for more than ten days. She was already halfway through that time when she escaped and came to us.

"It has grown into her brain in a way it was never intended to." The doctor shrugged. "My assumption is that they expected to be able to safely retrieve the vault physically, and that this was at least partially an intentional feature."

"What do you mean?" EB demanded.

"They likely believed that the vault could only be accessed by a physical probe and therefore removal was the only way to get at the data," Lan said quietly. "By rendering the vault unremovable without major damage to the victim, they created a security barrier against their more-moral enemies, at least, accessing the data."

"So, we can't get it out and we can't access it." EB shook his head. "Can we at least make sure any *other* security systems are disabled?"

"I do not believe there are any additional physical security measures," the doctor told him. "The most likely remaining measure is an overcharge function on the chip itself, which would only be triggered by hostile access."

"I could turn that off with *access*, but that's...bad," EB admitted. "I don't want Trace wandering around with a chip in her head that could kill her."

"I didn't say *we* couldn't access it," Lan said brightly. "I said that the traffickers likely believed physical access was required. *I*, however, am significantly better at this than they are."

EB waved away the imagery of file structure of Trace's headware storage and looked at Lan's scans. A three-dimensional hologram of the teenager's brain, at roughly one-to-three scale, now hung above where she lay on the bed.

"The vault is here," Lan told him, highlighting the invasive chip in bright red. It was about a centimeter away from the sphere EB recognized as the ATP converter—barely three millimeters in reality. "The cloned tissue is here, as much as it can be distinguished from her original tissue."

A hazy orange sphere appeared around the chip.

"Any attempt to *extract* the chip would require severing the neuron connections formed between the cloned tissue and her tissue," the doctor continued. "Given the complexity of the human brain, even I could not project the consequences of that. She might lose her memories of age three. She might be fine.

"She might lose her ability to unconsciously control her breathing and die on the operating table."

"You said we didn't need to do that," EB pointed out.

"Yes. But I wanted you to understand the level of danger involved in what they *expect* us to need to do," Lan told him. "And, unfortunately, you can likely assume that the *traffickers* assume we have accessed this chip the direct way."

EB winced. He'd figured the traffickers would assume *Evasion*'s crew had copied the vault. Now he knew what copying that vault entailed in the traffickers' minds—and that Lady Breanna assumed that *anyone* would have just...done that.

"Better to know the mind of our enemy, I suppose," he whispered. "But how do *we* get in?"

"You do not ask what I did before I joined you, and I appreciate that," Lan told EB calmly. "But I have several tools amidst my kit that are not standard for the Rim, let alone the Beyond. Among them is an active nanotech neural probe."

"Those words make sense to me, Lan, but the combination doesn't," EB admitted.

Lan sighed and shook their head.

"To make a connection with the chip, I need to find its physical port," they explained. "That requires examination at a closer level of detail than external scans can give me. My normal option, without extraction, would be to examine the chip with a neural probe.

"But the tiniest and most flexible probes available would *still* risk severing neural connections between the chip and her brain," Lan continued. "While *I* might be able to establish a connection without injuring Trace, I would not put the odds in my favor, and I would, frankly, assume any other surgeon would fail."

EB had never asked Lan to do more than basic surgery, cybernetic repair and trauma medicine. The level of confidence his ship's doctor was bringing to *neurosurgery* was new to him. He'd seen Lan be less confident about setting a broken leg!

"So?" he finally asked.

"An active nanotech probe uses a series of wirelessly linked nanites to form a connection from the exterior of the skull to the target zone," Lan told him. "I can then send several nanites to search the surface of the chip in a manner that will definitely *not* risk damaging the neural tissue.

"Then, once they have found the ports, we can establish an indirect wireless link to the chip, relayed through the nanotech probe. The nanites' wireless signals are so low as to pose functionally zero risk to Trace, where even if the chip was capable of it, a direct wireless link would be risky."

"Okay." EB exhaled. He understood most of that. "And the catch?"

"The chip is, at this point, integrated into her brain. If the software activates a burnout function, it will kill Trace. That part...is beyond my skillset."

Evasion's captain nodded and squared his shoulders.

"It's not beyond mine, my friend. Let's do this."

36

EB DIDN'T GET MUCH of a look at the case that Dr. Lan Kozel pulled out of their cabinet of wonders. He *did* get a glance at the symbol on the front, which was probably more than Lan would have preferred. The Star Kingdom of Griffin was a long way Sol-ward from *Apollo*, let alone the very edge of the Rim where he'd found Lan.

The case held six identical syringe-like devices with a green readout on their side. Lan tapped one, clearly linking the nanites to their headware, and then crossed back to Trace.

"The anesthesiologist stupid says we want to bring her back up in thirty minutes at most," Lan noted. "There's some oddities in her reaction to the current dosages, but we've got too much already in her to switch medications.

"Nothing that will be a problem, but it limits how much longer we can keep her under."

"We should be good, though, right?" EB asked. "How long should this take?"

"It's been...some years since I did this," Lan admitted. "Though..." They swallowed. "EB...this is an interrogation tool. The last time I used one of these probes, it was absolutely critical that the patient never realize we'd accessed his headware."

They spread their hands, the probe syringe in their right hand.

"The two factors should wash," they stated. "We should have plenty of time. I'll transfer access to you as soon as I have it."

"First priority is to disable security," EB said aloud, watching as Lan knelt next to Trace and readied the syringe. "Once that's done, we should just be able to copy the entire vault and decrypt it later."

"That is your area," Lan told him. They ran their finger along Trace's jawline, finally settling their index finger at the hinge of her jaw, beneath her ear.

The syringe-like probe went in next, replacing the doctor's finger right at the base of the girl's ear. EB twitched, resisting the urge to swipe the dangerous-looking device away from the child.

"We begin," Lan said calmly. There was no visible action on the probe, but EB had to assume that the nanites were now moving out from the tip of the probe and into Trace's brain.

The sickbay was silent for at least a minute, Lan staring blankly at the hologram of the teenager's mind hanging in the air.

"We've found the cloned tissue," they announced, their tone distracted. "It's slightly less dense than the organic tissue, which makes this part easier." Pause. "I've made contact with the chip itself.

"It's a standard Artemis Tau Technologies four-hundred-terabyte secured data chip," Lan continued. "I know where the contact port is. Stand by for connection, Captain."

EB nodded, linking into his *own* datavault—which was, to his shiver of awareness, *also* an Artemis Tau Technologies secured data chip. He wasn't sure how Lady Breanna had sourced the Rim-manu-factured datavault, but the chips were small enough that even a single container would fill her needs for a long time.

"I have the port," Lan declared. "Wireless connection stable. Establishing link to your system now."

The new data feed appeared in EB's headware and he focused on it. His tools were laid out around him, an array of virtual icons representing the software he expected to need.

"I'm ready," he told Lan.

"Activating the port," the doctor told him.

EB had it. The saving grace of his tools versus the security was that the chip didn't *have* its own operating system. It needed to be loaded in and accessed via an external system. The security software needed that activation to do anything.

If it wasn't activated exactly the right way, by software that knew the security system was there, it wouldn't even ask for a password or decryption key before burning out the chip. And right now, that would kill Trace.

But *EB* had the tools to run a scan of the chip's data architecture without actively reading it. To find the security software—and to erase it from the chip before ever doing anything the software would recognize as activating the chip.

"Chip is safed," he said aloud. "Taking a second scan for any software that could activate a burnout."

He also took a moment to disable the original software that gave the chip the *ability* to burn out. They couldn't disable the hardware pieces, and it was possible that some of the security measures would have their own code, but many would rely on the original Artemis Tau Technologies code.

The worm his scan *did* find, buried inside the encryption protocol, didn't. Any attempt to decrypt the data without using the right software as well as the right key, let alone a brute-force decryption attempt, would trigger a chip burnout.

Since EB wasn't planning on decrypting the data while it was inside Trace's head, that wasn't an issue...but he sliced that code out anyway. He wasn't leaving *any* code in the kid's head that could hurt her.

"Security disabled. Initiating copy sequence," he told Lan. "I make it...fifteen minutes."

The chip held over three hundred terabytes of data. Just what the hell had Lady Breanna *put* in Trace Finley's head?!

37

TRACE WOKE UP SLOWLY, groggily.

The first thing she registered was that someone was holding her hand, a solid reassurance against fears of the *last* time she'd woken up from anesthesia. She opened her eyes, blinking against the sickbay lights to see EB sitting in the chair next to her bed.

The *second* thing she registered was how awful she felt.

"I think I'm gonna puke," she said aloud.

"Right here," Vexer said from her other side, handing her a bag.

Trace stared at the bag for a few seconds before she managed to swallow her nausea.

"Alternatively, pass her this antinauseant and glass of water," Lan said from above Trace's head.

Vexer chuckled and followed the doctor's orders. EB helped her sit up, and for a moment, despite the nausea and the stomach cramps, Trace just...took in the presence of the two men flanking her.

Taking care of her. She'd done *nothing* to deserve that, she was sure of it. Yet here they were.

She accepted the pill and the glass of water from Vexer and leaned on EB as she swallowed down the medication.

"What happened?" she asked.

"You had a minor allergic reaction to one of the medications we used," EB said quietly. "Nothing severe, but Lan warned you'd wake up sick to your stomach. Figured we'd keep an eye on you."

He nodded toward Vexer, the two of them layering their hands over Trace's free hand and squeezing. She leaned against the upright bed and exhaled a sigh of relief as the medication took effect.

"I don't *think* I'm gonna puke on you now," she conceded. "Did it... Did it work?"

"The vault is still in your head," EB warned her softly. "We couldn't extract the physical chip without hurting you. We were able to access it and I disabled anything that could endanger you, but you still have the vault itself in your head."

"Oh," she whispered. She'd hoped that the *thing* the traffickers had put in her would be gone.

"We have a full copy of the data," he told her. "We'll learn what we need to know, and I'll be able to give you the decrypt protocols once I've cracked them. In the long run, that chip will just become part of your headware. You'll be able to wipe it, use it for storage, whatever you want."

EB sighed and squeezed her hand.

"It's not the best result, I know, but it's all we could do."

"If we have the data...why are you here?" she asked. Surely, they had better things to be doing—decrypting the vault, flying the ship, novaing away from the route to Star Plaza.

"We didn't want you to be alone when you woke up," EB told her. "Lan would have been here, but...none of us thought you'd want to be left with just them."

"Not even me," Lan agreed. "White-coat syndrome can be severe enough in people who were not actively hurt by those supposed to help them. In your case, I would recommend against you being alone with a doctor until such time as *you* are absolutely sure you are okay."

"Huh." It wasn't fair to Lan, even Trace knew that, but she was surprised to see that level of concern from the ship's doctor.

"What now?"

EB and Vexer shared a long look across her bed.

"A lot depends on what's in the vault," EB admitted. "I have some brute-force decryption protocols running right now on a secondary copy. They don't really need supervision, but they're going to take a while to crack it."

"We're heading away from the mapped nova point at full thrust," Vexer added. "It'll make it harder for us to move on when we decide our next destination, but it keeps us safe for now.

"No one is going to bother us for a bit."

"Still back to Denton?" Trace asked. She still wasn't entirely sure how she felt about that, but she knew that was what *Evasion's* crew thought was appropriate.

"Depends on what's in the vault," EB repeated, looking uncomfortable. "Right now, if we hand you back to your foster family, I'm pretty sure Lady Breanna's people would be kicking down the door inside a week.

"That's not safe for anyone."

Trace winced at a sudden vivid image of several of the guards she'd known on the Cage bursting through the door of the Vortanis' gorgeous townhouse, shouting and shooting.

"I hadn't..."

"Us either, until this started getting bad," Vexer said. "We can't take you home until this whole mess is dealt with."

"Home" was a strong word for the Vortanis, Trace knew, but it was the best anyone could do for now. A new wave of nausea swept over her and she cringed forward—only to find EB's arm wrapping her in a solid half-embrace.

"Antinauseants have variable effects for the first few minutes," he reminded her. "We've got you."

This time, she didn't manage not to throw up. Vexer managed to get the bag to her in time to catch most of it, but she also got vomit all over the navigator's arms.

"I'm sorry!" she exclaimed.

"Not the first time someone's thrown up on me," Vexer replied. "I'll go clean up and deal with this bag. You got her, EB?"

"I got her," EB confirmed.

The two men shared a firm—if *very careful*—forearm grip before Vexer ducked out of the immediate area to wash up.

"I'm sorry," Trace repeated miserably.

"Worse things have happened to Vexer," EB told her. "And me." He paused, a long dark silence that felt filled with *something* to Trace.

"And you," he finally said.

That sounded new. Like there was something *else*, something on top of the hells Trace had been through.

"What?" she demanded.

He swallowed, glancing at the doctor behind Trace, then shrugged.

"Did you know your foster father was using your headware implants as an installation test for new operating systems and updates?" he asked bleakly.

Trace stared at EB. That... That made no sense. And yet...it would explain part of why and when John Vortani had spent time with her and why he'd talked so much about headware with her.

"Isn't that..." She trailed off, not even sure what words to use to describe that.

"Illegal. Wrong," Lan said, stepping into view. "A violation of his oaths as a doctor, his principles as a neurosurgeon and his duty as a father."

Trace hadn't had much of a chance to get to know the dark-skinned doctor, but the anger in Lan's eyes touched her heart. EB didn't look any happier with Trace's supposed father figure either.

"I didn't know," she whispered. "I just thought... I thought everyone's headware software was randomly glitchy and went through adjustments as they grew up."

"No," Lan said flatly. "The fundamental architecture of your implant, Em Finley, is approximately twelve hundred years old. *Sixty generations* of humans have grown up with the implants in their heads.

"While your headware hardware and software are continually upgraded as you mature, there is no point at which those adjustments should be more than an expansion of what you already have. There are no *glitches* or *adjustments* for a *child's* headware, Em Finley.

"The kind of work Dr. Vortani did on you is reserved for isolated, unimplanted headware suites or adult volunteers," they told her. "Very, *very* occasionally, research work is done with children to allow for improvement in pediatric neuro-cybernetics. That work is done under the most careful supervision and ethical constraints.

"It is absolutely *not* done to an unconsenting child, in secret, by their legal guardian."

Lan was *very* angry, Trace realized.

"We're going to deal with the Lady Breanna situation, Trace," EB told her softly. "One way or another. Then... Then we'll need to work out what *you* want us to do with you.

"Until the traffickers are either dealt with or outrun, there's nowhere safe we can leave you, anyway."

Trace swallowed. That was...terrifying.

"So, where do I go?" she asked.

"With us," EB told her firmly, squeezing her hand again. "Your enemies have decided they're our enemies. So, we stand together. Until it's over.

"I promise."

38

EVASION WAS a long way from the mapped area of the official trade route stop now. They could still see what was going on there and *be* seen, but the time lag was such that EB was comfortable assuming that no one would pursue them.

Or, at least, had been before he'd finally cracked the encryption on the datavault.

"EB?" Vexer asked. "EB?"

EB swallowed and looked up across the bridge at his lover.

"We're in deep shit," he said, as levelly as he could. "I cracked the encryption."

He looked at the *map* spreading out in his headware. Stars. Worlds. Nova routes. Contact names. Passwords. Key phrases.

"What did we get?" Vexer asked.

"Get everyone to the mess," EB ordered. "We're so deep, everybody needs to know what we've got."

Because EB was staring at the network update intended for a senior syndicate officer. There was *so much* data there that he was still vaguely flipping through sections of it when he sat down in the mess hall and found Trace handing him a coffee.

"Thanks," he muttered.

He glanced around. Lan was the last person to drift in, the doctor taking a glance around the room and pouring two coffees. They handed the second one to Joy, then took a seat next to the environment tech as everyone waited for EB to start.

EB looked at Trace, remembering a name she'd used and using it as a keyword. He sighed.

"Amelie was the woman who recruited you, right?" he asked softly.

"Yeah," Trace said, shrinking back slightly. Vexer had a hand on her shoulder instantly, reassuring her—and nodding to EB to reassure *him*.

"Her real name is Irina Yakova," EB said. "She's been an active recruiter for the Siya U Hestî Cartel for eleven years, and is the only 'Level-Six,' whatever that is, among Denton's recruiters. The head of the Cartel on Denton is only a Level-Seven, so I'm guessing Yakova is one of her top people."

A chill silence fell over the room.

"That was in the datavault?" Vexer asked.

"Real and main false identities, contact protocols, pass phrases and digital drop points for contacting every Level-Six, -Seven, and -Eight in the Siya U Hestî Cartel in thirty-two star systems," EB said quietly.

"It looks like it's *supposed* to act as a database update, but they're basically transferring the entire database each time as an integrity check. Plus, contact protocols appear to be updated every six months," he continued. "If they're assuming we have this vault, the contact protocols and pass phrases and such are probably being updated as we speak.

"The names and identities might be useful to the Trackers or local law enforcement in those star systems, but they're useless to *us*," he admitted. "What's of value to *us* is the maps."

"Maps," Ginny echoed. "Nova maps?"

"Nova maps," he confirmed as he opened that piece of data and then linked it to the mess's holoprojectors, filling the air around and above them with a map. "Twenty-two systems on this side of the Fasach Expanse, ten on the other. Both official routes, as kept by people like the Transporters' Guild, and the Cartel's own routes."

Each of the mapped route stops was tagged with the information of where it had come from. Assuming that Breanna's people had every-thing the Nigahog Transporters' Guild had for maps, well, those maps had *not* been worth the hassle he'd gone through trying to get them.

"I'm not certain where Trace was intended to go," EB said levelly. "My initial impulse is to assume that the key was in the head of another victim going to the same place and that there was some metric the recipient boss knew to use to identify both the key and the vault."

He shook his head.

"Might have been as simple as 'one of the blondes has the vault' and 'one of the redheads has the key,'" he admitted. "Scanning for the chips, if you knew they were there, would be easy enough."

"Surely, they would have been more careful with something like this," Vexer asked.

"Victims like Trace aren't supposed to escape," Reggie said quietly. Every eye turned to the weapons tech, and he shrugged awkwardly. "They aren't. Even without the vault in her head, they had every reason to keep her under lock and key. And while the traffickers assume a certain loss rate...it's not usually in transit."

EB shivered at Reggie's cold, angry tone. He knew Reggie hadn't been directly involved in trafficking...but it sounded like he'd been a *lot* closer to it than EB had suspected.

And hated everyone involved in the sick trade all the more for it.

"Most people would never have realized there was anything added to Em Trace's headware," Lan said. "Without the oddities of her own headware architecture, the flashes of additional information that she received would never have happened.

"Without those flashes, I'm not sure even we would have thought to investigate. Given a few more weeks, the chip will be completely integrated with her existing neural pathways and almost impossible to detect."

The doctor shook their head.

"Even someone like Lady Breanna will expect law enforcement to hesitate to inflict critical brain damage on a rescued trafficking victim, regardless of suspicion or proof," they concluded.

"Plus, in all honesty, their encryption is better than I'm inclined to give it credit for," EB admitted. "I hit it with some of the best software protocols from the Mid-Rim, and it *still* took thirty-eight hours to crack."

There was a long silence as EB's crew looked around at each other.

"So, what do we *do* with this?" Ginny finally asked.

"I don't know," EB admitted. "The route maps are useful. We can get to Blowry or Poberin while bypassing Nigahog now, I think."

He gestured to Vexer.

"I'll download all the maps into the nav computers," he promised his lover. "That gives us a lot of options. The problem is that every one of those options is to get to places we know a syndicate that wants us dead is operating."

"There's only one answer," Reggie said. "The underbosses, these Level-Sevens and -Eights…they don't care. They don't know that we have the data or likely have more than enough security and cutouts in place that even handing those files to their local government won't do more than inconvenience them. It might be worse for some than others, but they won't really think to chase *us*.

"Lady Breanna is unlikely to tell them that there's *been* a security breach, let alone *who* has that data." The tech shrugged and pointed to Star Plaza on the map. "Normally, you cut the head off a snake like this, three more rise.

"But for *us*? Those three new heads won't give a shit about us. We have to kill Breanna and take out the leadership of this Siya U Hestî Cartel. Cut the head off the snake, and the new ones will fight each other, not chase us."

"Except nobody knows where she is," Vexer pointed out. "I asked a lot of questions and poked a lot of news sources on Nigahog. Lady Breanna is a known name, and she gets away with that by being *utterly* uncatchable. If she ever enters 'civilized space,' it's behind so many layers of fake identity, they can't link her.

"That EB met her at all is only because *Evasion* is fucking *perfect* for her needs. She wanted the ship and she wanted EB, the ex-nova-fighter pilot.

"Sure, we have the data to fuck over any six of her bosses, but we don't know where *she* is."

"She's at the Cage," Trace said. Her voice was very small and afraid, and EB had knelt down and reached out to take her hands reassuringly before he even realized what he was doing.

"'The Cage,' Trace?" he asked gently.

"It's where they take the...high-value prizes for extra training," she whispered. "The ones they think will be worth more if they know what they're doing...at one skill or another."

Trace was shivering and EB squeezed her hands. That seemed to help, and she took a great, shuddering breath.

"I saw her there," Trace said. "More than once. It was...a *treat* for the cooperative prizes to dine with her."

The chill silence returned to the mess hall.

"I have spent the last few years doing everything within my power to avoid getting any more blood on my hands," EB said, and he *knew* what his tone sounded like. "But I am going to *enjoy* killing this creature."

He was already searching through the maps.

"Here." A red diamond blipped up on the screen. "The Cage is at a black nova point, halfway between Star Plaza and Nigahog."

He checked the map.

"We could head there right now," he admitted. "But we'd be fucked. I've got passcodes and authorization phrases, but we have to assume those have been changed, and there are some clear and distinct notes here about defenses."

The hologram zoomed in. And in. And in, until it was focused on the space station hanging in deep space.

"It's not much of a station, all told," EB said, looking at the skeletal structure. "Looks like it was assembled out of standard ten-meter-units cut open. That said, it still couldn't go nova."

The Cage looked like a lumpy crucifix in space. A T-intersection of short "wings" marked the top, each roughly twenty meters by fifty meters—the same size and shape as *Evasion*'s cargo hull. Then a narrow pillar hung "down" from the intersection, clearly made of a chain of single five-meter-wide TMUs, linked to a longer wing that was twenty meters across and a hundred meters tall.

"The bottom part is the Cage itself, where the *trainees* live," Trace said quietly. "I...saw most of the inside, at one point or another. I was there for four months and I was *very* well behaved."

She collapsed forward into EB's chest, sobbing as he wrapped his arms around her and gently rocked her, looking up at the others.

"The station is armed and has defensive satellites," he told them. "*Evasion* doesn't have the firepower, and the eight of us can't storm a station stuffed with Cartel security. But Reggie's right. Breanna will chase us to the ends of her power and beyond. We've rejected her, defied her, escaped her... Her ego won't let us go. And she can't risk that we have this data."

"So, what do we do?" Vexer asked, kneeling next to EB and gently rubbing Trace's back.

"We weaponize our enemies," EB said as inspiration struck. "This region has a multi-system bounty-hunters' guild, and Lady Breanna is a known crime lord.

"Somehow, I have to believe that *her* bounty is higher than ours!"

39

TRACE WAS a kid in a giant mall with her dad's credit account.

Quite literally, in fact, though she knew that calling EB "dad" was stretching things. Still, she had a healthy credit account on the Poberin System's Spacer's Orbital Bank, permission to spend it wildly, and Ginny was taking her to Poberin Mall One.

Massive screens declared that Poberin Mall One was "the largest shopping experience in six systems," containing over five thousand stores and virtual kiosks with "artificial stupid delivery functions."

"This takes up a third of the space station," Ginny said, the engineer looking across the massive mezzanine gallery at the heart of Mall One. "Most counterweight orbitals have some shopping, but I'm not sure I've seen *this* before."

"Denton Counterweight Station is *boring*," Trace proclaimed, with the certainty of thirteen years of age and exactly *one* exposure to said station. "This is...well."

She looked around the massive, advertising-saturated, semi-open space and giggled.

"This is too much. It's..." She stretched for the word. "Null-born?"

Ginny gave her a pointed look.

"What?" she asked.

"That's a slur for 'space-born,' Trace," the engineer said calmly. "In most systems I've been to, anyway. And given that *half the crew* is space-born…"

"Fair, fair," Trace said swiftly. "It's almost as gaudy as Star Plaza?"

Ginny laughed aloud.

"That's fair. Come on, I see a teens' clothing store, and I *know* the only things you have to wear are shipsuits!"

———

ON BLACK OAK, Trace had been the foster child of a wealthy politician and doctor. They'd expected her to live up to the weight of that, including in her dress. Her nanny had taken her shopping at least once a quarter, making sure that she was up to date on the latest styles and fashions.

Trace herself had gone along and eventually built the eye and the habit of dressing like that herself. She'd *also* paid attention to how the young woman who had taken her shopping had dressed, learning how someone with *incredible* esthetics and a limited budget made it work.

Within a couple of minutes of walking into the store that Ginny had picked, she had fifteen different outfit ideas. All of them would be stylish, all of them would be cute…and not one of them would be sexy. Eleven would go over a shipsuit and use it as a base layer, relying on its covering and compression to minimize certain features.

All of those outfit ideas fell out of her mind as she hit one of the most basic displays in the store and half-froze. There was nothing special about the display of underwear. It was just the exact kind of briefs that most preteens would wear.

Multicolored, covered in fun patterns, full of cheer and completely sexless. Her underwear options had been disturbingly sexed-up lingerie when among the traffickers, and then plain fabricator-made underclothing on *Evasion*.

The concept of fun, colorful, comfortable underthings…

"Hey." Ginny's hand was on her shoulder, the engineer looking past her at the plain underwear and the cartoon-laden matching t-shirts.

"I have no idea who any of these cartoon characters are," she noted after a moment. "I *like* the robot and the wrench-person, though."

Trace giggled.

"Me too," she admitted. "And, well, *all* of the ones with puppies and kittens. Though I'm looking at..."

She trailed off, gesturing at the comfortable-looking underwear.

"I know," Ginny told her. "We can get whatever you want. As many as you want. I'm not going to pretend *anyone* thinks fabricator-made clothing should be used for inner layers. Fabricator patterns do...sturdy. Not soft, not fun, and not generally comfy."

"And these look fun and comfy," Trace agreed, the shock fading into sheer glee at the fact that *yes,* she could get them. All of them. She was not just able to be a child, she was *encouraged* to be.

"Let's get at least a few," she said firmly. "Though there might be some other cool designs elsewhere, and we have to carry everything!"

Including, though she wasn't going to say so aloud, the military-grade wide-beam stunner she knew Ginny had concealed under her green leather jacket.

ONCE SHE GOT over the initial realization that she could literally buy *anything* she thought was cool for clothes, Trace made herself exert a *bit* of control. Still, by the third store, she was wearing a green leather jacket of her own to match Ginny's over a black T-shirt with a neon pink unicorn.

Both of them were eating oversized ice creams, and Trace giggled as part of Ginny's flopped onto the floor.

"These things have got to be a major hygiene hazard for the sta— Oh."

The engineer hadn't even finished speaking before a small artificial stupid zoomed across the floor to start cleaning up the spill.

"Someone saw that," Trace said with a chuckle. Studying her ice cream for a second, she took a careful half-bite, half-lick to contain the part about to slide off.

"Speaking of 'saw,' we're being followed," she continued quietly, half to the engineer and half to the air. "Two dudes, old, blue track-suits. They're buying ice creams now, but they're watching us."

"I see them," Reggie's voice said in her ear. "And they're younger than *me*, let alone EB."

"Please, I *am* old," EB said on the channel. "I also see them. Why did none of the rest of us spot them?"

"Because *I* let myself get talked into running watch for Siya U Hestî before I knew what they were," Trace replied. "And they move like the cops that came for Amelie a couple of times."

"If they were going to move in, they'd have done it by now," Ginny murmured. "What are they waiting for?"

"Reinforcements, most likely," EB said. "They're Trackers, not cops, which means they also have to worry about mall security unless they've bought it off."

"Thanks, I needed the nightmare of paid-off mall security," Ginny whispered. "What do we do?"

"Keep shopping," EB told them. "You're not even a quarter of the way through that credit account, which tells me that you need to be a *much* better influence on young Trace, Ginny."

"I don't think Trace is interested in expensive jewelry," the engineer said. "Or fancy dresses."

"I can be sold on both," Trace said levelly. At one point, she'd dreamed of being a dress designer, after all. Among about five hundred *other* things… "Fashion designer" had stuck around almost as long as "starship captain."

"All right, then. Directory says that La Chappelle's is the best fancy clothing store in the mall," Ginny told her, clearly having looked it up a while before. "Shall we go get matching diamond earrings?"

Trace tapped the plain fabricator-made studs currently in her ear-piercings.

"Now that you mention it, I can use an upgrade," she noted. "Do we think La Chappelle's sells ones with built-in blasters?"

"BLUE TRACKSUITS HAVE MADE some friends and we've picked up some extras," Trace warned as she and Ginny made their way down a wide, sloping ramp. "Two girls and a guy with the tracksuits. And then there's a group of four pretending to be a double date over to my left, but they're watching us *way* too much."

"Sorry, Ginny, you aren't *that* hot."

Her companion chuckled at that—but also stepped in closer to Trace. With two groups of bounty hunters closing on them, things were starting to get dicey.

"We've got eyes on them all," EB told them. "There's a third group on the level above you. Only the two in blue tracksuits are being conveniently uniformed for us, but the team above you moves like they're boosted.

"They're going to literally jump you when they see the window," the captain continued. "I'm guessing they can take the impact and keep moving. That's...a lot of bodies."

"How much *is* the bounty on Trace?" Reggie asked.

"Don't know, don't care," EB replied. "Trackers' Guild wouldn't talk to us, so this is our only option. Everyone ready?"

Ginny "accidentally" bumped into Trace, tucking a blocky hand stunner into the teen's shopping bag.

"You shouldn't need this, but it auto-aims," the engineer whispered. "We're ready," she told EB over the channel.

"I'm good," Reggie replied. "What about mall security?"

"Handled," Vexer said, speaking for the first time. "Not *cheap*, but handled."

"Wait for them to move," EB ordered. "They want Trace alive, and that will open them up."

Trace grimaced. She'd *volunteered* for this, but there was a vast gap between agreeing to be bait and actually being hunted through a mall by over a dozen bounty hunters.

"There's La Chappelle's," Ginny said loudly, gesturing toward what was probably the least gaudy store in the entire mall. It was a plain black-and-white storefront with the name in white text on the sign.

With the shopping trips Trace had done on Denton, she could

recognize the kind of store that didn't *need* to do anything more to attract its target clientele. The two men standing in front of the store, however, didn't look right at all.

The clothes looked right, but the men inside them didn't. They looked, in fact, like hulking killers stuffed into ten-thousand-mark suits.

"Danger up front," she whispered, feeling in her bags for the stunner Ginny had given her. "I *don't* think those are Trackers."

The larger man saw her and pointed. There was no subtlety to it. No maneuver or attempt to avoid detection. Both men advanced toward her—and the weapons they were drawing were *not* stunners.

The entire plan of using Trace as bait had been based around the assumption that the Trackers would be using stunners—but they had forgotten to consider that Level-Eight Nosizwe Sauvageot, Poberin's Siya U Hestî leader, *had* to have operations on Poberin System Orbital One.

And it seemed that Sauvageot's people knew enough to flag Trace for a kill order!

For a moment, everything froze. Trace stared down the emitters of two blasters and knew they'd screwed up everything—and then someone they *hadn't* been watching moved.

Trace hadn't flagged the woman in the shipsuit and hooded sweater as a threat. The style was common enough in the mall that she hadn't *noticed* the stranger's face. She *definitely* noticed when the woman was suddenly between the two Cartel thugs, a stunner in each hand.

The Cartel operators were almost certainly boosted and might have stood up to most stunners at any significant range. They didn't stand up to *those* stunners at under half a meter. Mountains of muscle in ten-thousand-mark suits, they crashed to the floor as Captain Lisa Zelda threw back her hood and walked toward Trace, her eyes flat above her veil.

"Please, Em Finley, let's not make this messy," she said calmly.

"Agreed," Trace told the Tracker—and then dropped her shopping bag to free her hand stunner.

40

"TRACE IS DOWN!" Ginny barked over the radio.

"Move!" EB barked. He, Lan and Reggie were hidden in the crowd, facial holoprojectors—courtesy of Lan— concealing their identities from anyone looking for them.

EB *really* wanted to ask his ship's doctor just what the enby had been doing before they'd joined *Evasion*. First, the nanoprobes for accessing locked headware, and now illegal disguise hardware?

All of his people were proving willing to pull out the stops to protect the teenage stowaway they'd picked up. Including, he had to admit, EB himself.

He was close to the two men in blue tracksuits that Trace had originally flagged. They'd picked up three friends since, and *all* of them had body language radiating that they were armed. As stunner fire crackled through the mall, all of them turned toward La Chappelle's as one, like a well-trained hunting pack.

EB's hand was on his stunner before they started moving. He gave them a second to get going before he stepped behind them and swept his leather jacket aside to expose the weapon. On maximum power and dispersion, the beam swept through the five Trackers like a scythe through wheat.

Four of them went down, but the girl who'd joined them was wearing a long faux-fur coat—and that coat was clearly concealing body armor. She spun like a scalded cat, the coat flashing through the air in a practiced gesture that absorbed EB's second shot.

He shoulder-checked her as she completed her turn, sending her stunner—a carbine-scale weapon probably *at least* as capable as his own massive one-handed weapon—scattering across the floor.

She repaid him by slamming an elbow into his face—and then sweeping his legs out from under him with a kick he never saw coming.

EB hit the ground like a sack of bricks, his own stunner sliding across the floor toward the woman's. He managed to twist around as the Tracker came at him, and took out *her* legs with both of his.

She went down next to him, and EB had his second stunner out. His left hand grabbed her wrist as she also produced a second weapon and he fired his light stunner into her face.

The bounty hunter could conceal armor under a fancy coat without too much difficulty, but she couldn't easily shield her face. She twitched and went still as the beam took her, leaving EB breathing heavily and lying on the floor next to her.

"I am too old for this shit," he said calmly into the radio. "First bogies are down. I *really* want to hire this woman for this mess."

"Boosted team on the upper floor has been convinced of the error of their ways," Lan said in their calmly precise tones. "One will need to see a sickbay sooner rather than later. He went over the edge despite my best effort."

EB looked around the rapidly emptying concourse and winced as he saw the Tracker in question. They'd only fallen four meters or so, but they'd already been stunned when they went over the safety barrier.

"I'll check his vitals in a moment," EB said calmly, already bringing himself to his knees and checking the vitals of the woman he'd just stunned. "Reggie?"

Silence answered him.

"*Reggie?*" he snapped, coming up to his feet and grabbing his heavy stunner as he swept the area, looking for his gunner.

"Got eyes on. He's down," Ginny finally told him. "Dropped into the middle of half a dozen Trackers. He stunned them all, but they got him."

"What about Trace?" EB asked.

"Captain Zelda showed up again, stunned the Cartel thugs, then asked Trace to surrender," Ginny said. "Trace drew on her, and she was *not* expecting it."

The engineer paused, then chuckled.

"They stunned *each other*…and I feel like that's a lot more of an indictment of the *bounty-hunter starship captain* than it is of the *thirteen-year-old kid*."

EB laughed.

"All right. Vexer, we got wheels? None of these people are staying down for long."

"Strangely, I appear to have rented a mall security vehicle," EB's lover replied as a station transport pod trundled up the concourse. "It should suffice for about a dozen of our new friends…in its quite secure-looking transport section."

"Get Zelda, this girl and the wounded man first," EB ordered. "Then whoever's convenient. But this one almost took me down with her bare hands, and Zelda has a *ship*."

He didn't explain why the actually *injured* Tracker was a priority—and no one argued with him, either.

41

LISA ZELDA, EB noticed, was *very* good at pretending she was still unconscious. Unfortunately for the veiled bounty hunter, the cuffs his people had put on her were providing him with her full vitals and warned him when her pulse accelerated.

"I know you're awake, Captain," he told her. "And I'd like to note, for whatever resembles the record in this mess, that you were taken down by a thirteen-year-old girl using a stunner I bought in a convenience store."

There was a long silence, then the Tracker reached up to touch her face.

"You left the veil on," she observed. "Not many people would have that respect."

"I may not be very impressed with you, Captain Zelda," EB said, "but I'm not your enemy. You're working on that, but we're not there yet."

There were a *lot* of religions out there that would call for a woman to veil her face. Even the modern versions of most of them would probably be more okay with an unveiled woman than that woman being a bounty hunter capturing children, but it wasn't for him to judge.

"Bardacki," she guessed aloud. "We're in a transport pod, so you didn't apply tranquilizers after I was stunned. But I'm cuffed and you clearly think you're in control of the situation."

"We may have left the veil on, but I had a female crewmember search and scan you," EB told her. "There's a safety wrap around your left arm, if you haven't noticed yet."

The wrap would prevent her activating any cybernetics—like, say, the blaster concealed in her artificial hand and forearm. The arm had likely suffered the same fate as Zelda's ear.

"I see."

She was silent, her eyes slitted as she glanced around.

"This pod has a prisoner-transport section," she observed. "But I'm not in it."

"We ran out of space," EB told her. "I sent most of my team back by other means, to make sure Trace was safe, but you're not the only Tracker I picked up today."

"Interesting," she murmured. "I hope you realize that those two thugs were *not* Trackers?"

"I got that from the blasters, yes," EB said. "I suspect they work for the people who put the bounty on myself and Trace, though I didn't exactly ask. You might have been in trouble for stealing her from them to deliver her to them. I *told* you what this was about!"

"I have no reason to trust you. I deliver to the Guild," Zelda said flatly. "The *Guild* is supposed to make sure the bounties are legal."

"And you know *damn bloody well* that this one isn't," EB snarled. "So, that protestation isn't getting you very far. If I didn't know you had one of the more capable ships in this region, I'd have left you for the fucking Siya U Hestî to carve up for parts.

"Am I clear?"

Zelda swallowed.

"Al'ama," she whispered. "You're lying. The Guild wouldn't...but those men..."

"The Guild did," EB told her. "The bounty on myself was set by a woman named Lady Breanna. The bounty on *Trace*, I'm not sure of the *exact* source of, but it was set because she was an escapee from the Siya U Hestî's human-trafficking network.

"So, *that*, *Captain* Zelda, is what you were trying to return her to. For money. How's your moral vacuum handling *now*?"

The pod's forward compartment was silent. Reggie was driving, but he was leaving this conversation to EB...and unlike Zelda, they *had* gassed the people in the prison compartment.

EB had multiple reasons for keeping this conversation separate.

He'd been surprised to see Zelda there in the first place. It made sense—the black Cartel route they'd used to get to Poberin had stretched their ability to nova without discharging static, and Zelda had left the nova point almost two days before they had—but he still hadn't expected to see her.

But her ship was *exactly* what he needed for what he was planning. He needed mercenary ships to take the Cage, and he suspected *Zeldan Blade* was one of the best out there—plus, Trace had recognized her because she was on a list of *enemies* of the Siya U Hestî Cartel in the database.

Any attempt to collect the bounty on Trace or EB would likely have ended badly for Captain Zelda.

"I figured she was a runaway and her parents had posted the bounty," Zelda said quietly. "Or that *you* had kidnapped her."

"And now?"

"Most kidnappees don't stun the people who come to rescue them," the bounty hunter told him drily. "So, I am...reassessing."

"I'll confess to not being impressed with your assessments so far," EB said. "But I need you."

"You need me?" she asked. "And what exactly do you think that's going to entail, Captain Bardacki?"

"You promising that I can take those cuffs and that safety wrap off without you shooting me, to start," EB told her. "Then you convincing a transport pod full of stunned Trackers to sign on with the two of us, and then all of us making a great deal of money while making this region of space a better place."

Zelda chuckled mirthlessly.

"I'm prepared to promise that I won't shoot you, Captain," she told him. "That's about all I'm willing to put on the table so far."

"Not even that you won't try to take my or Trace's bounty?" he asked.

"I'll promise that I'll do some of my own research before I leap down that hole again," Zelda conceded. "And I'm sure as al-Nar not going after your hell-ship on your own ground."

"And what if I told you I can find where the head of the Siya U Hestî hides?" EB replied. "I know where she indoctrinates her trafficking victims and the headquarters of her entire criminal empire.

"I can hand you Lady Breanna of the Siya U Hestî on a silver platter, Captain Zelda. I just need a fleet and a landing force. My ship won't exactly cut it for either."

The compartment was silent again.

"The Cage is a rumor," Zelda finally replied.

"Trace was there," EB countered. "That's not the source of our information, but she's seen the interior of the station, knows its layout. She was one of the trafficking victims being *trained* there.

"So, it's no rumor, Captain Zelda. It's a horrific reality, a traffickers' prison and paramilitary headquarters hidden away in the void two novas from any star system.

"I have the nova route to get there. I have passcodes and IFF frequencies and a dozen other pieces of approach data that I expect to be obsolete when we arrive but will add to the confusion no matter what."

Zelda had fully opened her eyes above her veil now, her gaze entirely focused on EB as she seemed to assess him.

"I feel like it's a safe assumption that there is a bounty on Breanna?" he asked softly.

"There are fourteen," Zelda told him. "And if she's the only person on the Cage with a bounty, I'll eat my *ship*. And that's disregarding rewards for the return of kidnap and trafficking victims."

"I'm guessing just handing this over to one of the system governments won't do me much good?" EB asked.

"No. She owns them all," Zelda admitted. "If you want to take her down, you need mercs and Trackers. You made the right call, even if your approach was…perhaps a tad confrontational."

"Your Guild was hunting me first," EB pointed out.

"Fair."

"We're here, boss," Reggie said from the front.

"Well, Captain Zelda?" EB asked. "Do we have a deal?"

"I need to see everything you have on the Cage," Zelda told him. "Then I'll need to make some calls, see who I can bring in. But...the Siya U Hestî *hate* me, Captain. And the feeling is *very* mutual.

"So, yes. You have a deal."

"Good."

EB gave the mental command to unlock her cuffs.

"Then we have work to do."

42

TRACE PERCHED on a chair on the edge of the main mess, massaging her temples and nursing a sweetened coffee as she watched Captain Zelda with a baleful look.

Being stunned had turned out to be much less unpleasant than she'd expected—the headache was real, but so were several leftover tingling sensations that she could easily see being enjoyable under other circumstances.

She still wasn't a fan of it, though she *was* entertained to know that she'd successfully shot the elite mercenary captain who'd drawn on her. Of course, *she'd* been using an auto-targeting stunner fired from the hip that had really only needed a clean line of fire, but the victory remained.

"So," Zelda said, studying the hologram. "Two hundred meters tall, a hundred and fifty wide at the cross, roughly twenty meters thick most places. Not a small installation, but not as big as I half-expected."

"Too big to nova," Vexer said. *Evasion's* navigator glanced over at Trace. He caught Trace's scowl at Zelda and waved a finger of disagreement.

She glared at *him* for a moment.

"No, assembled in pieces. Internal layout is...straightforward but still a mess. No internal map?"

"We have the data update meant for a planetary Level-Eight like Nosizwe Sauvageot," EB told her. "It doesn't look like Breanna wanted them to know about the layout of her bastion."

"Not much security in that. Most of the Level-Eights would probably be willing to just vaporize the Cage and call it a day if they turned on her," Zelda said. "I mean, my sample size is *one*, but Ernestina Hope is a stone-cold killer."

"She's the Level-Eight on Agasoft, right?" EB asked.

"Yeah," the mercenary confirmed. "How did you..."

"Full data update meant for a planetary Level-Eight," EB reminded her. "But that doesn't help the problem of finding our way around the interior of the Cage."

"Depending on the defenses and where she's put people, there could be a thousand or more guards aboard," Zelda told them. "I can't get you the troops to take a thousand guards."

"There aren't a thousand guards," Trace said flatly, glad to shut down the Tracker who'd shot her. "There are only guard barracks here and here."

She stepped forward, indicating two sections on the cross arms.

"You know the interior?" Zelda asked.

"I lived there for four months, and I listened to the other girls," Trace told her coldly. "*I* wasn't expected to service the guards, but some of them *were*."

She held the Tracker's gaze until the woman looked away, clearly understanding just what she'd been trying to return Trace to.

"Are we going to have a problem?" Zelda finally asked.

"That depends," Trace told her. "Are you going to try to sell me back into sex slavery again?"

"Nobody here is going to let that happen," EB said. "Please, Trace. You have every reason to be pissed at Captain Zelda, but we need her contacts and her ship."

"I know," Trace admitted, still glaring at the veiled woman.

Zelda lifted her head, her eyes suddenly fierce as she met Trace's gaze and went to one knee in front of Trace.

The teenager blinked and nearly stepped away before the mercenary took her hands.

"Tracy Finley, I have wronged you," Zelda said, her voice very quiet and very sad. "I made a horrible mistake and turned my skills, resources and talents to the very cause I became a Tracker and a mercenary to oppose.

"I swear to you, upon the names of Allah and Mohammed, upon the stars and void itself, upon my ship and my heart and the souls of my mothers, that no harm will come to you from me. And if by my blood or steel I can prevent harm coming to you from another, I shall.

"You have my oath. Inshallah."

Trace had *no* idea how to take that and let the Tracker's hands drop.

"I... I'll take that as enough," she finally conceded.

The mess hall was swept with silence.

"How long until the other Trackers wake up?" Zelda asked.

"Half an hour or so," EB said. "Lan is working on the injuries of the one they sent over a railing."

"Then we need to get the key concepts sorted out." She turned and bowed to Trace. "Em Finley, if you can give us an idea of the internal layout of the station, that may make this plan possible...and save lives."

"Okay." Trace swallowed and stepped up to the hologram, studying it. "Down here, the largest section? This is the prison area. It has more internal divisions than the rest of the station, keeping the various groups of conscious, cryo-frozen, control-chipped, et cetera prisoners apart."

"How many groups?"

"I'm not sure," Trace admitted. "I knew of at least four separate groups of us cooperative captives, plus at least one section of cryo-chambers and a barracks of control-chipped victims who supported the permanent crew."

"I feel the need to note, again, that I really want to kill a lot of these people," EB said grimly. "And I was considering complete pacifism a few months ago."

"The Lady Breanna has that effect on people," Zelda replied. "You didn't spend all your time in the prison, though?"

"No," Trace confirmed. "They moved us up through this narrow section here. The whole section is a security zone, with shifting gravity and..."

BY THE TIME she was done, Trace had added a lot of spaces and markers to the map they had of the Cage. Even she could tell that it was sparse intelligence for the interior of a space station two hundred meters tall, but it gave them a start.

"You don't know the guard numbers, of course," Zelda concluded, looking at the revised map. "But this is still a lot. You have good headware, kid."

"My headware was shut down the whole time I was in there," Trace said coldly. "That's just memory. It better be worth it."

The bounty hunter was quiet again, but she nodded.

"We can't change what they did to you," Zelda told her. "But we can make certain, inshallah, that it never happens to anyone else. Not *there*, at least."

That had to be enough, Trace guessed. It might even *be* enough. If this worked.

"Can we do it?" EB asked. "The first problem is the exterior defenses."

"They are almost certainly not ready for anyone to come in with proper jammers," Zelda pointed out. "Between your ship and mine, we can confuse them, baffle them...and destroy them. None of those stations are more powerful than a decent gunship."

There were, Trace judged, a dozen of the defensive stations. She didn't have the knowledge to judge *anything* about them—except the information that was in her datavault, anyway.

"Still, a dozen stations, twice that in automated satellites, and they are almost certainly figuring this data is compromised," EB said.

"Without knowing where the data came from, I can't be certain," Zelda admitted. "If the Siya U Hestî Cartel thinks the Cage is compromised, they may have reinforced. They may even be *moving* it—it was assembled from pieces that can be novaed, after all."

"So, there will be ships at the very least," EB warned as Trace grimaced.

If the people who'd kidnapped her and wrecked her life got away, Trace wasn't sure she'd ever be safe. Even aboard *Evasion*...

"I will need to call in other favors," the mercenary captain warned. "Everyone's portion of the payout gets smaller, the more people we bring in."

"We need a fleet and an assault force," EB countered. "The shares were always going to get spread out. I hope the bounties are enough to make it worthwhile despite that."

"They are," Zelda said flatly. Her eerie gaze settled on Trace, and Trace glared back at her. "None of the system governments will have the nerve to join us, but they have certainly committed the money to make this happen.

"And even if they hadn't...against the Siya U Hestî, I could find ships and soldiers who would do this for free."

43

EB HAD a cargo hold stuffed with groggy not-quite-enemies. He hadn't really planned on stacking this many unconscious bounty hunters and mercenaries in his ship, but once they'd stunned them all and had the transport space to haul them...well, he couldn't argue with Reggie's point that it would have been a waste to leave them behind.

Still, he pushed a cart of coffee and donuts ahead of him as he entered the hold, glancing around the cavernous space to locate where they'd ended up.

"What the *fuck* is going on?" a voice snapped. The woman who'd worn the faux-fur coat—now tossed aside to reveal a tighter-than-usual armored shipsuit.

"What's going on, my friends, is that everyone here stalked a thirteen-year-old girl through a mall with the intent of capturing her and delivering her back to the human traffickers who kidnapped and abused her," EB said calmly.

"One of your companions"—he nodded toward the team of boosted mercs—"is in my sickbay. He broke three ribs and an arm when he went over the railing in Mall One, but he's going to be fine. My doctor is just finishing up the bonding injections and wanted to double-check their work.

"The rest of you are here because I'm hoping you have enough soul and scruples to feel at least a modicum of guilt for what you were doing," he told them. "Because if you were *knowingly* planning on handing that kid back to the Siya U Hestî, with everything they do, I'm not sure you're much use to me."

Or anyone else. While EB definitely didn't have it in him, he was quite certain the galaxy would be better off if he spaced anyone who met *that* description.

"The Siya U Hestî don't place Guild bounties," the woman who'd spoken snapped at him.

"How would you know?" EB asked. "The Trackers' Guild anonymizes all bounty sources, don't they? How do you, em bounty-hunter-on-the-ground, ever know who you're retrieving people for?"

"The Guild has a code," one of the boosted Trackers said grimly. "We trust them to do the work."

The speaker was probably the smallest of the collection of metal-and-flesh mountains that made up that team, but EB realized the rest were looking at him. He shrugged massive shoulders as he rose from where he'd been sitting against the wall.

Now EB realized that the four remaining boosted Trackers had been trying to open up an access panel in the hold's bulkheads when he came in. They might even have had enough brute strength between them to manage it.

"Kemp is awake," the speaker declared aloud. "Or, at least, awake enough for his implants to talk to me and confirm that he's fine. I know your man didn't *intend* for him to go over the edge, so I'll hear you out.

"But if the Guild has violated the bounty standards, we have a bigger problem."

"We have a bigger problem, Naveen."

EB felt a bit slighted that *he'd* brought coffee—but every eye was on Captain Zelda when the veiled mercenary captain stepped into the room behind him.

"You're sure," Naveen replied. It wasn't a question, and the entire tone of the conversation had changed.

The original woman sighed and grabbed a coffee from the cart EB had brought.

"At least you know the way to a Tracker's heart," she told EB. "Kick her ass, then offer her coffee. If Zelda buys your story, I'm listening."

"You may as well give them the spiel, Captain," Zelda told EB. "But I can assure Naveen and Tosta that I've double-checked key parts of Captain Bardacki's information.

"While I can't confirm whether this is *new*, our Guild accepted at least two contracts from the Shadow and Bone. One on Captain Bardacki himself, and one on Em Tracy Finley."

"Shadow and Bone" was the English translation of "Siya U Hestî." That apparently meant something to the Trackers as well.

"And the fact that *any* of you were hunting Trace makes me very, *very* angry," EB told them. "Because that kid has had a horrific time and you were all ready to hand her back over for twenty bits of silver."

The woman with the coffee cup—Tosta, EB presumed—took a long swallow and sighed.

"All right, my soul is *definitely* feeling that modicum of guilt," she told him. "So, tell us what you want."

IT TOOK ABOUT fifteen minutes for EB and Zelda to lay out the details of how Trace had ended up with a bounty—omitting some key parts, of course. The Trackers, including Zelda, didn't need to know about the datavault—and what the data EB had enabled them to do.

"We're in," Tosta said, as soon as EB had finished laying out the plan. "Assuming someone can give my team a ride, I'll be *delighted* to kick the Siya U Hestî in the nuts with a blaster or six."

"My team are in as well," Naveen agreed, the boosted Tracker looking perturbed. "We will have some *words* for the Guild when this is done. We have our own ship and can contribute to the space battle as well."

"There aren't enough people in this hold to carry this attack," Zelda reminded them all. "Tosta, your people are worth the fuel to carry. You can hitch a ride on *Blade*. Naveen's people and their gunship will help, but we need at *least* half a dozen more gunships.

"Shares are by standard merc code," she continued. "Ship crews split sixty percent; ground teams split forty. Any org in both counts in both.

"But every one of you needs to shake the orbitals for every friend you can find. I figure we take a week and meet in Nigahog. Six is big enough to discharge and far enough out that the good captain won't draw local attention."

EB grimaced. He didn't like the fact that the Nigahog system government was probably pissed at him. But the only way they could make it to the Cage and back was to discharge static at either Star Plaza or Nigahog.

The station was deep in the Expanse, its isolation and secrecy its first layer of defense.

"What happens if one of your contacts sells us out?" he asked Zelda. "That's a pretty wide net to spread."

He needed the reinforcements. His own estimate was that they needed half a dozen ships and two hundred ground troops to capture the Cage. The bounties on Lady Breanna would cover the cost, but they were asking a lot of people to buy in on spec.

Selling the entire mission out to the Siya U Hestî was going to sound like a much-easier payout to at least some of the mercs getting calls.

"I'm keeping the calls to the people I trust, and I expect Tosta and Naveen and Iris to do the same," Zelda told him, gesturing at the three team leaders in the hold. This had gone from prisoner release to strategy meeting with surprising ease.

It helped, EB suspected, that Lan had spent a good bit of energy patching up Naveen's injured trooper.

"But it's possible that someone will sell us out," Tosta agreed. "We need a plan to deal with that. We definitely don't tell anyone where the Cage actually is until we're at Nigahog VI, and I'll happily hunt down anyone who sells *me* out, but that won't protect us much."

"Unfortunately, that threat and our trust in our contacts may be the only shield we have," Zelda said grimly. "Which means we all undersell the resources we're bringing to the party and try to find *more* than anyone thinks we have.

"That way, even if someone *does* sell us out, there's no way Breanna is seeing us coming."

It wasn't enough...but EB didn't see any better options himself.

"Then I guess everyone gets to work."

EB ESCORTED the mercenaries off the ship and was surprised by Tosta hanging back as even her people left the ship. The Tracker waited until the two were basically alone and then winked at him.

"Em Tosta?" he asked. She was older than he'd thought at first glance, he realized. Not as old as him but closer to Vexer's age than the late twenties he'd initially flagged her as.

"Traveling on *Zeldan Blade* will get us there, but you also have a lot of space to work with," she told him. "My team could certainly fit in here, along with some extra toys. We could discuss it over dinner?"

"Dinner, Em Tosta?" he echoed carefully, his brain taking several seconds to catch up with what she was implying.

She laughed.

"Tosta Hallman, Captain Bardacki," she said, listing her full name. "And while I am thinking in terms of operations, I'm *also* asking you on a date. Not many men hold their own against me in a fight—and not many who can are sane enough to have a kid!"

EB chuckled softly.

"I'm flattered, Em Tosta," he said. "Though Trace isn't my kid. She can't go home until this mess with the Siya U Hestî is dealt with, so she's basically crew till then. But I'm nobody's dad."

"And here I thought I got clocked by a papa bear," Tosta murmured.

That brought a full belly laugh from EB, and she looked at him in confusion.

"And *that* brings me to the other two reasons I'll pass on dinner, Tosta," he said gently. "I'm not interested in women...and I'm taken. I'm going to be busy enough taking care of my ship and crew as it is.

"I am flattered—truly!—but I'm afraid I'm not your type."

"Good ones are always gay or taken, aren't they?" she snorted.

"In my experience, they're *straight* or taken," EB replied. "It was a perennial problem until the last year or so. I'm older than you are, Tosta; you still have hope."

She laughed and blew him a kiss.

"You are *adorable*, Captain Bardacki," she told him.

"Please, call me EB," he instructed.

"I will, EB," she promised. "But may I offer a word of advice?"

"Certainly," he said.

"I don't know this Trace," she admitted. "I only followed her through a store, but...I know her story. And a girl like that needs a dad. Not a father. A *dad*. And if it isn't you...you damn well fight like it is."

44

WITH EVERYONE GONE, EB finally collapsed back in the mess and looked up at Vexer and Trace. The crew had left the three of them alone together, intentionally, he suspected.

"That's moving, then," he told them. "We're up to a corvette, a gunship and about a dozen sets of boots on the ground."

"We're going to need more than that," Vexer said bleakly. "And we need to consider priorities. The mercs and Trackers? They're going to go for Breanna."

"Who's going for the prisoners, then?" Trace demanded.

"We are," EB said flatly. He hadn't even consciously decided that until that moment. "Reggie and Vexer and I and at least one of the merc squads will have to hit the prison, secure control of it and its *systems* to make sure no one does anything stupid and vicious."

"Thank you," Trace whispered.

Vexer came over and started to rub EB's shoulders.

"I'm glad for that 'one of the merc squads' part," he admitted. "You and Reggie are capable enough, but I'm no soldier. I'm a decent shot, but assaulting a space station is a bit beyond me."

"We'll see if we can get you armor here in Poberin," EB replied.

"Reggie and I both have some, but real armor will make all the difference."

He leaned back against Vexer and looked at Trace. The young girl seemed calm and collected. She looked like she felt...*safe*. A thought that warmed his heart.

"We'll set up a firing range in the cargo hold as well," EB continued. "For you, my dear, if no one else."

Vexer laughed—but kissed the top of his head in thanks as well.

"I appreciate it."

"Can I use the range too?" Trace asked. "Because...I need to be there, EB."

"No, you *don't*," he countered without thinking. "I don't have anywhere safe to put you, so you're coming on *Evasion*, but I can't let you take part in a space-station assault!"

Trace smiled winningly and shook her head.

"EB...that map I gave is okay, but they're going to need a guide if they're going to make it to the Lady's quarters through the maze that is the upper station. Zelda and the strike team are going to *need* me." She spread her hands. "Better if I'm armored and armed than if I'm in a shipsuit and can't shoot for crap, right?"

"She's got you," Vexer murmured. "She's *definitely* got you."

"Fair enough," EB conceded, mentally poking at the surge of protectiveness that came up in response to the situation. "I don't like it, but you're right. Talk to Ginny and Tate, both of you. We need to source body armor and real guns.

"I'll get the range set up and see what I can program for tricksy targets." He grinned. "I have some practice with the concept."

If he was going to be sending Trace and Vexer into the fight, he was going to train them the way *he* thought people should train—the way the Apollo System Defense Force trained. And the ASDF's theory had always been that training should be more difficult and chaotic than a real battle, to build reflexes and instincts that would survive in the stress of actual combat.

HALF A DOZEN HOURS LATER, EB was sitting on a storage container, regaining his breath. There was a lot of space available in the pressurized cargo hold, though he couldn't set up any targets more than fifty meters away. Of course, it was unlikely that a space-station assault would involve any shooting at more than fifty meters.

Blasters could be set to a training mode that wouldn't actually do significant amounts of damage, but he'd still rolled a layer of energy-absorption blankets across the back of the cargo bay. That would soak up what little energy the training mode unleashed.

He'd arrayed a series of empty storage containers through the compartment and then set up a number of holoprojectors on artificial stupids. He didn't have a lot of the specialty components he'd want to use to set up a shooting gallery, but he'd made do.

"Okay, I'll admit, I was expecting something a bit more, uh...bottles on crates," Vexer admitted as the navigator wandered in. "This is slick."

"My training was more complicated," EB replied. "Full holographic shooting houses." He shook his head. "They weren't built for *us*, but the peltasts didn't use them all the time."

"*Peltasts*." Vexer seemed to roll the archaic Greek around his tongue for a moment. "You know, most systems just call them marines."

"And one I can name calls them weltraumsoldats," EB said. "It's not like you don't know where I'm from, Vexer."

"Fair." The navigator dropped onto the crate next to EB. "Just been thinking, lately. That's all. You saw where I'm from."

"Estuval," EB agreed. "There are worse places."

"Estuval is a Beyond agricultural world," his lover replied. "That I even made it to space made me one in ten thousand. The only reason we have ships and navigators is because the dukes are smart enough to realize that letting *all* of our economic lifeblood flow in somebody else's hulls was a dangerous choice."

"I wasn't paying that much attention to anything on planetary surfaces at the time," EB admitted. "Space infrastructure seemed... reasonable for the size."

Vexer snorted.

"And cut off," he said. "Estuval is neo-feudal, EB. Most outsiders don't realize it, because what you deal with in space is the two dukes who hold the orbitals. Even *I*, a trained navigator, was technically Duke Baard's chattel.

"I could work my way up to command a ship, maybe, but all we had were ten-kilocubic freighters running grain and grapes to other worlds." Vexer shrugged. "And the ship would never be mine. It would be Duke Baard's.

"Got on the wrong side of one of the duke's enforcers, looked for a way out, found you," he concluded. "You don't ask, EB, and I love you for it, but that's as complicated as *my* story gets. Some of the others… I'm not sure either of us wants to know."

EB considered the firing range and considered his lover and considered what Vexer had just told him.

"I didn't ask, you know," he admitted quietly.

"I know," Vexer agreed. "But we're getting to the point where I felt like you and I needed to know everything about each other. Things are on the verge of real complicated."

"This has been…less casual of late," EB conceded. "I'm your captain, Vexer. You know I've always let you lead."

"Which has been *damn* frustrating on occasion," Vexer told him. "But I get it and appreciate it. But yeah, this has been less casual of late. Since you found something to fight for. Or *someone*, I suppose."

"I'm not sure I follow," EB said.

"When I met you, you were like…this exotic, glorious thing," Vexer said. "You came from the stars, far farther than I'd ever gone. You'd fought wars and flown ships I could only dream of.

"And I loved you from the moment I heard you talk. But I realized pretty quickly, EB, that you didn't love yourself and that you didn't know who you wanted to be. Other than not what you had been."

EB waited in silence. It sounded like Vexer needed to get this out.

"All you were doing was running away," Vexer told him. "All of us on *Evasion*, really, were running away. And I loved what I saw in you… but you didn't see the same things. So, that's where we've been, EB. For a year. And then Lady Breanna tried to recruit you as a human trafficker."

"I was never going to work for her," EB said.

"No, you weren't," Vexer agreed. "So, you lied to the face of the most powerful crime lord in thirty star systems. Foxed her sensors, her followers and her plans, and stole your own ship out from under her nose.

"And then when a teenage girl fell into our care, turning a flight into a war, you didn't turn her away."

"I couldn't," EB whispered.

"No. *We* couldn't; you're right. But we could have kept running," Vexer told him. "Dropped her off with her foster family or, hell, brought her with us. The Siya U Hestî have a long reach but not an infinite one."

EB was silent, looking at the shooting range he'd built.

"Maybe," he conceded. "But knowing what they put in Trace's head...it both put us all at risk and gave us an opportunity. And... there are few things in this universe more evil than scum like this. Give me a chance to take them down, and that's a fight I'll take on."

"Even though you'd rather run. You've been running from the blood on your hands for as long as I've known you," Vexer told him. "I'm *guessing* you no longer think that was a worthwhile war. But this one? I don't think anyone's questioning much about the worth of *this* fight."

Vexer had put a verbal finger on something EB had been struggling with for years now, and he exhaled a long sigh.

"I was a nova-fighter squadron XO, Vexer," he told his lover. "I flew heavy fighters and electronic warfare ships. I was an ace, by the old three-kill standard, a dozen times over. I have killed thirty-seven other pilots in straight fights and contributed to the destruction of at least nine capital ships.

"The cap ships probably averaged a crew of two hundred apiece," he said. "Even giving myself only a tenth of the weight of those deaths, I've killed over a hundred and fifty people by my own hand.

"And at the end? My government, Apollo's much-vaunted Council of Principals, sold out everything we'd fought for and allowed our enemy to send assassins into our territory after our aces.

"Including me. And I killed one of those assassins with my bare fucking hands, Vexer," EB said, old memories rushing back in. "I snapped her neck and I looked in her eyes as the life fled them, and for the first time in my life, I *knew* what I'd done to those hundred-plus I'd killed before, with a starfighter or a blaster."

The shooting range was silent.

"So, yeah, I don't trust the worth of the war I fought, and I'm running from the blood on my hands, the knowledge of the lives I've taken," EB told his lover. "But against what was done to Trace? Against the knowledge of, what, a *thousand* kids trapped on that space station?

"I'll take that guilt on myself again. For a thousand innocents, I will stain my soul again with the blood of the guilty."

He ran out of steam, staring blankly into space.

"That's my story, I guess," he conceded. "The whole one. That's what *I'm* running from, Vexer."

"But you're not running from anything anymore," his lover told him. "You're standing up to fight for those who need you, even if they don't even know you exist yet. And we're taking care of Trace, and we're going to keep her safe."

"We are," EB agreed.

"And we're not taking her back to a politician that uses her as a trophy and a doctor that uses her as an experiment, are we, Evridiki?"

That was...an armor-piercing question, and *Evasion*'s captain sighed. His breath whistled in the cold cargo hold, and he realized *that* decision was already made, too.

"If she wants to, we could still," he told Vexer. "That's her call. But...no, I'm not inclined to hand her back to the Vortanis."

"Then we need to offer her an alternative, my love."

That word sent a shiver up and down EB's spine. He hadn't registered it in Vexer's earlier point, but it struck home now.

"What are you thinking?" he asked, very slowly.

"She needs parents," Vexer told him. "And, frankly, she imprinted on you like a lost puppy. The only reason she *isn't* calling you *dad* is because she thinks it would freak you out. And if you're her dad, EB... that makes *me* her dad, too.

"If we want to take it that way."

EB exhaled another long sigh.

"Keep her, huh?" he said aloud. "She's smart; she's got a good head for tech. She loves learning what all of us do. We'll need to get some educational artificial stupids, keep up her schooling in a way everywhere will recognize, but..."

"You're already sold, aren't you?" Vexer asked.

EB laughed aloud.

"I'm sold on you as my lover and I'm sold on Trace as my *responsibility*, if nothing else," he told Vexer. "So, if you think she wants gay space dads forever, I am entirely okay with offering that choice.

"Once this is over," he noted sharply. "We take her to the Cage, and we burn her bad memories in fire and steel. Then we offer her a home here. Not before. I don't want her to think she has to stay with us for us to finish this."

"My love, if you tried to turn aside now, I think the whole crew would mutiny," Vexer said. "We're all running from something, but like you and I, everyone else is down to fight for Trace. She may have latched on to you as her new parent, but it takes a village to raise a child."

"I don't have a village," EB replied with a chuckle. "But I do have a starship crew."

45

"EXHALE, STEADY...*FIRE.*"

A blaster rifle didn't have much in terms of recoil, but the jerk backward still surprised Trace. She'd been expecting it the last half-dozen times, but this time she hadn't.

"Nice shot," Reggie told her, pointing downrange. "A few more like that and we'll switch you to the pistols."

Trace followed his gesture and picked out the target she'd been aiming at. There were all sorts of complicated targeting games EB had set up in the range, but right now she and Reggie were working on basic marksmanship.

And she'd put the latest blaster bolt right in the center of the target.

"Okay," she exhaled. "I'm getting the hang of this."

The blaster rifle she was holding was brand-new. Captain Zelda had sent it over, presumably as an attempt to apologize for her involvement in trying to recapture Trace. Unlike the bulky over-charged heavy blaster rifles in *Evasion*'s armory, it was of a size and weight that a tall thirteen-year-old could use.

"Prove it," Reggie said. "Take another shot for me. Without me talking you through it."

Trace nodded and breathed in carefully as she steadied the weapon again. She located the target, aimed...and fired. And then again. And again.

Despite Reggie's request for another shot, she pumped *five* blaster bolts downrange in fifteen seconds, then put the rifle down. Her breathing carefully measured, she looked up at the weapons tech and grinned.

"Well?"

"Three hits of five, one on the center," he told her—without even looking at the target. Of course, his headware was linked to the impromptu range's systems. "Not great. Not bad, given that this is, what...the third time you've held a weapon?"

"I did some target shooting back on Denton," she admitted. "The Society for Creative Anachronism ran a bunch of free events for the orphans as a public-outreach measure."

"So, what, twenty-first-century high-vee firearms?" Reggie asked. "Late-era chemical, pre-magnetic weapons?"

"Everything, really," Trace said. "But I liked the late chemical guns. They had a reassuring *pop* to them." She shook her head. "How did you guess?"

"You were compensating high, expecting a lower velocity and bullet drop," he told her. "Once you adjusted for that, you got up to about what I'd expect for someone just out of boot.

"At this kind of range, a blaster *has* no drop, but even late chemical guns would have *some* at fifty meters," he continued. "Where earlier chemical firearms, say cordite propellant, would have even more.

"You weren't adjusting enough for cordite, but if you were used to mag-guns, the change going to blasters wouldn't have been noticeable at this range," he concluded. "So, I guessed."

Trace snorted.

"We're *all* full of surprises here, aren't we?" she murmured.

"That's the point of ships where we don't ask questions, Trace," Reggie told her. "How you came aboard means we know most of your secrets, but even the captain doesn't know all of mine. Or Ginny's. Or Lan or Tate's or...well, I figure he probably knows Vexer's."

"I know more than I admit, Reggie," EB said from behind them. "I didn't ask questions…but I also didn't take any of you at full face value. There are lines I wasn't prepared to let people walk back from."

Trace turned to look at EB. The captain had come in with Tate and Vexer—and two large, human-sized boxes.

"I'm guessing those *aren't* coffins," Reggie noted sardonically. "So, we got our hands on armor, did we?"

"Zelda put us in touch with a merc supplier," Tate said. "Most of what they had was what I expected, but we got lucky." The cargo handler gestured at the slightly smaller case. "Take a look, Trace."

Trace obeyed, running her hand down the side of the box to release its catches. The contents didn't look like much to her. It looked, well, like gray combat armor in her size.

"There's not much demand for power armor for kids, but there are some smaller people who still need combat gear," Tate noted. "Even Ginny probably has too much hips to get into this suit, but it'll fit Trace's measurements.

"Original owner might have blown away in a stiff breeze, but that also means that nobody was looking to buy it. It was the best suit in the dude's inventory, and we got a discount."

Trace studied the plain gray suit for a long moment. She'd never really paid that much attention to real-world combat armor. She'd looked at some of the armor that had coexisted with the late chemical firearms she'd enjoyed shooting—if she *had* joined the SCA, she'd have needed a costume—but there was only a superficial resemblance between the three-meter-tall powered tactical reconnaissance ordnance loadout suits of the late twenty-first century and modern combat armor.

"Bellicose Five combat armor," Reggie said from behind her. "Manufactured on Why Are We This Far Out. It's decent gear…for the Outer Rim."

"And at least twenty years more advanced than the gear we got Vexer," EB explained. He chuckled. "Plus, it was the only suit the armorer had that would actually *fit* Trace, so it wasn't like we had much choice.

"Come on, Trace, let's get the final fitting sorted out."

"RELAX," EB told both Trace and Vexer. "Let the suit's muscles do the work. You're only initiating and moving with."

Trace struggled to follow that instruction. She wanted to move quickly, to evade threats—and the Bellicose V suit enabled that. If she could work *with* it.

She started to move and failed to follow EB's instruction. The next thing she knew, she was six meters away from her starting point, embedded *in* one of the crates set up as a target on the shooting range.

"That wasn't relaxing," EB said with a chuckle, walking over to her and helping lever her out of the wreckage. "There's *nothing* in here that you can wreck that we care about, Trace."

That headed off her apology before it even started. She *carefully* released EB's hand and interrogated her headware, bringing up a series of feedback reports on what had just happened.

They didn't make sense to her, and she stared at them in frustration, looking for bits that *would* make sense.

"The suit is overtuned," Reggie said. "Someone was being *clever*."

"What does that mean?" Trace demanded. She didn't *like* feeling clumsy. There were days the only thing she thought she had going for her was her dexterity!

"There's a level of response that the suit has to your movements," EB told her gently. "There's a standard that most people train for, but you can tune it up or down. Tuned up, it turns small motions into larger ones."

"The standard tuning fits ninety-plus percent of people," Reggie noted. "See Vexer, for example. His suit is on standard tuning, and he's able to handle it with a few minutes of instruction."

Trace glanced over at her other dad—and then flushed, glad no one could see her face inside the armor *or* realize how she'd just mentally referred to Vexer.

Vexer was moving cautiously in his own armor, but he was moving. He hadn't sprung himself across a quarter of the cargo hold in a few motions.

"Overtuning can accelerate your reaction times and make dodging easier," Reggie continued. "But it's almost impossible for most people to manage, and it's actually harder to train someone who's used to regular tuning to use an overtuned suit."

"Can we change the tuning?" EB asked.

"Easily," Reggie said. "Tate, where did the external control box go?"

"Leave it," Trace told them. "If I have to learn it either way, I may as well learn the way that will help me survive."

She trusted her crew, but she didn't necessarily trust the mercs she knew she was going into the Cage with. Plus...going into the Cage... she wanted every edge she could get.

"It will take longer to get used to and for you to be ready to use it," Reggie warned.

"D—EB, how long do we have before we kick off?" she asked, surprised at what had almost slipped out.

EB smiled at her. Had he heard her slip? If so...he didn't seem to *mind*, did he?

Trace was conflicted and confused—and, though she wasn't admitting it to anyone, terrified of what came *after* the Cage. It wasn't an easy thing to measure, but she was half-certain she was *more* afraid of leaving *Evasion* than she was of boarding the space station she'd been enslaved aboard.

"Ten days, give or take," he said. "You heard her, Reggie. You have ten days to get her used to that overtuned high-performance piece of metal."

The captain's grin widened.

"*And* I want my guns in top shape at the end, too. Think you can do it?"

Reggie grinned from ear to ear.

"Of course, boss."

46

NIGAHOG VI WAS the outermost of the system's three gas giants. With *two* gas giants closer to the inhabited planet, the vast majority of the official infrastructure for both gas extraction and static discharge was around IV and V.

VI was quiet. A pair of monitors orbited just above the largest of the three moons, the sublight warships making only the most casual of interrogations of ships that arrived to discharge there. There was a warning that the monitors were not responsible for any damages incurred by using the gas giant to discharge, and that was about it.

Any actual attack would be responded to, EB assumed, as would an attempt to set up a pirate anchorage or something similar. As it was, the lack of facilities meant a lack of fees. There was nowhere in VI's orbit to refuel or restock supplies. Not even an enterprising sublight freighter.

Zeldan Blade had beaten *Evasion* to the gas giant, and Captain Zelda's ship wasn't alone. Two smaller gunships orbited with the mercenary corvette.

"Are we sure everything is aboveboard?" Vexer asked. "I mean, I give us forty-sixty odds at best versus Zelda's ship on her own. With friends..."

"If we can't trust Zelda, this whole thing is already fucked," EB admitted. "If we *can* trust Zelda, those gunships are fucked if they turn on us. So, let's make our way to the rendezvous and find out, shall we?"

His lover chuckled.

"Course active. What's left of the plan, love?"

The change in how Vexer addressed EB *still* sent warm shivers down his back, and he grinned at the navigator.

"We're waiting on at least a few more ships—I hope—and then we're going to swap around some people and gear," he told Vexer. "Trace is probably going to have to go aboard *Blade*, and I'm still figuring how to make myself comfortable with that.

"We'll pull some mercs aboard *Evasion* to back us up as we go for the prisoners. Next day or two, Tate and Ginny are going to finish sealing the main holds and bringing up gravity and atmosphere in there."

He shook his head.

"It's not going to be *comfortable*," he admitted. "But we'll be able to put a couple hundred rescuees in each hold. Stars know if we'll be able to find anyone to babysit and feed them—I'm hoping to pick out some responsible ones to handle that."

Vexer chuckled bitterly.

"Probably the ones with control chips, once we turn that bullshit off," he noted.

"Probably," EB agreed. "Every time I think about what these assholes are doing…"

He clenched his fists for a moment before exhaling a long breath.

"Let's invite Zelda and the gunship captains over for a meal once we're at the rendezvous," he said, as calmly as he could. "We'll need some logistical coordination if nothing else. The plan is…honestly pretty simple at this point."

EB MET with the three mercenary captains alone—but on *his* ship. If any of the two strangers caused trouble, they'd be stuck on *Evasion* and need to get past Reggie to get any reward or benefit from that.

He wasn't betting on their ability to do so.

"Captain Bardacki, be known to Captain Jonas Hayden and Captain Alojzij Holt," Zelda told him, the veiled mercenary gesturing to the two men. Both were on the small side, but Hayden was blonde and delicately built where Holt was dark and broad-shouldered.

"Thank you for joining me," EB greeted them. "I'm not sure how many other people we're waiting for at this point. Any idea, Zelda?"

"Naveen at least," she said. "*Daisy* will stand out when she gets here. She's a thirteen-kilocubic gunship and will almost certainly be the third-largest ship in our little fleet."

"Tosta?" EB asked.

"Already aboard *Blade*. She *says* she's got two more gunship captains coming, but in all honesty..." Zelda shook her head. "I will count on no one who isn't already here...except Naveen. You made quite the impression, Captain Bardacki."

"I heard the story from Naveen," Hayden said, taking a seat and grabbing a glass of water. "I'm *not* a Tracker, but even I assumed they had a better filter on bounties than that."

"I am primarily a mercenary," Holt noted, his voice hoarse and barely above a whisper. "But I hold a Tracker license to enable dealing with the occasional prisoner who is worth something to someone."

"I was given *lectures* about the integrity of the Trackers' Guild."

"We all were," Zelda replied. "And once this is done, some of us are going to have words with the Guild. Inshallah, they will in future have the integrity we were promised in the past."

EB winced. He could guess what kind of *words* the top Trackers and mercs were going to have with their organizing entity.

"We need to go over some of the details of the plan," he told Zelda. "It will be...interesting."

"The physical layout of the station and our respective targets do make certain suggestions," the mercenary noted. "The space battle will be...straightforward. The Cage is in deep void, with nothing nearby. There are no sources for complexity except for jamming and maneuver.

Without coordinated training, we will have to rely on visual identification and individual maneuver."

"My people are scanning your ships and plugging them into our computers right now," Holt said in his strangely quiet voice. "We'll want to target any defending spacecraft as quickly as possible. That will clear the battlespace for ease of identification."

"And that's about as much plan as the space battle allows," Hayden noted. "After that is your people's problem. I don't carry a boarding team."

"I intend to land as soon as the defenses are clear," Zelda said. "The team I lead will head directly for Lady Breanna. She is our primary target."

"I'm going for their prisoners," EB told them. "Those are the only other *important* targets on the table, I think."

"I agree," Zelda said. "The problem, then, Captain Bardacki, is a question of guides. We have a decent map of the prison section, but our map of the rest of the station is more vague."

The other two captains were quiet, clearly waiting for EB and Zelda to sort out the plan and then slot themselves into it. It was very clear to EB that so far as the mercs were concerned, *he* was the client—and *Zelda* was in command.

"You need Trace," he conceded to Zelda. "I'm just, frankly, not sure how to make myself comfortable with her being with you instead of me."

"I understand completely," she told him. "The only answer I see is reciprocity."

"Reciprocity?" EB asked.

"I will have your daughter with me," Zelda said calmly. "So, I will send *my* daughter with you."

EB opened his mouth to object to Zelda calling Trace his daughter, then shut up and sighed. For this discussion, it was probably accurate.

"Your daughter?" he asked.

"Leia is nineteen and almost ready to strike out on her own as an independent Tracker," Zelda told him. "Operating outside of her mother's shadow will be a useful experience and test for her—and the failures of the Guild we have learned of make me nervous about releasing her on her own without that experience and test.

"If you watch *my* daughter, Captain Bardacki, I will watch yours. Does this sound sufficient to ease your fears?"

"It does, actually," EB admitted quietly. "I still need a team. Even with younger Zelda, I can only muster four people for a boarding action. That won't free many prisoners."

"Perhaps we should wait to see which teams and ships arrive?" Holt asked. "We may not have the numbers to press both attacks at once. My own strike team is only eight mercs."

"It may be necessary, Captain, for you to secure the prisoners with only four sets of hands," Hayden agreed. "Of course, once we have secured Lady Breanna, we can work together to liberate them.

"The immediate concern is making certain that none of Breanna's people do anything horrific," he concluded bleakly.

At least the mercenaries recognized that as a threat that needed to be handled.

47

THE ONLY WORD that Trace could use to describe Leia Zelda was *cool*.

Zeldan Blade's shuttle had docked with *Evasion* to off-load the bounty hunter and pick up Trace herself. That was nerve-wracking, which Trace was doing her best to hide as she waited next to EB and Vexer, but the sight of the young woman she was swapping places with was still a surprise.

Like Trace, Leia Zelda was wearing her combat armor already, though they were both holding their helmets. The apprentice bounty hunter had twenty centimeters on Trace, though, and the extra height lent an impression of towering indomitability to the armor.

Unlike her mother, Leia didn't wear a veil over her face. She did, though, have her hair covered in a blue-and-silver cloth that Trace's headware told her was called a hijab. The same coloring continued down onto the body armor, an intricate fractal pattern of interlaced colors.

"Captain Bardacki," she saluted EB. "Permission to come aboard."

"Granted," EB told her. "This is Trace. She'll be going back to *Zeldan Blade* to join your mother."

The situation was akin to an exchange of hostages from one of Trace's fantasy novels, though with a slightly more positive spin.

Leia looked Trace up and down, smiling at her—then stepped forward and wrapped her in an armored embrace.

It took Trace a moment to get past her shock and return the hug, buying them time for the other woman to whisper in her ear.

"I'll take care of your dad if you take care of my mom," Leia promised. "Adults are what adults are, yeah?"

"Dads," Trace corrected after a second, with a glance backward at EB and Vexer that she turned into a nod. "But I hear you. I'll have your mom's back."

"Good. That'll help me breathe," the younger Zelda said, then she stepped back and examined Trace again.

"You got potential, kid," she said cheerfully. "I promise not to break your ship if you don't break mine, eh?"

"Of course," Trace said loudly, reiterating the quiet pact they wouldn't let their parents hear. Leia might be six years older than her, but the other teenager *got it*, in a way the adults didn't.

Regardless of what names or structures or anything else was in play, EB and Vexer were the closest thing Trace had to parents—and if Leia would help keep them alive, then she was Trace's new best friend.

The exchange got a chuckle from EB, who gestured both teenagers over to him.

"We've got a spare set of quarters ready for you," he told Leia. "You won't be with us for long—we'll be novaing in an hour—but a few days is longer than I'm going to make anyone sleep in armor!"

"I appreciate that, Captain," Leia replied. "From what Captain Zelda has said about these people, I'm looking forward to, ah, *meeting* them."

EB chuckled again.

"Vexer, can you show our guest to her room?" he asked.

"Of course."

Vexer took a moment to give Trace a quick hug himself before he led Leia away, leaving Trace alone with EB.

"You ready for this?" he asked.

"Going back to the Cage?" she replied, then shook her head as a chill of fear ran through her. "I don't know, EB. Armor, guns, weapons, allies… All of that *helps*, but that place is…"

"Going to feature in your nightmares for a long time," he suggested. "And that's healthy, in some ways."

He shook his head and Trace stepped forward before either of them could say anything, curling carefully into his embrace as she lay her unarmored cheek on his shoulder.

"Be careful," she demanded. "I... I..."

She didn't have words.

"I know," he told her. Trace wasn't sure if he was taking the *right* meaning...and yet she also *was*. "Zelda and I made a deal, Trace. I'd watch her daughter...if she watched mine. Be safe and careful yourself."

A sun of warmth suddenly exploded in Trace's chest and she realized she was suddenly blinking back tears as he called her his daughter.

"I will...Dad," she whispered in his ear.

"Go," he told her with a smile. "A whole fleet is waiting on that shuttle getting back to *Blade*—and Lady Breanna's long-overdue reckoning is waiting on that fleet!"

48

AN ARMED FREIGHTER, a corvette and ten gunships did not make up anything that EB was truly prepared to consider a fleet. Not even a task force, if he was being honest. A single squadron of Apollon nova interceptors, like the one he'd been executive officer of for the ASDF's 303 Nova Combat Group, would have obliterated the entire force EB and Zelda had gathered in a single firing pass.

But there *were* no nova fighters out in the Beyond. There were barely any real nova warships. *Zeldan Blade*, at twenty-six kilocubics and eight moderately heavy plasma cannon, was as powerful a nova combatant as most Beyond system governments could or would field.

That made the twelve ships of EB's little fleet a potent force by the standards of the region and, *hopefully*, enough to take down the defenses of a major interstellar criminal cartel.

"All ships have checked in; we are prepared for the first nova into the Expanse," Vexer told EB. "I have to admit, love, I'm impressed. I honestly didn't expect your stunt of stunning a bunch of bounty hunters and asking for their help to work at *all*."

"I didn't expect all of them to buy in," EB admitted. "Or for them to be quite so successful at convincing their friends to come along."

Only *Zeldan Blade* and *Daisy*—the largest and third-largest of the mercenary warships—were captained by people he'd recruited himself. *Smasher* barely edged out *Daisy* to be the second-largest, at fourteen kilocubics, but she was here because her captain had owed *Daisy*'s Naveen a favor.

"I just wish we'd found just as many ships and a few dozen more gun hands," he continued. The numbers on their assault force were far sparser than he liked.

"I take it we're not getting that squad of backup?" Vexer asked.

"We get Leia," EB said. "That's it. There's only seventy-two mercs for the assault contingent, and while Trace only *saw* barracks for about a hundred guards, the station could easily support three times that."

"I wish we had more to go on than her memories," Vexer admitted. "I trust Trace, completely. She's telling us what she knows—but she didn't have headware online at the time. We're going off pure organic memory and a database that was intentionally vague in its information on the contents of the Cage."

"It's what we've got. And the Cage has to burn," EB said. "These people have misled, kidnapped, abused and victimized children and people from thirty star systems.

"It *ends*, Vexer. It ends," EB repeated, his tone soft.

"And on that note...nova," Vexer said calmly. The gas giant behind them vanished, replaced by only deep void. "This is one of Siya U Hestî's black nova points. There shouldn't be anyone here."

"And I'm running the scans anyway," EB said with a chuckle. "No chances, no risks. Not until we're at the Cage."

"Forty hours and counting," Vexer noted. "Start the count, I suppose."

"IT'S weird not to have Trace around," Ginny noted as they gathered in the mess hall later. "No offense, Leia, but you're a guest. Trace is..."

"Family," Leia Zelda said, half-toasting with a coffee cup. "Details are irrelevant after a certain point. She's not even crew to you, I can tell."

"This crew isn't really just crew anymore," EB pointed out. "But you're right, Leia. How's the coffee?"

"Better than I expected," she admitted. "How'd you manage it?"

"Luck and sheer burning hatred of most coffee grown in the Beyond," Vexer said. "EB might prefer to find specific beer, but he still insisted we find something tolerable for coffee."

"Mom has a hydroponics array *specifically* for her coffee beans," Leia told them. "Apparently, it was grown from cuttings of a plant my grandfather had. He grew *his* from cuttings *his* mother gave him—and so on and so forth all the way back to Turkey, Allah knows how many centuries back."

"I don't have the background for *that* level of care," EB said with a chuckle. "Or the motivation. I just have a *minimum* level of coffee I'm prepared to drink—and while Vexer blames *me*, *he's* the one who sourced the beans."

"I am wounded by the one I love," Vexer claimed melodramatically, holding his hand to his chest.

"And the truth," Ginny observed.

The mess hall was silent again.

"She's going to be okay, right?" Vexer finally asked. "Your mother will take care of her?"

"She's the guide to get my mom to the biggest prize of the century," Leia pointed out. "*And* Mom feels guilty for trying to hand her back to the Siya U Hestî. *And* Mom gave her word."

The younger bounty hunter spread her hands.

"When a Zelda gives her word, we will move all the powers Allah gives us to keep it," she concluded. "If any power in the galaxy short of Allah can keep Trace safe, my mother will keep her safe."

"And then I guess we take her back to Denton," Reggie said slowly.

"Given what Dr. Vortani did to her headware, I question whether that is the best plan," Lan noted, the doctor leaning against the kitchen counter and watching a pot simmer. "That kind of nonconsensual interference in an individual's headware is a crime on most worlds."

"I'm reasonably sure it's a crime on Denton," EB told Lan. "But if she wants to go back to the Vortanis, we take her back to the Vortanis."

"There's a lot of weight hanging on that *if*," Tate replied, the logistics officer grinning. "I feel like I should be making some preparations for long-term crew."

"Plan for educational stupids," EB agreed. "*I* am going to need to research adoption paperwork in the Icem System."

"Why?" Leia asked. "What star is this ship beholden to, captain?"

"None," EB told her. "I mean, technically, I think *Evasion* is registered in Redward, but that's...two hundred and eighty light-years from here? Maybe two-ninety? I haven't exactly been keeping track."

"Then if you and Vexer consider yourselves her fathers and she considers herself your daughter, what paperwork is needed?"

"I figure it might help settle things in her mind," EB admitted. "To have it sorted out on her homeworld."

"I think she'll be fine," Leia told him, chuckling. "*Adults.*"

"*Teenagers,*" Vexer replied in the exact same tone.

EB had to smile at the exchange.

"One way or another, after this, Trace goes home," he told his crew. "I just have the feeling—the *hope*—that her home is with us.

"But that's her call in the end. And first, we have a battle to fight."

"And many innocents to rescue," Leia Zelda agreed. "The galaxy will be a better place when this task is done. That, I think, is the best that any of us can say for anything we ever do."

49

"NOVA."

EB let the word roll off his tongue slowly as *Evasion* flickered through space. With a twenty-hour cooldown on the nova drive, this was the die well and truly cast. If any of his mercenary and bounty-hunter allies were going to betray him, the easiest way would simply be to miss this final jump.

"Contact," he continued aloud, old habits taking over as he ran through the initial assault report. "Vexer, get me reports on our companions. I'm scanning the target."

The Cage itself was much as they'd expected. EB had looked at the schematics of it from the database in Trace's head so many times, it was hard to remember this was the first time he'd actually seen the two-hundred-meter-tall "crucifix" of the slaver station in person.

"Everyone is with us," Vexer told him.

"I'm honestly surprised," EB admitted. "I figured *someone* was going to betray us."

Even that complaint was absent-minded, though, as he brought *Evasion*'s scanners up to their maximum resolution. They were a bit over two light-seconds distant from the station, and he figured he had maybe a minute to get as much data as he could before the jammers inevitably came up.

"Fourteen defensive stations," he noted. That was two more than they'd expected, but all of them fit the model included in the datavault. "I also read two freighters and four gunships."

The freighters were a problem. There was a decent chance that the nova ships were carrying trafficking victims…but there was *nothing* EB could do.

"Transmitting Siya U Hestî identification codes and beacons," Vexer told him. "I'm taking us in nice and slow, just in case they do buy it."

"They're not going to buy it," EB replied. "But it doesn't hurt, I suppose."

If nothing else, three of the ships in their flotilla were listed in the datavault as internal bounties, vessels and crews that Lady Breanna would pay handsomely for the destruction of.

EB would be surprised if *Evasion* hadn't been added to that list since. There were very few ships in the Beyond of his freighter's size, which meant she was easily identified.

Still, seconds ticked by with no hostile response from the defenses, and EB studied the display in surprise.

"We are receiving communication from the station," Vexer told him. "Phrase is: *The dawn always sings*."

"Response is: *But the shepherd still is lost*," EB replied. "We sent the call-and-response list to everyone, right? I was expecting them to update it."

"Everyone has it, but we all received the same query," Vexer told him. "Transmitting the response."

"Captain?" Reggie asked. "We're not quite in range yet, even without jamming, but if they let us get to four hundred thousand klicks, both us and *Blade* can target those platforms with long-range fire."

The Cage *had* to have multiphasic jammers as part of its defenses. Those would frustrate every kind of targeting, including direct visual, at any significant distance. Once the jammers were up, EB's flotilla would need to get within half a light-second—one hundred and fifty thousand kilometers—to be able to target the platforms and ships.

Closer would be better against a maneuvering target, but the defensive platforms *didn't* maneuver.

"Lay in the shot," he told Reggie. "I can't see them letting us get that close, but if they want to bare their throat for us…let's tear it out."

The defensive platforms were vulnerable from lack of maneuverability, but they had just as much firepower as the gunships backing up *Evasion*. With eighteen platforms and gunships versus ten gunships, EB was going to take any chance he could to turn the odds in his favor.

"They seem to be buying the beacons, love," Vexer said quietly. "No further communication after the call-and-response. Gunships are engaging in basic evasive maneuvers, but those might well be automated."

"Get me Zelda," EB told his lover. "*Zeldan Blade* is the only other ship with the guns for a long-range strike."

Only a few seconds later, the mercenary captain's image popped up in front of him.

"So, is it just me or has Allah struck our enemies lazy and stupid?" she asked.

"I half-expect a trap," EB admitted. "They have to know these codes are compromised."

"Unless no one *told* the people responsible for security," Reggie interrupted after a moment. "This kind of mess keeps everything close. Military need-to-know is a leaky sieve compared to hardcore organized crime, boss.

"Adjusting the codes off-schedule shows fear and weakness, and the leadership of something like Siya U Hestî can't afford to show weakness."

"Well, if they didn't show it, they have created it," EB said. "Zelda, I believe you can hit them from farther away, but my guns can reasonably range on the defense stations at four hundred thousand kilometers.

"I suggest we synchronize our fire to sweep as many of the targets from the board as possible."

"Agreed," Zelda said instantly. "Inshallah, they will remain asleep until it is too late. I will take one through four, you take five and six?"

"Then repeated with seven through ten versus eleven and twelve," EB agreed. "And then you get the gunships and we'll handle the last two. I imagine they'll have jammers up by then!"

"One can hope, but Allah is rarely so kind," the mercenary told him with a smile. "Al-baraqa, EB. Strike hard, strike together!"

"Stars guide you, Zelda," EB replied. "Keep Trace safe."

"And you, Leia. I make it three minutes to four hundred thousand kilometers."

"And fifteen until we can dock," he noted. "Somewhere between here and there, this is all going to go wrong, isn't it?"

"Inshallah. We will overcome."

REGGIE'S TARGETING data flickered across EB's displays and datafeeds as the range dropped. At this range, there was no way to tell if any of the Cartel gunships or platforms were charging their weapons—but the inverse was also true. Their targets wouldn't know that the incoming flotilla had active weapons until it was too late.

Even if they *did* think *Evasion* and her companions were friendly, some level of additional interrogation was needed. Except that the people in charge of the defense of the Cartel's most secret base *knew* the Cage was secret.

Even in the Siya U Hestî, only nova-ship captains and high-level Cartel officers knew where the Cage was. The database they'd acquired had been meant for the head of Siya U Hestî operations on an entire *planet*, after all.

Whoever was in charge of the defenses was clearly assuming that the fleet was here for Cartel business. The only precautions EB could see were the automated maneuvers of the gunships.

"Lazy and stupid, as Zelda said," he noted aloud. "I don't like this. Reggie?"

"Sixty seconds to long range," the weapons tech replied instantly.

"My armor is just outside the door. As soon as the stations are down, I'm slaving the guns to the main console and heading for the airlock."

"Vexer and I will be right behind you. Young Zelda is already there," EB told him. He glanced back at where Ginny sat in one of the bridge's extra seats, the engineer looking nervous.

"The dock-and-withdraw is already programmed into the nav computer, Ginny," he told her. "You can fly the ship in empty space, I know that."

"Yep. I can even probably dock it on my own," the engineer agreed. "But as the person who has to *fix* it when I break it, that *probably* makes me uncomfortable."

"You'll be fine," he assured her.

"Twenty seconds to range," Reggie noted. "Targeted installations lined up."

EB nodded, keeping his focus on the enemy...and he saw when things started to change.

"Aspect change; gunships have gone to real evasive maneuvers and are headed in our direction," he snapped. "Someone finally woke up!"

His best guess was that someone actually cleared for the knowledge they'd lost a datavault had finally been informed of what was going on. That had taken a full ten minutes—ten minutes that were going to doom the Cage.

"Firing!" Reggie snapped. "Full-speed capacitor dump!"

Evasion had only ever fired both of her turrets at full power three times while EB had owned her. All of those had been tests. He'd never fully emptied the capacitors in a minimum-cycle salvo, and despite the artificial gravity and reactionless engines, he *felt* the freighter shiver around him as Reggie sent over thirty plasma bolts into space in under twenty seconds.

"*Blade* has fired," Vexer noted while EB was distracted. "Looks like she only had six shots per gun in her capacitor banks, but she split them the same as we did."

"Jammers live," EB said grimly, watching as their targets dissolved into chaotic static—and then hitting the button that brought up the same system on *Evasion*. "Follow the plan. Vexer, take us in, match Zelda's speed.

"Reggie, shoot anything that's in front of us."

Evasion was overpowered for her size by Outer Rim standards. By *Beyond* standards, she could outfly any of the warships she'd brought with her. If she stuck with *Zeldan Blade*, neither of them needed to worry about target identification.

Anything in front of the mercenary fleet was the enemy.

THERE WAS no way for EB to judge the success of their opening salvo. Everything within a light-second of the gunships was impenetrable chaos now—and so was everything within a light-second of *Evasion* and his allies' ships.

Once they were closer, automated telescopes and image analysis would start to build up a useful image again, but the range on that was limited. A flagged target could be tracked out to maybe seventy or eighty thousand kilometers, but without knowing where to look…

They'd be within fifty thousand kilometers of the enemy before the next phase of the battle was joined—and at that point, the Cartel gunships and defense platforms would be equally able to see and fire.

In the chaos of the battlespace under multiphasic jamming, it would fall to human intuition enhanced by cybernetic reflexes to evade incoming fire and land their own hits. Vexer and Reggie had the balance for *Evasion*.

For the first time in a long time, EB missed his nova fighter. Even his NEWAC nova craft had been designed for this environment in a way *Evasion* just wasn't. His freighter had the cannon to go toe-to-toe with any of the gunships in the mess, but she was no warship.

"Optical scans commencing," he announced aloud. "We might —*might*—process them out of the chaos a second or two faster than they find us."

"That'll be enough," Reggie said confidently. "I make it five minutes to likely range."

"Me too," EB confirmed. "Vexer, you comfortable with this?"

"Only one way to *become* comfortable with this, right?" his lover replied. "Better with a fleet of backup than on our own."

"Fair enough." EB stretched over to squeeze Vexer's hand, temporarily turning off his link to the crew channel.

"I love you, you know," he told the navigator. "However this mess shakes out, I wanted to say that first."

Vexer lifted EB's hand to his mouth for a kiss. His other hand remained on the joystick, continually slightly adjusting their course around their main vector.

"I figured, but I wasn't going to push you to say it," he admitted. "Space dads forever?"

EB laughed, shaking his head at his lover.

"That's up to Trace, but she seems okay with the idea," he admitted. "All we need to do to earn ourselves a grumpy teenage daughter is take down a crime syndicate that spans thirty star systems. You with me?"

"To the end, EB. Always."

EB squeezed Vexer's hand again and relinked to the network. From the network, he was able to tell that Ginny had been studiously ignoring their moment, focusing on the scan data around them.

"We have no link with the rest of the fleet," she reminded everyone. "I've got a subroutine processing their location, but it may well screw up. This isn't a clean environment for tracking."

"That's the point, Ginny," EB told her. "But let's try not to shoot our friends. They're in this for the money, and I'd very much like them to get paid."

"Hostiles are definitely inside our jamming bubble," Reggie reported softly as the rest of the crew chuckled. "I'm beginning to pick up intermittent contacts. They're ghosts, but there's enough of them that somebody is actually out there."

"And the station?" EB asked.

"Three hundred-twenty-five-thousand kilometers and closing," his gunner replied.

"Twelve minutes to dock," Vexer told him. "Do we take down our jammers at some point?"

"When we dock, if nothing else. We'll need coordination between boarders and ships," EB said. "Let's hope we make it that far."

50

EB HAD three different analysis programs running in parallel while scanning through the data with his mark two eyeball at the same time. Like Reggie, he could see the ghosts scattered across the jamming on the display.

The gunships were definitely coming out to meet them, which suggested that they'd succeeded in blowing away all of the defensive stations. But four gunships couldn't fight ten, and he doubted their crews wanted to die for the Siya U Hestî.

Though they might be terrified of the consequences if they abandoned the Cage.

EB shook his head.

"What am I missing?" he muttered. "Surprise, sure, that got us here, but..."

He studied the ghosts again. Range could be anything from eighty to a hundred and twenty thousand kilometers. The size of the contacts was all over the place too. There was no way to resolve anything solid at this distance, but...

But.

There were too many contacts and they weren't *big* enough.

"Oh, stars," EB whispered. "Vexer, take us to full evasive. Reggie, refine your targeting. Expect targets in the three- to four-hundred-cubic-meter range.

"The station launched sub-fighters."

Considered a crude desperate countermeasure to nova fighters in the Rim, a sublight fighter had the engines and guns of a nova fighter without the nova drive. They were maneuverable enough, but with SCD tech, they were badly undergunned for their mass.

But while very little of the Beyond was fully up to even Outer Rim tech, there were plenty of pockets of "better than SCD" tech out there, and the Siya U Hestî could likely access the best of the thirty-two systems they operated in.

"Understood," Reggie said calmly. "There's parameters in the system for them. Loading them up now."

And just in time. Two dozen tiny contacts solidified at the fifty-thousand-kilometer range—and any benefit that *Evasion* had from better sensors or computers was lost against the unexpected size of the fighter craft.

"They're firing; evade," EB snapped. "Reggie?"

"I've got them. Half-cycles, engaging now."

The turrets spun on their bases, cannon elevating and tracking with a speed EB had never asked of them. Reggie had very clearly been doing his job *perfectly*, as the guns acted exactly as they should and the gunner opened fire.

Vexer pulled the ship out of the sub-fighters' opening salvo, clearing Reggie to work his fire across the formation. Every ten seconds, a shot blazed out from each of *Evasion*'s turrets.

There was no way Reggie could hit with every shot, not even with near-lightspeed weapons, at this range. His first pair of shots obliterated its target, though—and then sub-fighters started maneuvering to evade the return fire.

EB's allies clearly hadn't been expecting sub-fighters. None of the gunships had detected them in time, and focused fire hammered the mercenary ships. Only the imbalance between the gunships' limited armor and the fighters' even *more* limited firepower saved anyone.

Three of the mercenary gunships came apart under the attack.

Others were losing atmosphere and had clearly lost guns when they opened fire a moment later.

Now that the mercenaries had identified their enemy, they accelerated their maneuvers, cutting around the Cartel fighters' fire. They'd been surprised, but EB's allies were clearly veterans of the constant low-scale warfare of the Beyond.

The sub-fighter pilots...weren't.

Their opening salvo had been devastating because only EB had seen them coming, but their formation collapsed as soon as they had to dodge around incoming fire. EB had seen the pattern before, at the beginning of the war.

The pilots had been well trained, but they'd never expected to face hostile fire and they hadn't been trained in a way that prepared them for it. They landed a solid blow, but when faced with real opposition, they just...came apart.

Reggie was working his way along their excuse of a formation, nailing a sub-fighter with every second or third shot. The gunships' weapons might be toys by EB's standard, but they were more than sufficient to take down nova fighters—and most of the pocket warships had as many of those popguns as *Zeldan Blade* did her heavier cannon.

"*Blade* isn't firing," Vexer said. "What's going on?"

"She shouldn't," EB told him. "Zelda built her ship with the heaviest guns she could find. She probably doesn't even have the tracking for sub-fighters—she got lucky hitting this place with support that did."

"So, what is she— Oh."

Zeldan Blade had plunged forward under the cover of Reggie's careful sustained fire, and *she* saw the enemy gunships first. Her heavy plasma cannon, as heavy as any Rim destroyer and probably any cruiser ever built in the Beyond, opened fire first.

The lead gunship never even had a chance to fire. The other three broke formation, maneuvering to clear their lines of fire—only to discover that *Smasher* had a similar limitation to *Blade* and her captain had made the same call.

Blade's armor shrugged aside the scattered fire the three gunships unleashed, and then *Smasher*'s tore apart a second gunship. *Zeldan Blade's* fire walked across the remaining two, failing to destroy either ship but distracting their sensors enough to force a miss.

Thirty seconds later, it was all over. Five mercenary gunships were gone, including Naveen's *Daisy*. Three of the others, including *Smasher*, were leaking atmosphere and fuel.

If *Zeldan Blade* had taken any damage, she didn't show it as she began to decelerate toward the Cage. *Evasion* matched vectors with the corvette, Vexer tucking the armed freighter into their companion without instruction.

"Kill the jammers," EB ordered. "Try to get a laser link to Captain Zelda."

He wasn't sure if the Cage itself had jammers—it was fifty-fifty in his mind. The Cartel hadn't *armed* the station, but they had stuck two dozen sub-fighters aboard. The fighters and the gunships and the defense platforms would all have jammers.

That last thought reminded him—just as Reggie fired the ship's turrets again. *Blade* opened fire a moment later.

"Defense platforms located," he reported unnecessarily. "And neutralized. Jamming is down; watching our allies."

An icon flickered up to tell him he had a link to Zelda.

"Captain, are we good?" he asked.

"We could be better," she admitted. "Half the upper assault team was on the ships we lost. Al'ama, I *liked* Naveen. He was good people."

"I figured most of the lot who signed on for this stunt were good people," EB told her. "I didn't know any of them well."

"I don't have decent coms with anyone except you, but the plan called for them to kill their jammers soon." She shook her head. "Hayden is still with us, so he'll fly overwatch while the rest of us offload.

"I wish I could say the hard part was done, Captain Bardacki, but I think this may have been the *easy* part."

"I know," EB confirmed. "But we'll get through. I'll see you in the prison decks once you've got the bosses in chains."

"Inshallah!"

51

ZELDAN BLADE HAD a custom-built boarding system, a combination of docking tube, airlock and fusion cutter that Trace guessed was meant to latch on to a hostile ship and slice its way in.

It also had a mustering area attached to it for Zelda's ground troops —and one armored but very nervous guide. Her helmet was on but unsealed so she could hear the troopers around her chatting as the range counted down—and watched the corvette's tactical feed on her helmet.

Zelda herself had made a real effort to make the teenager comfortable on the ship for the three-day trip, but Trace couldn't help missing *Evasion*. The freighter was home now, and she would have felt far safer going aboard the Cage with EB and Vexer around her.

Well, maybe EB and Reggie. Trace knew that Vexer was going aboard the station, but all *that* did was worry her. EB and Reggie were fighters. Vexer was...Vexer.

"Shooting's stopped. Space fight's over," one of the soldiers grunted. "How'd we do?"

"*Blade* is fine," Trace said instantly, before she could stop herself. "We lost...a lot of ships, though. *Daisy. Evermore. Lancelot Dancer. Shit You Not. Chamomile Star.*"

She'd only confirmed the IDs now as the jammers came down, but she could see the winces of the dozen armored mercs around her.

"Well, fuck us," the same soldier said bleakly. "Thanks, kid. You were keeping an eye on it?"

"The whole way in," she admitted. "Dad—EB—Captain Bardacki taught me how to run a sensor data feed to my headware, and Captain Zelda gave me access."

"That's half the landing force, isn't it?" one of the other mercs. "What does that do to the plan, Sarge?"

"Nothing," Captain Zelda declared, the intimidating Muslim woman striding unexpectedly into the holding area, her helmet under her arm as her eyes surveyed her people. "Every extra gun hand was valuable, but it's only the loss of Naveen's team that we're going to feel.

"Em Finley here"—she gestured to Trace—"is going to lead us right to the prize queen, and once we have her, we make her shut everybody else down. Clean, simple. And remember: stun if you can.

"There *are* innocents in this hive of scum—and the folk that *aren't* innocent are worth money to us if delivered to the Trackers Guild."

"I hope I'm allowed to use a real weapon when the stun *fails*," the man the others had called Sarge replied.

"You see armor, Sarge, you put a blaster bolt through it," Zelda told him. "But anybody out of armor? Stun them. If they stay up, blast them. That's why I bought you all underbarrel stunners, isn't it?"

"Yes, ma'am!" Sarge replied. "Contact in sixty seconds. The Moray is ready to feed."

"And four of the gunships are going to dump another thirty troops across the upper part of the station," Zelda told them. "Stun everyone we meet, cuff them, move on. We *don't* know where the station control center is, and until we take that from the Siya U Hestî, everyone we take aboard is in danger."

She turned to Trace.

"You ready, Em Finley?"

"I'm ready," Trace confirmed, mentally giving her armor the order to seal. She'd practiced enough now to be comfortable with the overtuned muscles and reactions of the suit. It had sucked up most of the last week, so part of her hoped to need it.

The more sensible part of her knew that she really, *really* didn't want to need that edge.

THE CUTTING EDGE at the end of the boarding tunnel made a horrific racket, even through the sound protection on Trace's helmet. It only lasted a few seconds before the first wave of armored mercs charged down the tunnel with Zelda in the middle of them.

Trace started to follow Zelda, only to find Sarge's armored hand on her shoulder.

"You're our guide and our charge, Em Finley," he said on a private channel. "You stick to me like you're magnetized, you get me? Captain and I will keep you alive. *Nobody* on this op wants to bring a kid into the middle of it.

"But we need you, so we're going to keep you safe."

Trace grimaced inside her helmet, but she let him hold her back as blaster fire echoed down the tunnel.

"Bravo team, go. Charlie team, on my order," Zelda's voice ordered over the network. "Leapfrog by squad. These people are *not* as scary as they think they are."

More blaster fire echoed.

"Charlie," Zelda snapped.

"That's us," Sarge told Trace, swinging a massive combined blaster and stunner rifle up to point down the tunnel.

"*Underbarrel* stunner" was not the correct description for Sarge's weapon of choice. It was the size of Trace's leg *in* her armor.

The last wave of mercs went ahead of Trace, with Sarge watching between their armored shoulders and Trace sticking right behind him with her own blaster rifle. *She* had an actual underbarrel stunner, an attachment about the size of her fist that locked on to the barrel and trigger guard of her rifle.

Sarge led her past the first two teams, each holding what limited cover they had been able to find. None of Zelda's people were down, but there were at least a dozen dead guards in familiar-looking red-and-black armor scattered around the space.

They had camo settings on the armor, Trace was sure, but the Cage's guards' job was to contain and intimidate the people the Cartel kidnapped. Intimidating color choices had been part of that.

The skill to stand against Zelda's battle-hardened mercenaries clearly hadn't been.

"Stop here," Sarge ordered, pulling up his team at an intersection. "Is this familiar, Finley?"

Trace looked around, trying to place herself. It took her a moment and a reference to the map she'd put together.

"Yeah, we're in the starboard wing," she told them. She gestured to the left. "That corridor leads to one of the guard barracks. I…"

She shivered as she remembered why *she'd* been to the guard barracks. The thirteen-year-old victim had too much value to make *her* service the guards, but she'd been required to watch on several occasions for "educational purposes."

And, Trace suspected, to make her understand the consequences of *not* being cooperative.

"And the other way?" he asked.

"I'm not sure what's behind us," Trace admitted, pulling her focus to the moment. "But to the right should lead to the central hub. Gravity switches over when you enter the hub. It's always to the exterior, to disorient anyone coming in from any of the arms."

"Of course," Sarge said. "Captain?"

"We can't risk anyone coming up behind us," Zelda replied. "We've seen less than I expected, so there may still be some people asleep in the barracks. Seal that corridor and we move to the hub.

"Alpha, we're moving up."

Trace stuck with Sarge as Charlie team pressed themselves against the edge of the intersection. Two of Sarge's mercs pulled components out of their armor storage and assembled some kind of device.

"Pass it here," Sarge ordered as Zelda led her team past them and toward the hub. He examined the device—Trace had *no* idea what it was—and then grunted his satisfaction.

"Deploy," he ordered, passing it back.

One of the mercs went about a meter down the corridor Trace had flagged as leading to the barracks and placed the device. A solitary blaster bolt flashed over the merc's head, and they tapped a button and swiftly retreated.

Trace never even saw who had fired the shot before the device activated, spraying some kind of foam in a semicircular pattern. One moment, there was just a collection of bits of gear sitting on the floor.

The next, a wall of foam had filled the entire corridor—and *then* some kind of catalyst sprayed over the foam and it turned pitch-black.

"They'll be better off cutting through the hull than going through that," Sarge said with satisfaction. "Barracks sealed, Captain Zelda."

"Understood. Bravo, move up and leapfrog!"

One threat was down, and Trace was starting to feel confident that she would really see this place of horrors burn to the void.

TRACE FOLLOWED Sarge forward as Charlie team leapfrogged past the first two teams. There'd been no resistance since the initial boarding, but if Trace's memory was correct, they were about to reach the central hub.

"Watch your step," she warned the team as they approached a sealed hatch. "There's a ninety-degree gravity shift on the other side of the hatch."

She'd warned them already, but no one seemed to object to the reminder as they took positions next to the door.

"Locked by whatever central control there is," a merc reported over the network as they knelt by the door, their armor rendering them all anonymous. "I'll sever it from the network and take control, but it will take a minute."

"Hurry up, Josiah," Zelda said. "I'm having difficulties establishing coms with the other teams. Even Bardacki.

"The station doesn't appear to have multiphasic jammers, but something is going on."

Trace grimaced. She was unsurprised that the Siya U Hestí's leader had more defenses than they'd thought of.

"Alpha, move up to reinforce Charlie," Zelda ordered. "We'll prep to make the first push into the hub. Bravo, cover our rear."

Trace watched as more mercs made their way up the corridor, and shivered. From what Sarge had said, Zelda's strike force was almost half of the remaining assault. If they weren't linked with the other thirty mercs...

Well, she was no soldier, but she suspected that was going to be a problem.

"Is that you, Tracy Finley?" a voice suddenly echoed down the hall, picked up by the armor's external microphone.

It was a warm voice, the kind that could calm a kindergarten classroom with a disappointed look and a few gentle words of remonstration. Even *knowing* who it belonged to, Trace could remember the urge to wrap herself up in the lie of it for comfort.

"It is, isn't it?" Breanna continued. "You don't have the armor of Zelda's thugs. Most wouldn't tell, but I have some quite handy internal sensors. You, of all people, should realize this is a doomed course."

Trace gritted her teeth and ignored the voice.

"Are you following this child's memories to try to attack me, Zelda?" Breanna continued, maintaining a soft "I'm not mad, just disappointed" tone. "Please. We don't need to be enemies. But if you push this, you will use up my patience."

"Ignore her," Zelda told Trace over the network. "She's trapped in a corner and she'll say *anything* to get out."

"You've noticed, I'm sure, that you can't talk to your friends," the crime boss told them. "I know you're clever enough for that. I was quite disappointed to realize that we didn't have proper jammers aboard, but I was able to manage *something*.

"Every meter you push into my station—*my home*—is an intrusion that grates on my nerves, Captain Zelda, young Tracy. You will not like what you find if you keep searching. I may be forced to punish not just you but others if you continue on this course."

Trace swallowed and looked along the row of mercs, not sure which one was Zelda, now that they were all in camouflage mode.

It became more obvious when she stopped and glared up at the ceiling.

"The teacher act does you a disservice," Zelda declared loudly. "We're coming for *you*. For the mind behind ten thousand kidnappings and the *bitch* behind a thousand murders. Your words will not change your fate today."

"That's such a shame. I suggest you say hello to my babies," Breanna said, her tone still warmly sweet. "They're just *so* eager to meet you."

There was only silence in the corridor—then the merc technician at the door raised a hand and made a circular gesture. Everyone else seemed to understand what they meant, as the mercs checked their weapons and took up positions.

Trace checked her own weapon and pressed herself against a wall. She didn't know what was waiting for them on the other side of the hatch, but she doubted it was going to be pleasant.

52

"GO!"

Trace winced as she heard the buzz of stunner fire as Zelda's Alpha team went over the top. The ninety-degree gravity shift between the station's thoroughfares and the hub's intentional gravity screw was disorienting enough just walking through the station.

She wasn't sure what it would do for an attack, but she doubted it was good.

"I've got human shields," someone snapped. "Multiple guards in armor, hiding behind unarmed civilians!"

"Stun them and blast the guards," Zelda snapped.

A sudden ice-cold chill ran through Trace. It was unlikely that the defenders had brought prisoners up from the cells specifically to be human shields, which meant the people in the hub were the control-chip victims used as servants in the living quarters.

And a control chip didn't necessarily need its victim to be *conscious*.

"Target still up, target still up!" another merc bellowed. "Finding co—"

That channel ended with a cold finality.

"Wait, wait—the hostages are ar—"

Another merc's voice ended sharply, and Trace shivered.

"Bravo, Charlie, move up and reinforce," Zelda snapped. "All targets are armed and hostile."

Trace *heard* the captain swallow.

"Take them down."

"They're control-chipped," Trace snapped on the channel before she could help herself, already moving with the rest of the Charlie.

"I know," Zelda said, her voice a hollow shadow of its usual enthusiasm. "May Allah forgive me; we have no choice."

There were no more stunners sounding when Trace went over the top with Charlie team. She'd done it enough times before that she didn't stumble—and managed to grab Sarge when the big merc *did* stumble.

Pulling him over the gravity-shifting edge turned into pulling him to the ground as blaster bolts cut through the air. Trace followed them back to their source and triggered her own weapon, spraying a salvo of plasma bursts across the room.

The hub was a cube twenty meters on a side. In the center hung a transparent five-meter sphere of water suspended by antigrav fields, that acted as an aquarium full of exotic fish from two dozen star systems.

There were maybe half a dozen red-and-black-armored guards in the room, but they were hiding behind and among at least twenty white-robed youths. Those were the control-chipped servants, lacking entirely in free will, who provided domestic and...other services to the guards and staff of the station.

And a third of those youths were now on the ground, dead or dying. So were several of Zelda's mercenaries, and there was very little cover in the hub.

The control-chipped servants weren't particularly good shots with the blasters they'd been given, but they were providing enough covering fire to keep Trace's allies down while the guards shot to kill. In the middle of the formation, Trace was covered by enough of the mercs to keep her somewhat safe...and allow her to aim carefully.

It was just a shooting range, she told her head. Just one of the random targets EB had programmed. *Exhale. Steady. Fire.*

A red-and-gold guard staggered as her blaster bolt took him in the upper chest. She shot a second time, the recoil a familiar friend now, and his stagger became a fall.

She rolled sideways on instinct, the overtuning of her armor allowing her to cross several meters and come up on one knee before the blaster bolt even hit where she'd been lying.

The shooter was one of the servants, and she couldn't bring herself to shoot them. Her sight picture twitched sideways onto a guard, and she fired three times.

She missed the first two times, but the third bolt punched directly into the guard's throat and sent him to the ground.

Then a new cascade of fire took the defenders from behind as the team from *Smasher* burst out of the other side of the hub.

The silence that descended a few moments later was heart-rending. Trace rose to her feet, looking at the scattered array of white-clad bodies on the ground, swallowing down a sob.

She should have turned away. She knew, in her heart of hearts, that looking closer could only break her heart. But she couldn't turn away. Part of her knew that someone who understood exactly what those people had suffered through needed to bear witness.

And the first face she saw was Ben. Ben had been one of the older boys who Amelie had lured onto the same ship as Trace with sex and drugs. He'd been chipped before they'd ever made it to the Cage, turned into an attractive house servant for the Cage's guards.

Swallowing her tears again, Trace looked slowly across the faces, recording all of it in her headware. If nothing else, it was one more piece of evidence they could give the courts when they handed Breanna over to the law. Ben was the only one she knew by name, but she knew at least a quarter of the faces.

"She will pay for this," Zelda told her, stepping up behind her. "I'm sorry. Allah, am I sorry."

"This was her, not you," Trace replied. "And we are going to bring that monster in. Promise me, Zelda. She doesn't get away with this."

"She doesn't."

The two merc groups were combined now. Over forty armored

soldiers made their way to the access to the "top" portion of the station.

"There was no control center in either wing," one of *Smasher's* mercs reported. "It has to be in the crest."

"Then we take it from her," Zelda replied. Trace was a step behind the mercenary captain now—she'd lost Sarge somewhere in the fight, and she was sticking with the one anonymous suit of armor she could ID.

But when they reached the hatch in the "floor" of the top part of the hub, there was someone waiting for them. A dozen stunner beams sliced through the air before anyone realized that the image of Lady Breanna was a hologram.

She was still a mousy, motherly woman, but something about the hologram drew attention to the harsh chill of her eyes as she glared at the mercenaries.

"This is as far as you come, children," she said, her warm tone breaking into a disconcerting chill. "If you open this hatch, I open the other one. I have already sealed the prison section from your intrusions—if I read the cameras right, I've even trapped some of your friends in it.

"They're not escaping. Their armor will keep them alive for a time, but if you push forward, they will have a front-row seat to the death of every single one of the slaves you came to rescue."

Breanna shook her head sadly.

"I didn't want it to come to this," she told Zelda and Trace. "But you leave me no choice. Your attempts to secure control of this station have failed. You might still be able to capture *me*, but how much more death are you prepared to embrace for that goal?

"Are you prepared to sacrifice your *daughter*, Captain Lisa Zelda?"

An image of a painfully familiar hallway appeared above Breanna's hand—and Trace recognized the mismatched armor of three people in it instantly.

It was Vexer and Reggie and, yes, Leia Zelda.

Trace was close enough to feel Zelda freeze and see Breanna's cold smile.

"Well, Captain? Are you going to continue this disaster? Or shall we negotiate for the life of the only child you will ever have?"

Trace wanted to scream, to rage, to shoot the hologram out of anger —but then one question struck her.

Where was EB?

53

FOR ALL OF EB's assurances to Ginny that the computers could handle docking and undocking, *Evasion*'s final approach to the Cage didn't actually make contact. Harrington coils brought the freighter to a halt about five meters from the airlock they'd identified at the top of the prison section, and EB's small squad had to make the leap.

Leia Zelda led the way, the young bounty hunter clearly perfectly comfortable using her armor suit's jets to cross small sections of the void. She plugged a cable into the airlock and overrode it, opening the exterior hatch before anyone else moved.

Vexer went next, with EB and Reggie's assistance. The navigator's "jump" perhaps more closely resembled him being tossed by his lover and friend, but he made it into the airlock without issues.

Reggie was third, with EB only a few moments behind him. They were both almost as comfortable as Leia but out of practice on this particular maneuver.

"Close her up and get her out of here," EB ordered Ginny. "I'm dropping a coms relay in the airlock, just in case. Let me know if *anything* odd starts going on out there."

"I will," Ginny replied. "Everything looks quiet so far, though. It looks like we have control of this particular chunk of void."

"Good."

"Closing the lock," Leia told them. A moment later, the outer door of the airlock slammed shut and the space started filling with air.

EB took the time the airlock needed to cycle to place the promised coms relay, a fist-sized hunk of electronics that would help cut through any interference or radio-proofing on the hull and bulkheads.

His armor would now automatically deploy pin-sized sub-relays every so often as they moved deeper into the hull. It was a trick he'd learned from a peltast who'd served on his nova EWAC during the war, one that could overcome even multiphasic jamming if the intervals were short enough.

"Inner lock opening," Leia reported.

"Reggie," EB ordered. He didn't even specify what he wanted the weapons tech to do—he didn't need to. By the time the door had opened a centimeter, Reggie's massive assault cannon was pointed inward.

The compartment on the other side was empty.

"Where are we?" Vexer asked.

"Top security section on the prison area," EB replied. "Kill zone. Watch for auto-weapons."

The open space was designed to funnel anyone trying to escape the prison into the narrow tunnel of the main connector, but the lower segment of the station had also needed an airlock. To maintain security, the designers had put it in that section.

"Yep, stunners in the walls," Reggie noted. "Shall I?"

"Feel free," EB said.

The assault cannon's four barrels hummed ominously for a quarter-second, then the tech walked a carefully measured trail of fire across the walls. There might have been more-lethal weapons hidden among the stunners, but it didn't matter. Within a few seconds of Reggie's scan, the room was secure.

"One door into the top half of the station, one secured airlock into the cells," Vexer told them, the navigator having pulled up the map. "We should be able to override and open both doors of the lock to save ourselves."

"Do it," EB ordered. "I'm going to check in with Zelda."

His lover crossed to the airlock and attached a cable. Vexer wasn't as good with computers as EB was—and even if he was, EB had better software that he literally *couldn't* share—but he was good enough for that task.

"Zelda, come in," EB requested over the channel agreed on. Static answered him, and he did a quick scan of the channels. "Damn."

"Boss?" Reggie asked.

"Someone has recalibrated the station's transmitters for a short-range, wide-band transmission," EB explained swiftly. "It's just garbage, but it's going to muck up any long-range coms inside the station.

"The defenders can link in to the hardwire network, but we need to be careful with our relays."

He switched to another channel.

"Ginny, come in," he said.

"I'm here," she replied instantly, but a layer of static undercut her voice. "What's going on?"

"Station is jamming most coms," EB told her. "Not heavy, but material. I need you to stay inside a thousand klicks."

There was a pause.

"That wasn't the programmed course, boss," she said.

"And we both know you can fly the damn ship; you're just scared of it," EB barked. "I *need* you to keep her closer, or we're going to lose touch.

"Warn our mercenaries they'll need relay networks when they go aboard."

"It may be too late," Ginny admitted. "*Blade* was just asking if I had contact with the elder Zelda."

"Voids," EB cursed. "All right. Warn the merc ships, establish laser links if you need to keep in touch. It's not multiphasic jamming, but it's a pain in the ass."

"Understood. Keeping this channel open," Ginny promised. She sighed. "And I'll fly the ship in. I promise."

"I know. I trust you," he said. "I'm just watching for the other shoe at this point."

"We're through," Vexer reported.

Both doors on the airlock slid open simultaneously, clearing the way for EB's team to head down the corridor. EB gestured for them to head on as he checked the position of his coms relays, a task that took barely five seconds.

Five seconds in which that other shoe dropped in the form of a pair of emergency security doors that slammed down on both sides of the airlock, putting two layers of solid starship armor between EB and his three companions.

"WE'RE OKAY," Vexer told EB instantly from the other side. "But there was nothing about a *security door* in the system I cracked. I didn't even see command cabling for it."

"Entirely separate links, I suspect," EB replied. "Dammit, I should have had you handle the coms." He swallowed his next words.

"It's fine," he told Vexer instead. "You three sweep for any security on that side and start releasing prisoners."

"There is one very large security measure that I dislike extremely," Leia noted. "One that Trace probably didn't have enough starship experience to recognize at the time."

"No. They did not..."

EB trailed off. He could guess.

"From here, it looks like the entire bottom section of the station can be opened to space," the bounty hunter confirmed. "There are probably other segments as well. I imagine they are directly linked to the secured control center, like the security door we missed.

"This whole structure is set up to dump its atmosphere on a single command. Not every prisoner would end up in space...but all of them would die regardless."

"That won't happen," EB promised. "Start breaking them out, people. I've got the door *and* that horror."

"How?" Reggie asked.

EB looked at the single corridor that led to the rest of the station.

"They gave themselves a nice secure access and then jammed our coms...but that also means that the *only* way they can get a control command down here is through the data couplings in that connector.

"And I'm going to take control of them."

He was already running. Like Zelda, he knew how starships were built. He could guess where the data couplings had to be, and whatever security was on the panels couldn't stand up to the powered muscles of his armor.

It took him ten seconds to strip off enough paneling at the choke point where the ten-meter-wide connector linked to the prison segment to find his prey. There were a dozen different sets of piping and conduits running along that connector, carrying everything from power to oxygen to sewage.

There were three sets of data conduits, each containing thousands of fiber-optic cables. All were probably fully redundant, which meant the *first* thing EB did was cut one of them. The blade concealed in his armor could cut through a lot more than a few cables, after all.

The two unnecessary data couplings severed in seconds, and he was turning to the last one when the door from the main station slid open and things went to hell.

A blaster bolt took off the blade millimeters from his hand, and EB ducked forward *into* the shooter. Heavy power armor hit light unpowered armor and a blaster went flying from a badly bent wrist.

Then a boosted set of limbs twisted in a seeming impossible way, and both EB and his attacker went hurtling apart, both hitting the ground in the wide-open kill zone between the prison cells and the data couplings that EB *needed* to access to save his friends.

"I was wondering if you were involved in all of this," the stranger told EB, rising to his feet with catlike grace.

EB's armor had him on his feet with similar speed and he faced down the man grinning at him with impatience...and then fear.

Ansem made up what he lacked in EB's armored height with sheer bulk of boosted muscle. He wore a light armored shipsuit, with visible plating but no enhanced muscles. The augmented gunslinger bodyguard was watching every movement the freighter captain made, and EB returned the favor with careful regard.

The other man was favoring the right hand EB had smashed into, but his left was already hovering over the remaining blaster—a heavy hand cannon, probably more than overpowered enough to blow through EB's armor.

EB's rifle was on the floor near the data coupling. His only other weapon was a similar heavy pistol to Ansem's, concealed in a gauntlet storage compartment on his left arm.

He *knew* how fast he could draw and fire the pistol…and he suspected that Ansem could draw and fire significantly faster.

"I warned her the moment you walked out that you'd never take her deal, Captain Bardacki," Ansem told him casually. "She should have let me kill you then. But she wanted a fighter pilot and a military officer. She saw a lot of value in you—I agreed, but I *also* saw you were a threat."

"But you're just a dog, aren't you?" EB asked. He was calculating angles, time, distance…all of the calculations were ending in the same place, though: Ansem putting at least two blaster bolts through EB's chest before he finished drawing his own blaster.

It was *possible* that if he shot the coupling, he'd melt the right contacts to prevent the prison being opened to space. Unfortunately, it was also possible that Breanna could cut the jamming long enough to send the command wirelessly.

EB needed to have control of everything going through that cable, to assume control of the computers in this section of the station and prevent Breanna doing *anything* down there, to make sure his people were safe.

"Yes, I am a dog," Ansem told him, surprisingly unbothered by the taunt. "I am Lady Breanna's dog, bound to her will in exchange for my life. That was my oath, Captain Bardacki, and it means you die."

"Then what's keeping you?" EB snapped.

"Nothing, really," the gunslinger said with a chuckle. "But until she actually gives the word, this is just a game. And I'm curious to see how long it takes *you* to make the plunge."

"You're that sure you can outdraw me?" EB asked.

"Yes," Ansem said calmly. "There is a blaster in the storage compartment under your left forearm. It's designed to be drawn with your right hand and takes approximately point three seconds to open.

"If you're as fast as I think you are, it will take you just under three-quarters of a second to draw, aim and fire," the gunslinger continued. "That's fast, to be clear. Of course, without the mechanical limitation of the storage compartment, it will take *me* under a quarter-second to draw, aim and fire.

"You're already dead, Captain Bardacki. You were dead the moment you refused her offer. Everything since then has just been spinning wheels."

EB watched Ansem drum his fingers on the handle of the blaster and shivered—concealing a silent headware transmission in the shiver as a plan dropped into place.

"Ginny, I need you."

"I'm here," her voice said in his head.

"So, I take it changing my mind isn't an option at this point?" he asked aloud.

"I need you to take control of the guns and fire on my coordinates," EB ordered.

"Breanna might give you a chance," Ansem told him with a chuckle. "But I know folk like you. Anything you say to folk like us is a lie. You'll never join us. Never be us. We are too tainted for you, on your high-and-mighty horse."

"Are you insane?" Ginny demanded, the three-way conversation confusing even to EB.

"Desperate. Give me a three-count and do it," he ordered.

"You're not wrong," EB admitted.

Three. The count wasn't verbal. Just a data transmission, counting seconds.

"I'm disinclined to a life of kidnapping and torture."

Two.

"But I think you underestimate my high horse," EB told Ansem.

One.

"I suspect there is *far* more blood on my hands than yours."

Firing.

It was only a single shot, but it hammered into the link between the connector and the prison cells like a falling star. Chunks of hull and sparks of fire blew inward, spraying hell across the already-scorched security zone.

Ansem was only lightly armored, but the shipsuit would protect him from the debris of the hit. He still jerked away, shielding his eyes and body from the impact.

EB, on the other hand, *knew* his armor could protect him from the secondary damage of a plasma-cannon hit. He ignored the strike, going for his gun the moment the station started to move. Ansem realized what was going on too late, and EB's hand snapped out in a perfect form that would have delighted his long-ago instructors.

Three blaster bolts blazed across the room. Two hammered into the gunslinger's torso, sending his own gun flying from nerveless fingers and Ansem crumpling back into the wall he'd tried to take cover behind.

SILENCE FOLLOWED. The cannon blast hadn't fully severed the prison segment, and automatic systems hissed into motion a few seconds after the breach, covering the hole with foam as EB crossed to the data conduit and started locking his own connectors on to the fiber-optics.

He needed time. Time to find the right datastream. Time to crack into it.

"It's datastreams forty-two, fifty-seven and eighty-three you want," a weak voice told him.

EB looked up at the gunslinger and realized that Ansem was still alive. There was a large-enough smear of blackened blood on the wall behind the man to suggest that might not last very long, but the gunslinger was speaking.

"What do you mean?" EB snapped.

"There are one hundred and eleven separate datastreams running through that coupling," Ansem told him, before a gasp of pain interrupted him. "They're labeled clearly enough. If you want to secure the dump system, it's streams forty-two, fifty-seven and eighty-three. If you want to unlock the security seal, it's stream one oh five and one oh nine."

"Why the void should I trust you?" EB demanded—but he was also instructing his connectors to search for the usual identifiers and find those three streams.

"You shouldn't," Ansem agreed. He then coughed and grimaced. "If I was any less boosted, you'd have killed me," he continued. "As it is, if I do anything except sit here and talk in the next twenty or thirty minutes, you *still* will have killed me.

"So, my part in this is over."

The fiber-optic cables were, in fact, divided into one hundred and eleven datastreams. EB could eliminate half of them as automatic station-management streams with a momentary review. The remaining fifty-five were all encrypted to various levels, but forty-two, fifty-seven and eighty-three all appeared to *share* an encryption that wasn't present elsewhere.

"You can probably crack it on your own—you gave us enough trouble on the Plaza—but the key is Alpha Seventeen Kappa Two Five Lambda Mu Mu Zed Nought Seventeen," Ansem continued.

EB wanted to distrust the man...but he plugged that key into his decryption software anyway. A moment later, he was in the link. A dozen cyber-worms unleashed themselves a moment later, cutting into the systems and diving down.

The second set of channels broke under his codes a moment later, and the security seals slowly began to open.

"I have control of the prison," EB observed.

"Good, good," Ansem said, his voice fainter now. "I'd...appreciate it if that was enough to buy my life, Captain, but truth is...I didn't bargain and I won't ask for mercy. I was one of those kids once...made a different deal than most."

He chuckled, but there was clear pain in it.

"Worst part of it all, Captain? I was head of this station's security... and I had more in common with our control-chipped slaves than most of the guards I commanded."

He was silent after that. EB crossed over to him as the station seal finished opening and checked his pulse.

Whatever system was keeping the gunslinger alive had decided that keeping him *awake* was too much effort. He was breathing right then, but he'd taken a lot of damage.

EB sighed and pulled a spray bandage out of his armor's storage compartment. He'd still probably hand Ansem over to the authorities...but the cyborg would be *alive* to be handed over.

54

THE MERCENARIES slowly spread out around Trace and Zelda in deathly silence. No one made the first move toward the hatch, and the holographic crime lord just...stood there. Waiting. Smiling.

"We've no contact with the ships or Captain Bardacki's team," Sarge reported over the network. "We can send people back to act as relays to try and make a link to *Blade*, but...that could take more people than we can spare."

"That depends on what the Siya U Hestî have left, doesn't it?" Zelda replied. "Those prisoners are a huge asset to this monster, her grotesque stock-in-trade. She wouldn't threaten their destruction unless she'd run out of other choices."

"She has a few bodyguards left, nothing more. But we can't sacrifice those innocents, either."

"Well, Captain?" Lady Breanna finally asked. "Should I vent a few cells to get your attention? I don't *think* I can just vent little Leia without losing my entire inventory, but I can definitely give up a few dozen units to make my point."

"What do you want?" Zelda finally asked, activating the external speakers on her suit. "Because I promised a lot of people that you were going to Nigahog in chains. Your little *business* ends today."

"Well, that's not happening, dear," Breanna told them. "Not unless you want the blood of a thousand or so slaves on your hands *and* to lose your daughter. While her father wasn't worth the blaster bolt that killed him, my understanding is that you can't make another one anyway."

Even Trace winced at that. That struck her as something that Zelda's enemies shouldn't get to know and throw at her.

Before Zelda could respond, the entire station reverberated like a rung bell. *Something* had hit the station, though nowhere near them.

"Sounds like you might be having an even rougher day than you think," Zelda told Breanna. "Are you sure you don't want to change your opening position?"

"If your ships are trying to sever the prison segment to prevent my activating the dump protocol, you should probably warn them that there are secondary structures in place to assure my control," the crime lord replied cheerfully. "I mean, if you *want* to directly kill off my inventory, I suppose I can't stop you.

"But unlike you, I have far more resources than are here. Those ships that fled, those freighters full of slaves you decided were an acceptable loss? They'll be bringing reinforcements back. The entire Nigahog fleet is available for rent, as I understand."

"Do you really trust that Level-Eight Basia Kovačić is that strongly your friend?" Trace interrupted softly. "We had access codes, IFFs, call-and-response phrases…" She shook her head at the hologram.

Part of her was absolutely certain that EB had a plan. That *something* was going on in the lower reaches of the station—and that all she and Zelda needed to do right now was *buy time*. And while she didn't have *perfect* access to the datavault in her head, it had been decrypted for her and she could access chunks of it if she tried and had the context. Which meant she could ID the Level-Eight on Nigahog easily enough…

"Are you so certain that you know where that came from? Because Basia gave us *everything*. She's just waiting for you to stumble."

The hologram of Breanna stared at Trace for several long seconds—seconds she *wasn't* looking at the image of the prison hallway she was transmitting to the mercenaries.

Seconds in which the security doors on the edge of the video slid open and the three mismatched attackers began breaking open cells. Whatever lockdown Breanna had imposed on the prison bloc had just been lifted.

"And I think, my Lady Breanna, that you just stumbled," Trace told her, then switched to the armor network. "Zelda, EB's broken the prison lockdown. We have to trust... We have to *go*."

"Sarge. The hatch," Zelda snapped as Lady Breanna spluttered.

Before the big merc even reached the heavy security hatch in the floor, it began to move. It slid aside in front of them, taking Breanna's hologram with it as the crime lord's private part of the station finally opened to the mercenary strike.

———————————

"GO! GO! GO!"

Sarge's bellow echoed in Trace's ears as she followed the mercenaries "over the top" of the gravity shift and into the access corridor. Blaster fire flashed down the hall at them as concealed automated turrets jumped out of the walls.

Trace surprised herself by nailing one of the turrets with a spray of half-surprised blaster fire. The rest didn't last much longer as the far-more-experienced mercenaries around her followed suit.

"Josiah, Trent, you're hit; fall back," Sarge snapped. "Re-form by team. Alpha, Bravo, Charlie—rest of you are Delta."

The other mercs fell into place around Zelda's people at the end of the hall. A single security hatch waited at the end.

"Other side is a decorative garden," Trace told them all. "'Lady' Breanna would host the selected cooperative indentures in her dining room to the left. I haven't seen what's through the other five walls, but she always came from a door on the other side of the dining room.

"I *think* her quarters are back there and the control center is straight ahead."

"Clear the garden, then we split up," Zelda ordered. "Alpha, on me. Bravo, Delta, Charlie, follow on the fives."

"The door?" Sarge asked.

"Blow it," Zelda replied. "On twenty."

Zelda started a countdown on the network, and mercs scrambled to both place explosives and get clear before they went off.

Twenty seconds, it turned out, was plenty. Everyone was clear before Trace saw the timer hit three seconds, and the explosives detonated at zero. The entire door went flying into the gardens, likely shredding the delicate bonsai trees that Trace remembered.

"Go."

Zelda led the first team through the door.

"Contact!" one of her Alpha team mercs snapped. "No armor!"

"Stun them."

Bravo team passed Trace five seconds after Alpha charged out, and the buzz of stunner beams echoed through the crack of blaster rifles—and then silence descended.

"Secure," Zelda snapped. "Delta, Charlie, move up."

Trace stepped into the garden a moment later. She remembered the delicate Japanese-style tea garden that Lady Breanna had used to give the impression of refined culture to her slaves.

It was gone now, wrecked first by a flying steel door and then by an intense, if short, firefight.

"No injuries," Sarge reported as he and Trace caught up with Zelda. "These weren't guards."

"Station staff," Trace said quietly. She vaguely recognized a couple of the unconscious forms. "Some are probably mid-ranked Siya U Hestî."

"We'll scan them for bounties later," Zelda said. "I see three doors, two stairs. Left was her dining room?"

"Yes, Captain," Trace confirmed.

"Sarge, I'm keeping Trace," Zelda told her subordinate. "You're taking Charlie and heading straight ahead. Hopefully, that's the command center. Lance, take Bravo and swing right. We'll see what's there.

"Calverin." She turned to face the leader of the other mercs. "You got an org to split on or is everyone just following *Smasher*'s lead?"

Calverin, Trace presumed, was the head of *Smasher*'s ground team.

"Naveen was supposed to lead our second echelon," Calverin

replied. "But I can split off a team under Kaapro from *Intensity*. One up the stairs, one down the stairs?"

"Exactly," Zelda agreed. "Alpha, on me. Stunners at the ready but don't put the blasters away. Whatever is left with real gear is going to be around this *bitch*."

Trace stepped up beside Zelda and checked her own weapon, a shiver of fear running down her spine. Everything she saw in this place was giving her nerves. There was *nothing* about the Cage she ever wanted to see again.

"Let's go," Zelda ordered.

———

THE DINING ROOM sent even more chills through Trace. It was there that she had sat, smiling prettily, while Breanna and several of her aides had taught her perfect etiquette and how to read people. How to use that reading to make herself more appealing—and how to maintain that etiquette and appeal under various forms of stress.

Now she was using that same training to remain calm in the face of the stress of combat. It seemed Breanna had done her at least one real favor.

Still, the dining room was empty, and the mercenaries moved through it ahead of Trace. One checked the first door, then turned back and shook her head.

"Kitchen," she reported. "Looks like exits out the other side. Check it or seal it?"

"Seal it for now," Zelda said. "We'll sweep the whole station later. Right now, we need Breanna."

The door slammed shut and a portable welding torch emerged from the mercenary's armor. By the time the rest of Alpha team reached the other side of the dining room, the door was welded shut.

The double doors at the far end were where Breanna had always emerged when Trace had dined there.

"I've never been further than this," she warned Zelda. "But that's where she came from."

"And that's where we hope to find her," Zelda agreed. "Amina,

Palu, flank it. Hewey, Morana, prepare to breach. Semele, Jyoti, with me and Trace. Everyone else, covering fire."

The mercenaries spread across the room, blasters and stunners trained on the double doors. Trace joined Zelda in overturning the big table and using it as cover. It wouldn't stop a blaster bolt, but it would conceal them.

"Breach."

The two mercenaries Zelda had indicated went forward at full speed, powered muscles smashing armored shoulders through even the reinforced doors. Stunner beams crackled on the other side, followed by blaster fire from the covering squads. Trace tried to find a sight picture, but it was already over before she located either of the two bodyguards.

She recognized them both. They were the junior members of Breanna's trio of hyper-augmented bodyguards.

"Well, it seems we have reached the final denouement," Breanna said calmly. "I don't like this option, but it turns out that if you build a bunch of thermonuclear weapons into the structure of a space station, you have *all* kinds of possibilities."

Trace joined Zelda in walking into the room beyond the double doors. It was apparently a mix between a comfortable sitting area and an office. There had been a collection of plush armchairs around a small table and a faux fireplace—now wrecked, though it appeared the armchairs had contained concealed anti-blaster armor.

It just hadn't been enough to save Breanna's bodyguard.

The mousy crime boss was seated in a tall-backed chair that made her look even smaller, behind a desk scaled to the chair, and she was leaning forward on one hand, studying her intruders.

"Please, Lisa, Tracy, you may as well take off the helmets so we can have this discussion like civilized women," Breanna told them. She held up her free hand. "The entire station is currently wired to explode and on a dead-woman switch. You kill me, you die with me."

"I wasn't planning on killing you," Zelda replied. She hadn't taken off her helmet, and Trace followed her example, approaching the desk with her armor still on and her weapon in her hands. "I wonder how well your hardware handles *stunning*, don't you?"

"Please, Captain, let us not get in to such excesses," Breanna said. "I've lost. I can't dispute that. But I can make you lose with me. You gain nothing if you die along with all your friends and family and the slaves you came to rescue."

Trace was looking at the woman's face, running a scan on her armor's sensors to see if it could help her suspicions.

"At least you realize you've lost now," Zelda said. "Surrender and this will go much less painfully for you."

"Lisa, Lisa, Lisa," Breanna intoned. "We both know that I own the law in the systems around here. And Tracy here can tell you everyone who entered my service did so voluntarily. They may have misunderstood the terms, but I can't be held responsible for tha—"

Trace's underbarrel stunner crackled in the office, the beam taking Breanna at the base of her throat and silencing her instantly as it sent her nervous system into temporary overload.

The whole room was silent, and Zelda turned a faceless helmet to Trace in an obvious questioning gesture.

"She was lying about the bombs," Trace noted calmly. "I was *pretty* sure...and then, well, she *kept* lying and it was easy to tell."

55

EB WAS *REASONABLY* sure that he was no longer persona non grata in Nigahog. He suspected that whatever mercenary organization they'd got on the wrong side of was still angry at him, but the Nigahog government was currently in a state of half-delighted, half-over-whelmed shock at having eleven hundred and forty-six kidnapping victims delivered into their care.

Humanitarian concerns aside, the diplomatic and public-relations coup EB had just handed them was a golden opportunity, and he had every impression they were planning on using it.

Still, the government hadn't *paid* him for that. He probably could have talked them into something, but he'd been under the impression he didn't need to—which was why he was waiting outside the Track-ers' Guild office in Talson City.

It was a far less obtrusive facility than the Transporter's Guild. Several floors of a generic office tower were given over to the bounty hunters' home office, and the main entrance was even on the same floor as a small restaurant.

That allowed EB to get a coffee while Zelda dealt with her Guild. He'd just ordered his second pair—he'd ordered two to have one for

Zelda and then drank them both—when the mercenary captain finally emerged with a large security case in her hand.

She spotted him instantly and crossed to him.

"Good news and good news," the veiled mercenary told him. She passed him the case, and he grunted at the weight of it.

"What's in it?" he asked.

"Seven point six kilograms of third-party stamped lanthanum," Zelda said with a chuckle. "You had a share as an attack ship and as a boarding party, added up to ten percent of the total. Between Breanna, Ansem and a dozen others we took alive, I don't think the Guild has ever paid out more bounties in one shot before.

"They *really* didn't want to give us anything in stamped elementals, but I insisted on it. So, well." She waved at the case. "That's most of what they gave us in elementals. Most of the rest of us can draw on Trackers' Guild accounts, but I don't get the impression you're sticking around."

"No. *Evasion* doesn't stay in one place," EB told her. "I've got a line on a cargo for Blowry. Then we move on."

"Not a life I'd choose," Zelda said. "But I can see the appeal." She reached into her jacket and pulled out a small velvet-wrapped package.

"What's this?" he asked.

"Trace's payment for serving on *Zeldan Blade*'s crew," the mercenary explained. "Plus a bonus for being a guide. Two hundred grams of lanthanum. I can trust you to give it to her, right?"

"On my life," EB confirmed.

"Thank you," she said. "Other good news is that I got the bounties on you and Trace revoked. I need a couple more Trackers on side to force a full audit to make sure there are no more organized-crime bounties, but the wheels are rolling on that, too.

"We'll clean up our own backyard, Captain Bardacki."

"Please, Zelda, call me EB," he insisted. "After all of this…"

He shook his head.

"I'm sorry I ever came after you," she told him. "And, inshallah, I'm going to make damn sure it doesn't happen to another captain, EB. You have my word."

"Thank you." EB tapped the case. "This helps make up for the running around and chaos that bounty inflicted on my life, too. And the costs of going after Breanna."

"*She's* not getting out of jail anytime soon," Zelda said with satisfaction. "And thank you for that, too. I owe you more than this, though I have no idea how to repay it."

"Don't worry about it. I'll keep moving on," EB said. "Vexer and Trace and I have a galaxy to see."

"So you do," she murmured. To his surprise, she leaned into his personal space, pulling her veil slightly aside to kiss his cheek. "You take care of that kid, you hear? She's lucky to have you and Vexer."

"As I understand it, a father's job is to make sure *she* thinks that," he told her. "So, we're just getting started."

"Fly safe, EB. You've helped make this region of the Beyond a better place. Not sure there's any higher praise I can give."

EB RETURNED to *Evasion* to find Ginny and Trace sitting outside the docking tube connecting the ship to the orbital station. The two women had acquired folding chairs from somewhere and were watching the crews of the other ships walking past toward the main body of the station.

"Harassing our fellow Guild members?" EB asked them.

"What, we're Transporters' Guild now?" Ginny replied.

"Bought a year's membership," he confirmed. "I doubt we'll be in their territory long enough to renew it, but it seemed the easiest way to get a cargo."

"Have you managed that yet, Dad?" Trace asked.

That descriptor still sent a warm flush down his spine. She was a damn good kid, and he was *damn* proud that she wanted to stick with him and Vexer.

"Not quite yet," he admitted. "But be careful with that word; you might end up giving me a complex and make me keep you."

The teenager laughed.

"Dad, Dad, Dad, Dad, Dad, Dad, Dad," she immediately chanted. "Is that enough to get to stick around, or should I keep going?"

EB ruffled her hair with an affectionate chuckle, a gesture that got his hand gently slapped.

"Told you once, I told you a thousand times, Vexer and I are your dads as long as you want us," he told her. "Here."

He passed her the velvet package Zelda had given him.

"What's this?"

"Your share of *Zeldan Blade*'s share of the bounty payouts," he said. "I haven't calculated ours yet, but you'll get a chunk there, too."

"I think this might be more than I ever got as an allowance from the Vortanis," Trace said, staring at the stamped ingots in the package.

"Given that it's more than most people's annual salary, I'd *hope* so," Ginny told her. "Be careful with that. You never know who's watching."

"I'll take it back aboard ship," Trace promised. "Need to drag you back aboard ship, too, Dad."

"Oh?" EB asked. "That's where I was headed, but..."

"Someone showed up ten minutes ago, said he'd wait for you. We sent him to the mess with Reggie to keep an eye on him," Ginny explained. "Little old guy... Said he owed you and you'd know him."

"Lear Naumov sound familiar, Dad?" Trace asked.

JOIN THE MAILING LIST

Love Glynn Stewart's books? To know as soon as new books are released, special announcements, and a chance to win free paperbacks, join the mailing list at:

glynnstewart.com/mailing-list/

ABOUT THE AUTHOR

Glynn Stewart is the author of *Starship's Mage*, a bestselling science fiction and fantasy series where faster-than-light travel is possible–but only because of magic. His other works include science fiction series *Duchy of Terra*, *Castle Federation* and *Vigilante*, as well as the urban fantasy series *ONSET* and *Changeling Blood*.

Writing managed to liberate Glynn from a bleak future as an accountant. With his personality and hope for a high-tech future intact, he lives in Kitchener, Ontario with his partner, their cats, and an unstoppable writing habit.

VISIT GLYNNSTEWART.COM FOR NEW RELEASE UPDATES

CREDITS

The following people were involved in making this book:
    Copyeditor: Richard Shealy
    Proofreader: M Parker Editing
    Cover art: Elias Stern
    Typo Hunter Team
    Faolan's Pen Publishing team: Jack, Kate, and Robin.

facebook.com/glynnstewartauthor

OTHER BOOKS
BY GLYNN STEWART

For release announcements join the
mailing list or visit **GlynnStewart.com**

STARSHIP'S MAGE
Starship's Mage
Hand of Mars
Voice of Mars
Alien Arcana
Judgment of Mars
UnArcana Stars
Sword of Mars
Mountain of Mars
The Service of Mars
A Darker Magic
Mage-Commander
Beyond the Eyes of Mars (upcoming)

Starship's Mage: Red Falcon
Interstellar Mage
Mage-Provocateur
Agents of Mars

Pulsar Race: A Starship's Mage Universe Novella

DUCHY OF TERRA
The Terran Privateer
Duchess of Terra
Terra and Imperium
Darkness Beyond
Shield of Terra
Imperium Defiant
Relics of Eternity
Shadows of the Fall
Eyes of Tomorrow

SCATTERED STARS

Scattered Stars: Conviction
Conviction
Deception
Equilibrium
Fortitude
Huntress (upcoming)
Scattered Stars: Evasion
Evasion
Discretion (upcoming)

PEACEKEEPERS OF SOL

Raven's Peace
The Peacekeeper Initiative
Raven's Course
Drifter's Folly
Remnant Faction (upcoming)

EXILE

Exile
Refuge
Crusade
Ashen Stars: An Exile Novella

CASTLE FEDERATION

Space Carrier Avalon
Stellar Fox
Battle Group Avalon
Q-Ship Chameleon
Rimward Stars
Operation Medusa
A Question of Faith: A Castle Federation Novella

SCIENCE FICTION STAND ALONE NOVELLA

Excalibur Lost

Made in the USA
Las Vegas, NV
13 April 2024